Abdulrakhmanov ... ... Pitman by the shou ... ... ild, and led him to a wooder ... ... the wall. On it was engraved, as if with a pen-knife, in fantastic lettering reminiscent of the Far East, the following text:

1 Discredit good
2 Compromise the leaders
3 Shake their faith, deliver them to contempt
4 Use base men
5 Disorganize the authorities
6 Sow discord among the citizens
7 Incite the young against the old
8 Ridicule traditions
9 Dislocate supplies
10 Let lascivious music be heard
11 Spread lechery
12 Lay out money
13 Be informed

'These,' said Abdulrakhmanov with satisfaction, 'are the thirteen commandments that I have taken from Sun Tzu . . . But Sun Tzu says and says it again: "In war, the best method is to take the enemy intact; destroying him is but a poor alternative." That's what we are going to do to France, my Iakov Moiseich all-of-ruby: we shall pick it off intact.'

THE SET-UP

Vladimir Volkoff

A novel of espionage

Translated from the French by
Alan Sheridan

Methuen

If I were to assert that *The Set-Up* is simply the product of my imagination, no one would believe me.

Let me therefore here express my gratitude to the many and various comrades upon whose expert advice I have drawn.

V.V.

A Methuen Paperback

THE SET-UP

Originally published in French as *Le Montage*
Copyright © 1982 by Julliard/L'Age d'Homme
Translation © 1984 by Alan Sheridan
First published in Great Britain 1984
by The Bodley Head Ltd
This edition published 1985
by Methuen London Ltd
11 New Fetter Lane, London EC4P 4EE

British Library Cataloguing in Publication Data

Volkoff, Vladimir
  The Set-up.
  I. Title   II. Le Montage. *English*
  843'.914[F]   PQ2682.04

  ISBN 0-413-58060-1

Reproduced, printed and bound in Great Britain by
Hazell Watson & Viney Limited,
Member of the BPCC Group,
Aylesbury, Bucks

Contents

1 The Setting   7

2 The Divine Skein   56

3 A Day in the Life of Aleksandr Dmitrich   96

4 One Last Little Service
   (*Operation Pskov, Stage 1*)   141

5 Something for a Rainy Day
   (*Operation Pskov, Stage 2*)   192

6 The Turn of the Screw   236

7 Hard Sign   281

8 The Pearl   316

9 'Going Home'   355

Your aim must be to capture intact
everything that is under heaven.

Sun Tzu

I
The Setting

On 30 April 1945, after nine days of fighting, street by street, building by building and, in the end, staircase by staircase and room by room, the Russian flag—for a time we no longer said Soviet—was hoisted over the Reichstag.

On 2 May, Berlin had fallen and, for the third time in History, the victorious Russian troops marched through the Brandenburg Gate.

On 9 May, Iosif Vissarionovich Dzhugashvili, better known as Stalin, addressed the nation: 'The heavy sacrifices we have made for the freedom and independence of our country, the innumerable privations and sufferings endured by our people during the war, the effort and labour that have been laid, at home and at the front, on the altar of the Fatherland have not been wasted: they have been crowned with total victory over the enemy. The age-old struggle of the Slav peoples for their existence and independence has culminated in our victory over the German invaders and German tyranny.'

The very same people who bawled the *Internationale*, as they seized power in the name of the universal union of the working classes, now regarded the war that they had waged and won as 'patriotic', and renounced the use of the term 'Soviet'.

For a time.

Among those who were most struck by these events, were, of course, the Russian émigrés, the so-called 'Whites', some of whom had chosen to fight for Germany, preferring the devil to the Communists, while others had chosen to serve the Soviet Union, preferring the devil to the Germans. There were, I know, those who were too intelligent, too faithful, too cynical, too desperate; but in the hearts of all the others the victory of the Russian forces aroused an enthusiasm that was neither surprising nor entirely impure. National pride, coupled with a sense of compensation for the ordeals endured for twenty-five years, played a part in it, but there were also three reasons, of varying degrees of importance, that some, because of their own frivolity, might find frivolous.

First, this victory of Eternal Russia over Germany appeared to the émigrés as a victory of Holy Russia over the Bolshevik usurpation. Yes, the flag that fluttered over the Reichstag was just a red flag and not white-blue-red, but the Soviet soldiers we met talked of Russia rather than of 'the Union'. They were aware of having fought for land, not for an idea; their good, simple mugs reminded our elders of those of the Ivans they had commanded during the other war; in other words, the body of the fatherland seemed to have spontaneously eliminated the antigens that had been introduced into it. We had not cured Russia—Russia had cured herself, unaided. This gave us a humbler, healthier joy than if we had plied the scalpel ourselves.

Secondly, in France, for instance, the ambassador of the Soviet Union started regularly attending the services at the cathedral of St Alexander Nevsky: there was something rather splendid about seeing this devil on such hallowed ground and telling oneself that he did not look too wicked a devil. Many émigrés were more attached to religious freedom than to the political order of the Tsarist régime: if the Church had resumed her rights, that was all they needed to become once again loyal subjects of the Empire, whatever strange name it might go under. And the Church was there, gilded, mitred, bearded, melodious and aromatic as ever. Yes, she had been subjected to martyrdom, and we were not forgetting the priests crucified with bayonets in the porches of their churches, but all that was in the past: the new régime had at last realized that the faith was an integral part of Russian reality and would have to adapt to it.

The former seminarist who had led Russia to victory was now beginning some of his speeches with 'Brothers and sisters', instead of 'Comrades'. What more did we want?

Lastly, there was a visible, tangible sign of this rebirth of our Russia, of its internal restoration. Strictly speaking, this sign affected more particularly the soldiers, but what was the emigration if not military in its vocation? Moreover, that sign had cost so many lives and so much suffering that, even for minds that cared little for external marks of respect and honorary symbols, this rectangle of cardboard covered with material and fixed on the shoulder by means of a copper button, had assumed as much meaning as crosses of this or that shape, cockades of this or that colour, berets, fezes, tattoos, excisions, in short, whatever is the mark of an assumed difference, must have had at other times. Already, under the Old Order, to remove the epaulettes from an officer was to dishonour him. Under the New Order the Reds carefully transferred, with a knife, their prisoners' crowns and initials on to their shoulders. So as not to have to wear a uniform without epaulettes, the captive Tsar went on wearing the Cherkesse tunic, which had no epaulettes anyway. Indeed, after 6 January 1943 for the army and after 15 February for the navy, the converted Reds formed up and marched with that stiffening, that dubbing on their shoulders. The nostalgic tyrant, to whom various designs for uniforms had been submitted, had chosen one that differed by only two buttons from those of his youth. We were not so petty as to make a fuss over two buttons. The epaulette was rising from its ashes; some of us might have been forgiven for thinking that the civilization it represented was also rising once more. The nightmare, we fondly dreamed, was drawing to a close.

To these reasons for hope was added an opportunity: the amnesty. The government was allowing its former enemies to return home. Amnesty is a generous, imperial word. It implied, it seemed, not a pardon, but the forgetting of past conflicts. Victors and vanquished would go and serve their common fatherland side by side. The first to join the *vozvrashchentsy*—we had coined a new word for them—was a metropolitan who could hardly be suspected of connivance with anti-Christ: it was he who had set up the Academy of Orthodox Theology in Paris, he who had prevented the cathedral of St Alexander Nevsky from being handed over to the Soviets for use as a cinema. Symbolically, the metropolitan Eulogius was given Soviet passport no. 1. It was true that he died before leaving the West, and some people later saw this as the intervention of Divine Providence, but, for the moment, the fact remained that one of the White spiritual leaders had chosen the path of reconciliation.

The first batch of 're-immigrants' boarded the train at the Gare du Nord with joy in their hearts and tears in their eyes. Somewhat anxiously we waited for news of them: even the most convinced of those who stayed behind were not sure that an execution squad did not await their friends at the frontier. After some months, letters began to arrive. The amnestied had been scattered throughout the country; they had been given manual jobs; they asked for nothing, except, occasionally, mittens or balaclavas. A civil war that had seemed implacable appeared to be drawing to an end. Other candidates for repatriation rang the bell at the once accursed bottle-green doors of 79 Rue de Grenelle.

One of them was a naval man, Dmitri Aleksandrovich Psar, or Midshipman Psar, as he liked to introduce himself.

Dmitri Aleksandrovich was a small man of about fifty. He would like to have believed that he had been an officer in the Tsar's navy; in fact he had sworn his oath of allegiance only to the puppets of February 1917, which, as it happens, made it very much easier for his conscience. A monarchist out of loyalty rather than conviction, he had fought under Wrangel and, after the defeat, found himself dying of hunger, in very good company, on the Turkish island curiously named Antigone. He had to get out of there. But how? Where to? Some dreamt of the Americas, because they were thinking of the future and the sun travels from east to west; others had tender memories of the Fraülein who had taught them *der*, *die*, *das*. Psar, like many, was attracted by France.

This was not only because he knew French as well as he knew Russian, and because he had been lulled to sleep by the stories of the Comtesse de Ségur, because he could recite *Les Pauvres Gens* by heart and because he had a romantic admiration for Napoleon. In his eyes France was the ally *par excellence*; she could not have forgotten that two Russian armies, sacrificed at her request at Tannenberg in a gesture of insensate generosity unique in History, had enabled Joffre to save Paris.

The middle-men arrived, their cardboard briefcases bulging with work contracts. Their job was easy enough; the least of their propositions was worth a fortune to the starving men on Antigone. The supply was called 'nine million dead'; the demand was called 'I'm dying of hunger'; no problem coming to an arrangement.

Midshipman Psar accepted a job as a stable-boy in the Ardèche. He was not a cavalry officer, but he knew that in working with horses one did not lose caste and that—he was still at the beginning of his tribulations—still meant a lot to him. However, France turned out to be less grateful than he had expected. Instead of remembering Tannenberg or even the expeditionary corps that had been massacred in Champagne in order to show the Allies how the Russians could die, he was bitterly reproached for the loan that had not been repaid: 'Oh, yes! Your Russia is all very fine, but it's costing me a lifetime's savings.'

At first Psar felt so embarrassed that he would have tried to compensate the good people out of his own pocket if it had not been empty; fortunately his employer fed him, but he did not pay him.

'And anyway,' the regulars of the little café in Chomérac continued, 'when you'd had enough of the war, you lot pulled out!'

Psar then tried to explain that neither he nor his emperor had been responsible for the separate peace of Brest-Litovsk signed by Trotsky, that if His Majesty had stooped to such a cowardly act he would probably still be alive and on his throne, that the real Russia could not be accused of abandoning her Allies. On the contrary, it was the revolutionary internationalists who had denounced the Alliance after being paid off in Reichsmarks. Such justifications did not convince those penniless pensioners. And when Psar tried to show them that if, as Foch had demanded, the Allies had intervened in support of a sovereign who had done so much for them, the emblazoned bank-notes exhibited on the bar would no doubt have recovered their value, they replied half-craftily, half-self-righteously: 'All very well for you boyars—but the people lived in misery.'

No arguing with them!

Dmitri Aleksandrovich was not a boyar, but nor was he used to working in the fields. 'Groomsman' was no more than a title: he had been recruited as a farmhand, yet he had never lifted a pitchfork-load of firewood weighing practically half his own weight. The sailor lurched and staggered and the peasant who had hired this exotic muscle at the cheapest possible rate took a dim view of these wayward movements. There was one scene in which the employer threatened the employee with a kick in the rear, so that the employee, with neither gloves, card, nor witnesses, was forced to make an oral challenge to a duel; the challenge was vigorously declined. Spending his last few centimes on a third-class railway ticket and wondering whether or not he had been dishonoured, Dmitri Aleksandrovich allowed himself to be sucked into the vortex of the time, Paris.

The vortex had two irreconcilable centres: the Prefecture of Police and the Renault car factory. One could not be hired without a work permit, but to get a work permit one had to be hired. This meant not only that you seldom ate, but that sometimes you were taken to the frontier and kicked out into some neighbouring country, which then took you back to its own frontier and kicked you out, and so on. The job/permit dilemma was resolved for Dmitri Aleksandrovich through the good offices of an understanding Frenchman who had delivered dozens of work permits to innumerable secretaries, private tutors, managers, governesses, lady's companions— an entire fictitious staff who were never to clap eyes on this penniless gentleman's country estate.

Facetiously engaged as piano teacher, Dmitri Aleksandrovich, who would have looked for Middle C in an atlas, was able to gain the favours of the Prefecture. The favours did not amount to very much. The precious worker's identity card was issued for one year. To renew it, one had to go back to the Prefecture and queue up for hours: a day's work lost. When one finally reached the desk, the grumpy clerk in charge of foreigners—'Well? Don't you understand French?'—handed over a receipt of application. Then, some weeks later, a summons arrived through the post and one set off again: métro, queue, day's work lost without pay, grumpy clerk and, at the end of the tunnel, the priceless bit of paper, folded like a concertina and complete with a profile photograph, 'showing the right ear and the eyes raised upwards' (*sic*).

In the first year, the expatriate Psar Dmitri forgot to renew his card at the proper date. The scandal! The offender would be taken to court. He, who had gone into the thick of battle without blenching, fell sick at the very idea of appearing before magistrates: he was expecting a trial rather like the Karamazovs' and prepared a defence in which the battle of Tannenberg was to play its part. In the event he was merely asked to state his name and date of birth; in any case, among his co-defendants, who numbered about a hundred, he had seen some of his acquaintances, which reassured him somewhat. The fine that he was called upon to pay amounted only to one franc; he went home relieved and grateful, his digestive tract having resumed a more or less normal shape. He earned 16 francs 75 centimes a day; his hotel room cost 10 francs, plus another franc for the service; so a fine of one franc simply meant that he would have to go without breakfast for one day. Oh the magnanimity of French justice! Ten days later he received a bill that somewhat diminished his admiration: the franc referred to in the fine was a gold one and had to be multiplied by eleven, making 11 francs, in other words, three or four meals. And why not, after all? Dmitri Aleksandrovich had committed an offence, he was not surprised that he had to be punished. But when he discovered that in addition to the fine of 11 francs there were another hundred to cover legal expenses, he did feel disheartened for a time.

The other centre of the vortex was the Renault factory, which proved more hospitable. No doubt the forty-eight-hour week still seemed an absurd mirage. The best one could hope for at that time was a fifty-six-hour week; Saturday was a working day like any other; the year pursued its course without interruption from holidays; one was not allowed to sit during work, which did not do the spine much good . . . but what of it? It was still better than being back home with the 'comrades'.

Psar's relationships with other workers was marked by surprise on both sides, but there was no hostility. His workmates would ask questions like: 'Is it true, Monsieur Dmitri, that you eat candles?'

One of them, trying to be friendly, brought one to Monsieur Dmitri, who felt obliged to accept it, in order not to hurt the giver's feelings. One got used to the obligatory round of drinks on Saturday. The wives' hold on the weekly pay packet—hundreds of them were waiting for their husbands at the gate and they did well to mount guard between the factory and the bar—did not bother Psar, who was unmarried. His cleanly habits caused some offence, but in the end he was forgiven his eccentricity. The cross he wore round his neck upset only the most rabid anti-clericals and even they relented on the grounds that an Orthodox 'pope' was not quite as black as a 'crow', the nickname they usually applied to a member of the Catholic clergy. A mutual tolerance, that was not without a touch of warmth, even gave a certain charm to these relationships, based as they were on services mutually rendered. At least no one in the Renault factory blamed Psar for the Russian loan.

Anyway, whatever happened during the week hardly concerned him; he really only came alive on Sundays.

On that day, he would get up a little later than usual, have a good scrub at his basin, sew on his buttons and nail irons on to his shoes. He would then repair to the Rue Daru, lend an ear that was more patriotic than religious to the *Gospodi pomilui* of the choir and, having performed his devotions, spend an hour or two in the cathedral courtyard hanging Bolsheviks and restoring the Tsar. He would fetch up in what he called a family, i.e. a group of about ten men with no families in the room of the only one among them who had a wife. For twelve hours on end, this woman never stopped pouring out tea for her husband's brothers-in-arms. In that cramped, ugly backroom, overlooking the courtyard, in the heat of the icon lamp and teapot—they were still too poor to have a samovar—everyone was sure of sharing in what really mattered: a faith. For what, in some cases, could have been merely ambition, habit, a way of killing time, vulgarity, could be here transmuted into a single, pure, sacred essence.

An old five-kopek piece now assumed the inestimable value of a relic. The St Andrew's flag, a blue cross on a white ground, which, flying over the Tsar's men o' war had once trapped in its fold the breeze of battle, was transformed into small enamelled badges that signified no more than fidelity, sacrifice and, for their humble maker, a living.

It was at one of these Sunday reunions, as midshipmen and ensigns, already some twenty-five-years-old, replaced ministers and generals and tirelessly replayed the civil war, each in his own way (the only rule being that their side had to win), that Dmitri Aleksandrovich learnt that Elena Vladimirovna von Engel, his fiancée, was still alive. Not for much longer, probably: she was dying of starvation and cold in a communal apartment in ex-St Petersburg.

The von Engels were Russians—and woe betide anyone who said otherwise. They were in favour in the eighteenth century and owned a wide assortment of country estates, town houses, dachas—but the explosion of industry in the late nineteenth century had done them no good. Dmitri Aleksandrovich remembered them as a flock of nightbirds who understood very little about the approaching dawn: they ran from one side to another, waving their long arms, gently surprised at seeing hussars dressed like dragoons, women with short hair or gentlemen in the Duma. With amusement and without illusions, they accepted that they belonged to a species condemned by progress: for mankind, there is no ecology.

Elena von Engel, slim, pale-skinned and fair-haired, had aroused in the youthful Dmitri one of those 'northern' attachments that are neither of the heart, nor of the senses, nor of the brain, nor of the entire being, but, apparently, of some mysterious, specialized organ. He liked to skate with her in Taurida Park and he liked to listen to her running through her somewhat approximate arpeggios in the twilight. They had gone to the same *Tanzklass*, dancing quadrilles together and, occasionally, as if by some providential stroke of luck, sharing a mazurka. No promise had been exchanged—that would not have been right—but there had been a little squeeze of the hand in the winter gardens of the Princes Shch . . . Ever since that day, Dmitri regarded himself as engaged, in honour bound. The revolution had come and made his love unrealizable and therefore ineluctable.

The idea that his fiancée had escaped the massacre threw Dmitri Aleksandrovich's existence into turmoil. When the possible (so flat-footed) meets the necessary (so intransigent) the result is seldom happy. In the midst of all the danger and butchery, the volunteer in Wrangel's army sometimes told himself that he was serving his white-skinned Elena. Russia, which has never known chivalry, never ceases to dream about it. But since he had been working nine hours a day operating a lathe that left metal dust in the skin of his fingers, Dmitri had not had time to dream of the girl whom he had begun to call his fiancée without even letting her know. And now she had turned up, absent, but no less real for that, having lost everything, family, position and possessions—and, quite simply, starving. His duty was not to take up the cudgels on her behalf, but to make sure that she had enough *boeuf Stroganoff* or at least macaroni. This was no doubt all very shocking: ladies were supposed to feed themselves in secret, so as not to offend their knight by the sight or even the idea of their manducations; but Dmitri Aleksandrovich had already learnt to give precedence to life over literature. He decided to get Elena to France.

At this time, the Soviet Union badly needed foreign currency. A scale had been set up enabling émigrés to free their relations or friends legally, providing they paid to the State a certain sum of money. Let's call it a ransom, for that is what it was. Grandmothers did not cost very much; it was quite possible to pay for one even with a Renault worker's wage, providing one cut down on one's own expenses. Boys were priceless; one had to be as rich as Croesus to get one's son out of the people's paradise. Girls cost somewhat less, but they were quite beyond the means of a mere lathe operator. Dmitri Aleksandrovich would have to change his job.

His health and small stature put the best-paid jobs, like that of a coal-miner, for instance, out of reach. There was only one solution: taxi-driving. A lot of émigrés had decided to become, as they themselves put it, coachmen. In this way they escaped the production line and, by working extra hours, managed to make a decent living. There was one snag, however—the tip. Could an officer accept tips, like a flunkey? *Centurio in aeternum*. Some had openly snubbed middle-class customers about to proffer their tips, but their French colleagues protested; these Russians had no right to overturn the practices of the profession. In the end they resigned themselves to the tip, some humorously, some bitterly, some irritably, according to temperament.

'This is for you,' said a passenger to one of my cousins, handing him a ridiculously mean tip—two sous, I think.

'And this is for you!' retorted the driver, tossing fifty at him.

The humiliation always hurt. The hand would take the money and put it away surreptitiously; if one wore a signet ring, one would slip it off before taking the wheel. Never mind, Elena had to be saved. But it was with some regret that Dmitri Aleksandrovich gave up his laborious but dignified job for this shameful sinecure. To his surprise, however, he soon got used to the humiliation of taking money and, after a few months, even began to get irritated with customers—the ones he used to like best—who paid just the fare and no more. After all, it was important that his nest-egg grew and that, every fortnight, he was able to send off his food parcel.

He began to write love letters to his 'fiancée', using the rather simple code often resorted to by the émigrés: in order not to arouse the suspicions of the Cheka, one of whose tasks it was to 'look through' all letters from abroad, he gave women's names to the men about whom he provided or asked for news. He himself cleverly signed his letters 'Dina'.

After three years he had saved up the sum required and handed it over to the lawyer who would act on his behalf, for he did not imagine that it was possible for him to be in direct touch with the 'comrades'. Anyway, he harboured no bitter feelings and even considered that he had been lucky:

'Supposing I hadn't been able to drive? Or if stateless persons did not have the right to drive taxis?'

The great day came at last and he rented a second room in his small hotel in the Rue Lecourbe. He cleaned it from top to bottom. He bought real flowers from a real florist and, having brushed his only suit as if he were going to church on Easter Eve, he got into his own taxi and drove off, without slowing down when people hailed him from the pavement.

'Can't they see my flag is struck?' he muttered to himself.

Elena's arrival was nothing like an Easter service. On the contrary, what they had both expected to be a feast of the resurrection turned out to be a recognition of death. If only they had admitted it to one another! But they felt obliged to keep their word and, gritting their teeth, married.

For Elena, Dmitri had represented the past, that is to say, security, comfort, the tender care of family and friends—and that romantic time of late adolescence when happiness and tragedy seem equally attractive to a noble soul. Meeting him again in Paris, she imagined she would be picking up her life in St Petersburg. Indeed, in his letters, he had complained of nothing, partly out of politeness, but also to avoid giving the impression that paying the ransom was in any way a hardship. So she imagined him to be well-off, which was natural enough. The French could not be so stupid or ungrateful as to fail to do their best by an officer of an Allied army. If, from time to time, he had talked jokingly of his job as a taxi driver, she had imagined that this was all part of the code to fool the censors: in fact, he was probably the aide-de-camp of some French general and accompanied him on his travels.

Dmitri's well-worn little suit, with its frayed cuffs, the taxi, a common or garden taxi, in which, on other days, any lout might ride, the hotel room, without right angles (they were cheaper), but possessing the supreme luxury of a partly half-partitioned-off section with the wash basin and obscene bidet, all that struck Elena Vladimirovna von Engel as incredibly sordid. Where she had come from, she had nearly died of hunger, while here Dmitri lived and even claimed to live quite well; but over there, it was the greatest revolution of all time, a still smouldering civil war, an Apocalypse . . . while here it was the clothes line slung from one nail to another in a corner of the room at night, so that the manager would not know that they had washed their own 'smalls', in defiance of the regulations. And that smell on the landing . . .

'One gets used to it,' said Dmitri, like Devushkin in Dostoievsky's story, but it was a foolish thing to say.

For Dmitri, Elena, too, stood for the innocence of the past. He had expected to find once again the fair-haired child whose fingers he had squeezed in the winter gardens, that most poetic of all places, and perhaps in her company revert to being the smart naval cadet that he had once been. But he found that her hands had been spoilt by icy water and her feet by chilblains; the expression in her eyes was alternately shameless and timid; she lied; she repeated at every end and turn the vulgar proverb: 'A handful of wool on a scabby sheep is worth the taking.' Dmitri Aleksandrovich reproached himself for reproaching her with these faults: 'She was such a sensitive plant! What she must have been through!'

But he could not get used to seeing her daub herself with cheap make-up, any more than she could get used to the fact that he didn't buy her better.

Life together, in the tiny apartment that had replaced the two hotel rooms, proved a disappointment for the couple. He considered that, once he had a wife, he ought to provide a home for the thirty-year-old ensigns and midshipmen who did not have one, feed them on Saturday night and all day Sunday, invite them, whenever they felt like it, to come and cheer themselves at the sight of a young wife bent over her needlework, or, before long, over baby clothes. It was with such expectations that when they moved he had fixed the traditional icon and oil lamp on the wall: 'They'll have their little bit of Russia in our home.'

But Elena refused to spend her life slaving over a hot stove to feed a dozen useless mouths:

'You'll be asking me to mend their socks or the seats of their breeches next!' (Yes, she actually used the shocking word—'breeches'—the Soviets had done their work!) 'What good are they, these old tramps of yours who can't even offer a lady a decent bouquet of flowers?'

She was right: an ensign might bring a rose, a midshipman three carnations, and some of them brought nothing, but just stood there, bemused, stroking their bald pates.

The marriage lasted just long enough for Aleksandr Dmitrich to see the light of day. Elena had hated her pregnancy, and the attentions required of a newborn baby exasperated her. The child was uncared for and became daily more repugnant to her. Elena combined the tastes of a well-bred woman with the sloppiness of a common one: naturally enough, she could not bear the result.

For Dmitri Aleksandrovich, on the other hand, the birth of his son was an unadulterated joy, a redemption: the name had been handed on; when the Tsar recovered his throne, he would have one more devoted servant. He who had lived through the horrors of the civil war, was moved at the sight of that tiny parcel of human flesh, that still delicate skull, those tiny hands that, one day, would bear arms and also the immortal soul that he could sense behind the milky eyes. He fussed over the child—and washed his nappies.

'My wife is not in good health,' he would say, by way of excuse.

Elena Vladimirovna disappeared one day with an open touring car, a moleskin coat and a former midshipman who now worked in rather daring women's lingerie. She left a note: 'I know what you will think of me, but I want to live, to live! Try to understand: look after the boy.' Sometimes one tells children whose mother has died that she has gone away. Dmitri Aleksandrovich did the opposite. With a crooked finger he stroked his son's cheek and murmured: 'Mummy has died, Alek. We're orphans now.'

When World War II broke out, new hopes ran through the Russian colony: surely the régime would not survive the upheaval. Yes, but Russia colonized by that race of pork butchers! Dmitri Aleksandrovich kept out of these discussions. He was not a man of superior intelligence, but the trials and tribulations that he had lived through had left him with a fatalism or perhaps a despair that was his way of reaching the truth. Nowadays he no longer expected a restoration of the Old Order, he no longer believed that his will or that of his friends, the forty-year-old midshipmen and ensigns, could do anything to alter History. A single hope still burned in him, that he would not die an exile: 'I shall go home to die. Of that I'm sure,' he often said.

It would happen of its own accord. One day.

The status of stateless persons in France was complicated. Some were called up for the army, others were not. Psar was asked to give up his taxi and to put his skill as a driver at the services of a munitions factory. Some officers started talking to him again about the Russian loan, but, apart from that, he did not consider that he was looked upon with disfavour. When France fell, the factory retreated to the south-east.

'But I'm a foreigner,' he objected. 'In wartime I don't have the right to travel in French territory.'

'That's nothing to do with us. If you don't turn up at Tarbes, you'll be regarded as a deserter.'

After several days spent in the Prefecture, Psar got the necessary permission, but he had no sooner arrived at Tarbes (at his own expense) than the Armistice was signed. The munitions factory disappeared. The only course open for Dmitri Aleksandrovich was to go back to Paris and look for work.

Work? When we've lost the war because of these dirty foreigners, out of the question, my friend. But he still had to eat and, above all, feed young Aleksandr. There was only one solution, sickening though it was to a midshipman: follow the example of large numbers of the natives and accept a job offered by the occupying authorities.

There are two kinds of Russians: those who admire the German machine that produced Goethe and Krupp and those who, since Alexander Nevsky, detest it. Unfortunately for him, Dmitri Aleksandrovich belonged to the second category: for him, to serve the Germans was to betray the 1,700,000 who had died in World War I and the hundreds of thousands of others killed over the centuries by the crusader knights or by Napoleon's auxiliaries. However, once again, he submitted to necessity. He spoke German, he was well treated, his wages had tripled. But he was one of those for whom moral discomfort is more harmful than material: the two years spent driving a German truck were the most destructive in his life. There was one bright spot: he consistently rejected any more responsible or better paid job. He could have worked as an interpreter, a pen pusher, or an employee of the intelligence services; he might even, if he had put on the grey-green uniform (and very becoming it was, too!), have got back his old rank, but he steadfastly refused. Bzar Tmidri may have compromised himself, but the midshipman remained as pure as an icon.

No one, at the Liberation, thanked him for this self-denial. The administration was in the hands of those who had joined the Resistance at the eleventh hour, and who had no other way of proving their patriotism than by attacking anyone who was at their mercy. Besides, the heroism of other resisters, many of whom were Communists, imposed on France a feverish honeymoon with the Soviet Union: in these circumstances, the presence of white émigrés was almost intolerable. A stateless person who had been in the pay of the enemy was a ready target for all insults, a providential scapegoat for a nation that had committed the supreme sin of doubting itself.

For Dmitri Aleksandrovich the situation became, in the strict sense of the term, untenable: administrative harassment on the one side, unemployment on the other. And, from time to time, he had to put up with the gentleman at the end of the bakery queue saying, 'Go home, dirty Russkie.'

The idea of doing precisely that, of going home, not by an act of Providence, but out of choice, began to surface in Dmitri Aleksandrovich's mind. Nowhere could he be poorer, more despised than he was here. And when, in the out-patient's department of a hospital, a doctor told him that he was worn out, that the cells of his body were betraying him, he felt choked by a more potent nostalgia than any he had previously known. As on that other occasion, he gently stroked his son's cheek and said: 'We're going home.'

Aleksandr, taciturn as ever, said nothing.

Dmitri Aleksandrovich no longer had any illusion as to what he would be going home to. He did not hope to find the 'glittering St Petersburg' of his childhood. But he would hear his mother tongue spoken all around him, his native soil would receive his flesh when he had given up the ghost.

'Even the Reds can't refuse me that.'

Anyway, could one still speak of Reds? One could not deny all legitimacy to a State that had so gloriously repulsed the invader. Independence was more precious than liberty.

In any case, liberty was not a word that brought joy to the midshipman's soul. He came from a long line of men whose glory it had been to serve; to be free would have seemed to them the ideal of a slave. And if there was no private property over there, Psar could manage quite happily without it: for him, it was more important to belong than to possess. What a relief it would be to throw that passport of nowhere, that 'Nansen passport' as it was called, into the fire! And Aleksandr would grow up in his own country, which he, too, would learn to serve, perhaps become a cadet, for there were new ones, which they called *suvorovtsy*, 'Suvorov's lads'.

It was strange for Dmitri Aleksandrovich to make contact with the 'comrades'. When he pressed the bell of number 79, he almost expected the world to explode, as it would if a particle of matter came into contact with a particle of anti-matter. But the world did not explode and the Soviets seemed to the émigré more or less like any other of his compatriots.

'You know,' he later recounted to his real comrades, the ensigns and midshipmen, who were now getting on for fifty, 'they don't have horns on their heads or cloven hooves.'

On the other hand, what astonished him was the bureaucratic arrogance, the deliberately displayed sense of superiority that he met with. It was made clear to him that this would in no way be a reconciliation, rather an absolution. And to obtain it, he would first have to abase himself, recognize his mistakes, not only in politics, but in every domain. Dmitri Aleksandrovich's manners, for instance, reflected his long moral decay and one day he even licked his fingers to turn the pages of a volume of Lenin.

'Never do that. We regard that as very bad manners,' his appointed catechist declared severely, fixing on him an aquiline nose and menacing spectacles.

To start with, the new recruit had to fill in pages of forms that were contained in a file marked 'Investigation'. Not only had he to confess his own sins against the Soviet government, but he also had to write out a complete list of all his relations, of whatever degree, and sketch their biographies. He cut short his own exploits and declared that all his relations were dead. The obsession of the 're-immigrants'—not to do anything that might harm those who had found a way of surviving over there—became his: 'Should I have mentioned cousin Alosha as dead or not mention him at all?' he would ask himself, waking up in the middle of the night.

Next came the period of rehabilitation. Having confessed his sins and being apparently absolved, the prodigal son had to undergo an initiation into the correct doctrine. Evening classes had been organized; émigrés who hardly dared to look at one another met three times a week, taking in lectures on the misdeeds of the Tsars, learning by heart the 'thoughts' of Marx, Engels, Ilich and, of course, those of the greatest genius, the greatest general, the greatest philosopher, the greatest economist, the greatest leader of the peoples of all time, the man whose Christian name and patronymic were spoken only with a mixture of obsequious tenderness and male deference, Iosif Vissarionovich. It was unthinkable, of course, that this liturgy should be treated with the slightest degree of humour: the revolutionary style is, first and foremost, a serious one.

Having no training in economics and feeling no concern for the interests or virtues of the bourgeoisie, Dmitri Aleksandrovich was able to take part of his examination without 'betraying his soul': he recited with some satisfaction the list of the marshals of the Union and their victories; with a lump in his throat he recounted the Battle of Stalingrad. But he had to make several attempts at repeating, under his catechist's demanding spectacles, the words 'Nicholas the Bloody' or even 'Leningrad'. The other candidates listened to him without looking at him, in the silence of shared shame. It was then their turn to parrot phrases like 'the hordes of White guards' and 'the shameless marauders of Counter-Revolution'. The session ended with them singing *Katiusha* together: it was Soviet without being Communist, heroic and sentimental, in other words, Russian. One felt better afterwards, as if one had been cleansed.

If Dmitri Aleksandrovich had imagined that for so little effort he would be given his passport and be able to declare to the French that he, too, now had a country, a government, an ambassador, he was mistaken. He now had to give proof of his sincerity. On Sunday mornings, he skipped church and went and applauded propaganda films like *The Hot-head* or *The Oath*, which were shown precisely to coincide with the hours of mass. He took part in organizing balls in honour of the October revolution. He drank toasts to the memory of the ineffable Ilich and to the health of the greatest of all great men. He even forced himself to pronounce in the Soviet way the two apparently innocent words, 'bus' and 'library', that mark off the Russians on one side of the divide, from those on the other. Yet another sacrifice, he thought, and he would be able to board that train . . . home.

At long last he was summoned by his catechist, who declared: 'Citizen, we are now convinced that you are a true son of our Soviet fatherland.'

The green passport lay on the desk in front of him. Dmitri Aleksandrovich could pick it up, check the stamps, the photograph, the signature. The modern spelling of his Christian name and patronymic still irritated him, but that was only a detail; besides, he had almost got used to it, ever since he had been crossing out the hard signs and Latin 'i's on the forms he filled out.

'Thank you, thank you!'

He felt that he had become a whole man again. He would go out into the Rue de Grenelle, head held high. When stopped and questioned by a policeman, he would now reply proudly:

'I am a Soviet citizen.'

To be a citizen seemed to him almost as honorable as being a subject.

'When can I go home?'

The catechist gave a tug at the passport that Dmitri Aleksandrovich seemed hesitant to let go of.

'This must be put away here, for the time being.'

He got up and placed the passport on one of the shelves of the safe embedded in the wall.

'Of course, you'll go home one day. But, for the moment, you'll be more useful to your Soviet fatherland staying where you are. You know the French, you're used to them, and they to you.'

Dmitri Aleksandrovich did not realize at once that the end of his dream had just been announced to him. He clung to the words 'of course' and 'for the moment'. He fixed his prematurely aged eye on the little patch of green that he could still see at the back of the safe.

'But . . . the passport, give it to me,' he begged.

'What for?'

'I can't live in France without proper papers.'

It was not the only reason: he wanted to take the small green booklet back with him, holding it tenderly to his heart and, when he was alone in his room, kiss it, and keep it as material proof of what he had become once again.

'That will present no problem,' said the catechist, with a severe glint of his thick glasses. 'You will not tell the French authorities that you have obtained Soviet nationality. You will continue to live under the Nansen Régime.'

And, since he saw that the poor man's heart was breaking, he added, whether out of cunning or out of charity: 'In this way you will render the greatest services to your Soviet fatherland, which, in spite of all your wrongdoings, has opened its arms to you.'

Dmitri Aleksandrovich was not to live much longer and no one asked him to perform any service for his Soviet fatherland. His cancer progressed, from that moment on, at redoubled speed. He had never been a great drinker, but he now began to drink as if he wanted to finish himself off. Nightwatchman, dishwasher, porter, sweeper, he lost all his jobs and found only temporary ones. Now that he knew that he would never 'go home', he wanted only one thing: to be buried in the cemetery of Sainte-Geneviève-des-Bois, where so many Russian corpses have rotted away that the very soil has become Russianized. The ensigns and midshipmen, now in their fifties, having condemned the treason but not the traitor, clubbed together to realize the humble posthumous dream of a man whom they still called their *odnokashniki*, a word difficult to translate, but which means someone with whom one has shared meals.

Dmitri died in hospital with little medical care, for, on that day, the nurses were on strike.

'I shall not go home, Alek,' he told his son. 'You will go in my place.'

Those were his last words. He raised his hand to stroke

26

Alek's cheek with his knuckles, but could not reach it.

The funeral took place in the cemetery chapel consecrated to the Dormition of the Virgin. Since it was a very hot, June day, the priest put a lot of incense in his censor. They sang the *Among the Saints*, the *Eternal Memory* and the *How Glorious*, the last one being reserved for military funerals. The coffin was lowered into the grave by means of embroidered cloths lent by an old general's wife to whom they had to be given back, so that, contrary to the custom, they were not left to the grave-digger. Anyway, what would he have done with them? The clods of earth broke on the deal coffin.

Aleksandr Dmitrich, fair-haired, distant, observed all this with apparent impassivity. The father's friends felt more distrust than sympathy for the son: he, too, had made a request for repatriation, he, too, haunted the embassy. Could it be that they had a real little Red there? Their wives, on the other hand, were moved at the sight of the thin face with its lined eyelids and the youthful neck that emerged from the white shirt worn without a tie (Dmitri Aleksandrovich hated that particular ornament) under an old blue linen suit, a present from some better-off cousin or perhaps from some international charity.

'How old do you think he is?'

'Nineteen? But he looks younger, the poor boy!'

A young man whom no one seemed to know had attended the funeral. Several times he had crossed himself at the wrong moment. He had a round head and small, round, spectacles, that gave him a benevolent air. He wore a brown jacket, baggy fawn-coloured trousers and stout shoes. As Aleksandr was about to leave the cemetery—he had refused to wait for the bus with the others and intended walking in the full heat of the sun to the station—a car stopped in front of him. The door opened and the driver said: 'Jump in. I'll take you back.'

It was *that* man.

Aleksandr hesitated a moment. Then he realized that this offer might be an order, though politely expressed.

'Thank you, Iakov Moiseich.'

He got in.

As a child Iakov Moiseich Pitman had often been told of the deeds of the valiant Red Chekists in saving the Revolution. Without them, the White Guards would have triumphed. So Iakov dreamt of one day joining the People's Commissariat for Internal Affairs: it was there, he thought, that he might be most useful to his Party and Country.

Iakov Pitman knew that he was of Jewish origin, but that seemed hardly more important to him than if he had been a Tartar or a Georgian. He was proud of belonging to the country that had produced Pushkin, Tchaikovsky and Peter the Great. He loved Russian folklore; he was perfectly capable of singing *Once at a Ball* with the required degree of longing in his voice or of executing a frenetic Cossack dance. Not that he rejected his parents: on the contrary, he was very fond of them, but their concerns seemed to him to belong to another age. When not at home, he would eat pork without the slightest remorse: indeed, he derived particular pleasure from doing so. Like Chekhov's characters, he yearned for an age in which men would love one another and be happy, but he had the advantage over Chekhov of knowing that this age was about to dawn.

The driving force of this future that was approaching full steam ahead was the Party, and Iakov felt for the Party an affection and a gratitude that often brought tears to his eyes. It was thanks to the Party that the fatherland would become the most powerful country, the greatest force for good, in the world. Under the Party's guidance, the Soviet people were working together to build a new world of justice and prosperity. Naturally enough, Iakov wanted to be in the front rank of the workers.

There was nothing against his being accepted by a service that preferred to recruit its members from among young men who had most to expect from it. His father, Moisei Pitman, was a little tailor, as *his* father had been; the mother and grandmothers also belonged to humble families from Berdichev: so the investigation, over two generations, revealed almost impeccable proletarian origins. At that period, Jewish 'nationality' was still regarded as a guarantee of worth, rather than as a taint. A revolutionary uncle added some improving touches to the picture. So, on leaving University, Iakov

Pitman, his heart filled with gratitude and joy, entered the school of Belye Stolby, where his two-year course focused largely on counter-espionage. Because he could speak French, he was then attached to the fifth department of the first chief directorate. With the end of the war, he was given a post at the embassy that the government was reopening in Paris. His enthusiasm knew no bounds: he would be working with all his strength to make France a sister nation of Russia, as free and as happy as she—a younger sister, of course, who would have to obey her older sister's orders for her own good.

In spite of all these good intentions Lieutenant Pitman found himself on the verge of dishonour and recall after a year.

Though shocked by the vulgarity of his colleagues, most of whom were careerists out for a good time, everything went well for him at first. His boss was in charge of relations with the 're-immigrants', drug-addicts and other degenerates, the remnants of Wrangel's thugs and Kolchak's butchers: the Soviet régime must have been tender-hearted indeed to amnesty those henchmen of reaction! Pitman was at once intimidated, disgusted and, as it happened, intensely curious, when for the first time he found himself in the presence of a real prince. He almost expected an ogre—or a superman. But Prince O. was hunchbacked, frail, as poor as a church mouse, took no drugs and had certainly never flogged anyone. Evil incarnate did not always manifest itself in a form as easily discernible as Pitman had at first believed. But he was very willing to learn. He possessed a rapid, adaptable intelligence and above all a certain intuition where people were concerned. He was soon given the task of selecting those of the candidates for return who might be suitable as *seksots* (secret collaborators).

The amnesty was not entirely disinterested, as one might imagine. Most of the 're-immigrants' would not go back: they would stay in France, their numbers serving as a cloak to cover the activities of those who would be given specific missions. One of Pitman's best recruits was a former member of the Resistance whose sister was studying atomic fission. There could be no question of letting such people go back— they were there, already in place, with a sort of legal-illegal status, and could easily be pushed into applying for important posts. But in order to confuse the surveillance of the French authorities, the old taxi drivers, old gypsy musicians and old theologians—for whom, in any case, there was no work in the Soviet Union—would have to spend the rest of their days rotting in exile.

Pitman made a good job of this selection and, in order to give him an opportunity of acquainting himself with every aspect of the intelligence service, the resident transferred him to another section, where his boss was an old blue-nosed Chekist whose exploits in pursuit of his duties (and of his dubious pleasures) were the frequent subject of discussion when the vodka was flowing.

Pitman's first mission in his new post was to take part in the kidnapping in the streets of Paris of a former colonel in the imperial army who had tried, once the war was over, to relaunch the *Union Interarmes*, an organization that had been successively run by Kutiepov and Miller. It was not that the old man was dangerous, but the *Union Interarmes* had to be decapitated, as tradition required. Indeed, this time there would be no need for complicated preparations. With the agreement of the French authorities they would simply have to 'collect' the colonel at home, just as people in Moscow or Nizhni Novgorod were 'collected', preferably at the hour when the body's temperature is lowest, and consequently, the powers of resistance at their weakest.

Iakov Pitman felt no scruples as he got into the black Citroën that had been hired for the occasion. The colonel was a despicable, but embarrassing trouble-maker. He had no doubt been ready enough to hang Red prisoners twenty-five years earlier. He must be prevented from sowing confusion in what was soon, very soon, to be the earthly paradise. Because he had never been a Soviet citizen the French were reluctant to hand him over openly, but they would not be averse to closing their eyes while his compatriots grabbed him. After all had they not fought together against the Germans?

It was Pitman who pressed the doorbell. Since this seemed to produce no sound, he knocked, politely but firmly, with four taps of the knuckle of his right index finger, which he repeated four times. As he did so, he noticed that the old door was losing its varnish. The Chekist was breathing vodka down his neck; one of the two strong-arm men had stayed on the fourth floor, the other had gone up to the landing on the sixth, where he could observe the scene, ready to intervene in the event of trouble. Not that any was expected: the concierge's wife liked the Russian gentleman who always wiped his feet before going up the stairs, but her husband, a former member of the Communist maquis, now a policeman, had promised to keep her quiet.

'If you go on tapping like that,' said the Chekist, 'he'll think you've come to borrow ten francs—which he hasn't got.'

And he began to hammer the door with the flat of his hand. When this failed to elicit an immediate response, he kicked it a few times.

Suddenly Iakov felt as if a great void was opening up before him. Yet the door remained shut. He never knew where that sensation came from: perhaps it was a draught . . . Suddenly, the concierge was yelling excitedly up the stairs:

'Comrade! M'sieur! Captain! Something terrible has happened!'

When Iakov saw that thing on the pavement, that human pancake with a bit of beard on the chin, those broken legs, one bone sticking out through the meat and the patched pyjamas, he stepped back and started to vomit, quite openly, shamelessly. And when there was nothing left to bring up, he went on heaving.

'Milksop! Sissy!' the Chekist spat out.

He then gave up insulting his assistant and just stared at him, glancing up occasionally at his two henchmen, as if calling on them to witness the scene. The concierge kept in the background and shook his head, torn between instinctive pity for the victim, a nervous desire to laugh at the sight of that stinking buffoon with his goatee laid out there on the pavement, and profound disappointment: he had always believed that the Russian comrades invariably pulled off their coups, but a right mess they had made of this one! From that point on, his faith in Marxism declined rapidly: two years later, touched by grace, he was attending mass and voting to the right.

The Chekist got his revenge on his hapless subordinate. In his report the entire failure of the operation was attributed to Lieutenant Pitman, who had knocked on the door for so long that the subject had had time to jump out of the window. The lieutenant's subsequent behaviour proved that he had acted in this way out of a lack of physical courage.

In a single day, Pitman, who had seemed to have the wind in his sails, was doomed to failure, to ignominy. People no longer shook hands with him. When he came in, they turned away. It was now only a question of time—of administrative delay—before he would be removed from the prestigious first chief directorate, perhaps even from the Geebee itself. Cowards don't wear the sky-blue piping of a KGB officer. When he timidly asked for an explanation—he had not been allowed to read the report—the resident looked him straight in the eyes:

'In your place, I'd be ashamed, Pitman. I'd go away and hide myself.'

So he did begin to be ashamed—for the Geebee, inspired by an infallible Party and an absolute doctrine, could not be wrong—and hide himself, for the unconcealed contempt of his comrades hurt him too much. Moreover he was not given any more work: he had no alternative but to bury himself in some corner and await his recall.

Iakov Moiseich Pitman was deeply wounded, wounded in his ambition, in his desire to serve, in what had been his purpose in life. He knew that once one belonged to the Geebee, one could make a number of mistakes that would be passed over out of *esprit de corps*, but what he was being reproached with was a mere weakness. It must be, then, that he had never really been accepted by his peers, that he was being rejected as undesirable. He was also wounded in his love: the gentle Elichka wrote him letters full of tenderness, emotion and hope, but could he bear the thought that his fiancée might blush on learning the truth about the man she loved? He contemplated breaking off the engagement. He even contemplated suicide.

Then, one day, an orderly, who, knowing that he was in

disgrace, dared not look him straight in the eye, came for him: 'Comrade Abdulrakhmanov wants to see you.'

Abdulrakhmanov, a giant of a man, with a sugar-loaf head, had been nicknamed Stalagmite by the young men of the embassy, not only on account of his extraordinary height, but also because he looked more like some natural phenomenon than a human being. This nickname never gained currency, however: for some time the staff had avoided referring to him by any name at all, as if the slightest allusion to him might trigger off heaven knows what cataclysm.

Abdulrakhmanov probably belonged to the Geebee but no one seemed to know in what directorate or department or what his precise duties were. He was shrouded in mystery. Nothing was known about him, not even his rank: he would answer just as readily to 'Comrade Captain' as to 'Comrade General'. He did most of his work outside normal working hours, ferreting around in every office, including the ambassador's—some person had evidently provided him with master keys to the entire building. He was assumed to be either an inspector who had to account for his actions only to Comrade Beria himself, or a high Party dignitary responsible solely to Iosif Vissarionovich. For a man in Pitman's position, to be summoned by Abdulrakhmanov was like a prisoner in death row being knocked up at four in the morning.

Having been given permission to enter, Pitman stood to attention, in typically clumsy fashion, on the threshold of a bare, commonplace office, in which, quite clearly, little work was done. He expected to be met with a soldierly bark or an icy whisper, but all he heard was a melodious voice reciting over and over: 'Before even there was blood on my sword, the enemy surrendered. Before even there was blood on my sword, the enemy surrendered . . .'

In front of the sugar-loaf head an index finger was raised in a schoolmasterly gesture, but there was nothing threatening about it.

'Do come in, Iakov Moiseich of my heart. And pray rest your seat upon a chair. Do you happen to know Sun Tzu?'

The terrifying Comrade Abdulrakhmanov certainly did not speak like an officer of the Geebee. He did not even speak like an ordinary Soviet citizen. He had a deep, musical voice, which he exploited to the full, using the methods of the most refined diction. He played on it like an actor, but his polished pronunciation suggested rather a university professor under the Old Order. Indeed, the words 'Old Order' sprang readily to mind as soon as one saw this courteous, easy-mannered, almost unctuous man whose presence suggested nevertheless such an impression of power. Iakov Pitman would have been shocked by this quite unrevolutionary style had he not been in the grip of quite different emotions: it was the first time for two months that any man had had a kind word for him and now he would have to disappoint him, for he had not the slightest information concerning this Sun Tzu, who must be some lackey of Chiang Kai-shek.

'No, Comrade General, I'm not in the sixth department, Comrade General. And this Sun Tzu, I . . .'

'But do be seated, Iakov Moiseich. The three of us must be better acquainted.'

Pitman looked around him, but he saw no third person in the room, unless one counted Feliks Edmundovich on the wall, but he was everywhere: not a single office of the Geebee escaped his riveting gaze.

'Tell me first what you think of this noble yet—how shall I put it?—surreptitious idea.'

Once again the unfortunate lieutenant was to disappoint this superior, who seemed nevertheless to be so well disposed towards him.

'What idea, Comrade General?'

He said 'General' because that was the highest rank, but he had never seen a general so polite.

'The one I've just quoted: "Before even there was blood on my sword, the enemy surrendered." What do you think about it?'

It was a tricky question, even for those who were anxious to think in the correct fashion at all times. Perhaps Lenin had said somewhere what one should think of that idea, but if he had, Pitman had forgotten it. Overcome with guilt, he took refuge behind a pitiful 'I don't know, Comrade General.'

'Listen,' said the man nicknamed Stalagmite, 'before we meet Comrade Sun Tzu, we shall have to take a few decisions. To begin with, you and I are much too "cultured", as those who are not put it, to feel obliged, at every end and turn, to bombard one another with expressions of our political faith. So you will now cease, my affable Iakov Moiseich, to address me as comrade. Secondly, we are too intrigued by the truth about things and men to attach any importance to superficial and superfluous social stratifications. So you will cease, my inestimable Iakov Moiseich, to address me as general. Lastly, since I take the liberty to call you Iakov Moiseich, I should be much obliged if you would do me the honour of calling me Matvei Matveich.'

'But no one, Comrade General, calls you that.'

'My precious Iakov Moiseich, the comrades who surround us have their uses, undeniably so, but they have nothing to teach Matvei Matveich and nothing to learn of Matvei Matveich. So, in the circumstances, I care not whether they call me the first thing that comes into their heads. If one of them were to say to me, "Come here, Ivan the Simpleton", I would go if I had a mind to do so. Have you heard of Einstein? Don't worry, I've no intention of having him arrested,' he added with an ironic smile, which he immediately suppressed.

'Yes, Matvei Matveich, I have heard of Albert Einstein. However, it is not yet certain whether his doctrine conforms to the basic axioms of Marxist-Leninism.'

'Rest assured: it will. What has to be done will be done. Well, my dear Iakov Moiseich all-of-emerald, what Einstein is as a physicist, I and a few others—for we form a consistory, an areopagus, of which, God willing, you will one day be part—are as strategists. We have discovered the relativity of the art of war. Sun Tzu says: "In the art of war, the supreme refinement is to attack the enemy's plans." Unfortunately Sun Tzu was unable to put his genius into practice.'

Pitman plucked up enough courage to ask: 'Why not?'

'Because, my Iakov Moiseich all-of-silver, Comrade Sun Tzu went up in smoke some two-thousand-five-hundred years ago. Well . . .' (To say 'well', Abdulrakhmanov used the contemplative *nnu-s* of the Old Order, a term forbidden under the New Order on account of the polite particle *s*.) 'We are able to carry out Sun Tzu's ideas, and not only to attack the plans of the general staff, which would not require much effort, but all the plans of the enemy, whatever they may be, from birth-control to literature, sexuality to religion. Let us hope to God that we make full use of the sage's ideas.'

Suddenly Abdulrakhmanov stood up or rather rose to his full height. He was not a man, but a tower, dominating everything around him. He repeated, in the same intonation one uses to chant in church:

' "Before even my sword had blood on it, the enemy surrendered." Do you know anything more elegant or more effective? Ah! Let us settle one detail. I know everything there is to know about you. If you'd been allowed to do it your way, you would probably not have scared the old ass, and he would be braying in the Lubianka now. It's all the fault of that son-of-a-bitch who was so keen to get blood on his sword. I shall show him where the crayfish spend the winter. And if you have a rather delicate stomach . . .'

Pitman felt the need to justify himself: 'It wasn't so much that I was sorry for him, it was the sight of that beard on the pavement. Such a pitiful beard . . .'

'For you, it's the beard, for another something else—no matter. If our qualities were measured by the resistance of our digestive tube, Henri IV would never have become king of France. I'm a recruiting sergeant: I have seen your notes and I'm annexing you.'

There was something terribly greedy about his choice of the word 'annex'. Standing there, with his strangely small hand resting on his desk, Abdulrakhmanov looked like some pterodactyl about to swoop down upon his prey.

'I am very honoured, Matvei Matveich.'

'You are wrong to be so. Are you honoured to have brown hair and to be rather short-sighted? You have the abilities I need in this new apothecary's shop I am setting up. You lack others. But that is no bad thing, since they are mutually exclusive. Think it out, my Iakov Moiseich all-of-diamond. Is it very likely that I shall find in the ranks of this service men possessed of a virtue that is indispensable to me, namely sympathy? Courage, yes, and devotion, and guile, and cruelty, these qualities are to be found among our comrades, but the ability to put oneself in the place of another, to leap into the consciousness and even into the unconsciousness of another, as one would leap to the controls of a vehicle? Come over here.'

Abdulrakhmanov walked round his desk, took Pitman by the shoulder, as if he were a child, and led him to a wooden plaque on the wall. On it was engraved, as if with a pen-knife, in fantastic lettering reminiscent of the Far East, the following text:

1 DISCREDIT GOOD
2 COMPROMISE THE LEADERS
3 SHAKE THEIR FAITH, DELIVER THEM TO CONTEMPT
4 USE BASE MEN
5 DISORGANIZE THE AUTHORITIES
6 SOW DISCORD AMONG THE CITIZENS
7 INCITE THE YOUNG AGAINST THE OLD
8 RIDICULE TRADITIONS
9 DISLOCATE SUPPLIES
10 LET LASCIVIOUS MUSIC BE HEARD
11 SPREAD LECHERY
12 LAY OUT MONEY
13 BE INFORMED

'These,' said Abdulrakhmanov with satisfaction, 'are the thirteen commandments that I have taken from Sun Tzu. I amused myself carving them into this hard-grained olive wood so as to engrave them the better on my memory.'

Pitman looked up to this man who seemed to be laying down for himself the laws by which he lived. With that pale, yet sallow skin, that head shaped like a howitzer pointing to the sky, those hands of a Cherkess princess, those huge feet screwed to the ground, that oriental name, that speech of another century, Abdulrakhmanov seemed to him like a compendium of the Soviet Union, or rather—for union always implies disunion—what was once called the Russian Empire.

' "Those who are expert in the art of war make the enemy host submit without a fight," ' continued the compendium. ' "They take cities without mounting an attack and overthrow a state without prolonged operations." What finesse! What grace! Quite evidently this ideal cannot be shared by our professional sabre-rattlers, who indeed think only of mounting attacks and prolonging operations, either to collect medals and promotions, or for the sheer pleasure of it. But we, my dear Iakov Moiseich all-of-gold, are not here for the pleasure of it. We are here to take over the world. Ay, there's the rub, as Shakespeare put it, or, as we say, this is where the dog is buried. Well, are you interested?'

He did not wait for an answer, but continued: 'I am setting up within the first chief directorate, a Department D. I need someone to be in charge of French affairs. Our techniques are fairly esoteric, but you will learn them on the job. As soon as possible, we'll be peppering your shoulders with stars, to impress the gullible. You are young and at first they will even impress you: don't be taken in by them. The stars are means and not ends, that's what our sabre-rattlers fail to understand. And to have their stars they are determined to get blood on their swords. But Sun Tzu says and says it again: "In war, the best method is to take the enemy intact; destroying him is but a poor alternative. That's what we are going to do to France, my Iakov Moiseich all-of-ruby: we shall pick it off intact.'

A week later, Iakov wrote to his fiancée: 'My Elichka all-of-sugar, I have met the most wonderful man you can imagine. He's Karl Marx and Santa Claus rolled into one. Believe me, I'm not being disrespectful, on the contrary. He is going to teach me certain techniques, which I may not talk about, not even to you, but which will make it possible to do good to men without harming them. Now, the main thing is I've been promoted to captain and will be able to get married as soon as I get leave, which I hope will be soon. Tell me that you hope so too, you little monster.'

Transferred to Department D and promoted, Pitman could now shake as many hands as he wished. Good-natured soul that he was, he forgave his comrades their ill-treatment, but he no longer sought out their company: he plunged himself more and more in the exceptional mission with which he had been vested—condemned, by the fact that it was not so much secret as incommunicable, to increasing isolation. Indeed, he was not even aware of this isolation, finding as he did so much illumination and warmth in the affection that Matvei Matveich had lavished on him from their first meeting. Quite apart from exchanges of a professional nature, a rare friendship was to bind these two men together over the years, the distance of a generation between them adding to the interest each found in the other.

Major-General Abdulrakhmanov—he had finally revealed his rank—was interested, among many other things, in the 're-immigrants'. After hastily skimming through their files, he put his finger on the 'investigation' concerning Dmitri Aleksandrovich Psar: 'Go and see the son. I shall want a detailed report.'

A month later, Pitman handed in his report. Young Psar, sixteen years old, was an intelligent boy, proud and uncommunicative, with literary interests, and he spoke perfect Russian. He showed no hostility towards his political monitors, but appeared to be bored at their lectures. When asked why he had made an application for Soviet citizenship at the same time as his father he replied: 'I want to go home.'

Abdulrakhmanov asked for a photograph of the boy and, at the first glance, exclaimed: 'He is beautiful and he will be superb.'

For Pitman female beauty meant very little, male beauty nothing at all. Indeed what connection could there be between an agreeable physique and the relativity of the art of war? But he concealed his astonishment.

'*Nnus*', murmured Abdulrakhmanov, leaning back in his chair, which creaked as he did so. 'What is your opinion?'

'If you're thinking of making him an influence agent, Matvei Matveich, he would not be suitable.'

'Why not?'

'Because, as you have said, you are looking for men who "radiate". He doesn't radiate, or, if he does, he radiates inwards, secretly.'

'All you'd have to do is kick over the bushel.'

'The bushel?'

'I know what I mean. Carry on.'

'How can I explain? He isn't a Red? Never *will* be. I tried to "surround him ideologically", as the *Vademecum* recommends—and do you know what he did? He learnt by heart

39

the principal chapters of *Das Kapital*. By heart! What insolence!'

'My Iakov Moiseich all-of-gold, what a pleasure it is to deal with a man of your intelligence! However, I would like you to persist. Reread the pages on entryism and make a friend of the boy, or rather become his friend. Flatter him until he drops his guard. And remember that one must always stroke a cat's fur in the right direction.'

Pitman took some time 'to catch the subject on the human plane' (that was the technical term), but by dint of taking him to the cinema to see non-Soviet films, inviting him to cafés and not trying to get him drunk, and talking to him sometimes about Russia, but never about Marxism—what he began to call in his own jargon, 'to titillate the birch-tree syndrome'—he began to draw the boy out.

Aleksandr felt for his father a pathetic mixture of admiration and contempt; he did not miss his mother, and he hated France, 'that nation of petty bourgeois'. He wrote poetry and even prose; in the end he showed Pitman a few of his writings, admitting that his ambition was to become a great writer. As for the dream of 'return', he talked about it as if it were some sacred hope, but he seemed to realize, far better than his father did, that it would happen in the distant future, if at all.

Abdulrakhmanov read *The Four Seasons* and one of the *Tales of Uncle Stepan*.

'His prose is really quite remarkable, especially for a boy born abroad. The poetry is more ordinary. Iakov Moiseich, fill in his background for me.'

Pitman was surprised that his boss still wanted to get something out of this dry, twisted vine, but he filled in the background.

The Department had a long arm. In spite of the prohibition that generally operated against any direct exploitation of the 'corporation', the necessary contacts were made at a very high level and, in the end, an unknown gentleman 'one of your father's friends', turned up one day and asked young Georges Puch what he thought of the White Russian in his class.

'The Ruskie? He's too much! Top of the class in everything! He's not quite your universal genius, but he's not far off.'

'You don't like him that much?'

'It's not that: he's a straight enough guy. Not a teacher's pet. But we're getting a bit tired of "First: Psar" . . . Of course, we call the little fellow "Tsar".'

'You try to needle him, is that it?'

'We have to watch it, though.'

'Why?'

'He doesn't often lash out, but when he does, he really lays it on. Only Coroller is stronger than him, but he's really a gentle guy . . .'

A French teacher, a thin, crusty, dapper little man—and a Communist—was also interrogated.

'Tell me about your pupils.'

'Which ones?'

'All of them. You see our future leaders among them?'

The teacher talked at great length; he was flattered to be asked his opinion.

'Is that all?'

'There's the boy who's top of the class, but he's a White Russian. Believes in God and all that.'

'He's intelligent?'

'Ye-es, but he'll never make a poet. Too uptight. He lives in the past.'

Pitman reported his findings to Abdulrakhmanov.

'Silly ass! On second thoughts, no! He made a point. Talk to our young protégé about God. And another thing: you're engaged, I think? What is your fiancée's name?'

'Elektrifkatsia Baum.'

'Of course. "All power to the Bolsheviks and electrification of the countryside!" You call her Elektra?'

'Elichka, Matvei Matveich.'

'Elichka? Charming. Talk to this boy about Elichka, my friend. I'm asking you to do this as a personal favour. And mention his father as often as possible: twist the knife in the wound. And one day start asking him if he'd agree to help us and in what capacity.'

Pitman talked of God and Aleksandr replied: 'We've fallen out.'

'But you believe he exists?'

'Oh, no! That would give him too much pleasure.'

Pitman talked about Dmitri Aleksandrovich: 'A naval officer who spends his time scrubbing the deck is a teratological phenomenon!' declared his son sententiously. 'Besides, it reveals an utter lack of competence on the part of the French: they imported an element of human capital of unusual value and what did they do with it?'

Pitman hazarded a confidence to his young friend: he was in love, he was going to marry and have lots of children. Aleksandr received the news superciliously: he alone had a soul delicate enough to understand what love was.

Eventually, Pitman came to the point: 'You have asked "to go home", but you must realize that our country could use you here. Have you any idea of the kind of work you might . . .?'

Aleksandr assumed a stubborn air: 'I have some idea.'

He did not seem too enthusiastic.

Shortly afterwards Abdulrakhmanov disappeared from the embassy without warning anyone. Pitman began to worry. Usually the Geebee, nicknamed *patria nostra* by its more cultivated members, protected its own, even against the Party, but not always successfully, and sometimes important Chekists did fall through the floor, as it were—one never knew why—and were never seen again. The arrival of a handwritten letter soon reassured the over-sensitive Iakov. The spelling was modern, devoid of any reactionary letters, but the tall, sloping, elegantly flowing handwriting, as legible as if it had been printed, might have been that of an imperial civil servant.

'My dear Iakov Moiseich, the inevitable has been fulfilled: I have been enrolled in the consistory of those whom we officially call the Conceptuals, but whom our younger comrades, thinking in their mischievous way of those Russian tales in which one finds headgear that confers invisibility on those who wear them, have dubbed the Hidy-hats. So now and henceforth you will have a friend among the Hidy-hats.

'The nickname is not entirely inapt: we know so much of things past, present and to come that we are no longer permitted to leave the territory of the Union. This excess of honour will deprive me therefore of the pleasure of seeing you as often as I would have wished, so, by way of compensation, you will have to come to Mohammed, since Mohammed will never be able to come to you again. I take this opportunity to confess to you, from the height of my recent greatness, that my true, first-name-patronymic is Mohammed Mohammedovich: the other names were chosen so as not to disturb the peace of mind of those colleagues of ours who think that to be a good Bolshevik one must first have been a bad Christian.

'For you, the time has come to begin your training as an influence agent, to bring some order into the notions that you have acquired in the field and to embark with all the assurance required on the career that will be yours. Meanwhile, I am asking you to prepare for me a list of about fifteen candidates for the various posts of influence agents planned for France: we shall keep, I think, some six or seven, whom we shall point in the directions for which they seem best fitted. On the whole, avoid candidates of Russian origin, Psar excepted, whom you will include in the fifteen. I have great hopes for him.

'You will of course be given leave at the end of your training, and I suggest you spend it here. In this way I will be able to enjoy your company and you will have the opportunity of marrying the exquisite Elichka, whom you will then take back with you to France, where she will stop you playing Casanova and falling under the influence of some lisping Mata Hari.'

Department D was destined to enjoy an exceptional future. In ten years, it was to become the independent directorate A and the members of its Consistory were to acquire an importance that was all the more decisive for being relatively concealed. For the time being, it was already distancing itself from the plebs of the Geebee. Only a covered passage way linked the blue town house of the Counts Rostopchin, where the department was housed, to the twin buildings of Dzerzhinsky Square: the headquarters of an insurance company in pre-revolutionary days, in the depths of which was now to be found the prison known as Lubianka, and the building that was completed by German prisoners to house the headquarters of a service employing a few hundred thousand individuals.

Among the gilt, the cornices, the candelabra and marquetry of Rostopchin House, Major-General Abdulrakhmanov seemed to be in his element. The only concession to his colleagues was the ubiquitous portrait of the atheist monk hanging prominently in his office: large, well-defined cheeks, teeth that looked as if they were braced behind the heart-shaped lips, a full moustache, a goatee twisted like a dishrag, lower eyelids that seemed to crush the eyeballs, a gaze that was still hypnotizing the world a quarter of a century after the death of its emitter, just as we can see the light from long extinct stars. A gilded plaque listed the virtues of Feliks Edmundovich Dzerzhinsky: 'Terror of the bourgeoisie, loyal knight of the proletariat, the noblest of those who struggle for the Communist Revolution.' The piece of olive wood on which the text of Sun Tzu had been carved faced the portrait.

'My son, I am happy to see you,' said Abdulrakhmonov. 'I have prepared a few trifles for Elichka: they will be my wedding present.'

The discussions concerning the French candidates took nearly a month, which, fortunately, was added to Captain Pitman's leave. They had to fill posts for a future deputy, a future bishop, a senior civil servant, a non-Communist trade unionist, a film director and a journalist. Late one afternoon, when these decisions had been taken, Mohammed Mohammedovich Abdulrakhmanov sent for tea and broached the subject of Aleksandr Psar.

Snow covered the city and, under the street lamps that were just coming on, it took on strange lilac glints. Steam was rising from the glasses of tea in their silver holders. Pitman was thinking how pleasant it would be, in an hour or two, to dash outside, the cold pinching his nostrils and, like a man in the prime of youth, to run helter-skelter for refuge in the Baums' pleasantly overheated apartment.

Abdulrakhmanov clumped up and down the room, like the statue of the Commendatore, treading heavily on the rugs with their polygonal motifs.

'Did you know that they all come from my country? This one is a blue Bokhara. Iakov Moiseich'—he clasped his hands behind his back—'I have read your report on Psar, and I entirely agree with you, except for one thing. I take the opposite view. If you apply my *Vademecum*, you are right, but one must also learn—and I hope one day you will do so—to disregard the *Vademecum*. You're a young officer. You're not only ambitious, but also, indeed, above all, anxious to serve. Quite understandably, you have certain anxieties. I would like to free you of them. I am telling you now that you will be a success in your career in the Department, that one day you yourself will be a Hidy-hat and that, as such, your cranium will be one of those in which the politics of our country, and therefore of the world, will simmer. Think of me as an old fortune-teller or an astrologer with a pointed hat, and whenever you feel uncertain of yourself, think of my prediction and be reassured. Having said that, you must inscribe the following on your nose: you have a terrible defect, Iakov Moiseich . . .'

'What defect, Comrade General?'

'You do not think freely, you tie up your kopeks with roubles, you give things a nudge when you ought to leave matters to the earth's gravity.

'I recruited you because, being green in the service, you had not yet had time to lose all sense of pity and humour. In our enormous organization, we in the Department are the only ones for whom pity and humour are not only permitted, but indispensable: indeed it is only because they are indispensable that they are permitted. Without pity, which is understanding of other people, we would be nothing; and without humour, which is an understanding of oneself, we would try to be everything. Cultivate your pity and humour, Iakov Moiseich. Try to be detached. Others may do better by keeping their noses to the grindstone, but we require a certain distance and magnanimity, we owe it to ourselves to breathe more deeply.

'You have handed in a thirty-page report on Psar and you end up with the same conclusions as you expressed in your first report. If this is the result of blindness, then let us say no more about it: we all make mistakes. But if it is because you are afraid of contradicting yourself . . . He is not a Red, you say, he does not "radiate".

'To begin with he is very good looking and, in the intermediary echelons of our profession (not yours, fortunately, or mine: we fly too high), physical beauty is invaluable. Secondly, when I went to see him at one of our evening classes at the embassy, I sensed in him a very great, but captive force. You remember the fairy tale in which the giant ties up his own death in a sack and throws it to the bottom of the sea in order to become invincible? One only had to dive down and free the poor thing and Koshchei would perish. For Psar the opposite is the case: it's his life that is in a sack at the bottom of the sea. I am ordering you to go and drag it out, to turn him into a sun.

'To begin with, you will put him through an influence test. You will give him a limited, precise mission, to be carried out in his lycée or even in his class. If he fails (but I do not think he will) I shall give up the plans that I have for him. The mission you give him must not be a political one, or at least not a Marxist one: I want Psar because, in the long run, his background cannot fail to inspire confidence in the West. I shall go further, because, as you correctly observed, he is not a true Red. In the task that I have in mind for him, a true Red would be of much less use.

'It is in this delicate domain, I grant you, that you, my Iakov Moiseich all-of-silver, have made a mistake. And yet the *Vademecum* is quite clear on this point: influence is always exercised through intermediaries. It is only through the interplay of these successive fulcra that the arrow-opinion can reach the target-society. We are not in the propaganda business. Minds like yours and mine would be quite incapable of the arthritic discipline required of that necessary, but crude occupation. Our way is to lean on Psar's resistance, not to weaken it. The only question at issue is whether he will serve us faithfully, which brings us to an examination of the motives that might lead him to accept the casting—I use the word in the theatrical sense—that we might offer him.

'On that point, your report contained two positive answers. On the one hand, young Psar is boiling with a will to power that makes him want to serve those whom he regards as tomorrow's victors, namely us; furthermore, he wants "to go home". Well, personally, I think these two motives, in a vehement spirit like his, may be sufficient mainsprings to make the mission I have in mind viable. The influence agent, after all, does not have to make a superhuman effort. He floats above dangers, he operates in the open air, in sight and sound of everybody, he runs the risk neither of torture nor of death. Against whom will young Psar be called on to work? Against the French, whom he detests. And why does he detest them? Because they are witnesses to, if not actually the cause of, his father's downfall, because they treat even him with contempt, because they have disappointed the hopes that the émigrés had placed in them, because they were given a licking by the Germans. Psar, I think, is of an irritable temperament: he cannot but detest what he sees every day and does not admire. You fear that he is not sufficiently with us because we are his class enemies, but at least we are Russians: the bourgeois who surround him are just as much his class enemies—and French.

'You may be thinking that I like to sail too close to the wind, that I enjoy walking a tightrope by employing the offspring of our hereditary enemies. Yes, it is true. But without such pleasures, our profession would be as dull as any other. And, anyway, I'm keeping a little surprise up my sleeve for that aristocrat who deigns to soil his hands in our company in order to settle a few old scores. Of course, we will lead him to believe that he will be able to go home when he wishes and that we will unroll the red carpet for him when he does. In fact, when we have exploited His High and Mighty Birth to the full, we shall drop him like an old rag at the feet of France. If he dares to boast that he has been our agent, it will make not the slightest difference, for, between now and then, our techniques will already be known to the specialists and, as far as the public is concerned, we shall so arrange things that it refuses to believe in their existence. Does that seem too good to be true? See how the prince of this world operates: he has never been so successful since the day he pretended that he did not exist. And what if I'm wrong and Psar writes his Memoirs? He will demonstrate that, for thirty years, we have manipulated French opinion. That will merely deepen the panic that will reign in the West as the year 2000 approaches. No, no Iakov Moiseich, we have nothing to fear from Psar, provided we make sure that he doesn't drop us on the way. Now put that in your pipe and smoke it.'

As soon as he was back in France, Pitman carried out the influence test with all the intellectual honesty at his disposal.

As a first test—he had decided that there would be three—he asked young Aleksandr to give up being top of the class: 'Be among the top five, never the first.' This would have two effects: first, his classmates would no longer be constantly irritated by his prowess and, secondly, he would show that he was capable of that self-effacement, that lessening of self (the theologians call it 'kenosis') which no secret agent of any value can do without. Pitman knew that this sacrifice would go hard with Aleksandr: being first in everything took the place, for him, of pocket money, holidays, membership of the Racing Club, girls, everything that brought *joie de vivre* and prestige to a teenager. Other, still deeper susceptibilities would be affected: it would be as if he were betraying his country of origin, whose ambassador in space and time he felt himself to be. How could he bear to drag down a name that meant so much to him? Pitman guessed all this and pointed out to the young man the romanticism of the enterprise:

'You will be preparing yourself for what the Germans call a "lord's profession". You will be a masked lord.'

He quoted Sun Tzu, of whom he, too, had become an adept: 'The entire art of war is based on deception.' He pointed out that by imposing this restraint on himself Aleksandr would already have begun to serve, that his father, whom he would take into his confidence, would reproach him with nothing, that any initiation involves some kind of ordeal and that this ordeal would have the supreme elegance of remaining secret.

'I shall have to endure their sneers,' Aleksandr reflected. 'They'll be so delighted to see the mighty one fall.'

'I'll tell you a story. Once upon a time, there was a Chinese prince called Mo Tun. His neighbours, the Hus, in order to test his mettle, sent him emissaries who declared: "We want to buy the horse of a thousand lis." This horse was a most

48

unusual stallion who could cover a thousand lis—500 kilometres—without water or forage. The prince's advisers were indignant at this proposition, but Mo Tun replied that he did not want to give offence to anybody and he sold the horse of a thousand lis. The Hus then demanded one of the royal princesses. Mo Tun's advisers were scandalized, "Demand a princess! We beg you, Prince, to declare war on these miscreants." "One does not refuse one's neighbour a young woman," replied Mo Tun. And he sent the princess. The Hus, emboldened by what they took to be marks of weakness, then demanded part of the prince's territory: "You have a thousand lis of land that we would like to have." Mo Tun assembled his ministers once more. Some recommended firmness, but others, in order to please him, advised him to hand over the land. The prince first had these flatterers decapitated, then jumped into the saddle, gathered his army around him and crushed the Hus, who were caught unprepared. In this way Mo Tun reconstituted the kingdom of his ancestors.'

Contrary to his own expectations, Aleksandr derived a certain pleasure from introducing mistakes into his Latin translations and his quadratic equations: he did so deliberately, of course, after indulging in the additional luxury of turning out a perfect translation and equation for his own satisfaction. Not only did relations with his classmates improve, but he despised them all the more. He was beginning to find his feet as a secret agent.

As a second test, Pitman asked Aleksandr to abandon his solitary habits, to learn to dance and to get himself invited to what were then called, somewhat paradoxically, surprise-parties. A humiliated Aleksandr replied furiously: 'What do you want me to go in, this?'

He pointed at his old blue serge suit and his worn out shoes. Pitman took out his wallet.

'You're not my uncle. I can't take money from you.'

'But I'm not giving it to you,' said Pitman, with a kindly smile. 'You'll have to sign a receipt for it.'

Satisfied, Aleksandr signed. He was thus officially recruited under the pseudonym *Oprichnik*, not on the staff of the Department, of course, but among the occasional informants of the KGB. Dmitri Aleksandrovich was no longer in a position to approve or disapprove: he would get drunk, sleep it off and get drunk again.

Young Psar never liked dancing: he could never let himself go. He got invited all the same. The attention that he had always refused his comrades and which he now gave them flattered them; their sisters found him good looking and their parents liked his rather old-fashioned manners. In a few months he had a circle of friends and even his teachers, who had always found him respectful almost to the point of impertinence, began to say: 'Psar is getting quite human.'

Then Pitman proposed the third of his influence tests. It was the time when public opinion was divided on the death sentence passed on the Rosenbergs, who were thought to have given American atomic secrets to the Soviet Union. Associations were formed to demand that the sentence be commuted.

'What do you think of this affair?' Pitman asked.

'If I were one of the Rosenbergs, I would have acted as they did. If I were the President of the United States, I'd send them to the electric chair, and I'd sent Gold, Borthmann, Greenglass and the whole clique with them.'

'Perfect. You will start an association in your *lycée* demanding the death penalty for the Rosenbergs.'

'But . . . they're working for us!'

'You surely don't imagine that a petition from a few French schoolboys will have the slightest effect on the fate of Comrades Ethel and Julius, do you? In the meantime, we shall be preparing a cover for you as a man of the right that will be useful to you later.'

Believing that an openly bloodthirsty organization had no chance of success among young people who had been rendered incorrigibly sentimental by Christianity, romanticism and democracy, Aleksandr called his group the 'Association for Limiting the Proliferation of Atomic Weapons'. It was quite bad enough that the United States possessed bombs capable of blowing up the world, but if other countries, traditionally less peace-loving, got their hands on the same weapons, how could a universal holocaust be avoided? By giving the Soviet Union, whose expansionism was becoming quite overt, parity of terror, the Rosenbergs had put the whole of mankind in peril. At the very least, one must make sure that this sort of treason is not repeated: an exemplary penalty would be the only guarantee of that.

The argument appealed to those who had a hysterical fear of the nuclear apocalypse, those who wanted France to become a power in the world of culture only, those who liked the Americans, those who hated the Russians, those who feared the Communists—not to mention, of course, a few right-wingers who didn't give a fig for the proliferation of atomic weapons, but wanted to see the Rosenbergs fry. To this last group, Psar hinted that he shared their opinion, but that what mattered above all was to get as many signatures as possible: they signed, with a wink. Perhaps even more important than the arguments was Psar's personality, the calm way in which he could say: 'You know me. I don't get excited easily. But you have to do something, or before you know it, Monaco will have the bomb.'

He derived great pleasure from this, for him, new role of leader. The association voted to charge its members a fee, and, in accordance with the practice of secret agents, Aleksandr, handed over these few francs to his case officer. How he tried to conceal his triumph and how badly he succeeded! With the required degree of seriousness, Pitman took the money and wrote to Abdulrakhmanov:

'Dear Mohammed Mohammedovich, you are right, as always. *Oprichnik* is like our *Ilya Muromets*: he needs time to get going, but, once he starts, there'll be no stopping the clapper, and the bell will sound loud and clear. He is not one of those natural leaders who spontaneously thrust themselves forward, but who do not always have the necessary stuff to face up to the responsibility that they so lightly take on. To begin with *Oprichnik* must overcome a certain aristocratic nonchalance that reminds me a little of Oblomov, perhaps a certain shyness. But for such temperaments it is enough to be given a mission: in carrying it out they find the quantum of energy required to free the energies they all unwittingly carry within them.'

Abdulrakhmanov smiled at the style of the letter, which Pitman had tried to make literary out of piety rather than out of a desire to flatter, and sipped his tea, which smelled strongly of tannin.

'Come and see me again,' he replied. 'We must now find a mission worthy of my protégé.'

This time, it was spring; huge ice floes, some of them bringing branches in full leaf with them, struck each other with terrifying abandon on the Moskova. Elichka was delighted to see her parents and sisters again; she had brought presents for everyone from Paris. Iakov, wreathed in smiles, was introduced into the majestic office that he already knew. The major-general embraced the major.

'*Nnus?*'

Pitman loved the way Abdulrakhmanov said *Nnus*: it conjured up a world of smoking jackets, book-plates, brandy balloons and borzois.

'It seems clear to me that we ought to exploit the boy's literary talents, Mohammed Mohammedovich. Imagine a great writer of undeniable quality, who attacked us systematically, thereby bringing disfavour upon himself and on all who shared his opinions. It would be easy for us to float an idea for him to attack, thus ensuring its immediate popularity. A reactionary writer manipulated by us could do a great deal of harm to the reactionaries.'

'No, I don't agree,' said Mohammed Mohammedovich mildly, squinting at the cigarette that he was inserting into his tortoiseshell cigarette-holder. 'I don't agree, my Iakov Moiseich all-of-silver, and for three reasons: primo, we have no reason to harm the reactionaries as long as they have no greater audience than now. Secundo, any writer who is manipulated loses whatever talent he may have. Look at our literature: it's enough to make one weep. Tertio: do you know what I did? I took your samples of Psarian writing to Comrade Bernhardt. After all, he's the specialist. He read it all, with great attention. At last he emitted one of his rumblings, like a bunged-up bugle, and handed the pages back to me: "For a seventeen-year-old, it's remarkable, but he'll never be a writer." "Why not?" I asked. "Because, to begin with, there is nothing original about any of this stuff—the prose is pure Gogol and the poetry pure Tiuchev, though inferior—and, secondly, he writes in Russian." "So what?" "You say this boy lives in Europe and is not expecting to come here soon—so how will he publish what he writes?" "I don't suppose he's thought of publication yet, only writing." "That's exactly what I'm saying—he isn't a writer. A real writer thinks of publication, then writing." "Are you not exaggerating, Comrade Bernhardt?" "Not really. The vocation of the born writer is to become a public figure. Scribbling is his way of getting there." He didn't relent and, all in all, I don't think he was wrong—suppose we bank on Psar's talent and he doesn't have any?'

'What is to be done with him, then? He isn't a politician: any collective activity from team sports to universal suffrage bores him. A soldier, perhaps? He has it in his blood. A general of ours in the French army . . .'

'Who told you we didn't have one already? Besides, their work is penetration, not influence. I don't intend doing the work of Directorate S for them. Anyway, whom do you expect a general to influence? The colonels waiting for him to retire so that they can become generals in their turn?'

'A journalist, then?'

'We have plenty already, my Iakov Moiseich all-of-brass. We can't have our influence agents meeting one another too often—they might give each other a fit of the giggles, like the Roman haruspices. No, I will tell you what we will do with our Psarchik—he will become a literary agent. Are you familiar with the species? Neither am I, but our colleague who works on America has explained it all to me.

'A literary agent is a man who cannot write a thing himself but who gets others to do so. He solicits manuscripts, puts a few finishing touches to them, to sustain the illusion of his usefulness, presents them to publishers and pockets a percentage of the royalties. He may also act as a scout for publishers, especially when a publisher is interested in a particular subject. In which case he then pockets a percentage of the profits. That's how things work in America and we're going to introduce the same system into France.

'For, don't you see, if one cannot be a genius to order, one can encourage geniuses, put them on the right path, help some to blossom, stifle others, organize publicity or silence, in other words, carry out through intermediaries what one cannot achieve oneself. Re-read the chapter on the Lever in the *Vademecum*, my Iakov Moiseich all-of-pearl. Talking of pearls, we'll never make fine pearls, but what's wrong with cultured pearls? And most contemporary writers, you will agree, are merely cultivated oysters, which is why ours won't stand out. So that's it, Psar will not be a writer, but an incubator of writers.

'Now tell me what you think are the danger zones of his personality, those that could lay him open to being turned, so that we can prepare our counter-measures?'

'I see two, Mohammed Mohammedovich. First, military service. If he does his service in France, he only has to meet an intelligent officer and he might change allegiance. With such traditions and atavisms—well, what are often called atavisms—one does not remain entirely unaffected by the hoisting of the colours every day. If *Oprichnik* feels he is becoming a Frenchman, he will not be bound by any political loyalty to us.'

'He'll get an exemption. The other zone, I suppose, is the fair sex?'

'Yes. It is very difficult to get him to say anything on this subject: he immediately assumes a superior air, or, if one makes a rather crude joke, he blushes, but out of anger, I think, rather than shyness. I'm inclined to think he's a romantic, a true Russian romantic, rather in the style of Pushkin's poor knight, rewritten by Dostoievsky. He has been known to use the word "soul-mate", but, as far as I know, he has not yet met his.'

Pitman talked of these matters with delicacy, as if handling a butterfly. And, as he spoke, he thought with gratitude of the friendship that bound him to Mohammed Mohammedovich: in front of what other officer of the Geebee would he have dared to abstain from sarcasm?

'In short, he's a virgin?'

'I presume so.'

'*Nnus* . . . his soul-mate must turn out to be a Greater Russian. Otherwise, we shall have to watch for absorption by the female: Latin women, it seems, are very good at that. We will have to see what we can do for the pure little gentleman.

However, hold off until further orders. Just keep me informed.

'And, meanwhile, find me a suitable opportunity to recruit him into the Department. We're not going to hold him with the few *sous* you gave him to dress himself decently. An influence agent, Iakov Moiseich, is not an informant, whom one holds on a leash and from whom one asks only one thing—a steady supply of information. He will have to fly on his own wings. That is why the first inspiration you will breathe into him will be as determinant as baptism for a Christian or circumcision for a Jew. But take care how you handle my new pet—I don't want him damaged.'

Pitman returned to Paris. He could not puzzle out the constant hostility with which Abdulrakhmanov spoke of young Psar, while at the same time harbouring such great hopes for him, but he carried out the orders he had been given, with competence and devotion.

The timely death of Dmitri Aleksandrovich provided the necessary opening. He contacted his boss by scrambled telephone and got his agreement. Pitman chose the place, the time and the ingredients of the initiation ceremony. On the day of the funeral, he got into his car and set off for Sainte-Geneviève-des-Bois.

2

The Divine Skein

After the funeral, Iakov Moiseich Pitman began by taking Aleksandr off to lunch at the *Coq d'Or*, a Russian dive on the edge of the Latin Quarter. The walls and low ceilings were daubed with subjects taken from folktales; waiters of various origins tried to pass themselves off as former hussars.

'I'm not hungry,' said Aleksandr.

'One must honour the dead,' Pitman replied.

He ordered vodka and made the sign of the cross before drinking his first nip. Aleksandr looked at him sarcastically: 'You believe in God, and in the Christian God at that? You, a Chekist?'

'How imbued you are with prejudices, my young friend! To begin with, the Cheka disappeared long ago. The Committee of State Security is not at all the same thing, though we would not dream of denying our grandmother. As for God, how shall I put it? I can see that men need God and I think that this need is already God himself. Of all the gods, the most divine was for a long time that of my people. Compare him with that philanderer Jupiter. But there is progress among the gods as there is among men, and just as the Geebee is an improvement on the Cheka, the god of the Christians is a new improved version of the god of the Jews. You are surprised to see me making the sign of the cross? But that's because I'm thinking of your father. I would touch my forehead and breast to honour a Muslim and, when I'm on leave and stay with my father, I don't ask for pork and I twiddle my thumbs on Saturdays.'

Aleksandr began to drink, too, and when confronted with the zakuski, he more than recovered his appetite. To eat and drink in memory of the dead was to celebrate life, solemnly, while respecting the mystery of death. After a few nips, the son even found that he was able to talk of the father, who had already begun his decomposition under the sun at Sainte-Geneviève.

'He didn't go home. He commanded me to go home in his place.'

'I shall help you to carry out his wish.'

After lunch they walked through the hot, dusty streets. They felt closely bound together by the strange sacrament that they had just shared.

'Have you even seen Paris from up there?' Pitman asked, pointing to the towers of Notre-Dame.

Aleksandr shook his head. They started to climb the narrow spiral stairs. Pitman went up first, his dumpy legs soon feeling the strain and his bureaucrat's lungs soon aching with the unaccustomed effort. Aleksandr climbed blithely behind him, glad of this physical exercise that enabled him to burn up in himself the excess of grief and vodka.

They climbed the two hundred and fifty-five steps that led to the gallery. After a few moments' rest, they visited the bell-tower, a strangely theatrical space, all ladders and cat-walks, with, in the middle, the huge, motionless god-child of Louis XIV and Maria Theresa. A guide, with the rough accent expected of a minor functionary, explained that the bell weighed thirteen tonnes, that molten gold and silver had been incorporated in the metal, that it could be heard ten kilometres away four times a year. He pointed out the spaces between the oak and chestnut timbers of the supporting structure.

'They serve as baffles, as it were, to deaden the vibration. Otherwise when the bell rings it would bring down the church.'

Back on the gallery, he pointed out to the visitors the crouching monsters that devour one another for ever in the Paris sky.

'The celebrated medieval gargoyles,' Pitman remarked, appreciatively.

'Ah, no, Monsieur! The gargoyles are water-spouts and they empty the guttering. These are Viollet-le-Duc's chimeras and they are hardly a hundred years old. Look at that one, the one with the three heads. Do you know what it symbolizes?'

He might have been a teacher addressing the class dunce.

'I don't know,' Pitman admitted meekly.

'It symbolizes the architec', because the architec' creates in three di-mensions: length, breadth and heighth!'

Having extended their knowledge, Aleksandr and Pitman went and leant over the parapet. One could breathe better at this altitude than on the asphalt, but one could almost feel the heat refracted from the rooftops. Tourists, who were still rare at this season, were not a hindrance to meditation and, for some time, the youth and the young man, standing side by side, elbows almost touching, their eyes full of the Paris spread out before them, but their attention turned back to their inner landscapes, said nothing. Aleksandr was thinking of his father, Pitman of what he called the 'sacred moment' of recruitment. They surveyed, without really seeing them, the cupolas, towers, domes and steeples and the swell of roof-tops, subliminally recognizing the tiara of the Invalides and the skullcap of the Panthéon, the carcase of Saint-Eustache and the play of cubes of Saint-Sulpice, the floating island of the Sacré-Coeur and the compass needle of the Eiffel Tower. Gradually, however, the landscape, at once grandiose and refined, seemed to rise up towards them as if on a huge service hatch. Suspended above the world, they stood on their balcony, with, behind them, this dizzy wall, and the world advanced to them vibrant with its greys and verdigris, its chalky or livid whites, its dust and its patina, its differ-ences and similarities. At last Pitman broke the silence: 'Have you read Balzac?'

'You're thinking of Rastignac, defying Paris.'

'It would be agreeable to possess all that is here.'

Aleksandr did not react. Pitman went on: 'Oh! I'm not talking about bourgeois possession: it is childish to imagine that one owns a particular square of land because one pays the ground rent. I'm thinking of a deeper relationship. If the French king had come up to this gallery and seen what we see, he would have said to himself: "All this is mine", and yet none of these houses, apart from the biggest one, over there, belonged to him.'

'There are no kings any more,' Aleksandr said coldly.

'Oh yes there are! There always will be. And even . . .'

Pitman felt his heart beating faster. Any time now the 'sacred moment' would begin. Only he could delay it, but in a second it would be too late. He felt like a Victorian young man about to request a girl's hand in marriage.

'And it even depends on you whether you are to be one or not,' he concluded.

'It's not only Balzac you read, Iakov Moiseich, but the Gospels, too, it seems. Isn't that rather frivolous for a Marxist? Is it to lead me into temptation that you have brought me "to the pinnacle of the temple"?'

Pitman was annoyed at being found out, but he hid it.

'The day to which you allude, Jesus Christ committed an inexpiable sin against mankind. You see, I read Dostoievsky as well: he sensed that, but in his day he did not dare to say it, or perhaps even to see it very clearly.'

Aleksandr did not answer.

Confronted by so much reticence, Pitman wondered if it might not be better to beat a retreat for the time being. Originally the tempter had wanted to play on the mythological association without the tempted being aware of it: in this sense, he had misfired. Yet should not the burial of that beloved father and that fierce decision to 'go home' be exploited without delay?

'Aleksandr Dmitrich,' Pitman resumed, in a different tone—he sometimes affected to address his junior with the courtesy form of first-name-patronymic—'do you know what the oldest profession is?'

'Yes, but if you're thinking of ending the funeral celebration in a house of ill repute, then go to hell.'

The prudishness of the term was typical of young Aleksandr's usual tight-lipped attitude.

'You've got the wrong profession, but to go to the place you mention you would still need to know the address. It's an old joke among us intelligence officers—we like to think that ours is the oldest profession.'

Aleksandr stared straight in front of him.

'I see. You've chosen today to recruit me once and for all. And how do you know if I've any talent for intelligence, or

59

even if I'm interested in it? I don't wish to hurt your feelings, Iakov Moiseich, but for me that profession smacks too much of the copper's nark. Send me off to break a few bones somewhere—that would be more in my line. If I'm not mistaken, Lysenko has demonstrated the inheritance of acquired characteristics, and for twenty generations my family has had no other occupation. No Bolshevik, I take it, will reproach me with that. I would even go so far as to say that we can probably agree best on that point—and so much the worse for the bourgeoisie!'

'Any fool can go and get himself rubbed out, though I would imagine that it's more satisfying to get rid of others,' Pitman replied, smiling broadly, as if to apologize for the bluntness of his language. 'But we are no longer living at the time of Prince Serebrianny or our *bogatyrs*: then a naive outlook and a heavy blungeon were enough to win wars. Unfortunately, as far as your ambitions are concerned, the future no longer belongs to such a primitive art of war. The Americans have the atomic bomb—and we shall have it soon. Result: no more idiots usefully bumped off. Oh! Here and there in the world, there will always be trials of strength, with a few dead, unfortunately, and acts of heroism and, of course, atrocities, but without any real consequences: exchanges between pawns at the outposts, nothing more. Real modern warfare, Aleksandr Dmitrich, will occasion few deaths, hardly any torture and no material destruction. It will be perfectly economical and will enable the victor to take possession of territories and peoples more firmly than kings ever could. You and I are at the dawn of the deployment of a new weapon, which is all the more effective in that it does not kill. If you want to wage a war that pays, you must give up your dreams of bloodshed and wounds and become an officer in that cavalry.'

Pitman was sincerely moved and he was banking on that sincerity to make his emotion contagious.

'You're free, of course, not to follow me along the path that I have indicated, but you will see in twenty or thirty years from now that I was right today: armies will be larger and better equipped, but they will not fight any more. They will be great sabres kept permanently in their scabbards.'

'I see, in short, you want me in intelligence.'

'Aleksandr Dmitrich, I shall now explain something to you.' He paused. 'What you vaguely call intelligence takes two forms . . .'

'I know: espionage and counter-espionage.'

Pitman smiled indulgently.

'Espionage and counter-espionage are two stages of the same aspect, which is not unimportant, far from it, but which remains all the same somewhat simplistic. To try to know what the enemy is doing, to prevent him from knowing what I am doing, all that is relatively passive. Things get interesting when I suggest to the enemy certain aims which he then tries to carry out. Imagine Kutuzov commanding the Grand Army through Napoleon, or, since you're a sailor's son, Rozhdestvensky at the head of the Japanese fleet at Tsushima. Doesn't that make your mouth water?'

Young Aleksandr looked up; his brown eyes seemed to be veiled.

'It could be amusing,' he muttered.

'That's what we call the active aspect of the secret operations usually known by the generic name of intelligence.'

'And you think that one really can . . .'

'Our comrade Mao Tse-tung says that we must "mould" the consciousness of the enemy's masses: in so far as we design the mould, we will have them at our mercy.' Pitman pretended to hesitate. 'I don't think I shall be revealing any secrets if I tell you that we distinguish five methods that enable us to get the enemy to act as we want. First, white propaganda, a game two can play, and which consists simply in repeating "I am better than you" over and over again. Secondly, black propaganda, a game for three players: one attributes to the enemy fictitious statements intended to annoy the third party, for whose benefit this comedy is being played. Then there is intoxication, a game for two or three players: the aim is to deceive, but by more subtle methods than lying; for example, I would not give you false information, but I would arrange for you to steal it from me. Then there is disinformation, a word that is now used to denote all these methods taken together. In the strict sense, disinformation is to intoxication what strategy is to tactics.'

Pitman fell silent. He looked at the Seine, a mirror losing its silvering. A *bateau-mouche* crammed with tourists wearing a riot of colours was about to pass a barge festooned with drying shirts and underpants.

'And the fifth?'

The fish was biting.

'The fifth method is secret, Aleksandr Dmitri. We are the only world power that has developed certain methods . . . If I told you what they were, it would be as if I had given you the secret of the atomic bomb five years ago.'

'In that case, tell me nothing,' said young Aleksandr resuming his icy composure.

Pitman corrected his aim.

'What I can say is this: the fifth method is called influence, and the other four are child's play in comparison. I am now going to say something that may shock you. You remember Karl Marx's observation: "The time for revolutions by surprise attack, carried out . . ."'

'. . . "by conscious minorities at the head of unconscious masses, has passed." I know your multiplication tables.'

Pitman lowered his voice slightly.

'Well, it's no longer true.'

'So the prophet slipped up?'

'He was right for his own time, but that time is passed. Sociology has made some progress since then, and we now know that a revolution may be triggered off not only by objective socio-economic conditions, but also by a public opinion conditioned to believe that they exist, even in the face of all the evidence.'

'You mean we no longer need hens to hatch eggs because we have incubators.'

'I mean that we now have incubators that not only hatch eggs, they lay them. The revolution corresponded, according to Karl Marx, to a certain historical moment determined by a previous development; it was supposed to replace an old order with a new one, the blueprint for which already existed, and it was necessarily a violent episode, a convulsion in History. That no longer corresponds to the realities of the twentieth century.'

Pitman had never much believed in Aleksandr's conversion to Marxism: young Psar would enter with more enthusiasm a system in which the Jehovah of Trier was subject to revisions.

'At the present time, we trigger off the "historical moment" by ringing Pavlov's bell—Karl Marx couldn't foresee that. We have discovered that no "new order" ought to be offered in exchange for the old order, because that makes it a target at once. Frankly, nothing is more annoying for us, than the foreign Communist parties—the "corporations", as we call them—that endlessly repeat that the Soviet Union is a paradise. It is not a paradise, as anyone can demonstrate— and as our enemies never fail to point out. We believe that it will be a paradise, but that is an act of faith, and one cannot ask the majority to sacrifice a society it knows for a gamble of this kind. What we must do is to undermine the old order without proposing anything very precise to replace it: it is only when it has become completely incapable of defending itself that one can introduce the new order. Moreover, nothing is more old-fashioned than the scheme by which one first makes propaganda, then triggers off an insurrection. In fact terror is indispensable, but only to set off the explosion, which need not itself be violent. Karl Marx was still thinking in terms of the Encyclopedists-Jacobins binomial, but we have made some progress since then: now terrorism has no other use than to provide us with opportunities of exerting what we call our influence, and we do that through technological means that Karl Marx could not even dream of: the mass media.

'In the Middle Ages, the murder of an individual, a prince, say, could transform the history of a country; then peoples came on the scene and this kind of isolated action no longer served any purpose; today we are striving towards a period when the individual will once again be determinant, not on account of his own qualities, but simply through the new factor of information. I don't know whether you realize it, but the human face, which has already been multiplied by press photography and the cinema, will be multiplied again, in the next quarter of a century, by television. I don't think I'm mistaken in saying that in twenty-five years the seizure of a hostage or the murder of some nobody will have wider repercussions than a colonial war in the nineteenth century.

'It's that train, Aleksandr Dmitrich, that I should not like to see you miss.'

Aleksandr turned his white, bony face towards the Paris that still seemed to rise up towards him. As the afternoon wore on, it appeared more and more clear to the youth that one of the great duels of his life had begun.

What was at stake was the return that had been a desire and had become a duty. And then other interests were at work in that imagination, which was all the more fertile for being confined in an affected coldness. If modern psychology and sociology really did make it possible to rule over people's souls, then young Psar was not a man to refuse the risk.

'It's rather intriguing, isn't it, this . . . influence,' he said.

Pitman pointed his small round nose to the sky. He was looking for maxims and riddles. He knew that at this stage he must intrigue, rather than instruct, but, at the same time, burning with all the passion of the neophyte, he longed to convey his passion to this boy, for whom he felt affection if not sympathy, and even a sort of respect.

'In the Department,' he said as last, 'we have a handbook that contains our doctrine or, at least, that part of it that can be passed on to our agents. This handbook was written by our bosses, for the most part, I imagine, by the greatest of them. Perhaps one day you will be fortunate enough to meet him, as I have done.'

Pitman gave a naive little laugh of adoration. 'He's a big man in both senses of the word.' He saw the form of his benefactor rising before him as tall as the gallery of the Chimeras, as high as the spire of Notre-Dame, even higher. Matvei Mateich held the world in the palm of his hand. And yet was he not the most affectionate of men?

'He calls his handbook *The Vademecum of the Influence Agent*. It's a joke: *Quo Vadis? Mecum*, my pet, *mecum*! And he beckons you with his finger. Of course, we all go *secum*, you'd better believe it!'

Pitman had always been susceptible to the generous emotions of apotheosis, even if his Latin left something to be desired.

'What about this *Vademecum*?'

'I don't think it will be regarded as a great crime . . .' Pitman, at once devious and candid, exploited his own weaknesses, like the great case-officer that he was. '. . . if I reveal to you . . . You know, looking at that three-headed chimera, it occurred to me that there was a certain resemblance between it and us. Our doctrine is one, but it takes on a triple form. The main thing, as I have already suggested, is that nothing we do may be done directly. You saw that bell: one does not strike it with one's fist, one sets it going by means of a rope. Our rope, Aleksandr Dmitrich, is long, very long, and without it we would be nothing, just as a man who tried to sound that bell by striking it would merely damage his knuckles.'

'There must be more to your doctrine than a rope.'

Pitman guessed that Aleksandr was cleverly trying to get him to talk; Aleksandr guessed that Pitman had guessed. He guessed, too, that Pitman wanted to excite his curiosity and that in order to do so, he had to initiate him, at least up to a point. Pitman, for his part, guessed that Aleksandr wanted to learn a great deal and promise little, but neither of them found this game uncongenial.

'Yes,' Pitman agreed, 'there is more to it.'

He was still very young, which, naturally enough, Aleksandr was not aware of: for him, thirty was already quite old. Not for Pitman, who felt, as he had put it, that he was at the dawn of a great adventure. He had his doubts about the abilities of Aleksandr Psar, not about the quality of his own faith. In this first initiation, he refrained, of course, from going beyond the permitted limits, but what was to stop him going up to them? His Master, the man-mountain, would not reproach him with that.

'Our doctrine, as laid down in the *Vademecum*, consists of three archetypes, though the word archetype is not part of our vocabulary. Let's say, three articulations, three images. These images are at once so secret that I ought not to reveal them to you and so precious that I can't stop myself doing so. Despite all our differences you and I have common allegiances—Russia, our political beliefs . . . We both know that it is Red Russia that will save the world. And there is something else: the very simple fact that we are here, standing here together, in this late afternoon, looking at the same landscape, feeling the same admiration—and the same exile. We have set sail on the same boat—and we were destined to do so from the beginning of time.'

Pitman was getting excited and he knew that it was good to get excited (up to a certain point) and Aleksandr, young as he was, knew that Pitman would not get more excited than he wished. As for the boat, it was true: yes, here, between earth and sky, one might well have been on the bridge, perched on a ship carrying with her a microcosm, like Noah's esoteric ark. Aleksandr kept silent, knowing that if he asked questions, Pitman would have an opportunity of refusing to answer. Pitman realized that this silence was not indifference, but a ploy, and he had decided to feed this ploy, one titbit at a time.

'I can, I suppose, give you some idea of these three archetypes, but afterwards—I'm sure a generous nature like yours will understand—you will have to give me an agreement, your word . . . This would be a very suitable day to do so.'

Spontaneously, Aleksandr looked for the south, for Sainte-Geneviève, for that grave, that coffin, that body.

'The three archetypes are . . .' Pitman began.

And it all seemed so beautiful, so nourishing, that he half closed his eyes and refrained from speaking for a second, not, this time, out of calculation, but rather out of respect and a sort of sensuality.

'. . . the Lever, the Triangle and the Wire.'

Aleksandr looked surprised. He found these images very pedestrian.

'I shall expand on that a little,' said Pitman, moved by his own gospel.

The pigeons were flying about below. The deserted Seine reflected the passing clouds. The hovels at the other side of the square would soon be breathing the cool air of the evening.

'The first image is that of the Lever. The greater the distance between the fulcrum and the point of application, the greater the weight you can raise by the same force. One must steep oneself in the idea that it is distance itself that forms the lever and, consequently, one must always seek to increase it, never to reduce it. From this it follows, in the domain of influence, that one must never act oneself but always through an intermediary or, preferably, through a chain of intermediaries. Let me give you a historical example, for the great men of the past sometimes had an intuition of our methods, even though they never gathered them together in a body of doctrine. Philip of Macedon wanted to take Athens. Was he going to practise white propaganda and say: "You Athenians would be happier if you let yourselves be governed by me"? No: he was content to infiltrate Eubulus' pacifist party and Athens fell into his hands like a ripe fruit. This party was Philip's lever. Indeed the use of pacifists has become a classic tactic, as I shall show you if you undergo training with us. When one wants to take over a country, one sets up a peace party, which one tries to make popular, and a war party which discredits itself, because few reasonable people actually want war.'

'When I was small, many French parents didn't give war toys to their boys. The poor fellows grew up without lead soldiers and Eureka rifles.'

'In France the propaganda for peace was an influence operation carried out by Hitler who, in Germany, encouraged the cult of the army. Result: the collapse of France in 1939.'

'And we're doing the same thing, on a much greater scale, with the Stockholm appeal?'

Pitman burst out laughing into his clenched fist.

'You've seen that poster showing a mother holding a child in her arms, with the slogan "Let us struggle for peace"?'

'Of course.'

'The idea emanated from our Department. In the Soviet Union, to support the same appeal, we have a poster with the same slogan, but do you know what it shows? A Red Army soldier cradling a machine gun.'

'And it's the poster that is the lever?'

'No! The lever is the naïve individual who looks at the poster and repeats the message: for example, the journalist of good faith, who believes in the virtues of peace and cannot help but believe in the sincerity of whoever demands it. As you know, it is very easy to say one thing and do the opposite: providing you shout loudly enough, it's what you say that gets noticed, providing public opinion has been suitably prepared; what you do passes unnoticed. That's why the ideal lever is the press—and will soon be the other mass media. Once the preparation has been done, one no longer has any need to orientate information: one just has to let it "reverberate". For example, you have decided to terrorize a particular population. You arrange for an isolated terrorist act to be committed. The conservative press violently condemns that act, but the more it condemns it, the more importance it gives it and, better still, in the end, it's working for you.'

Up until that day Aleksandr regarded himself as a future great writer. Indeed, not just a future one: he had written poems, short stories and two novels, which he was quite satisfied with. But Pitman was suddenly showing him another area, which struck him as infiinitely more tempting. What a poor empty thing the theatre of shadows, with its imaginary characters, seemed, when one might organize real murders and real love affairs! What more sublime kingdom could there be than that of souls and wills? What could be more delectable than to take Guildenstern's pipe and to get Hamlet and all his Danes to dance to one's tune?

'In short,' said Aleksandr, seeking an ironic tone, but not finding it, 'the Pied Piper of Hamelin belonged to your Department?'

'Except that we have more noble ambitions than to rid the world of rats. Think how fortunate it is that it was we, and not the capitalists, who discovered that pipe music. You know, Aleksandr, I don't think that's an accident. In a way, a certain determinism and a certain Providence are the same thing, don't you think?'

'You said that public opinion had to be prepared if such coups are to be carried off. How do you prepare public opinion, Iakov Moiseich?'

Pitman sighed; he was about to discharge more ballast.

'By the method of tendentious information. To do that one infiltrates some highly respected newspaper. If one refrains from compromising it overtly, the entire press falls

68

into step and multiplies the information you provide ad infinitum.'

'And what exactly does this tendentious information consist of?'

Aleksandr tried to look unconcerned. Pitman pretended to fall into the trap.

'The *Vademecum* gives ten recipes for the composition of tendentious information. Would you like to know these ten recipes?'

'Sure.'

'*The unverifiable inversion of the truth, the true-false mixture, the distortion of the truth, change of context, blurring*—with its variant *selective truths—exaggerated commentary, illustration, generalization, unequal parts, equal parts.*'

'Could you give me some examples?'

'I shall try and repeat the exposition given me by my own mentor. "Take the following historical fact," he said. "Ivanov finds his wife in Petrov's bed." 'Aleksandr stiffened; he did not care for dirty jokes. The French could not do without them, but with a Russian he expected to be spared them. Quite obviously, he was wrong. Pitman seemed to like that sort of thing. 'I shall now show you the various ways in which this fact may be treated, if, for some political reason, you wish to present it in a tendentious manner.

'First case. There are no witnesses. The public doesn't know what happened and has no way of finding out. You simply announce that it was Petrov who found his wife in Ivanov's bed. That is what we call a *non-verifiable inversion of the truth*.

'Second recipe: There are witnesses. You write that Ivanov and his wife are not getting along and you admit that, last Saturday, Ivanov surprised his wife with Petrov. It is true, you add, that, during the previous week, it was Ivanova who surprised her husband with Petrova. This is the method we call the *true-false mixture*. The proportions may of course vary. When the lads in "deception" want to bring down the enemy, they mix up to 80 per cent truth with as little as 20 per cent lies, because, at their level, it is important that one particular untruth should be regarded as true. We "disinformers" and influence agents bank on quantity and we find, on the contrary, that a single true and verifiable fact can gain acceptance for a great many that are neither.'

'Just as the founders of the big bell we saw just now put a bit of gold in the bronze.'

'Exactly.

'The third trick. You accept that Citizen Ivanova was found at Petrov's last Saturday, but you refuse to take the question of the sleeping arrangements seriously. The furniture, you say, has nothing to do with it. Ivanova was probably sitting in a chair, but it would certainly be Ivanov's way—after all, he does tend to roll under the table—to calumniate his unfortunate wife. What was she to do? Put up with the beatings of her drunkard of a husband? She may have thought that it was her duty to take refuge at Petrov's and, more than likely, she took her young children with her, for we cannot accuse her of leaving them to the mercy of that brute. There is no evidence either that Citizen Petrova was not present at the Ivanova-Petrov meeting, indeed it is quite likely that she was there, since the scene took place in the bedroom that the Petrovs occupy in the apartment they share with the Ivanovs. This is the trick of *distorting the truth*.

'Fourth artifice.' By now Pitman was counting on his fingers. 'You have recourse to *change of context*. It is quite correct, you will say, that Ivanov found his wife in Petrov's bed, but everyone knows Petrov—he's a notorious philanderer. It is quite possible that he has been condemned fourteen times for rape. That day, he met Ivanova in the corridor, threw himself on her, dragged her into his room and was about to rape her, when, by good fortune, worthy citizen Ivanov, returning from the factory (where he had once again carried off the prize for screwing three thousand screws in two hours and twenty-five minutes), broke down the door and saved his chaste wife from a fate worse than death. And the proof, you will shout from the rooftops, is that the initial information contains no criticism of Ivanova by Ivanov.

'Fifth method: *blurring*. You drown your true fact in a mass of other information. Petrov, you will say, is a Stakhanovite, a renowned harmonica player and a draughts champion. He was born at Nizhni-Novgorod. He was in the artillery during the war, he gave his mother a canary for her sixtieth birthday, he has mistresses, including one Ivanova, he likes garlic sausage, he swims well on his back, he is good at making Siberian *pelmeni*, etc.

'We also have a trick that is the opposite of blurring, *selective truths*. You select from the incident that you have to report certain true but incomplete details. You say, for example, that Ivanov entered Petrov's room without knocking, that Ivanova was startled because she is nervous, that Petrov seemed shocked by Ivanov's bad manners and that, after a brief exchange on the moral decline that is one of the legacies of the Old Order, the Ivanovs went home.

'Sixth method: *exaggerated commentary*. You change nothing in the historical fact, but you draw from it, for example, a criticism of communal apartments, which are rapidly disappearing, but in which encounters between lovers and husbands still take place more often than is provided for in the Five-Year Plan. You then describe a modern city in which each pair of turtle doves has its own studio flat where it can coo to its heart's content and you paint an idyllic picture of the enviable lot awaiting the Ivanovs.

'The seventh trick is another form of the sixth: *illustration*, in which one moves from the general to the particular, rather than from the particular to the general. You may develop the same theme: the happiness of couples in the new cities built thanks to the beneficent efficiency of the Soviet régime, but you end it with some such exclamation as: what an improvement on the old communal apartments in which deplorable scenes took place, like that of Ivanov finding his wife in his neighbour's bedroom!

'The eighth tactic is *generalization*. For example, you draw from Ivanova's behaviour incriminating consequences concerning women's ingratitude, infidelity and immorality, not to mention Petrov's complicity. Or, on the contrary, you lay into the vile seducer Petrov-Casanova, and you might acquit (cheered on by the jury) the unfortunate representative of a shamefully exploited sex.

'The ninth technique is called *unequal parts*. You address your readers and ask them to comment on the incident. You publish one letter condemning Ivanova, even if you have received a hundred such letters, and ten supporting her, even if these ten are all you have received.

'Lastly, the tenth formula is that of *equal parts*. You commission from a university professor, a competent popular polemicist, a fifty-line defence of the lovers, and you ask some village idiot to condemn the same lovers also in fifty lines, which establishes your impartiality.

'So there, Aleksandr Dmitrich, you now have some idea of what tendentious information is and of the exercises that you will be taught to do, though of course on rather more serious subjects.'

'I think I know a French paper that does precisely what you say,' said Aleksandr. 'But . . . didn't you also mention something called the Triangle?'

'You're insatiable. D'you really imagine that I'm going to reveal all our doctrines like that, on this balcony, simply for the fun of it?'

'Goodness! Could you really, if you wanted to, tell me everything before they close the towers?'

'No, of course not. I've given you ten childish recipes, as an example. We have worked out hundreds of such methods that we could use together or separately, a whole interpretation of history, a whole *Weltanschauung* of influence, I would say almost a cosmogony . . .'

'Well, let's have the Triangle, then? Just the Triangle.'

'Very well, briefly. Again it is an application of the basic principle: nothing direct, always intermediaries, never fight on one's own territory or on the enemy's, deal with him elsewhere, in another country, another social context, another intellectual domain than the one in which the conflict actually takes place. This view presupposes three participants: us, the enemy and a foil, that is to say, an element that relays our manoeuvres. Supposing I want to attack a large empire: I don't attack it directly; I discredit it among its allies, its clients, all those on whom it bases its world power. You will see how, before long, the very existence of the under-developed countries will give us extraordinary opportunities for anti-American influence. Suppose now that I have designs on a particular country: I shall make a great show of my friendship for that country and undermine it from within, until its structure is so rotten that it will collapse of its own accord.'

'How would you undermine it from within?'

'By methods that can be learnt, Aleksandr Dmitrich. To begin with, one has to have a perfect knowledge of the society on which one is working. That's why the methods that we have discovered and which our enemies will discover after us will be of no use to them: capitalists are much too lazy and self-assertive to learn to be "like fish in water" in an alien environment. One must make the effort to know the target-society better than its own members know it. To do that we have techniques that I shall not explain to you today, but which might be grouped together under the name of "entry-ism".

'Suppose I decide to extend my influence over a certain country. The triangle will be made up of the authorities of that country, its people and myself. I shall not regard the people as the enemy, but as the foil. I would have three aims: first, to break up the traditional references—those groups that might protect the people from my actions; secondly, to discredit my adversary, the authorities, by action on the foil, the people; thirdly, to neutralize the people itself. Special procedures would be implemented for each of the three stages of my action. In order to break up the traditional groups, I would first try to portray them as guilty, in their own as well as in others' eyes: I would get the rest of the people and the weakest members of those groups themselves to believe that they have acted wrongly in the past and are still doing so; then, ignoring the contradiction, I would show that these groups are useless, parasitical, illusions rather than realities. In this way I shall dig a ditch between parents and children, employers and employees, leaders and led. My agents will have a triple slogan: good faith, good law, good sense. From this position of strength they will attack the authorities, attributing to them all the real ills existing in the target society, not to mention other, imaginary ones. A truly authoritarian society will find means of repression that will provide me with martyrs and enable me to stir up world opinion. A liberal society will succumb even more quickly, for, having demonstrated that it could be attacked with impunity—that is the real principal objective of terrorism, intelligently understood—I shall arrive at the third stage of my action. Before then, I shall do a little propaganda by projection, that is, I shall accuse the enemy of using the methods that I intend to employ myself: in this way I shall appear in a state of legitimate defence. Don't forget, Aleksandr, unlike revolutions in the past, modern revolutions are conducted against the majority and not against a minority. And we shall have that majority in our hands when we have brought it to a general state of paralysis. This can be done in various ways. It is sometimes possible to transform a majority into a gigantic sports club: raise the right leg, they raise it, raise the left, they raise it; raise both legs—and they find themselves on their backsides. Sometimes, on the other hand, one has to split up the population into millions of individuals, each citizen finding himself alone confronting the Gorgon's mask that is presented to him, feeling disarmed and ready to surrender. One creates this dumb panic by propagating the myth of the superiority of the enemy, by a little terrorism, by that fascination that the snake exerts over the frog. Sometimes one adds a whole pseudo-supernatural apparatus, with prophecies, visions and various Rasputinades. In any case, when one speaks of "mobilizing" the masses, one has in fact only one aim: to immobilize them. When one has succeeded, that is, when the foil is petrified, the real enemy falls into your hands like a ripe fruit.

'That, in brief, is the theory of the Triangle.'

'You also mentioned,' said Aleksandr, 'the Wire.'

This time Pitman really did hesitate. He walked away a few steps then turned back. The guide was looking at his watch. The coaches, having regurgitated the Barbarians, were now moving off in the direction of the Opéra. The light was changing colour as it changed height. It was no longer white, though not yet golden; it was as if it were falling on the great battleship Notre-Dame through some imperceptibly tinted window.

The three principles of the *Vademecum*, explained without the techniques for applying them certainly did not constitute a complete initiation: indeed, it was only the beginning. But a beginning had been made. Aleksandr Psar, though a Soviet citizen, came from a reactionary family, had been brought up in France, and might have hidden links with the enemy that the investigations had not revealed. The day would come when the doctrine of influence would be known throughout the world but, for the moment, it was still one of the régime's greatest secrets. It fell to young Iakov Moiseich Pitman to reveal this last article at the risk of its being betrayed, or to conceal it at the risk of losing his protégé forever.

'Look,' he said, coming back to lean again next to Aleksandr, 'I can't do more than just touch on this subject. The image of the Wire comes from the fact that, in order to break it, you have to bend it in both directions. We are coming close here to the very essence of our art—I use the word advisedly. The influence agent is the opposite of a propagandist, or rather he is the absolute propagandist, the one who practises pure propaganda, never *for*, always *against*, with no other aim but to weaken, soften up, loosen, untie, undo, unscrew. If you are still interested in our work, I shall lend you a book by the Chinese thinker Sun Tzu, who lived 2,500 years ago. He was the Clausewitz of his time. Among other admirable things, he says this—he is talking about the disposition of troops before the enemy, but it describes us perfectly: "The ultimate finesse is not to present a shape that can be clearly defined. In this way, you will escape the indiscretions of the most perspicacious spies, and the most sagacious minds will be unable to draw up a plan against you." For example, the Soviet influence agent will never appear to be a Communist. He will systematically cut through the existing order, sometimes with the left, sometimes with the right. That is all that he is supposed to do and, in this role, he enjoys absolute impunity. No law, Aleksandr Dmitrich—I mean no Western law—forbids one to undermine the society in which one lives. One only has to play the red and the black, *pair* and *impair*.'

Aleksandr was watching the sun move obliquely to the West, like a ship making harbour.

'One day,' he said, 'when I was small, my father took me to a fun fair. We stopped in front of a lottery: a great wheel divided into red and blue sections. You put your money on one or the other. The prize was a fish in a bowl. I wanted that fish and my father found enough money in his pocket to back both ways. "You take the red and I'll take the blue," he said. "That way, we're sure to win." The fish cost less than the two bets, probably less than one. Nevertheless I wondered if our tactic was very honest. But I said to my father: "All right. Let's go." He won the fish and gave it to me. I was happy.'

Aleksandr fell silent. Pitman waited for a while before asking: 'Am I to take this story as an answer?'

The younger man smiled sadly: 'Yes, on one condition. I shall serve you faithfully, with no effort spared, and with no thought for my own life, for thirty years. But before I reach the age of fifty, you will let me go home, as I wish and as my father commanded me.'

'You have my word as an officer and a Bolshevik,' said Pitman, holding out his hand.

'*On ferme*,' yelled the guide, in his thick accent, yawning.

When the recruiter and the recruited left one another that evening at the foot of the spiral staircase, Pitman rushed once again to his telephone: 'Mohammed Mohammedovich. We've got him!'

Aleksandr went back to the room he had shared with his father and wept over the death of the poor old midshipman, of course, but much more over the loss of his own innocence. He had been reading Goethe and knew perfectly well what he had done up there, 'at the pinnacle of the temple'. To deprive men of their freedom of action is regarded as sufficient evil in itself, but his purpose went deeper. He would replace that voice within us that says: 'I choose.' Stretched out in the darkness of his bed with its broken springs, his eyes riveted on the indigo trapezium that the window projected on to the ceiling, he murmured, with the grandiloquence of his age: 'I shall be the incubus of French thought.'

It is possible to be grandiloquent and not to lie.

Not long afterwards, as a would-be conscript, he was summoned to appear before an army medical board. On the appointed day, he stood, naked, in front of the officer, Major Nanan, who was fully kitted out in jasper-brown uniform, garnet-red *képi* and gold braid.

Some years earlier, Nanan, dissatisfied with his pay, had spent the empty hours of garrison life working as an abortionist. He was saved from prosecution only by the intervention of a Communist deputy and, ever since, lived under a dual subordination. He would fail candidates at the medical to order and, since such a practice was by no means unheard of in France, did quite well out of it. Psar Aleksandr was one of the few beneficiaries who nearly got him into trouble:

'Me? Not fit? I demand a second opinion!' Aleksandr spluttered, insolent in his naked whiteness.

Pitman had to intervene. He had made a mistake. He should have asked for a sacrifice instead of rigging it behind the boy's back. He had to explain that there was no time to waste: Aleksandr could not spend months polishing his gaiters when the Soviet fatherland needed his services. Aleksandr gave in, but for a long time he held a grudge against his masters: he forgave them only when, towards the end of 1968, he was co-opted into the rank of second-lieutenant of the KGB—and therefore got his epaulette, or near enough.

For the rest, he obeyed the slightest injunction. He was told to take a course in French literature at the Sorbonne and he passed with distinction: he regarded these studies as a reconnaissance mission in the enemy camp. This did not prevent him, however, from later launching, through one of his 'sound boxes', the slogan 'Standardized spelling is discriminatory, repressive and reactionary, it is the last bourgeois chain that the proletariat has yet to break.' Further studies were then arranged for him at Columbia University and he set out for New York without taking his leave of a single person.

'That will be my Egyptian campaign,' he remarked to Pitman, with all due modesty.

'Not entirely. First, you must really master the American language: otherwise, you'll never be anything but a lame duck in the modern world, my Aleksandr Dmitrich all-of-gold.' (Pitman confined himself to the metals.) 'Besides, if you want to know precisely what a literary agent is, it's from the Americans that you must find out; so you must do your apprenticeship there. Lastly, it will be an excellent opportunity to "launder" the funds that you will need when you set up your own agency: you'll make out that they're your savings.'

There was a fourth reason: if Aleksandr left France for a few years, he would feel like a foreigner when he got back and a reversal of allegiance would become that much less likely. Pitman considered that being away from France might have the opposite effect, but he did not regard it as a serious threat: too many resentments and humiliations from the past would colour his memories of France.

Aleksandr, as apparently phlegmatic, submissive and elusive as ever, got his degree at Columbia *summa cum laude*.

One day he went into a snack-bar on 43rd Street for a frankfurter. He sat on one of the tall stools at the counter. The stool next to his was empty and, of course, Aleksandr fully expected that some ravishing girl would come and sit there.

A ravishing girl did come and sit there. She shot terrified glances around her. In hesitant English she ordered an ice-cream. Aleksandr observed her with all the discretion and trembling respect of a Russian in love.

Her eyebrows were very long, almost framing her green eyes; her long neck gave her a certain distinction; her pale lips suggested no sensuality; her oval forehead, Aleksandr thought, called for a diadem. She probably had a body, but he did not particularly notice it.

She was the first to finish her snack and made to pay the waitress, who refused and, with a lift of the chin, indicated the cashier. With a lump in his throat—he had never, in all his life, spoken to an unknown woman—Aleksandr explained what she had to do. 'Tank you,' said the young girl, with a shy glance from her large, frightened eyes. He followed her over to the cashier, driven by two contradictory feelings: 'I hope she doesn't think I'm trying to follow her' and, 'What a crime it would be to lose her if she is It!'

She opened her purse and peered into it, short-sightedly. She found only a few copper coins.

'Not enough!' the ill-tempered cashier repeated.

When the girl realized at last that she did not have enough to pay the bill, she exclaimed: '*Bozhe moi*!' (Oh, my God!)

The rest was easy. The young couple spent three hours

walking in the Park, which, in those days, one still had a chance of leaving alive. She was called Tamara Shch. Aleksandr did not fail to recognize her illustrious name. She was a singer in a folk choir. (Pitman had suggested a dancer—the Soviet ballet companies often travelled—but Abdulrakhmanov had objected vehemently: 'No, no, Iakov Moiseich, no bare thighs! Our young friend is a man of great delicacy!') That evening the choir was not singing. Tamara had escaped from the surveillance of the 'interpreters' because she had wanted to see the real New York. Like Cinderella she had to be back at her hotel at midnight. And what did they talk about? Russia and love. They separated without a kiss.

Next day he went to hear her and, although she was in the choir, he thought he could recognize her voice in the moving rendering of *Luchinushka*. The next day the choir left for San Francisco.

Aleksandr did not write to Tamara, so as not to get her into trouble: serving the régime as he did, he had no illusions as to its liberalism; that may even have been the reason why he served it. He could have explained to the authorities that he, too, worked for the cause, but he was already too imbued with the importance of his own clandestinity. And what of Tamara? He had recognized her as the One. He loved her and he would never see her again: that was simple enough for a Russian.

The years passed and one day Abdulrakhmanov said to Pitman: 'A nightingale can't be fed on fables.'

Indeed, Aleksandr's chastity had in a sense become exhausted and he then resorted, with detachment, to the mistresses that the Geebee placed at his disposal. None of them was French: a carnal link must not be allowed to be created between him and the country against which he was working. None of them, of course, was Russian: he would marry a compatriot when he 'went home', but, for the moment, he had to separate clearly what would be 'the real thing' and what was a matter of mere hygienic necessity. Furthermore, Aleksandr never had overriding physical needs; he did not always avail himself of the opportunities put at his disposal.

He was twenty-seven years old and a graduate of Columbia: he had done his apprenticeship as an influence agent in a secret school in Brooklyn and his apprenticeship as a literary agent with an agency in Madison Avenue, when he stepped down, feeling not unlike a conqueror, from the plane that had brought him back to Orly. What had been said, one June afternoon, eight years before on the towers of Notre-Dame, had already cut into his soul as a ring cuts into the flesh of a finger. He had come to pay off old scores with France and to make it dance to his tune.

Pitman still had his post in Paris and the two men, whom the relativity of age had already begun to bring together, were pleased to see one another. From the outset Aleksandr treated Pitman not as an adoptive father, but rather as Mephistopheles to his Faust and Pitman, benevolent and skilful as ever, did nothing to disabuse him. While remaining the only true professional, the older man was supposed to have certain foibles that forbade him the centre of the stage, where his junior was supposed to shine: 'But you are an aristocrat, Aleksandr Dmitrich . . .' Pitman quipped, but not without a certain deference. Aleksandr replied: 'Iakov Moiseich, you really ought to learn to spit your olive stones into your fist,' but not without humour. There was a certain trust between the two men, based on mutual recognition of their qualities and even a certain warmth, because Aleksandr was easy-going and Iakov felt sorry for him.

Contrary to the usual practice, Aleksandr's recruiter was his first case-officer and their mutual affection veiled their professional relations. A sudden jolt might upset the apple cart.

It was agreed between them that Aleksandr's life must be clear of all suspicion and that, consequently, there could be no question for him of crossing the so-called Iron Curtain before completing his mission: any reasonably attentive policeman might wonder what a White Russian was doing in Red Russia and an influence agent functions to the full only as long as no one asks any questions about him. But suddenly Aleksandr Psar took it into his head to ask for leave, which he wished to spend in the USSR.

Pitman, sensitive as ever, passed on the request to Abdul-rakhmanov. The Man-Mountain turned into a Man-

Volcano: 'I thought I told you, my Iakov Moiseich, all-of-papier-mâché, that the aristocratic little *katsap*'—that is to say Greater Russian—'was to die on the dung-heap of exile!'

The artist-manipulator then demonstrated his true genius: 'Aleksandr Dmitrich, this thirty-year-mission that you have agreed to, ending with your rediscovery of the fatherland, what a fine love story it was! And now what are you suggesting some sordid flirtation?'

Aleksandr Dmitrich, humiliated at allowing this side of things to be pointed out to him by a man whom he regarded as less subtle than himself, never again mentioned the matter of a temporary return.

Shortly afterwards Colonel Pitman was appointed to Department headquarters. He would still travel, but could no longer direct his agents at close quarters. A new case-officer, 'Ivan', was assigned to influence agent *Oprichnik*. There was a little friction at first, but this was soon sorted out and, to mark his esteem for his guide, Aleksandr accorded him the patronymic Ivanich. With the next case-officer, who also claimed to be called 'Ivan' and whom Aleksandr called 'Ivan II', things went badly from the start: the KGB officer treated *Oprichnik* like an ordinary agent, all stick and carrot; *Oprichnik* demanded the recall of the uncouth individual. Pitman, a gentle man, hesitated, but he mistrusted his own gentleness and his first reaction was a violent one: punish Psar or dismiss him for good.

'There can be no question of that, old son,' said Lieut-General Abdulrakhmanov, emitting circles of blue smoke. 'There are cases when violence is not enough and only brutality will do.'

'You don't mean . . . Department V?'

'No, my Iakov Moiseich all-of-cardboard. You must understand that you have committed a serious error in appointing such a dunderhead to run *Oprichnik*. You will award yourself a collective, patriotic reprimand, immediately recall this idiot and send him where Makar himself never pastured his calves. I am grateful to you for not trying to hide this business from me: otherwise, it would have been you, my lad, who would have been sent to sow disinformation among the Buriats.'

Ivan II was replaced by 'Igor', whom Aleksandr baptized Ivan III: 'If they don't tell me their real names, I shall call them all the same, like chambermaids.'

Ivan III got on well with Aleksandr and even adopted some of his ways of looking at things.

'Doesn't that pose something of a risk, Mohammed Mohammedovich?' Pitman asked.

Mohammedovich sighed.

'Does *Oprichnik* give you satisfaction? Yes. Do you keep an eye on him? Yes. Has he been turned? Not as far as you know. So stop fretting like a shopkeeper. It is hardly surprising if this man, who "radiates"—as we know, because that's why we chose him—exerts some influence over the subordinates entrusted with the task of reflecting his sun. Influence is the poor fellow's job. Rather than reduce it, take it into account, subtract it from the overall weight as one does with the tare. And, in order to be quite sure that you are not making a mistake, assign him case-officers who will definitely be influenced by him—not just influenced, but charmed, possessed by him. Whenever you feel you must keep a tighter rein on him, simply change the case-officer.'

Having completed his time in France, Ivan III was replaced by Ivan IV, an odd, but warm-hearted individual, who was also accorded by his agent an honorary patronymic. Ivan IV deeply revered *Oprichnik*, but that did not stop him doing his job, that is to say, transmitting the directives and funds in one direction, the receipts and reports in the other. Pitman smiled behind his thin-rimmed glasses; his only wish was that everybody should be happy.

Aleksandr Psar was forty-three years old and had the rank of 'co-opted lieutenant-colonel' when Ivan IV, an ordinary bon vivant, a run-of-the-mill officer, a Parisian Geebee man, sounded the alarm. He had been summoned to the Directorate for his regular talk with Colonel Pitman (which he referred to as going to confession), and, although he answered with great volubility all the questions asked of him, he still seemed to be keeping something back. He got up, sat down, looked at the portrait of Dzerzhinsky, read for the tenth time the commandments of Sun Tzu that Pitman had had carved in imitation of Abdulrakhmanov, like a dog that could not settle down to sleep. Pitman decided to extend the interview until the fellow had unburdened himself. Meanwhile he asked innocuous questions that, together with their soothing answers, were supposed to have an absolving effect. Outside it was getting dark. Pitman still did not turn on the light. At last, in the half-light, Ivan Ivanich murmured: 'There is . . . something else. It probably doesn't mean anything . . . If I'm talking like an old fool, don't be mad at me . . . Just tell me: "You're a fool, a donkey that doesn't deserve his hay!" Just tell me, Comrade Colonel, don't feel embarrassed. But all the same . . . my duty as a Chekist . . .'

Pitman waited patiently.

'Comrade colonel, he is always . . . looking at young boys.'

'You mean . . .?'

Pitman gave a disgusted snort. Ivan Ivanich blushed to the roots of his hair and waved his hands about.

'No, no, not like that. You have children yourself, haven't you, if you'll forgive my asking?'

'Six.'

Elichka had done her duty.

'I have three cute little kids myself and, you may rest assured, they are convinced Bolsheviks. Three pretty, fair-haired *Bolshevichki*, the joy of my life—outside working hours, of course. Well, if I was his age and had no little blond head to stroke . . . Judge for yourself, Comrade Colonel . . . If a little boy walks by, a little girl, too, but especially a boy, he can't keep his eyes off him, and he seems to be turning something over in his mind. And something else—for some time now, he has been using more diminutives, whereas he used to make fun of them. I've carried out a statistical analysis: hardly an hour passes but he uses five or six diminutives as opposed to two or three last year.'

Pitman was moved, sincerely moved: that was his strength. He went and discussed diminutives and stroking young heads with the colonel-general, who, at seventy-five, was about to retire. To talk in peace, he had to send out the orderlies, who were busy rolling up the Bokhara rugs in his now bare-walled office.

Mohammed Mohammedovich reflected. His own private life was a mystery for his colleagues; some talked of a harem, some of eclectic sexual tastes, others declared that Stalagmite had become petrified by his job. His large face, which was hardly wrinkled, but which, with age, had taken on basalt-coloured highlights, betrayed nothing. However, after a moment's thought, he gave his decision:

'A woman. Not a "swallow", but an officer. Let him be quite clear on the matter. No marriage for the moment, but a son. You'll arrange a honeymoon somewhere and then set up a correspondence through the case-officer. No meeting. Not for five or six years. He will wait.'

'But . . . what then, Mohammed Mohammedovich? Will we let him come home?'

'Never. What Sun Tzu calls "the divine skein" will tighten around him all the better.'

Pitman still did not understand why the great man persisted in such petty rancour against Psar.

'Choose a woman with plenty of flesh on her,' continued the great man, who still had an astonishing memory. 'A woman less Platonic, so to speak, than the other one.'

And, as Pitman was leaving, he called out: 'And remember, a virgin. Or at least a woman who can pass for one.'

'But, Comrade General . . .'

'You're a Chekist: see to it.'

The orderly, who was on his way back in, gaped with amazement.

Alla Kuznetsova was twenty-four years old, had the rank of captain and fine grey eyes. She came from a peasant family of Great Russia; she had the stocky physique and rather austere grace of that nation. She could be much given to day-dreaming; she loved music and climbing trees; a mixture of personal ambition and inherited modesty had prevented her from devoting too much attention to men.

Aleksandr chose her as princes once chose their princesses: on the basis of photographs and information provided as to the health, education and character of the candidate. He had never had any desire to lead an ordinary life and it pleased him to be able to pick his fancy in this way. He also saw this treatment as a measure of the favour he enjoyed with his masters.

The successful candidate was presented to Abdulrakhmanov: 'A morsel fit for a king!' he declared, after testing the firmness of the muscles. 'The fellow has good taste.'

Pitman said nothing: any attractive woman aroused a feeling of tenderness in him and almost an excess of passion for his plump Elichka.

Innumerable precautions were taken so that the tryst should remain secret. M. Psar told everybody, even his faithful secretary, that he was going on a cruise to Norway, bought an air ticket for Senegal, and arrived in Yugoslavia in a BMW rented under a false identity.

The Geebee had done a good job. A small, romantic, but comfortable house, clad with Virginia creeper and possessing two bathrooms, perched on a hill overlooking the Adriatic, surrounded by a garden well stocked with flowers and shrubs, separated from the road by electrified railings, had been prepared for the colonel and his future wife. In a tiled living-room, with irregular walls pierced by loopholes, the floor was thick with rugs. (*Abdulrakhmanov:* Rugs are important: they make for spontaneity.) A grand piano occupied the corner, opposite the fireplace and, near a sofa strewn with cushions embroidered in cross stitch, a gramophone, provided with some fifty albums, awaited, with that pregnant silence peculiar to machines that produce music. (*Pitman:* Music is important: it makes for nostalgia.) The refrigerator contained, among other things, four sorts of caviar and twelve of vodka. (*Abdulrakhmanov:* And above all, see that they eat oysters every day. *Pitman:* I'll have a box of halva sent to them.) A bar was plentifully supplied with Caucasian brandy (for patriotism) and French cognac (for the taste). (*Abdulrakhmanov:* Do not forget the liqueurs! *Pitman:* They must have a bottle of slivovits.)

Nor had the decoration been left to chance. In the bedroom Abdulrakhmanov had hung Fragonard's *Stolen Kiss*, which, exploiting the privileges of his rank, he had borrowed from the Hermitage, much to the inconvenience of certain tourists (who still remember the bare space on the wall); Pitman decorated the living-room with romantic Russian engravings. To remind the lovers that they were still on duty, a portrait of Felix Edmundovich was placed above the mantelpiece: the ascetic torturer seemed to have his gaze fixed on a radiant future illuminated by burning stakes and, below the portrait, was the famous motto: 'Cool head, burning heart and hands always clean!'

The two sponsors took a paternal delight in feathering their agents' love-nest: 'I hope they will be happy,' said Pitman, with some emotion.

'They'll have no excuse if they're not!' Abdulrakhmanov concluded, with a fierce smile.

On arrival, Aleksandr contacted the old village woman who was to clean and cook for them. Having served Russian émigrés, she spoke the language fairly well and took pleasure in doing so. Aleksandr was touched to see that for this southern Slav who, in her Russophilia, confused the Tsars, the champions of Orthodoxy, with the Commissars, the avengers of the proletariat, the myth of 'Big Brother' in the North was a very real one. He soon got used to hearing himself addressed with tender respect as 'Your Lordship, Comrade Colonel.'

Aleksandr did not know Yugoslavia; the little he saw of it greatly surprised him. He had always felt that Slavs and Southerners belonged to two opposite worlds, but here he discovered the contrary: this country was both Central Europe and Antiquity, Orient and Occident, a little Russia opening out on to the Mediterranean, a synthesis of the ambiguity that characterized his own destiny.

He had his car filled with armfuls of flowers and set off for the station.

Alla, wearing a blue suit over a blouse with a broad white collar, climbed down from the carriage and walked along the platform with an almost masculine gait, shoulders thrown back and head held high, conscious of her beauty, but determined to set no store by it. The grey eyes expressed only the alertness expected of any officer confronted by one of higher rank, but there was a hint that they could also be teasing, dreamy, melancholy or angry. For the moment, they scarcely repressed the curiosity that was craving to be satisfied. She introduced herself with brusque efficiency:

'Kuznetsova.'

'You're exactly like your photographs.'

She eyed him critically.

'You're not.'

A hint of coquetry was discernible in her grey eyes.

'No?'

'Younger.'

He moved to relieve her of her bag.

'Leave it. I can manage.'

'I know you can, but I won't allow it.'

She let go the handle and, as she did so, their hands touched.

They walked in silence for a time, then he asked: 'Are you tired? Would you like to go to the house now? Perhaps you would like to sleep until tomorrow?'

She looked at him, her eyelids slightly creased: 'I'll do whatever you like.'

He stopped.

'Alla, let's make one thing quite clear. When I want you to do what I want, I shall tell you. When I ask you what you would like, I want a straight answer.'

'Right.'

He was shocked by this 'right', which he found rather common.

'So what is your good pleasure?'

'I'm not tired. I'd like . . . to see the town, perhaps? Walk around a bit? With you, of course.'

Aleksandr's irritation soon passed. Alla had both the amiability of a friendly dog—This street? Fine! This garden? Perfect!—and all the dignity of a bureaucrat. He found both touching. She was aware of belonging to the élite of those who know how to behave in society, die for their country and explain the history of the world in terms of the class struggle. She knew that she was respectable, respected herself and was respected by others. The idiots who use the word would have found her more 'élitist' than it is possible to be. 'I'd be more likely to shock her,' Aleksandr thought, amused, 'using some familiar term, or, at table, picking up my napkin with one hand.'

Having, for an hour or so, paid her respects to hierarchical reserve, Alla became more natural and threw a few tender glances in Aleksandr's direction. She was not trying to seduce him, she was no coquette, but she breathed like women who are used to being desired. And she had a way of slightly raising her right eyebrow, while making a hollow at the left corner of her lips, that made her particularly seductive.

They dined on the terrace of a restaurant under an arbour, looking out on to Ulysses' sea, turning violet at their feet. Alla laughed contentedly: 'It's romantic.'

Aleksandr observed her, not as a woman—from that point of view, she had passed the test with flying colours: in any case, Aleksandr was convinced that, in a sense, one woman was as good as another—but as a wife-to-be and especially as the mother of future little Psars. The efficiency with which he served world Communism had in no sense diminished in him the pride of belonging to a long line of leaders, quite the reverse, in that he believed that a Communist society was better placed to recognize—and to encourage—natural superiorities. He fully expected, therefore, that the young Psars that would spring from him would rise to high government posts and take up their rightful place in their country. This feeling had nothing snobbish about it. Aleksandr would not have minded if his wife had been a peasant woman, but she had to be of good birth, in the profound sense of the term, capable of perpetuating a certain quality of being, of which a noble name is no more than a symbol and never a guarantee.

He noted discreetly, he hoped, and in no particular order —the strong, but feminine wrists, the Soviet grammatical mistakes, the full-blooded way of speaking, without a hint of petty-bourgeois affectation, the absence of jewellery, a way of lowering the head while raising the eyes that might have been mannered, but which was not, her clean, close-cut nails, the care she took not to talk with her mouth full, her self-assurance at being right on fundamental questions, an amiable humility on secondary matters, her large, but not heavy feet, her temperance and her obvious love of food, a magnificent neck.

For her part, Alla observed him, determined to do her duty, but without losing the consideration that she had for herself, surprised by a kind of banter that she was not at all used to. Later, she said to him: 'You make fun of me all the time.'

While he, on the contrary, felt that he had been treating her with an attentive, almost exaggerated respect.

After dinner, they went and listened to some singing. Aleksandr was struck by the contrast between the Slav language and those Arabic melodies. Eventually they made for the house; at each turning in the road, the headlamps dazzled cascades of flowers, whose names Alla reeled off, though she could not see their colours, and went into ecstasies about them, perhaps to fill the silence. Aleksandr, indifferent as usual to the external world and incapable anyway of distinguishing between a violet and a gladiolus, was reflecting on the alchemy that was to unite his lineage with that of his wife.

Alla was delighted with the dacha, which was much more spacious than the two-roomed apartment that she shared with her mother in a Geebee building on the Stretenka.

'Do you know the Stretenka, Aleksandr Dmitrich?'

He explained that he had never been to the Soviet Union. She could not believe her ears: 'But you speak Russian perfectly! You use a few old-fashioned expressions, but you speak the language perfectly all the same.'

'Didn't they tell you that I was an émigré?'

It was the first reference that either of them had made to the circumstances of their meeting.

'I thought you left as a child.'

He recoiled slightly; he had always felt a double aversion to what was called 'the second emigration'. The Soviet citizen that he had become saw those people as traitors and the old émigré that he had been regarded them as an inferior species.

'I left before I was born,' he replied.

She sat down on an Uzbek rug and, despite the lateness of the hour, they began to talk about themselves, he with some reticence, she in a quite relaxed way. With her legs folded

89

under her, she sat erect, neither stiffly nor sloppily. She talked of her student days and of her ambitions, which happily coincided with a passionate desire to be useful.

'In our country, women can do anything. One day I might even be a general. You,' she added, diplomatically, 'will be a marshal. Would you like some tea? Or coffee, Frenchman that you are? I'll make you some.'

She took possession of the kitchen with determination and some degree of competence. She imagined that he would take whisky in his coffee, but he declined, without sarcasm. At last they could speak openly about their relationship. She was sitting, once again, on the floor, drinking her tea ('I drink it in the correct way, but I must admit, I have never been able to get my mother out of the habit of keeping her sugar between her teeth'), while he lay on the sofa discovering the opaque vapours of Caucasian brandy and deciding that there was certainly something to be said for French civilization.

They had in common a love of their country and the certainty of seeing the Communist system triumph throughout the world. This certainty aroused in Alla nothing but feelings of gaiety and self-righteousness: it would be like a fairy tale with a happy ending. Things were not so simple for Aleksandr, but he desired no less to see the victory of the faction with which he had thrown in his lot.

'We serve,' they both agreed.

Alla knew that marriages between members of the Geebee were encouraged and saw no objection in marrying a man who had been described to her as a hero, and whom she herself found to be attractive, courteous, pleasant, intelligent, almost as virile as she would have wished—not that Aleksandr was in any way effeminate, but there was nothing of the Herculean weight-lifter about him either. As for the idea of an arranged marriage, this very sensible girl was no more shocked than millions of women have been for centuries.

'For the first few years,' said Aleksandr, 'we shan't see much of each other.'

As far as he was concerned, he did not particularly mind such an arrangement. The idea of babies in nappies aroused in him a mixture of fear and repulsion; he did not mind that he would meet his son only when a boy begins to feel the need of a firmer authority or when one might play at toy soldiers with him. Meanwhile, of course, he would be deprived of Alla: Pitman had not given details of the number of meetings that would be permitted, but even at the very worst and supposing that the necessities of secrecy forbade any meeting, Aleksandr would be quite capable of bearing the separation. There would be no lack of temporary compensation if the need were felt. Alla, for her part, made no objection: she would raise their child until such time as his mission was completed and he would be able to take up his place in their family. In this respect, nothing had changed, since Prince Igor.

They slept apart that night. An engagement period, however brief, seemed appropriate to Aleksandr's susceptibilities. If, from this fact, Alla drew uncomplimentary conclusions about him, she soon had occasion to reverse them. At dawn they went down to the small beach nestling at the foot of the hill and bathed in the nude. Then he took her in his arms, religiously, just as at table he broke the bread.

'This is the first time,' he confided to her, with a quite untypical candour, 'that I don't feel that I have committed adultery.'

'Because we will get married one day?'

'No, because you are a Russian.'

The fact that she was Russian transformed for him the act of love: what had been only release or pleasure became a sacrament. The contempt that he had felt for other mistresses, the sense that he was using them, turned into veneration, into a sense that she was feeding him. The impression of fulfilling a destiny, of recreating order in the world, redoubled his vigour. He caught himself murmuring words of love to this woman he did not know. One night he whispered in her ear: 'It's as if I had already come home.'

Arranged marriages are sometimes the most poetic.

Alla was touched by the tenderness and respect of this man who was her senior by twenty years. She had expected something quite different; her women friends, who, bubbling over with laughter, recounted to her the prowess of their lovers, had never suggested that a man could be so trusting, so defenceless. She melted before this vulnerability. At the same time, she told herself that everything would have been quite different if he had been a true Bolshevik, and not a 'has-been' (a *byvshy*, as the Russians put it): hence that consideration, that solemnity even in the wildness of love. When, much later, she described this experience to her friends, who were at once sarcastic and sympathetic, she told them, her eyes wide in wonder:

'He kissed me as if I were an icon . . . And he never gave me one of those friendly slaps . . . And he knocked before coming into the bedroom . . . And he wanted to know if I was happy. I don't think a real man should be concerned about that. It's indiscreet and, anyway, why should he care?'

But, for the moment, she was in love with him, and threw herself into his arms with adorable ardour and gaiety. She burst out laughing when he asked her to choose between a dozen phials of scent; she laughed when she caught him polishing his fingernails; she laughed when he picked her up in his straining arms and threw her out of the window into a bed of carnations; she laughed at him in the water, because he swam less well than she did; she laughed when he claimed that she did not make *pirozhki* properly and that the Revolution had destroyed Russian cuisine; she laughed when he betrayed his ignorance of Marxism-Leninism; she laughed with pleasure whenever he mentioned their future: How many children shall we have? What shall we call them? Where shall we spend our leave? She laughed whenever she could tell by the look in his eyes that he wanted her again. But it was he, not someone given to riotous mirth, who nearly died of laughter, when, before collapsing in his arms on the rugs, she walked naked up to the portrait of Felix Edmundovich and turned it to the wall:

'I don't want the old man watching us.'

But she wept when they had to part: 'Sasha, I'm yours.'

He drove her to the station, saw her to her compartment and presented her with flowers and chocolates.

'Oh, and there's this. It's not much,' he said.

The case contained the most beautiful solitaire she had ever seen. She burst into tears, this time out of gratitude:

'I've only done my duty. You didn't have to thank me,' she said, in all simplicity, through her tears.

He replied, gravely, tenderly, with a touch of amusement: 'I'm not thanking you for doing it, but for perhaps taking some pleasure in doing it.'

A solitaire, he said to himself, as he drove back to the house, means nothing. On his return to Paris, this co-opted colonel of the Committee of State Security bought a signet ring and took it to a goldsmith to be engraved. On an oval ground were to appear the arms of the Psars, which would have scandalized any Western herald: Gules a dog's head facing to the sinister proper and a broom or in saltire. He would send it to Alla even before marrying her, as soon as their son was born.

Before finally 'retreating to his lair to die', Colonel-General Abdulrakhmanov, of the reserve, went to sun himself on the beach at Sochi. It was there that, nine months after the Yugoslav episode, Pitman went to visit him. For the first time the subaltern saw the huge body of his superior stretched out at his feet and almost naked. He was surprised by the brown colour of the skin—the head, however, had kept its olive complexion—by the hollows of the collarbones and by the thinness of the neck, which reminded him of a model in an anatomy class.

'Mohammed Mohammedovich, I'm terriby sorry . . .'

He felt that he himself was to blame.

'It's a girl.'

The colonel-general gave a slight tug on his faded red bathing trunks and gazed out into space. A sailing boat was visible out at sea. Abdulrakhmanov quoted Lermontov:

'The sail is white and solitary . . .'

He muttered something. Pitman stood very close to him, in uniform, with sand in his shoes. Palm trees nodded nearby.

'That won't do, my Iakov Moiseich all-of-enamel, that won't do at all.'

This man was born with the century. He had served under Lenin, Stalin, Malenkov, Khrushchev, Brezhnev. His bosses had been Dzerzhinsky (removed), Yagoda (shot), Ezhov (hanged from a tree in a psychiatric hospital), Beria (liquidated), Semichastny (dismissed), Shelepin (sacked), Andropov (how would he end up?). He had invented the absolute weapon of modern times. If his history were written one day, it would show that he had been the Sun Tzu of Europe. In a more mysterious way, which Pitman, who did not yet belong to the 'Conceptuals' of the Department, hardly glimpsed, this man may have ruled over the world, and yet he was no more than that, a very large brown body roasting in the sun.

'Of course,' said Pitman, 'they could try again as many times as necessary . . .'

But he already knew that this suggestion would not be accepted: every meeting endangered Aleksandr's mission and it was not even known whether he was capable of producing sons. And, in all probability, a daughter would not satisfy his need for roots in space and time.

Pitman may not have dared to resort to the obvious solution, but for Abdulrakhmanov it was quite simple: he had spent his life faking the reality of the world. He carried a military rank and he had served in a kind of police, but by vocation he was a sorcerer. He shut his eyes. His vast chest, striped with ribs, rose and let forth a sigh: 'Let it be a son.'

It was not so much an order as an incantation.

Had it been an order Pitman would not have felt obliged to obey it: in theory, Abdulrakhmanov no longer belonged to the service. But at the level at which they both operated, there was no longer any hierarchy in the strict sense, no longer any regulars or reserves, nothing but the Department, which one left only on departing this life (and even that was questionable): a sort of communion of saints. Between these saints reigned such professional trust that Abdulrakhmanov had not even thought to ask whether, by any chance, the father had been told of the birth before he had.

The young son of Lieutenant Ermakov, of the second directorate, was regularly photographed by the service and Captain Kuznetsova received precise instructions concerning the correspondence she would pursue with her lover. Of course, all her letters were regularly submitted to Colonel Pitman for approval. She did this without scruple. Young

Ekaterina was brought up by her grandmother, while Alla began to resent that gentleman of a certain age whom she had, in a way, loved, but for whom she found it somewhat excessive to languish indefinitely.

Aleksandr, duly disinformed, went to pay his respects to his father's grave at Sainte-Geneviève. He sat there, bareheaded, under the scorching sun: 'Now, papa, there's a new Dmitri Aleksandrovich.'

He thought that in a sense he had already carried out the midshipman's last wishes: a fragment of his body had 'gone home'.

3
A Day in the Life of Aleksandr Dmitrich

Thirty years, to the day, after his recruitment on the towers of Notre-Dame, Aleksandr Psar awoke in the apartment that he occupied on the eleventh floor of an expensive apartment building at Suresnes. He had not yet entirely resumed consciousness, but a strong intuition took hold of him: 'Today I start my homecoming.'

The bedroom was vast, net curtains billowed in and out across a wall made of a single pane of glass; one's toes sank into the silky depth of the wall-to-wall carpeting; the harmony of discreet blues and beiges betrayed the hand of a reliable interior decorator.

Neither in the bedroom, nor in the adjoining sitting-room, did one find any of those imprints of personality that indicate that, if the decorator proposes, it is the client who disposes. Even in the bathroom, the cakes of soap devoid of froth, the brushes with no hairs left on them, the spotlessly clean razor were arranged in line without betraying anything of their owner, other than that he was an orderly man of adequate means. The same could be said of the books in the sitting-room: the complete set of the Collection Pléiade, all unopened. Only one object escaped the all-pervasive banality of good taste and it was the first thing that Aleksandr looked at when he woke: this was a large electronic chess game, the pieces of which were made of precious wood. The small red light winked at well-spaced intervals.

'Haven't you found the answer yet?'

Aleksandr spoke Russian to the companion of his nights. He got up.

His decision had been taken long ago; he had no intention

of changing it. Yet it is not easy for a man of forty-nine to change his life from one day to the next, except in details. Over there he would not find the same well-being, the same comfort, not so much material comfort, for on the contrary, he would be well provided for, but those comforts that derive from familiarity and mastery. He would lose his tailor, to whom he was very attached—indeed, do they have tailors over there?—and he would have to get another car because of the spare parts. The network of relationships that he had patiently built up over the years would disappear like a spider's web under a broom; he would have to set about creating others, with men of a quite different kind—and the joys of a double life would no longer be his. It would be the end of a certain independence, for he had always been left as much rope as he wanted, and now it was he who was going to ask them to pull it in, and therefore restrict his freedom. He did not even know how he would stand the climate. But all that was as nothing compared with the fundamental matter, which was to carry out now what, thirty years earlier, he had decided he would do.

As he shaved, his mind went back to the strange scene that had taken place high up on Notre-Dame, that dazzling, dusty day of an exceptionally hot June. One could hardly say as much for this one.

As he came out of the bathroom, the computer announced by not winking its light that it had at last found the rebuttal.

'F 6: just as I thought.'

Aleksandr had found the next move the evening before and made it immediately.

'You'll have the whole day to think about it.'

He descended into the concrete bowels of the building to get his car. He was fond of his burgundy-coloured Omega, which he had bought recently, by way of symbolic humour, remembering the Alpha that he had acquired twenty-five years earlier. At that time the Alpha had been second-hand; now the Omega, which purred under his gloved hands, was not even an extravagance.

He stopped for a moment on a pedestrian crossing and lowered the window. The woman in the newspaper kiosk, who knew him, handed him *L'Impartial*. He would find the other papers at the office, but this one belonged to his 'orchestra' and he liked to skim through it in the traffic jams. As he drove, he felt with his right hand for the Books page. *L'Impartial* had not yet published an article on the *Dictionary of Dictatorship* and Aleksandr, who had sponsored the work at the Lux publishing house, had taken the trouble to call the paper's editor:

'The elections are over, the holidays are about to begin: it's the last moment, Jean-Xavier! People aren't going to read something so seriously documented on the beach at Saint-Tropez. You've no doubt noticed, by the way, that the *Dictionary* is exactly in accordance with your line. So . . .'

Jean-Xavier de Monthignies liked to pose as a man of the left; he ran a newspaper that was regarded as right-wing. His line necessarily zig-zagged.

'How do you reconcile all that?' people asked him.

He would reply proudly:

'I don't reconcile; I conciliate.'

And he believed it—or almost.

He had replied to Psar's objurgations with a sigh: 'I know what you mean. We both carry the burden of our past.'

That meant: you've just hit below the belt, by talking of my line. We both come from the exploiting classes.

Jean-Xavier de Monthignies would have been very sorry if one had forgotten that he came from the exploiting classes.

But he had given his word and, as editors go, he kept his word. Out of compensation for the delay, the *Dictionary of Dictatorship* deserved a half-page. 'An unusual approach,' wrote Hugues Minquin, a serious young journalist. 'In his introduction, the author codifies the perameters of the dictatorial régimes in, for example, the enfeoffment of the judiciary to the executive, the one-party state, discrimination of various kinds, the application of physical pressure during interrogation, or laws against deviant opinions. Then he draws up a catalogue of thirty-three nations to which, he believes, the term "dictatorship" may be applied and proceeds to examine them from the point of view of the predetermined headings. No one is obliged to share his opinions, but it is impossible not to recognize his punctilious objectivity. Indeed all the régimes incriminated are accorded the same number of pages (I know, I have counted them). In this area, we have to recognize that the USSR is given its full deserts . . .'

The shadow of a smile passed over Aleksandr Psar's long, equine face, shaded by a full head of brownish hair, with as yet no grey in it, which fell in curls with all the luxuriance of a latter-day Phoebus. The marvellous thing about his profession of illusionist was that one was never short of sub-illusionists only too delighted to carry on the work. And they were sincere, too, incredible as it may seem. The author of the *Dictionary* actually believed that he had shown objectivity by devoting as much of his attention to 'the material and technological base of Communism', with its 240 million inhabitants, whose declared aim was to impose its doctrine world-wide, as to Paraguay, with its 3 million inhabitants, whose sole aim was to survive. And Minquin, of course, had fallen for it. There was really nothing to be done but to let the Minquins get on with it. Iakov Moiseich would assuredly have quoted Sun Tzu: 'Use the situation as when one rolls a ball down a steep slope; the force required is minimal and the results incalculable.'

'That reminds me,' thought Aleksandr with scarcely condescending pleasure, 'I shall see Pitman again, the affectionate, clever Pitman.'

A certain warmth invaded his heart, which for so many years, he had kept in hibernation.

He went on leafing through *L'Impartial* on the seat beside him, crumpling the pages, then patting them smooth with his hand when his eye caught a headline, but, spontaneously, he was filtering. What amused him above all was noticing the work of his fellow 'team-members', whom he did not know, whom he would no doubt never know, for their common link protected them from any risk, and being French, they had no need to ask to 'go home'. Today he did not pick up any 'primary' items of influence; as for the 'secondary' and 'tertiary' ones, that is to say those passed through successive 'sound boxes', there was hardly anything else, which rather took the excitement away.

One paragraph, however, did attract his attention. A new page of a work entitled *The Russian Truth* had reached the

Seagull publishing house in Rome. The presumed author of the book was the prisoner of cell ooo of the Special Hospital in Leningrad, a psychiatric asylum frequently used to bring freethinkers to heel. The writer's anonymity, the mysterious circumstances in which a few purloined sheets of his manuscript had arrived in the West, and even the tenor of those pages—the style was reminiscent of oriental fables—had so whetted the appetite of the press that 'Iron Mask', as he had been nicknamed, had become, if not exactly a fashionable author, at least an infallible bait to catch the reader. Of course there was in the fate of this nameless, faceless man, imprisoned among mental patients, subjected no doubt to so-called 'treatment' that amounted to torture, all the terror and pity required not only of ancient tragedy, but also of contemporary post-romantic melodrama. Aleksandr, however, was interested in Iron Mask for professional, rather than personal reasons.

'Is all this coming from our Directorate?' he wondered. 'And if so, what is the purpose of the operation?'

Unfortunately, *L'Impartial* did not provide the text of the last message; all one knew was that there was something about a 'punished bell' (*sic*).

Aleksandr Psar's office was in the Rue de Verneuil, and the lease gave him the right to park his car in the courtyard of the noble old mansion that had been divided up between a number of questionable businesses. Aleksandr did not care for the Left Bank, too obvious a misalliance of the intellectual and the commercial, but he took great pleasure in mounting the late seventeenth-century staircase which, with its almost imperceptible steps, wafted him, transported him, one might say, to his floor, the first above the mezzanine.

Marguerite was already there, of course, in the larger of the two offices, which, with its Trianon-grey panels, some of which were not the original ones, its inside shutters, warped with age, its magnificent, but squeaky parquet floor, had a rather dilapidated grandeur in the best of taste.

Marguerite was forty; she had spent half her life in the Agency. Aleksandr remembered with horror the succession of inept secretaries during the first few years, when the Agency was still called Les Quatre Vérités, and occupied two

maid's rooms in the Boulevard Beaumarchais. He certainly
had a sense of failure at that time, not in his mission—the
Parisian intelligentsia threw themselves at the bait he held
out to them like a shoal of starving piranhas at a chunk of
meat—but financially. Pitman was very keen that the firm
should make a profit, but Aleksandr had a soldier's contempt
for penny pinching. Pitman then had a stroke of genius:

'Do you think a company, any more than a destroyer, runs
itself?'

And, in the end, Aleksandr put in the necessary effort and
even began to enjoy the running of a profitable operation.
Marguerite's arrival had coincided with this recovery, and
with the move to a literary quarter and the transformation of
the Les Quatre Vérités into the Agence Littéraire Aleksandr
Psar, which sounded more serious.

'All well, Marguerite?'

'Good morning, Monsieur.'

She was always standing when he came in, and gave him a
deferential smile.

'The mail hasn't arrived yet. There was a telephone call for
you from M. de Monthignies: he wanted to know whether
you were pleased.'

'Will you call him back for me?'

He went into his own office, a longer, narrower one than
the first. He had had the walls stripped and now the original
panels, a rhythmic succession of rectangles and ovals,
appeared in the warm, rosy splendour of the natural wood
On the mouldings of the cornices—a motif of ova and
fleurons—one could still make out the chisel marks of a
rather hasty worker three centuries earlier.

Aleksandr threw his heavy black briefcase on to the
Empire table and his gloves on top of that. Soon he would be
leaving this room. He had enjoyed working in it, but he had
not been taken in by it. He glanced up at the icon, which he
had hung, not in a corner, as was the custom, but flat against
a wall, in order to degrade it. It was a red-headed Saviour,
dressed in gilt silver leaf.

'You might have lent us a hand,' Aleksandr muttered, by
way of a morning prayer.

He sat down in his English leather chair. He knew that the

style of this room lacked unity, and derived a certain pleasure from the fact. The sofa, also in red leather, the lampshades and the dark green curtains, the mahogany bookcase, the Caucasian carpet that concealed the imperfections of the parquet floor, the pair of Cherkess kanjars on the wall, one large and one small, all this reminded him of the study his father would have had, in Kavalergardskaya Street, if only . . .

He glanced at his diary.

10.30:	Mlle Joséphine Petit (*Psychoanalysis of Terror*).
11.30:	M. Alexis Lewitzki, dissident (An idea. Refused to give details.)
1.00:	Lunch at *La Ville de Pétrograd*. Invitation from M. 'Divo', accepted.
3.10:	Showing of the film *Topaz* at the Cinéac. You said that you would stop by at the end of the day.

He glanced at his watch, then opened his file of letters awaiting signature. He carefully read and signed the two letters in the file. He then noticed the handwritten letter that had been lying for some days in the basket marked 'Pending'. He picked up his dictaphone.

'To Monsieur Valérii—watch the spelling, Marguerite, check against the original—Miagkoserdechnyi. Put today's date. Dear Sir, I have read with great interest—no: not great, just interest—your manuscript *The Decembrists*, comma, written in Russian, comma, which you were kind enough to send me. New paragraph. I do not think that it would be suitable for the series The White Book to which you refer and which is concerned with current affairs. On the other hand, comma, it occurs to me that it might find a place in the series Genesis of Revolution, comma, published by the same firm. Stop. As you know, I run—no, I . . . I . . . have some say . . . yes, that's it, have some say—in the running of these two series. New paragraph. However, I deeply regret that you take such a gloomy view of the heroes of the December Revolution. If, as you say, they showed great cowardice in prison and in exile, comma, if, on the other hand, personal ambition played a larger part in motivating some of them, perhaps it would be better not to stress these less savoury aspects of an enterprise that, when all is said and done, has aroused so much sympathy in so many quarters. New paragraph. On the other hand, perhaps one ought to put more stress on the abuses that those young men set out to correct, and not to give quite such weight to their incompetence, which in no way detracts from the nobility of their aims, or from the fact that they never dreamt of freeing their own serfs, which, you will grant, is irrelevant. New paragraph. Lastly, it seems to me that you might have made more of the repression—five executions, by hanging, exclamation mark. It would also be good to bring out the devotion of the wives, who insisted on following their husbands into deportation. The conditions, the comfort, the number of servants, et cetera, are beside the point. New paragraph. I am therefore returning your manuscript in the hope of finding it once again on my desk before long. Yours faithfully.'

The telephone buzzed apologetically.

'M. de Monthignies is on the line, Monsieur.'

'Good. When I've finished talking to him . . .'— Aleksandr looked at his watch; he was always looking at his watch—'get me Mme Boïsse.'

As usual, de Monthignies was all of a dither: 'Well, how did you find it? I did what I could, huh. I try to please everyone, huh.'

That was true.

'In fact I had a look at your tome myself. It's horrible, huh? The rack in Spain, ice-packs in Russia. We're living in horrible times.'

'I share your concern, Jean-Xavier. Things will get better when we've an R in the month.'

'Maybe for you—the hunger in the world doesn't bother you. Two people out of three are dying, Aleksandr, because they've nothing to eat. When I hear things like that, I just can't go on.'

'Don't let's exaggerate. At most it slows you down a bit.'

'Look, you're a Cossack, a born reactionary. It's not your fault if you have no heart, but some of us . . .'

'Jean-Xavier, I should like to thank you for the article

from the bottom of the heart that I don't have. Hugues Minquin did just fine. I particularly liked the passage on the politico-psychiatric hospitals.'

'Yes, you would, wouldn't you? You think of nothing but Soviet tyranny. But there are others, too, you know, and Minquin is quite objective.'

The conversation ended with a mutual promise to lunch before the holidays—what a drag they were!

'I'd like you to bring Minquin along,' said Aleksandr.

Hugues Minquin might conveniently be recruited, unknown to himself, of course, as one of his regular 'sound boxes'.

Marguerite announced, in a detached tone of voice: 'The telephone is ringing at Mme Boïsse's.'

The boorishness of getting a secretary to call one's mistress was calculated. Aleksandr did not question Marguerite's discretion, but he had been taught to take care with his covers, and he tended to overdo it. If his telephone was bugged, then fine: if it wasn't, Marguerite would at least know that he had an illicit and therefore innocent, rendezvous that evening.

'Jessica?'

'It's you?'

A smoker's voice. That had been a slight professional error on Pitman's part.

'How are you?'

'Very well, apart from a headache, a hangover . . . You're laughing, you brute! Yet it's all your fault.'

'I didn't get you to do all the drinking!'

'Yes, you did.'

'But I haven't seen you for ten days!'

'Exactly: I've been drowning my frustration in alcohol.'

'You won't be frustrated for much longer. Can I come round this evening?'

'My lord's wishes are my commands.'

'We'll open a bottle of vodka. There's no better cure for what you've got. It's called *opokhmelitsia*.'

'What a language! Fancy belonging to a race that invented Russian and the knout!'

'Seriously, Jessica, you aren't really ill?'

That sudden concern, which slipped out almost unwittingly . . .

'Don't worry: I shall be in top form this evening.'

Aleksandr hung up. Well, that was that. The first step eastwards had been taken. His finger had tickled the gear lever. Nothing irrevocable had been done, or so it seemed, but, in fact, the procedure—and the process—had been set in motion.

'I shall take the kanjars,' he thought.

Marguerite brought in the papers. Despite a certain heaviness around the bosom and hips, she moved with a grace that anyone other than her boss would have noticed. And she dressed well: well cut russet and dark blue dresses, good quality garnet-red twin sets, not overly severe bodices, grey flannel skirts bought at some well-known shop or perhaps, who knows, made to measure (Aleksandr paid her well enough for her to run to this), and above all, thank God, never trousers.

'Mlle Petit is a little early for her appointment.'

'What's she like?'

'Mmmm . . . about twenty-seven. Looks as though she knows what she wants.'

Aleksandr reached for the fat blue folder on which was written, in red capitals: THE PSYCHOANALYSIS OF TERROR Too perfect a manuscript suggests an author who likes to pretend that his book has already been published; an illegible one, on the other hand, that the author regards himself as a recognized genius. Joséphine Petit fell into neither of these two errors, and she had made her cuts with a felt pen so thick that there was no way that one could make out the original version. The first page began thus:

'There is the terror one undergoes and the terror one imposes. They are indissociable, but must not be confused. Imposed terror may come from on high, from a despotic government, or from below, from those commonly referred to as terrorists. They are two quite different kinds of terror. Terror undergone may reign below, as in a totalitarian régime; it may also reign on high, as in a declining liberal régime . . .'

Aleksandr had been both attracted and disturbed by this

clarity of thought and exposition, by this way of assuming the obvious in order to go beyond it. He was attracted as a lover of literature, disturbed as a professional in the field of influence. A conjurer by profession, he was more at ease amid confusion and gibberish. He himself had written in one of his first reports, when he still regarded himself as a theorist because he had not yet become a practitioner: 'I was taught that to attack freedom, one had to attack thought, but I shall go further: to attack thought, one would do well to attack language. Indeed, in spite of the hammering at the hands of the mass media, thought, at worst, remains protected within the fortress of individual intelligence, whereas language, being common property, is exposed to attack in open country. If thought could no longer find the medium of a sufficiently clear and rigorous language, it would be stifled and perish. So it is our duty to encourage by every possible means the decay of the target-languages, which will inevitably lead to the decay of the target-thought systems. To achieve this we must exert as tight a grip as possible on the practice of writing and on the educational system.' And he had concluded, with a strikingly juvenile fondness for the well-turned phrase: 'When our enemies have forgotten how to spell, we shall know that victory is near.'

Yes, despite Mlle Petit's lucidity of language, Aleksandr had concluded that *The Psychoanalysis of Terror* might have a good influence on the public. As in the *Dictionary of Dictatorship*, the formula of 'equal parts' had been used unconsciously to advantage. Mlle Petit was liberal in outlook; she was repelled by the principle of terror in all its forms. In an attempt to vary her examples, she had geographically and politically diluted her indignation. As a result, a handful of Greek colonels who had ruled for six years seemed to be as dangerous as an international party, with millions of members, that had been in power in Russia for ten times as long. Moreover, titles containing the word 'terror' sold well and Aleksandr was not averse to profit of this kind. There was one point, however, that he would have to insist on changing: the directives of the Department were categorical on the matter. But he anticipated no resistance; for all their bluster, authors really only wanted one thing: to get published. A strange form of exhibitionism indeed! Aleksandr recalled with a shudder of disgust that he too had once wanted to be in the public eye: what vulgarity!

'Good morning, Mademoiselle, it is Mademoiselle, isn't it?'

She was very small, hardly taller than a dwarf. She had short, stiff, brown hair, a small square face, with square nostrils, firm, but not coarse, lips; under bushy, stiff-looking eyebrows, her eyes looked out at the world with uncompromising intelligence. Mlle Petit was curiously dressed—curiously for Aleksandr—in a lace blouse and a full-length, stiff, blue denim skirt that beat around her ankles, revealing a pair of blue socks.

He stood up, held out his hand and said, deliberately radiating fellow feeling and hope: 'I'm sure we'll see eye to eye.' She looked gravely at this man who had it in his power to decide whether she was to belong to that race apart, published writers.

'Is this your first book?'

He had received so many, from beginners of every sex and type: the arrogant, the wheedlers, the over-familiar, the well-groomed, the slatterns, those who pretend to self-assurance or to shyness, those who offer to give up their royalties, those who have nothing to refuse you, those who have friends in the Académie Française, those who haven't eaten for three days, the crack-pots, of course, and those who inspire confidence at once because they know what they expect of you and what you expect of them.

'Yes.'

'May I ask you why you sent your manuscript to a literary agent and not directly to a publisher?'

'I didn't know you were an agent. I wrote to the editor of the White Books.'

He liked to know these details and, though he had already made up his mind, he had no desire to change his method. For a moment, he wondered: 'What will they do with the Agency? Will they hand it over to someone else or wind it up?'

He had sat down, now he stood up again, all youthful vigour, confident in his muscles and his brain.

'Ah! The White Books! Of course.'

This series had been his great success. He glanced across at the mahogany bookcase where the White Books published over the years stood side by side in battle order (it was the right word):

White Book on Racism.

White Book on the Exploitation of the Natural Wealth of Latin America.

White Book on Women.

White Book on State Education in France. (This book had become the breviary of the revolutionaries of May '68 and had led to Aleksandr being co-opted into the ranks of the Geebee and his first commission, not as a reward for his contribution to a failed revolution, but 'for having virtually put French universities and *lycées* out of action for at least a generation', as the statement passed by the Department authorities put it.)

White Book on Neo-colonialism.

White Book on the French Army.

White Book on the Catholic Church.

White Book on the Parallel Police.

White Book on the Penitentiary System in France.

White Book on the C.I.A.

White Book on the Rebirth of Nazism.

White Book on the Arms Race.

White Book on the Concentration Camps throughout the World.

White Book on Nuclear Energy.

He picked one out at random: they were weighty, but compact volumes, of small format, with white covers on which the name of the author and the title were printed in attractive black roman type: they looked like official publications. To be published in that series was, as people foolishly put it, an entrée into the so-called 'serious' press or the political clubs and, from there, of course, into the bureaucracy. How many authors would sell their souls to see their name on one of the famous consciously 'old-fashioned' white covers! How many had already done so! He flung the small, thick volume on the table and perched himself next to it.

'You see, Mademoiselle, a White Book at a first attempt . . .'

'What does that matter, if it's good?'

They talked for a long time. He raised various obstacles, only to drop them one by one. This girl, he told himself, would never be a good 'sound box'; she had too much independence and judgement. She had just the critical dose of pride and humility. He was tempted to get rid of her. But she would only take her manuscript to someone else, who would get the profit and, what was more important, publish it without the vital alteration.

She looked at him, apparently neither attracted nor repelled by his appearance, which was nevertheless quite striking. Perfectly proportioned, he seemed taller than he actually was; his thick, curly hair enhanced the energetic, almost brutal, but certainly not coarse impression conveyed by his long, bony, thoroughbred face. People tended to say of him, quite spontaneously: 'He's a bit of all right!' or, more modestly, 'He's not bad!' He dressed with a certain superannuated elegance, at once sober and flamboyant. Flannel suits of a dark grey veering to nut-brown, or nut-brown veering imperceptibly to mauve, double-breasted and flared from the waist, or single-breasted with a waistcoat, white shirts and starched collars, heavy gold cufflinks. On top of that, his body was in perfect condition: he attended a gym and one sensed that his calves were supple and his biceps firm.

'Well, Monsieur, what's it to be? Yes or no?'

He did not like being rushed.

'I do not deny, Mademoiselle, that your book is perfectly documented and well-written. It's perhaps a bit too theoretical, for the readers of the White Book, who are used to more strictly "factual" arguments. May I ask you what is your profession?'

'I teach maths.'

'Ah! In that case, you will probably have no particular reason for keeping the word "Psychoanalysis". In any case all our titles . . . It would be *White Book on Terror*, or something of the kind.'

She thought for a moment.

'You're right: "Psychoanalysis" might be misleading.'

'Good. I'll submit your book to our editorial committee.' (There was none.) 'Ah, just one thing.' (He thought that by now he had raised enough hopes, yet left them sufficiently vague to be able to approach the only really doubtful point.) 'You have made a study of what you call the "Leninist terror". I think it would be better to refer to the "Stalinist" terror.'

'Why?' Her dark eyes glinted. 'Lenin himself said: "Terror is a means of government." It was he who called his political enemies "noxious insects". It was he who advised Gorky not to "snivel over rotten intellectuals". It was he who wrote to the People's Commissar for Justice: "In my opinion, the application of execution by firing squad should be extended." And Vladimir Bukovsky has remarked: "Stalin and all his atrocities came straight, organically so to speak, out of Lenin's idea, of the very idea of socialism. It is no accident if the Party promoted him, precisely him." It's all in the book, with all the figures.'

She pointed to the manuscript.

'I know, Mademoiselle, but it isn't individuals you are attacking, I think, but principles. The most usual adjective is therefore the best one.'

'I don't see why I should call the terror organized by Lenin "Stalinist".'

Aleksandr could not say what the real reason was: he could not reveal that an instruction from his Directorate had been given to all 'fellow travellers': 'We're dumping Stalin. Blame him for whatever you like, but keep Lenin out of it! We must keep at least one god absolutely pure.' Pitman had commented with his mischievous smile: 'The most ingenious thing invented by my ancestors must have been the technique of the scapegoat.'

'Mademoiselle, the average Western reader thinks of Lenin as a liberator, not as a tyrant. Personally'—he glanced up at the icon and the kanjars—'I could hardly be suspected of indulgence towards the man who destroyed a civilization of which I am the posthumous son. However I must admit that Stalin killed more people than Lenin.'

'Because he was in power for thirty-one years and Lenin for only seven.'

'Yes, but you are not comparing the two forms of terror. What you mean is simply: the Bolshevik terror, which is usually called Stalinist.'

'I mean: the terror inaugurated by the leader of the Bolsheviks.'

Usually Aleksandr was quite capable of dispersing even fairly strong opposition with his own mixture of platitudes and good intentions. But in this girl he had met his match. He replied curtly:

'You're preaching to the converted, but publishers will tell you that the words "Leninist terror" will alienate the press and knock five hundred copies at least off your sales.'

'What if I tell them I don't care?'

'They will tell you that they do.'

He placed his hand on the blue folder, as if to hand it back.

Mlle Joséphine Petit got up and walked over to the window. His other authors, in such circumstances, tried to hide the struggle that was going on inside them. Not she: she hugged her arms close to her body and stared out at the antique shops and bookshops two floors below. Even her back showed that she was thinking.

She swung round.

'O.K. We'll settle for Stalinist.'

'Very well. I'll let you know when our editorial committee has reached a decision. Could I have your address?'

Marguerite should have taken care of that. Why did he feel the need to jot down Mlle Petit's address in his personal diary? Perhaps, in view of his imminent departure, he wanted to speed up the execution of the decisions that he had taken. Or was it last-act nervousness? He decided to watch himself.

She left, unsmiling. How strange these modern young people are who claim to be so 'relaxed', so 'cool', but who are in fact so ill at ease in life. Clearly one cannot abandon the spinal column of tradition, of *savoir-vivre*, without some loss.

M. Alexis Lewitzki, Aleksandr's next visitor, was a young man with full lips and gold-rimmed spectacles. He began the interview with a speech on the present state of Western knowledge—or rather ignorance—of what he called 'the Russo-Soviet fact'. What he said was not wrong, but the careless, ungrammatical French in which he expressed it irritated Aleksandr.

'We can speak in Russian, if you find it easier.'

'No, no thank you. I regard your troglodyte Russian, with its "gracious lords" and "deeply honoureds", as totally outmoded. I prefer to talk to you in French, a language on whom I speak at my ease. Is it understood of you that the West has built up for itself a Russo-Soviet myth that we must milk? You know what I'm talking about.'

'Sorry, not at all.'

'Do not play the fool with me. The Westerners imagine that nothing has changed in Russia. Either in 1917, or 1905 or 1861. Always the same conspiracy. So I have a magnificent subject on that conspiracy. I write in French, but if you want to hire someone to polish it up, then you must pay him. You agree, it is to your advantage.'

'M. Lewitzki, you must understand to begin with that I'm not a publisher . . .'

'I know what you do. You are on a percentage. But I have calculated that, as you know the ins and outs, it is fair.'

Aleksandr looked at his watch.

'Well, what is this subject?'

'I have taken out copyright, so I am quite willing to tell you about it. You can check at the Society of Authors. Of course you think you know what happened on 22 December 1849 at seven o'clock in the morning.'

'I haven't the faintest idea.'

'Calls himself a literary expert! In our country every schoolboy will tell you that at this historical moment Lieutenant-Engineer Fedor Mikhailovich Dostoievsky was tied to a stake to be executed, but that his penalty was commuted to forced labour, and that he went on to live forty-two more years. But the schoolboy would be wrong. The lieutenant-engineer was strangled in his prison and an agent of the Okhrana took his place. It was to him that General Rostovtsev announced, hardly able to get the words past his lips, that the Tsar had spared his life. It was he who did four years' penal servitude to justify his political transformation. It was he who wrote, in the glory of the Tsarist régime, such works as *The Devils, Diary of a Writer* and the rest. All of which, note, is very different from *The Poor, The Double, Netochka, White Nights*, etc., which were written by the real Lieutenant-Engineer Dostoievsky.'

'But what of the evidence of Herzen, who, if I'm not mistaken, witnessed the scene . . .'

'They had chosen an agent who looked like Fedor Mikhailovich.'

'But the family . . . Dostoievsky's brother, Mikhail . . .'

'Mikhail was in debt: they made sure that he kept quiet.'

'And this agent happened to be a writer of genius?'

'It has happened. Marlowe, Defoe, Beaumarchais, Greene . . . Of course, Nicholas did not choose an illiterate.'

'All right. And what are you going to write about this magnificent subject, M. Lewitzki? A pamphlet aimed at undermining the great counter-revolutionary authority, a historical novel, *à la Monte-Cristo*, a thesis?'

The gold-rimmed spectacles glittered; the small, plump hands parted in an eloquent gesture:

'Whatever you like!'

'And you have the material that . . .?'

'I have all the material. Of course, when I crossed the frontier, they robbed me of the Tsarist archives, which I had confiscated in the Lenin Library and various monasteries. But let us say that I took notes and, anyway, I have a photographic memory.'

Lewitzki lied without hoping or even wishing to be believed. But what did it matter? Archives could be manufactured, if need be, and they could be 'handed back' to him, probably 'under pressure of international opinion'. Any attack on Dostoievsky's reputation might prove useful. Having said this, even if it was a good idea, it might be worth passing it on to some sincere Frenchman, who would believe the archives to be authentic and would do a better job. If Lewitzki protested, the public would think that their work had overlapped. Yes, it was worth passing on to Ivan Ivanich. Even if nothing came of it, the hypothesis would amuse Pitman.

Lewitzki was led to the door with a promise that they would think about his idea.

'Do not take too long,' he rejoined. 'You are not the only literary agent at Paris.'

Aleksandr dictated two more letters. Then, glancing at his watch yet again—that lunch with Divo had him worried, but he could not turn it down—he went over to a cupboard and took out a pair of black kid shoes and a shoe horn. He took off the dark brown suède shoes he was wearing, put on the black ones, went over and put the brown ones back into the cupboard and got ready to go out. Marguerite put her head round the half opened door: 'Monsieur, Mlle Petit is asking to see you for a moment. I told her that . . .'

'I was going out, but . . .'

Mlle Petit slipped into the office, almost under Marguerite's arm. With as long steps as her ankle-length skirt allowed, she strode over to the desk, seized her blue folder with the hasty precision of a thief, pressed it to her bosom, held securely by both arms in the form of a cross and, having got what she came for, looked up at Aleksandr and declared: 'Monsieur, I have changed my mind.'

She beat a hasty retreat.

Aleksandr and Marguerite looked at one another in consternation. What had got into her? Really! Authors are quite mad. Those who work with them get used to it. Marguerite then caught sight of the black shoes. She then knew that her boss was lying when he said that he would call back in the afternoon: he would not be seen dead in the evening wearing brown shoes and, if he had already put on his black ones, it was because he would be going straight to his mistress's apartment after the cinema.

Aleksandr arrived at *La Ville de Pétrograd* on time, but Divo the least Parisian of Parisians, was already there. Divo could not do anything like anyone else. For example, he paid for every other meal they had together, whereas, being an author, he should have averted his eyes when the bill arrived at the end of every meal. It is true that the two Franco-

Russians had cordially disliked each other ever since their school days and saw one another only to discuss literary projects that never came to anything.

'Blinis-caviar, will that do? To tell you the truth I prefer red, but if you would rather have the black, proceed, as they say. White vodka, unless you're losing your taste as you get older?'

Always the same rather too pointed blows, the same slanted smiles. Always the same disturbing novels, the same semi-successes and the same mysterious sources of income.

'How are your scribblers getting on? What's the next White Book to be about?'

'I've got two coming up. One on God and one on the police.'

'What a combination! The police is to prepare the purge, is that it? But what has God ever done to you?'

Sometimes Aleksandr thought that Divo had seen through him and was overtly making fun of him. Sometimes, on the other hand, he told himself that Divo was just infuriatingly frank.

'The White Book on God will probably be the most interesting one we've ever published. Jeanne Bouillon and Patrice Duguest have done a remarkable job of demystification.'

Divo whistled.

'Demystification of God? Doesn't that strike you as a bit daft?—No, no, Mademoiselle, a whole carafe—Who do you take us for?'

'Daft? Why? I'm sure the book will be well received by a section of the Church. There are more and more priests who think that Heaven can be made on earth.'

'Then, let's face it, there was some good in the Inquisition, after all. Demystifying God! That strikes me as the peak of snobbery—and plain daft! All right. I've no such ambitions, but I've an idea for a novel that might interest you. That's why I asked you to spare me some of your valuable time. Let's drink.'

They tossed back their drinks like men well versed in the art, head thrown back, elbow scarcely raised, with a sharp flick of the wrist.

'You have your publishers, Divo.'

'Yes, but given the Great Fear of the Year 2000, which is striding towards us . . . Self-censing soon replaced by self-censorship . . . I have publishers as you say: I change them with every novel. Not so much out of disloyalty on my part, as prudence on theirs. I thought that you might point me in the direction of some three-stripe warrior. I know you're a "very Parisian figure" and all that, what I call a ripe Roquefort, but all the same your father sailed under the flag of St Andrew: you can't be all bad. Let's drink to the flag.'

'A Roquefort? What's that supposed to mean?'

'No, sorry, you're better than a Roquefort. Let's say a Tokay wine: aristocratic decay, you know. Anyway, would you like me to tell you my plot?'

'Yes, go ahead.'

They talked, as in their youth, a crazy mixture of Russian and French. Moreover, Divo took delight in pronouncing French words in the Russian manner and Russian words in the French.

'It's politics-fiction, you see. Suppose a country, let's call it the Confederation of Confusional Communes, is anxious to make the entire world benefit from its own political system. And suppose there is another country, whose strategic position is essential in order to realize this aim: let's call it Galatia. For fifty years the CCC has financed, encouraged, flattered and bolstered up the Confusional Party of Galatia. But in Galatia, the Confusionists, however frivolous the electorate may be, never gets more than 15 per cent of the vote. Besides, as a result of a number of factors, the popularity of the Confusionists has declined over the years.'

'What factors?'

'A writer expelled from the CCC publishes a horrific account of the régime there; in fact, this guy isn't revealing anything new, but he manages to get a hearing: that's the important thing. A group of philosophers, formerly Confusional, step smartly to the right. The international situation forces the CCC to intervene militarily in several parts of the world, which shocks the simple-minded; now, the simple-minded are always in the majority. In short, the Confusional vote falls from 15 to 14 to 13 per cent . . . and it becomes clear to the leaders of the CCC that Confusionism will never triumph in Galatia if democracy has its way.'

'Well?'

'Well, the more thoughtful members of the CCC leadership think up the following little strategem. They get some impossible clown made leader of the Confusionist Party of Galatia, who, whenever he appears on television, lowers still further the popularity of his clique. The percentage of the vote drops to 12, to 11, to 10.5 per cent . . . This has two results: on the one hand, Confusionism, which, not so long ago, still terrified the bourgeoisie, now makes it laugh; on the other hand, the fortunes of the other party of the left, let's call it the Syncretist Party—for, as you know, in psychology, confusionism is merely a particular state of syncretic thought —improve dramatically. The elections approach. To make quite sure that the outgoing president will not be re-elected, the CCC announce that it wants him to win, which obviously destabilizes his support on the right, and the Syncretist candidate comes to power on a landslide.

'Let's called this candidate Pushkin. He's an adventurer of average ability; not much is known about him, except that from time to time he organizes phoney attempts on his own life. And what's the first thing he does when he gets into power? He pardons the murderer of a policeman. The suckers on the right rub their hands with glee: Pushkin has alienated the police. What they don't understand is that any loss of morale on the part of the police destabilizes the republic and, consequently, encourages subversion. The second thing Pushkin does—in chronological order, not in order of importance—even though the Syncretists have an absolute majority and the Galatian people have given fewer votes to the Confusionals than ever, the new head of state recruits four ministers from that party which, under cover of muzzling it, actually rehabilitates it. You see the elegance of the manoeuvre: a group once thought to be both serious and dangerous, and which has been cleverly ridiculed in such a way as to lose both these characteristics, is now, thanks to Pushkin, getting back the first, its seriousness, despite the wishes of 90 per cent of the Galatians. Long live democracy! But Pushkin goes ever further: he plays the nationalist and distances himself from the CCC. So of course when it comes to distributing portfolios he doesn't give Defence or the Interior to the Confusionals—that really would make people suspicious. No, no, he gives them a few apparently harmless portfolios, among which he slips in that of Transport, whereas, of course, in a time of crisis, whoever controls Transport, controls the country.

'Pushkin's third action, though it only concerns terminology, seems to me to be just as revealing. You see, Galatia had at its disposal an efficient administrative system, composed of a body of generally respected men, known as the praetors. Well, Pushkin not only restricts their powers, in other words, encourages the disorganization of the country, but he gives them a typically Confusional title, which doesn't go down at all well with most of the population . . . He calls them . . . "Inquisitors".'

'His next action: whereas two-thirds of the Galatians demand the restoration of the death penalty, the Syncretist Pushkin abolishes it in flagrant disregard of the wishes of the people. This has one aim: to undermine authority, and no one sees what is perfectly obvious, because Pushkin himself represents authority and no one can grasp that this is merely a transitional authority.

'His fifth action, if I haven't lost count: In Galatia, there is a specialized court that deals with crimes against the State, that is to say, Society. Yes, you've guessed it. Pushkin can't wait to abolish that particular body.

'Sixth act: whereas the galette, the national currency of the Galatians, had reached enviable stability, Pushkin devalues it, quite against the interests of Galatia and of the agreements worked out with its neighbours.

'Seventh and for the moment last action . . . Ah! This is the juiciest one of all, the most aphrodisiac for a writer. Pushkin deliberately sabotages the Galatian nuclear industry, not at all with the aim of disarming the nation, for all overt war has become impossible, but in order to put Galatia at the mercy of the CCC, which finds it advantageous to sell its excess colonial gas and above all is delighted at having its hand on the energy tap of a country that is so important in terms of world strategy. This last action, my friend, might be what philosophers would call the ultimate cause of the entire manoeuvre.

'Well, Alek, you're no Aliosha, even if I'm something of an Ivan, but what do you think of the subject of my novel?'

Aleksandr said very gently: 'Novels without heroes don't sell well, Divo.'

Divo burst out laughing.

'Ah! But you've missed the point, my hero is Pushkin. Let's drink to Pushkin. Pushkin, whom the reader follows since he was a little lad in a sailor-suit; Pushkin, with whom he identifies, for whom he fears, with whom he haunts the graves of great ancestors, whose taste in sex and flowers he knows, whose fears he shares during his cosmetic surgery operations, with whom he pockets small ex-colonial gratuities, with whom he plunged Galatia into a hopeless *kerenshchina*!'

Laughing and drinking, Divo stared hard into Aleksandr's dark brown eyes, trying no doubt to make out the thoughts that lay hidden behind the veil that covered them.

'You mean,' Aleksandr said slowly, 'that Pushkin is a "mole"?'

'I think "submarine" is the traditional French term.'

Neither looked away. Divo was still smiling his slanted smile.

Aleksandr felt rising up inside him one of those inordinate fits of anger peculiar to men who constantly repress their true feelings.

'A pity we're no longer in the days when a little bloodletting was commonly resorted to, I would have known whom to inform of your case, friend Divo. Not that you are dangerous, but I find you irritating beyond measure.'

And yet, who knows? He might well have given a great deal to be Divo at that moment and not himself.

He said, in a detached tone of voice: 'I don't know whether *Seconde* serializes fiction: you might be lucky. I doubt if you'll get a publisher for it. Though . . . it all depends. You might even have found your bestseller at last. Who knows? And what's your politics-fiction going to be called?'

'I thought: *An Act of War*.'

'Mmmm, a nice title.'

The word war had just reminded Aleksandr that, over thirty years before, he had said to Pitman: 'But I want to make war!'

'Don't worry, you will,' Pitman had replied, allowing a twinkle to appear behind his small round spectacles.

Why had Divo instigated this meeting? Aleksandr took his leave without having settled the question. Perhaps that second-rater really imagined that the Psar Agency would help him to get his tedious story published. At school, Aleksandr remembered, Divo had always been at once brilliant and credulous. Hadn't they once convinced him that he'd find a Dodo in the Zoo aviary?

The day was not turning out as well as Aleksandr would have wished, since it was the first of his 'return'. First, there was that crazy cookie, then that ironic account of a whole life . . . never mind: now he had an hour of happiness in front of him.

He went into his favourite cinema, on the Champs-Elysées. That day they were showing *Topaz*, not Pagnol's, but Hitchcock's. He had already seen it twice. He took a seat near the exit. Five minutes went by, men and women made gestures on the screen, no one had come in after Aleksandr. He got up and, using the emergency exit, found himself in a small, sloping street. He spent five minutes on a café terrace, descended into a métro station, boarded a train, then jumped off just before the doors shut, got on the next train and repeated the operation. When he got to the Gare Saint-Lazare, he was pretty sure that he had not been followed, but he did not omit two extra precautions: he bought a ticket for Versailles, whereas he was going to Pontoise, and boarded the train at the last minute. What he was going to do that afternoon was strictly his own business and he felt a certain malicious pleasure at using against his employers, whom he thought quite capable of having him followed, the few tricks of the trade that they had taught him.

In *La Voix*, which he had bought on the platform (in preference to *Le Monde*, which was not part of his 'orchestra'), almost half a page was devoted to an article by Jeanne Bouillon called 'Demystifying Iron Mask'. In the middle, in a 'box' and heavier type, was a short text, 'The Punished Bell, extract from the ultra-secret work by the Anonymous Prisoner'.

He began with the article. Jeanne Bouillon was one of his regular, albeit unwitting, 'sound boxes', one of the loud-speakers who tirelessly dispensed to the French what he, Aleksandr Psar, decided—or, to be more precise, was ordered—to bring to their ears. 'The Directorate is concerned about the popularity of the Pope and about his insistence on the primacy of the spiritual,' said his case-officer. 'Have you any bright ideas?' And Aleksandr would invite Jeanne Bouillon to lunch at the *Antiquaires* and set one in motion: 'Jeanne, I thought of you for a new White Book: what about putting God in his place? It would be just up your street, wouldn't it?'

But this time Mme Bouillon was expressing her own ideas. Aleksandr had no reason to stop her. She was no vulgar propagandist and her usefulness was in direct proportion to the freedom she enjoyed. However it was a good idea, of course, to keep an eye on her work.

For years, the anonymous prisoner of cell 000, of the Special Hospital, Arsenal Street, Leningrad, USSR, has been passing on to the West—how, we do not know—startling political observations that suggest that he may be the equal of a Solzhenitsyn or a Zinoviev. He may even have the advantage over those two illustrious dissidents in that he offers positive solutions to the Soviet mess, instead of confining himself to denigrating the present or praising the past. His observations seem to be extracts from a longer work entitled *The Russian Truth*. One wonders, of course, where this work is to be found and how it is that the régime's psychiatrists and torturers—after all, they are the same—have not yet got their hands on it. Hence the legend that surrounds the man whom the press refers to now only as Iron Mask, an admirable individual no doubt, but one whom it is all the more important to demystify.

To begin with, why should one imagine quite improbable hiding places, worthy of the cunning of the

Sioux . . . or of Rocambole? The work may very well not have even been entrusted to paper: it may be that it has been wholly and entirely recorded in the elephant's memory of the prisoner, and that the loony psychiatrists are still looking for it there. We know from Solzhenitsyn what extraordinary feats of memory may be displayed by the oppressed.

But there is another question to be answered: who is this romantic Iron Mask?

M. Enzo Grucci, editorial director of the Seagull publishing house in Rome, which specialises in the reproduction of samizdat material, claims to know no more than the public, though he is the usual recipient of the mysterious correspondent, who, since 1975, has sent him the seven messages known to us. Two new émigrés, who have spent time in the sinister Special Hospital, have noted the existence of an isolated cell, bearing the number 000, where the only person ever seen entering was a psychiatrist of enormous height who did not belong to the normal staff of the establishment, and in which there was a confined prisoner, whom the other patients have never seen, but whom they, too, have nicknamed Iron Mask, the renown of Alexander Dumas being apparently as great on the far side of the curtain as on this. Only two nurses (both male) have access to cell Triple Zero and they have virtually no duties in the rest of the hospital.

However, strange rumours are circulating in the '*psykhushka*' (psychiatric prison): cell 000 is magnificently furnished; there is a television aerial above it; one of the two nurses has been seen cleaning a carpet, which was then taken back to the invisible resident; classical music can often be heard coming from inside; the food eaten by Iron Mask smells quite different from anything eaten by the rest of the patients.

Let us compare these observations with another series of facts.

On 13 July 1971, a certain Mikhail Kurnosov, born at Kostroma in 1926, disguised himself as a militiaman and fired on a car in which he thought Brezhnev was riding. In fact, Mr Brezhnev had taken another car, and only the chauffeur was slightly wounded. Kurnosov was apprehended and everyone wondered what horrible punishment awaited the unfortunate wretch . . . Shortly afterwards, it was learnt that Kurnosov had been handed over to the Serbsky Institute in Moscow for psychiatric examination. The reputation of the Institute is well known: it is the scientific branch of the horrible Lubianka.

It seems that Kurnosov was confined at the time in a solitary confinement cell dependent on the insulator of the fourth section. When the psychiatrists had decided that only a madman would make an attempt on the life of a benefactor of mankind, the prisoner escaped trial and, consequently, the execution squad. But what became of him, then? The question has been asked on several occasions by Western journalists, but the Muscovite sphinx has always kept silence.

Now—and this, perhaps, is the nub of the matter— the extracts from the psychiatric report released to the press stated the following: 'Mikhail Kurnosov suffers from paranoiac psychosis with a doctrinaire theme. One of his aberrations consists in believing that he is the inventor of a political doctrine destined to create an ideal régime in one country, which, as everyone knows, is entirely contrary to the sane views of Marxism-Leninism, which is universalist by definition.'

Well, what if the rumours that have been heard with ever increasing frequency in well informed circles are in fact correct? What if the prisoner of the cell Triple Zero is in fact Mikhail Kurnosov?

Indeed, one cannot but speculate on why the Soviet authorities are so pampering the enigmatic Iron Mask, instead of sending him to rot at Sychevka with the other irredeemables, supposing that no one has the courage to organize an escape for him that would have the expected result. If Iron Mask is Kurnosov, this might be the reason.

Increasing numbers of witnesses assure us that the USSR is the only country in the world where no one any longer believes in Marxism-Leninism. This fact is embarrassing for the members of the Nomenklatura, who do not believe in it either, but do not intend to lose their place in the sun. They might well, therefore, have set up an ultra-secret political bureau, entrusted with the task of working out a new doctrine that might replace at some stage a completely demystified Communism and, in this political laboratory, the original thinker, Mikhail Kurnosov, might have found his place.

This hypothesis of a doctrinal *sharashka* (prison-laboratory for philosophers, similar to the prison-laboratories for scientists that we already know about, thanks to Solzhenitsyn) might provide a rational explanation of why summary justice was not meted out to the unfortunate tyrannicide.

'I doubt if the explanation is as simple as Jeanne thinks,' Aleksandr said to himself, 'especially if Pitman has anything to do with it . . .'

The platitude of style of which Jeanne Bouillon was so proud always irritated him. But this time he was also needled by professional jealousy, which he preferred not to be aware of: by what right was one of his 'sound-boxes' repeating 'rumours', coming from 'well-informed circles', which he himself had never heard? Bah! What did it matter? He would be 'home' soon.

He read the 'boxed' statement, a French translation from the Italian.

WHAT DOES THE RUSSIAN TRUTH THINK OF THE MASS MEDIA?
or
THE PUNISHED BELL

In olden times, church bells were blessed, yes, and anointed with holy chrism. As long as they behaved themselves, they were revered. If they misbehaved, then watch out, my girl, lift your skirts: we're going to give you a sound thrashing.

The young Tsarevich Dmitri had his throat cut at Uglich in 1593. Apparently it was Boriska Godunov who had sent men with knives. Well, one might almost believe that the great bell of Uglich had started sounding the alarm of its own accord: 'Murder! Murder!'

Boriska became angry. On his orders the bell was taken down and beaten with rods. One of its ears was broken off, as one might have cut off the ear of a man, and it was exiled to Siberia, to Tobolsk. At first it rang out over the market place, from the church of the All Merciful. Then it counted the hours from the top of the tower of St Sophia. And it counted a great many: about two million, two hundred and forty-two thousand, five hundred and sixty.

In the year 1849, the Uglichians decided that the punishment of the bell had lasted long enough. They asked for it to be repatriated.

Well, it first had to be proved that the tradition was correct, that it was in fact the bell of Uglich that was counting the hours of its exile at Tobolsk. Then the amnestied clock could return home. It finally came back on 20 May 1892, three centuries less a year after its condemnation. Then, on 21 May, before a multitude of people the dove rang out again from its native tower.

This is the story of a judicial error, but suppose that it was not.

Without troikas, there would be no Russian soul. And without sleighbells, there would be no troikas. They are called the sleighbells of Valdai. Why?

The Grand Prince of Moscow, Basil III, having conquered the city of Pskov, sent his intendant Dolmatov: 'Listen, Dolmashka, bring me back the belfry bell.' The belfry bell was, one might say, the symbol of bourgeois independence.

On the way back, at the village of Valdai, the bell broke. The inhabitants picked up the pieces and melted them down to make sleighbells.

And what if the bell of Uglich had broken half-way from Tobolsk and sleighbells had been made of it and they had all chimed 'Murder' together?

That is what the Russian Truth thinks of the mass media.

'Stuff and nonsense!' murmured Aleksandr indignantly. 'The Russian Truth thinks nothing at all. This parable can be interpreted in any number of ways. Whether he's Kurnosov or not, this Iron Mask is a charlatan.'

When he got to Pontoise, he made sure once again that he had not been followed, and took a taxi to the shooting range.

'Ah, M. Alexandre! It's been an age . . .'

By means of a slightly touched up identity card, since conveniently lost to avoid trouble, Aleksandr Psar had joined the Shooting Club under the name of Alexandre Rsar, which had the double advantage of putting any possible researchers off the scent, since they would proceed in alphabetical order, and, since the name was unpronounceable, club members would call him by his first name.

A cheerful, plump retired colonel ran the shooting range, one of the most modern in Europe. He thought that he had recognized in M. Alexandre a true marksman and did him all kinds of favours. Perhaps, indeed, he was wrong, and M. Alexandre was merely a frustrated warrior. He lacked the cold passion for technique that characterizes the most serious —and deranged—members of shooting clubs. He did not use antique weapons or unusual calibres, he did not make ballistic calculations, he did not recite loads and velocities by heart, he did not regard himself as a master armourer and did not strip down the trigger mechanisms. He was not even what is called a crack shot, nor did he take part in any championships. But he experienced a certain restrained, but nevertheless visible pleasure in shooting; he respected the safety rules to the letter; he handled the weapons with respect; in short, everything suggested that, if he had not been a prosperous businessman, he might well have been a very good army officer.

The firing range for air-guns was as calm as an aquarium. Two marksmen were practising, but each was much too careful of his own concentration to interfere with that of the other. The little pops at intervals no more disturbed the quietness of the place than the movements of a fish's fins detonate in the depths of the sea.

Aleksandr concentrated: the preparation for shooting had something of Zen about it and something of the inner preparation that Stanislavsky requires of the actor. The hand closed placidly on the butt, the index finger rigid on the side of the trigger guard, the striped lead carefully inserted in the chamber, the muscles deliberately relaxed. All these had their practical purpose, but they were also rites that induced the required state of grace. Then, suddenly, one was ready, one raised one's eyes to the target: at that precise moment, only it and I exist in the world.

Aleksandr pulled the trigger slowly with the austerity appropriate to compressed-air shooting, which is to real shooting what a toccata is to a symphony. After each shot, he pressed the control knob and his target came back to him, travelling along the stretched wires the whole length of the range, as on a cable-car. He examined it carefully: 'Why so wide of the mark? Did I jolt?' He then sent the target back to its place to be shot through again. He took a deep breath, breathed out, breathed in again, half breathed out and, holding his breath, raised his arm, then lowered it, outstretched, but not to its full length, trained the bead on the bull's-eye and, finally, very gently, tightened his hand a little more, as over a sponge. The little click surprised him each time.

When he was satisfied with his score—he imposed this purification, this preparation, on himself, before the real shooting, rather as the Orthodox fast before Christmas—he returned to his locker, turned the combination lock and took out his ear muffs. At the bottom of the locker was a glint of blue: it was his Smith and Wesson, which Aleksandr never touched without an emotion that he could not entirely explain. To find a sexual symbol in a weapon struck him as ridiculous; similarly he refused to see anything sacred in an object that had never been used for anything but practice, for relaxation. But one day, this ascesis might come to an end. Aleksandr was descended from a long line of military men, who can only fulfil themselves completely through weapons as others do through tools, the pen, the cross, the banknote.

'Let's go,' he said in Russian.

A weapon is neither a hound nor a horse, but it belongs to the same family.

Why had he chosen to own a revolver rather than an automatic? Perhaps because he was as little interested in mechanics as in administration and because, despite its advantages, the automatic seemed to him to be too conditioned by the recharging spring, by the excessive, artificial safety-catch, by what amounted in a sense to a plethoric ingeniousness; the revolver had a simplicity of its own! And, in any case, the only weapon that his father had ever been given was a Nagant revolver: perhaps the more modern automatic pistol stood in his unconscious for a world in which people like him had lost, had got lost.

'The silhouettes, M. Alexandre?'

'No, I'll have a carton first, Colonel.'

He went into the real shooting-gallery. There was only one marksman there. He took up his position as far away from him as he could.

His Smith and Wesson fired the .357 magnum and the .38 special. Though by no means an expert, Aleksandr knew that, according to the cartridge used, the energy and velocity could be doubled. For the cartons, he used the relatively economical .38 special lead ogival bullets, cased with nylon.

He took up position in front of the target and let the weapon hang loose in his hand. With its four-inch long barrel—a combat weapon rather than a competition one, but bulky all the same, it weighed, when loaded, over a kilo. He allowed his body to get used to this new extension, this supplementary organ.

Then he cocked the weapon.

To fire at the cartons, he always used the simple action. It gave him pleasure to feel his thumb hook the hammer, the hammer resist, then yield and, inside, the tumbler lock into place.

He raised his arm solemnly as if to give a blessing and, at the same time lowered his left eyelid. Standing square, his hips and shoulders sideways, as in an Egyptian mural, it was as if his body had been flattened and no longer existed except in a single vertical plane perpendicular to the target. In this plane his arm came slowly down, like the vane of a windmill.

The sighting notch, regulated to perfection, framed the bead, the triangle of which seemed to be fixed in the black circle of the bull's-eye. Aleksandr had large hands. He hardly felt the weight of the weapon distend his palm. Trying, as the American experts recommend, to keep the index finger free, trying not to disturb in any way the miraculous architecture that he had just created, he pulled the trigger—that is, he drew it towards him.

The weapon spoke.

He began again. An internal—psychosomatic?—calculator kept him informed of the number of shots fired. After six he could eject the cartridges. He was pleased with his score. He turned to the colonel, who had been accompanying him from stand to stand.

'Now, Colonel.'

The silhouette room was normally reserved for policemen, reserve army officers and those, generally, whom one could not suspect of joining a shooting club in order to learn how to injure their neighbour. But M. Alexandre was allowed in. For the silhouettes he used the .357 magnum, not the still-sealed box that he kept, without quite knowing why, at the bottom of his locker, and which contained hollow-points, but semi-wadcutter, which were also fairly realistic. Having rotated the cylinder, he loaded the heavy pellets of death one by one into their respective cases. Soon the large snub-nosed bullets would leave the barrel at a speed of 500 metres a second.

'Ready?'

'Ready, Colonel.'

The silhouettes were not going to appear too quickly for him to use the single, much more precise action: but the double action seemed more suitable for this type of shooting. The instinctive shot at a silhouette is to the carefully aimed shot at a carton what platonic love is to ordinary love.

One short silhouette showed up on his left. Fire! Another, taller one on his right. Fire! He was relieved: he had got those two. Another, right in front of him. Fire! His finger had contracted too much. He guessed that he had touched that one only on the shoulder. And, before it swung away, he had time to correct his shot by getting another bullet at the level of the navel. One of those disproportionate flashes of rage.

'You thought you'd got away? Right!'

One on the right. Fire! One on the left. Fire! The colonel, his fat face creased in a smile, increased the pace. One on the left again. The striker hit at nothing. The psychosomatic counter had failed to work.

'Ah! Monsieur Alexandre, you won't listen to me. I've always told you that an automatic . . .'

'I know. The last one would have got me.'

He stared with hate at the jeering silhouette. He reloaded: peas rolling in their pod, letters sliding into their envelopes: could they reach their addressees?

He began again. It was an orgy of firing. He did not stop until he was exhausted: the heel of his thumb was strained; his index finger, tired by the extra effort of the double action, had lost its smooth movement. 'I wonder how the shooting ranges are over there? They must be as well set up . . .'

'Hey, Monsieur Alexandre, you brought down about fifty Viets. Take off your headphones and come and have a drink.'

He got back into the cinema through the emergency exit, which did not shut properly. That was why he went to see almost all the films shown there. Today he would have had time to see *Topaz* two or three times, because the showing was continuous. But that did not bother him: he had acquired the reputation of sitting through several consecutive showings if he liked the film. He left after the hotel sequence. He would leave the Omega where he had parked it and walk to Jessica Boïsse's.

June evenings are interminable. He made his way unhurriedly along the broad bourgeois avenues of the 8th arrondissement that he was so fond of. All those imposing residences, almost palaces, built for whom? Not great lords, but stockbrokers and bankers who still knew how to live. Those broad staircases, those squat loggias, those wrought-iron railings. (Aleksandr loved wrought iron.) Those gardens one glimpsed through the *portes cochères*. Those patches of ivy tumbling over a stone wall five metres high. The sober splendour of the side-avenues, their pavements crunching with gravel. Aleksandr thought he could make out the ghosts of horsemen and phantom barouches. His grandfather had walked around there wearing violet gloves, perhaps under those same trees, some eighty years before. It was the period of the alliance; the French republicans had no prejudices against the boyars, or, if they had, they hid them out of a liking for roubles. Then his father had been thrown up here, with an empty belly, knocking on one or two doors, to no avail. And now he had come to take his leave, treading the gravel in shoes made by the best Italian bootmaker in Paris. He walked head held high, stepping aside with exaggerated courtesy before each woman he met, whether she was a native of the quarter or a Portuguese maid.

Jessica lived near La Muette, in a very ugly, very comfortable building built just before the war. By leaning out of the balcony, one could catch a glimpse of the Bois de Boulogne. The Soviet embassy was a few steps away.

'So we're all dolled up, I see, Madame Boïsse.'

When he spoke to this woman, Aleksandr never managed to avoid a touch of boorishness that only she could arouse in him.

Jessica was dark, thin, beautiful perhaps, smelled always of tobacco and always wore black: today it was a négligé with flounces and lace, old-fashioned to a degree, transparent, held at the waist by a loosely knotted belt.

She led Aleksandr into the living-room; at one end black-and-white striped sofas, flanking a zebra skin; a glass table at the other end, laid with modern cutlery, huge plates for *cuisine nouvelle*, a bottleneck with gold paper round it, emerging from an icebucket; a table laid for two.

'I'm always willing to honour my contract.'

She toyed with her belt.

'No? You haven't changed your mind?'

He dropped onto one of the sofas. He would have liked to say something crude, but stopped himself.

'Well, what is it? Ivan won't be here for twenty minutes. Come on, tell me the truth: do I disgust you or are you impotent?'

She spoke with a slight American accent.

'My dear Jessica,' he drawled, 'experience shows that one is always wrong to mix business and pleasure.'

'When business is a pleasure, it can be marvellous, no?'

'But when pleasure becomes a business, what a bore! If, one day, you stop being my cut-out, we'll see. For the moment, don't tell me you're short of admirers?'

She must have been forty, but she did have what it takes, as they say.

She lit a cigarette; he made no pretence to help her. Yes, Pitman had made a mistake in assigning him this smoker: someone might notice that he hated women who smoked. On the other hand, Pitman may have done it on purpose: any complicity between her and him might have been damaging to the service. For the first time in the day he thought of Alla and felt a pang in his heart.

Usually he stopped himself from thinking of Alla and even more of young Dmitri. Even that morning, thinking about his forthcoming return, he had consciously erased them from his mind: 'Pitman holds me, but he mustn't hold me too tight . . .' But sometimes, in the middle of a sentence, when he was thinking of something quite different, it was suddenly as if a dyke had burst: 'Oh, my wife! Oh, my son!' He reproached himself for that moment of inattention. 'One must always hide one's feelings.' He looked at his nails. He had beautiful hands and treated himself to the old-fashioned luxury of having his nails manicured.

Jessica watched him and giggled: 'Not impotent and not disgusted, but just a little bit of a queen? They must say that about you in literary circles, no?'

'Those are precisely the circles where it would hardly matter,' Aleksandr replied, without contradicting her. 'I know perfectly normal writers who pass themselves off as homosexuals in order to gain good will. The West really *is* rotten, Jessica—it's not just propaganda.'

A Canadian born at Cannes, who had been married to an Italian count, an American impresario, and to a few others, Jessica Boïsse had access to the international jet set, without really belonging to it. From time to time she exhibited Alexandr at *Maxim*'s, or picked him up from this or that publisher's in her little white Lancia: that was enough to satisfy the curiosity of the Parisians as to the private life of Aleksandr Psar. What hold did Pitman have over Jessica? Money? Blackmail? Aleksandr had to and preferred to remain in the dark. It was even quite smart in his Directorate not to appear too well informed. 'Keyholes aren't our line.' What is the point of spying on anyone, even the enemy, when it is easier to give him instructions? 'The snake doesn't spy on the frog,' Pitman was fond of saying.

The door bell rang. Jessica went to answer it, adapting her walk to her dress, in imitation of the panther style of the *années folles*.

'Pleased to see you, Ivan Ivanich.'

'How are you, Aleksandr Dmitrich?'

Ivan IV was a broad-shouldered man of about fifty; thinning ginger hair, combed across his head, did not manage to hide his baldness; his face was pitted with small-pox marks; his pale blue eyes often had a despairingly gentle look in them. He wore a blue-and-white striped shirt, a brown suit and stout shoes.

They shook hands firmly. Ivan Ivanich observed his agent.

'You're looking well, Aleksandr Dmitrich. And you're still as handsome as a god.'

'A god's hand isn't a pump, Ivan Ivanich. Stop trying to prove to me that you could snatch my arm off if you wanted to and come and have a snifter.'

It was an old joke: to his great regret vodka did not agree with Ivan Ivanich.

'Come, come, now Comrade Colonel, it isn't fair to make fun of a poor dyspeptic.'

Aleksandr was a co-opted colonel; Ivan Ivanich a regular major.

'What? No PCMs?'

Aleksandr liked to show that he knew the Geebee jargon: a drink was a Politico-Cultural Measure.

'Ah! Not at all. You do go at it! Now if our young lady here had thought of champagne . . .'

Jessica interrupted: '*Champanskoie*? Yes, yes, there's *champanskoie*. I know my job.'

She went on in bad Russian: 'Gentlemen, I'll leave you to your business. If you want me, call me. But I get the impression that you'll be just as happy without me. If you decide to dance in the nude, draw the curtains. I've got neighbours.'

She went out. Ivan Ivanich winked: 'She'd have stayed readily enough, the trollop!'

'If you like that kind of thing, don't mind me.'

'Oh, what *I* like . . .'

Ivan Ivanich trotted over to the dining table.

'A spot of caviar! A little lobster! A little goose! I fear the expense-sheet will be not negligible!'

They sat down. Ivan Ivanich unfolded the heavy starched napkin and formed it into a triangle with the tip stuck between two buttons of his crumpled waistcoat. Emitting a 'ha!' of anticipation, he stretched his hand out towards the bottle. One sensed that he was a man in a happy frame of mind who would take delight in cracking the lobster's claws and the goose bones between his teeth. Aleksandr reminded himself, with a mixture of pity and satisfaction, that he was just about to spoil Ivan's appetite.

'Ivan Ivanich. It was not only to feed you on lobster that I sent out the signal "urgent contact requested". In fact, I have a few trifles for you, like, for instance, a defamatory historical novel about Dostoievsky, but that could have waited. What I wanted to let you know urgently was that I've finished.'

'Finished what?'

'Working for the Directorate. At least in France.'

'You've . . . what? You'll get me strangled, Aleksandr Dmitrich.'

'That's your business. I'm going home.'

Ivan Ivanich's clear eyes seemed to swim with tears.

'Sasha, Sashenka . . . You can't do this to me. I've got used to Paris, so has my wife . . . And, anyway, one doesn't interrupt a mission right in the middle!' Think of the Geebee, think of the Fatherland! Aleksandr Dmitrich, please, tell me you're joking, you old son of a gun. Tell me it isn't true!'

'Ivan Ivanich, I agreed to serve here for thirty years. Thirty years are up. It is time for me to go home.'

'Agreed, agreed . . .? There's no question of *agreeing*, my lad, you do what you're told, like the rest of us.'

'Wrong, Ivan Ivanich. When I agreed . . . I insist on that—the proposition was put to me . . .'

'Where? When? What proposition?'

'As I said, thirty years ago. Where? If you absolutely must know, on the towers of Notre-Dame, on the gallery of the Chimeras, to be precise, between the two towers. I accepted the proposition on one condition: I wanted to go home before the year of my fiftieth birthday. That condition was accepted. I have the word of Iakov Moiseich himself, you may not know this, but it was he who recruited me.'

Ivan Ivanich snatched his napkin and threw it on the table.

'It's scandalous! It's monstrous! I refuse to believe a word of it. We shall continue as before.'

Aleksandr stared at him.

'Ivan Ivanich, I am very fond of you, but remember, you amount to very little: a conveyor belt, nothing more. So do your job, convey!'

It was still daylight when Aleksandr got home, and yet it was ten o'clock. It was true that it was around midsummer and that at this time Parisian evenings remind one of St Petersburg nights.

A blue half-light floated in the bedroom. The electronic chess set was not blinking: it had solved the problem. Aleksandr sat down in front of the chess board to work out his next move. But his mind was not on what he was doing. Images passed before his eyes again and again. A fair-haired boy, whose photos he would have to destroy after committing every detail of them to memory. An old man dying in a hospital: 'I shan't go home. Alek, you go in my place.' And his hand fell back without the knuckles being able to reach the beloved cheek. A young woman with expressive, mischievous eyes. And then the huge ship of a church sailing through the sky, with two small figures clinging to the poop: a young man and his tempter.

Devastated as he was, Ivan Ivanich had no alternative but to transmit by radio *Oprichnik*'s request for recall, though he did lard it with excuses and justifications. The message fell on Major-General Iakov Pitman's desk.

At fifty-seven Pitman was the youngest member of the

Consistory of Conceptuals, those whom the really young called the Hidy-hats. The least of his responsibilities consisted in secreting the aberrations that the Soviet Union would get the world to believe in the next twenty years. Other, even more secret functions were revealed to him only through successive initiations, but already he was absorbing the sap of a higher truth, certain that if his life were to be of some use to mankind, it would be thanks to the most impenetrable mysteries of the former Department D, now known as Directorate A.

If Directorate A had respected the rules, Major-General Pitman would long since have ceased to concern himself with such trifles as an influence agent let loose in the world. He would have been concerned with administration below and politics above. But Pitman, bitten by the Sun Tzu bug, had taken upon himself the right to unwind to the end his own 'divine skein', the seven Frenchmen whom he had recruited in his youth. When he read Ivan Ivanich's message, he relived in a second the scene on the gallery of the Chimeras . . . He then reached for his *vertushka*, the telephone reserved for the princes of this world: 'Can I come?'

'I'll be expecting you.'

The official car was brought round. Pitman got in the back. He did not approve of the condescension of certain important individuals who sat beside the driver, but he had never had the audacity to demand what Abdulrakhmanov got quite naturally—the held door open for him.

'To Volkovo.'

Abdulrakhmanov had retired to a very old village, about a hundred kilometres from the capital, where the Geebee had built dachas for its members. About four hundred hectares had been closed off and were guarded by armed men and dogs. Within the compound reigned the peace of a nature left almost in its wild state. One could fish in the lake, go hunting or collect mushrooms in the forest.

Abdulrakhmanov's dacha had been built on the very edge of the lake, with the veranda almost overhanging the water. Built shortly after the war, the wooden house had already taken on an old Russian air, with its carved gables and warped wooden steps.

Abdulrakhmanov lived alone with a dumb orderly—no harem, no family. Pitman found the old man sitting on the veranda, in front of a chessboard with large old pieces, polished with use, and a small, badly printed sheet of paper containing chess problems. The sun was going down behind the trees and, as if for a rearguard-action, was shooting its rays between the trunks. Small explosions of light detonated among the branches. The lake was lead-smooth, colourless.

'Kenti, the samovar!'

But Innokenti, warned no doubt by the guard post, was already carrying in the big-bellied silver samovar, angrily spitting steam. He came back several times with small loaves of various shapes, *kalachs*, *bubliks*, pots of jam, honey and molasses, and cold sausage; he had a grumpy look, never once raising his eyes to his master or to the visitor.

'I always thought, Mohammed Mohammedovich, that you had specific plans for *Oprichnik*.'

Abdulrakhmanov did not stoop, but his shoulders had rounded with age, so that it was not only his head, but his whole body that suggested a gigantic sugarloaf. He bit into a cucumber. His huge teeth were yellow, but all present and correct. 'A very old ogre,' thought Pitman. 'An ogre of eighty-plus!'

'*Oprichnik*? Do you remember, Your Excellency, how you did not want to recruit *Oprichnik*?'

Abdulrakhmanov accorded Pitman the title that would have been his by right under the Old Order.

Pitman admitted his blindness and they went over, one by one, *Oprichnik*'s greatest successes. The first had been that novel by Emmanuel Blun, *Un Ami fidèle*, which no publisher wanted and which Psar had turned into a success, rattling a few skeletons in a few cupboards in the process and winning a major prize. Blun had been translated into several languages and, in the Soviet Union, had received an award named after one of the bloodiest butchers of mankind. Nevertheless Blun continued to be regarded as a liberal, even though his hero's faithful friend was an effective, if silent member of the Communist Party, who always arrived at the right moment to save the narrator from the perils that his generous, but blundering temperament got him into.

Then Psar had the idea of the White Books. They had had to stop him in his tracks with some of these: in particular, they had to forbid him to publish one on the Algerian War. 'You mustn't get labelled left-wing,' they had told him. 'Remember, you're an honest man who cannot deny what is self-evidently true, but whose natural sympathies are on the right . . .' There was another reason, of course, and he guessed it: the campaign on Algeria had been given to another agent and they had to avoid getting their wires crossed.

'But what about his White Book on State Education? The French are still licking their lips over that one!'

'His White Book on Women wasn't bad, either, Mohammed Mohammedovich.'

'Absolutely. Could one ever calculate the number of would-be French citizens who must have been returned to sender, thanks to him. Don't you think, Your Excellency, that limbo must be full of little bleeding French-speaking embryos, which would not have been sent there without *Oprichnik*'s intervention?'

Abdulrakhmanov buttered himself a slice of bread and, methodically laid rounds of sausage on it in a pattern of curves.

'There was also that business of *Russian for All*, Mohammed Mohammedovich.'

Yes, *Russian for All*, a four-year course, planned in the Soviet Union and containing capsules of propaganda in each reading, in each grammatical exercise, what a masterstroke! The political gain was immense, to judge by the financial profits.

'And the *Dictionary of Synonyms*, in which one looked up "exploitation" under "capital" and "revolution" under "proletariat"!'

'And the *Dictionary of Quotations*: twenty-eight from Jaurès, as against three from Péguy.'

'That was a slight error: it would have been better to enlist Péguy to our cause, doctoring the contexts as necessary.'

'You can't criticize Psar for that—he still lacked experience.'

The two men were fond of recalling the adventures that

marked the youth of the one and the maturity of the other.

'There were also the apocryphal prophecies of Guillaume Postel. Of course, he was forced to deny them afterward, but as the *Vademecum* observes, denials pass and lies remain.'

Yes, they had had a good laugh in Dzerzhinsky Square at the panic that had seized the French, always so Cartesian, on reading the Apocalypse of the Magus from Barenton: 'The old soldiers will drop their halberds, the bombards will swallow up their cannon-balls, the galleys will sink of their own accord and bags of gold will pour out their entrails into the sculleries the day that the Red Knight, shading his eyes with his hand, appears in the rising sun . . . And this will take place in the year 7488 from the creation of the world.' Was it conceivable that capital had left the national territory as a result of this Great Fear? Perhaps not; in any case, the psychological success had been delicious.

Suddenly the colonel-general became more serious and seemed to change the subject.

'*Nnus* . . . I think I detect in France a certain slide, not exactly to the right, but towards political cynicism, pessimism, a certain tendency to see facts as facts and not as applications of ideas. These are reactionary characteristics. This is not a criticism of you personally, Your Excellency, but it seems to me that, in my time, we managed to impose Marxism as a cornerstone, as a sort of absolute. Now I am told that one is no longer ridiculed for not being a Marxist in France. Is that true?'

Pitman put down the cold *pirozhok* that he had already raised to his mouth. Displeasing a superior was the terror of his life. This particular superior was also a benefactor. How could he bear to disappoint him?

'Mohammed Mohammedovich, nothing escapes your eye. I don't know whether I'm guilty of negligence, but I do my best, I do assure you. Indeed, according to the background information we are receiving, we no longer hold the French intelligentsia as we did under your direction. Perhaps we have relaxed our vigilance? In any case a contrary wind is blowing over Paris.'

Abdulrakhmanov sighed slowly, like the old man that he was. In thirty years of friendly relations, various acts of kindness, presents for that stupid cow Elichka, he had still not managed to cure Pitman of his delight in self-criticism which paralyses all totalitarian bureaucracies.

'Oh, it's not my affair any more,' he muttered.

But, in the Directorate, could that ever be so?

'However, if I were you, I would not neglect the contrary wind that has been sown very largely, by our own dissidents. French opinion still carries weight in the world. I would suggest getting a firm grip on things. Very firm. And the dissidents themselves are beginning to deserve a punitive expedition of some scope. The two operations might be carried out as one.'

'Have you any particular suggestion, Comrade General?'

The sun had disappeared. The lake had become tinted with patches of red that would vanish in an instant. In the distance, a fish leapt out of the water and fell back with a heavy plop. Ripples spread outwards, becoming less and less marked. Pitman thought that he could hear them lap against the piles that supported the verandah.

Abdulrakhmanov did not answer. He stared out in front of him. Perhaps he was trying to hear that noise or some other, equally elusive, rising towards him from the depths of the future.

'What do you expect to do with *Oprichnik*?' he asked at last.

'I have come to ask your advice, Mohammed Mohammedovich. *Oprichnik* is your child, in a sense.'

Abdulrakhmanov nodded slowly.

'Listen,' he said, 'do as you wish, but personally I've always liked divisions which leave no remainders—and shirts that have as many buttons as buttonholes. You don't know what to do with *Oprichnik* . . . You don't know how to regain control of the French and the dissidents . . . It's simply a question of putting the right nut on the right bolt . . . Tsar Ivan was ready to raze Pskov to the ground to teach its inhabitants a lesson. A Pskov operation might be desirable . . . From what I know of young Psar, I think he would be quite capable of playing his role in some rather exquisite little set-up. Does Your Excellency wish to know more?'

4
One Last Little Service
(Operation Pskov, Stage 1)

The University of Leningrad would soon be closed for the summer vacation, but Gemma would not be going back to Italy; she would continue with the mission that she had given herself—to struggle against oppression.

She had declared war on Communism, just as, during the Nazi period, she would have tried to assassinate Mussolini, just as, in the nineteenth century, she would have thrown bombs at kings and ministers, just as, during the French Revolution, she would have stabbed Marat. It was because of all this that she had learnt Russian and with a passion for clandestinity, she had chosen the cover of a student of literature in the Soviet Union.

She had a beautiful face—she was Tuscan—but dirty hair. Her large bust bulged out of shapeless sweaters. She wore ill-fitting trousers that seemed about to split with every step she took. Yet she was very successful with the men: a swarm of students, claiming more or less to be dissidents in order to win her over, buzzed around her, but to no avail. Gemma was unapproachable: she lived only for the struggle.

While awaiting more violent activity, she had set up a network for the clandestine export of samizdat texts, and was happy enough to devote herself to this for the time being. The network had already been functioning for over two years. Her organization dated from one evening when she left a party of friends, and had been unable to find a taxi to take her home to Marat Street. (Superstitious, though an atheist, the would-be tyrannicide regarded it as an excellent augury that she had managed to find such an address in a city where the housing shortage had reached crisis proportions). It was cold, the thick snow stuck to her over-shoes. Most private motorists, Gemma had been told, would be very happy to take her home for a few roubles. She stopped the first vehicle she saw.

It was a huge truck, bearing in white letters on a blue ground the unlovely word *Sovtransavto*, with two arrowed Cs superimposed, the second reversed, and a telephone number —2213653—that Gemma immediately committed to memory because, in preparing herself for her secret war, she had trained herself to remember series of numbers. The enormous mass, jolting through the night, screeched, panted and came to a stop. Gemma climbed up into the over-heated cabin.

'Where to?'

'Near Moscow Station.'

'Five roubles.'

She took out the money from her pocket without bargaining.

'You speak Russian well, but you're a foreigner.'

'Italian.'

'No! I've just come from Italy.'

The driver was a tall, square-faced young fellow, with small, squinting eyes, always half-closed, as if irritated by a non-existent cigarette. He left the Soviet Union with a load of chrome and came back from Europe with spirits.

'A real carrier pigeon.'

She removed the hand that had been placed on her knee and launched into a headlong attack on the Soviet Union for its shameless transgression of the Helsinki Agreements. The driver emitted a few hums without actually committing himself either one way or the other. At Marat Street, he muttered, without conviction: 'Can I see you again?'

Gemma, who was already imagining all the services that she might be able to extract from him, agreed. The following Sunday, they went to Petrodvorets. Viacheslav was put out to find the fountain, where he had been told a mechanical dog chased artificial ducks, frozen. Gemma launched out once more on her propaganda and, this time, got some limited agreement:

'I'm an educated man. I'm not too badly off. But, it's true, for a guy earning 75 roubles a month, when a pair of boots costs 150 . . .'

The following Sunday they went to Pavlovsk. Viacheslav was curious to see the Lions' Steps, which are wider at the bottom in order to give the illusion of being higher than they really are.

'We Russians didn't have to wait to be Communists,' he commented, 'before becoming clever.'

His conversion then seemed to Gemma to be sufficiently under way for her to ask him to take one or two manuscripts on some of his journeys. He agreed without asking for the slightest thing in exchange: 'I do that for the love of freedom, as you might say.'

Gemma took the first plane to Rome. She knew Enzo Grucci, a small impecunious publisher, who published books at the author's expense. She explained her plan to him, got his agreement and left him what she called her 'breviary', that is to say, a list of meeting places and a series of passwords and codes to indicate the days and times. Pleased with the professional way in which she operated, she immediately returned to Leningrad. There would be no shortage of manuscripts: samizdat was the LSD of the Russian students.

A week later, Gemma telephoned 'Uncle Enzo', telling him that she had had her 'first meeting' with a Soviet young man, that she was reading a book published in '1825', the spelling of which puzzled her, and that she had to take an exam 'Tuesday or may be Wednesday'.

Signor Grucci, still sceptical, consulted the breviary and took the trouble to get his heavy carcass under the Arco di Tito the following Thursday at 1825 hours. That day he drew a blank. But he came back again at the same time on the Friday and immediately caught sight of a tall fellow with a short bust and long legs, who was walking up and down with a parcel of old *Oggi*s under his right arm. Conscious of the absurdity of the situation, but sensing profit, Signor Grucci approached the unknown man and repeated distinctly a call to murder borrowed from the libretto of *Norma*:

'*Strage! Strage! Sterminio, vendetta!*'

The man, half-shutting his eyes, handed him the parcel of

*Oggi*s without a word. Inside, Grucci found an envelope and, in the envelope, a pretty smutty story which, when translated still more smuttily, would keep the Seagull publishing house afloat for six months.

The system continued to operate. Without counting the great commercial successes—and he did have some—Signor Grucci could always sell his publications to an unchanging clientèle, which, at worst, enabled him to cover his costs: Russian émigrés, university libraries (especially American ones), intelligence and propaganda services, the first keener to get their hands on the originals, the second more interested in translations, made the Seagull publishing house into the main source of samizdat for export, all thanks to young Gemma, who, without any reward, guaranteed the publisher's prosperity. The authors, of course, were not often in a position to demand their royalties; when, most unusually, Grucci had to resign himself to settling with some of them, he did so only after overcoming innumerable 'difficulties', meanwhile making the money work for him. The strange alliance between the libertarian virgin and the beneficiary of subversion prospered.

Every day, on her way to the University, Gemma called at the meeting places that she had assigned to the people whom she called 'the members of her network'. There were two on the Nevsky Prospekt, one on the Field of Mars, one on Palace Square, one in Gorky Park, one in the Square of the Decembrists. That morning—it was June and the sun (like an adolescent suffering calf-love) had stayed up all night—she found a diamond shape drawn in chalk on a bench in Gorky Park. That same evening she pushed open the door of a bar on the Nevsky Prospekt above which a laconic notice proclaimed: *Pivo* (beer).

Dunduk, big, red-haired, his white overalls visible through the open raincoat that he had stupidly put on to hide them, was already there. There was no *Pravda* on the table. Gemma had brought her own and, normally, they would have exchanged copies. Perhaps he had not brought a new page of *The Russian Truth*, but why then had he asked for a meeting?

She sat down. The carafe was three-quarters empty.

'You don't read the paper any more? Don't you care what is happening in the world?'

She spoke harshly: you have to give the Russians a good shake; Slav equals slave.

He chuckled soundlessly and, into his gaping mouth—the uvula was clearly visible—he dispatched another tot of vodka.

Gemma got up.

'We can do without drunks.'

He was still chuckling soundlessly, as in a silent film.

'If you knew what I've got here,' he said, in a stage whisper, 'you wouldn't go.'

'What have you got?'

He opened his raincoat, overalls, jacket, shirt, and pulled out a brown-paper parcel.

'This time, we've got them.'

'Them' meant the Party, the government, the powers of this world.

'What do you mean? What's this crumby parcel?'

He was still chuckling.

'Ah! He's a deep one! Do you know where he hid it? In the panelling of his television set. There's room. The set *they* gave him to keep him quiet. He's finished it now. The end. Then he said to me: "Dunduk, I know you love our little Mother Russia. Take it." There is no other copy in the whole world, Gemma! What I, Dunduk, have here is the whole of *The Russian Truth*.'

He was tightly clutching the brown parcel to him with one hand. With the other he rewarded himself with another tot.

Gemma made to grab the parcel. Then she remembered the security measures that she had herself drawn up.

'If anyone sees you give it to me . . .'

Dunduk stood up, tottering on his feet, and made a deep bow: 'Here, fair maiden, allow me to present you with . . . two rotten herrings and a dead mouse. Pray accept, beauty of my heart, this sacrifice from a noble soul.'

He thrust the parcel into her hands while performing a few uncertain bows. Someone laughed; a boy yelled out: 'If you've had enough of this tottering wreck, let me take his place.'

Gemma looked at the thing she held in her hands; she was convinced that *The Russian Truth* would turn out to be as important in the history of the world as *Mein Kampf* or *Das Kapital*. She felt a sudden upsurge of gratitude: it was she, with the help of this old anti-Communist drunkard, who had brought the first pages of this work into the West. It was only just that she should bear the responsibility of getting the entire book out of the country.

She left, more intoxicated than Dunduk. If she pulled it off, she would not have lived in vain.

The first thing to be done was to produce several copies of the manuscript. Thus God, the God in whom the Catholics believed, had made copies of Adam. Photocopying machines were watched, but Gemma had photographic equipment hidden in her apartment. She had learnt how to develop photographs and bought film only in small quantities, in various shops, so as not to attract attention; she also got film sent in from Italy.

In Marat Street, shut up in her room with the old battered, Dostoievskian furniture, which she was very fond of, she undid the precious parcel. Dunduk had kept his word. One day, he had come to see her:

'Are you the Italian girl? People have told me about you. Whatever I can do against them . . . They killed my father and mother . . . Would you be interested in a great political thinker locked up in a psychiatric hospital? I'm his nurse and he trusts me.'

Since then, seven messages had reached the West, thanks to Viacheslav.

The new pages were similar to those that she had already received and sent on: thin as cigarette paper, covered with blue ink, a compact, sloping hand, with tall ascenders, sometimes almost as in an illuminated manuscript, tiny but only to save space: one sensed that the man who was unrolling this microscopic reel would have preferred to write on the finest parchment with wide margins, well spaced lines and plenty of indentations for paragraphs. Instead of that, the spring was tightly wound. Gemma read Russian as easily as Italian. She quickly skimmed through the introduction.

It is not for nothing that the Teutonic peoples have two verbs for the Latin *facere*: *tun* and *machen*, 'to do' and 'to make'; that the Spanish peoples have two to signify 'to be', or that the ancient Greeks had three nouns to express the notion of love: *agape, eros* and *file*. We Scythian barbarians have *svoboda* and *volia*, and they both mean *libertas*; we also have *pravda* and *istina*, both meaning *veritas*. I don't think this is an accident, for we are also the only people in the world, to my knowledge, to possess a word to denote not inaccuracy, or lying, or error, but quite specifically the contrary of truth: *krivda*.

Yes, my lords and comrades—for they amount to the same thing—we Russians are drunk with truth. (Yes, and with freedom, though freedom is merely an application of truth: the truth will make you free, said Jesus Christ in St John, and Solzhenitsyn teaches us 'to live without lying', because this is the only freedom.) Even more than the God-bearing people of which Fedor Mikhailovich dreamt, we are the truth-bearing people, the people pregnant with truth, big with truth. We bear the truth both as a cross (on our backs) and as a child (in our womb).

Now, the devil being as clever as he is, it is laid down that whoever bears a thing also bears its contrary, and that is why we are the greatest purveyors of *krivda* in the world. Such are the laws, convex/concave, of the Apocalypse.

Our official newspaper is called *Pravda* because it carries the reverse side of truth. One has only to read it in a mirror to see our true Mother Truth.

From the mid-eleventh century, Kievian Russia possessed a collection of wise and moderate laws that bore the sublime name *Russian Truth*. And we have all heard those folktales in which the Tsar summons Ivan the Simpleton and sends him out into the world, ordering him: 'Bring me back the truth.'

Cinderella is a Christian truth. Faust is the German

truth. Don Quixote is the Spanish truth. But the Russian Truth is Ivan the Simpleton going off in search of the truth.

Now, Ivan the Simpleton, dear reader, is you and I, God help us!

That is what the Russian Truth thinks of Russian truth.

Gemma was as susceptible to the *Arabian Nights* style as to independence of thought: the anonymous prisoner did not cite Marx, Sartre or Heidegger; he recognized his roots (Russian: folklore; Christian: St John), but from these roots he flowered freely, which confirmed Gemma's intuition that true freedom can be reborn only in the totalitarian drama, not in the democratic operetta.

She shut the opaque blinds and drew the curtains, darkening the room. The boys would knock on her door in vain—she would be in better company.

'And what about him?' she wondered, as she set up her projectors and tripod, the wise madman, in his padded cell, guarded by Dunduk, the good warder, and by the other, wicked warder. How did he spend his hours, this man who knew that his life's work was in the hands of a foreign woman? 'Have no fear,' she murmured in Italian. 'No one in the world could be more faithful to you than I.'

Outside there was no twilight, no night and no dawn; the sky hardly darkened. Gemma thought that death must be that: a darkening, and one did not even know that one was dead. But she had a dark night of her own making, cut through by the beams of her projectors, independent of the rest of the world. Her night for his light. One by one she turned the pages and the camera clicked and *The Russian Truth* became immortal.

When the last page had been photographed, Gemma got the developing baths ready. She would make three copies from each negative. She felt an almost maternal joy when she saw the Cyrillic text appear again and again on the fine glossy, damp sheets. This was how the Ten Commandments had appeared to Moses, engraved in stone by an invisible hand working from within.

'I'm reproducing and I shall have triplets,' said Gemma.

When she had finished the developing, she lit her welding torch. Before embarking on her adventure, she had learnt a score of different techniques that, she thought, might be useful to her underground. She had a small cupboard full of food cans. She filled three of them with a copy of *The Russian Truth*: it would be the food of truth. She sealed the lids, melting the metal in the throbbing blue flame.

Then she picked up a bound volume of *The Complete Works of Lenin*. She had already stuck together and then cut out the pages so as to make a box. In it she placed the second copy and lightly stuck the cover to the fly leaf so that the box would not open by accident.

She then pulled out one of the skirting boards that ran along the walls of her room. She had removed several bricks to make a hiding place, which was already piled high with several works. Gemma had not put them there to hide them, but, on the contrary, to compromise herself: if she was ever arrested, she wanted those who searched her room to see at once the extent of the blows that she had struck at the régime.

The original—she always sent off the original so that there could be no doubt as to the authenticity of her find—she put into an envelope and stuck it between several copies of *Ogoniok*, which she cross-tied with string.

Meanwhile, she had given no thought to the possibility that she might be apprehended at any moment: Leningrad was a city of conspiracies and the militia intervened only when it really could not do otherwise. But now, for several minutes, *The Russian Truth* was to run considerable risks and Gemma unlocked her door with a rare degree of anxiety.

The corridor was empty; the neighbours who shared this communal apartment with Gemma were sleeping the sleep of the just or the unjust, snoring or not snoring as the case may be, but, in any case, were quite unconcerned with what she was doing. She hid the Lenin on top of the cistern in the lavatory: even if her room was searched, there was still a chance that this copy might not be discovered. She went back to her room, threw the parcel of *Ogonioks* into the corner, got a string shopping bag, put the tin cans into it and went downstairs.

A light that hardly altered with the hour glowed gently at the corners of the apartment buildings and Rastrelli palaces. There was no one in the streets, except for a few drunks sleeping in doorways.

Gemma reached the Griboiédov Canal, whose tamed waters flowed between two rectilinear quays, with ordered, administrative violence. At the corner of the Bank Bridge, she looked around her. She was not being observed. She dropped the cans into the water, one after another. Hardly a gleam from the tin remained visible through the grey-brown water. If everything went according to plan, this copy would rest in the mud until the day when the canal was drained or perhaps even until the Last Judgement of works of art.

Gemma went home, picked up the Lenin, which had lain undisturbed during her absence, and set off for the University. She had not slept all night and she had no breakfast. She felt both exhausted and light-headed.

Her admirers were waiting for her; they came up and surrounded her, making a fuss of her as they did every morning. One had brought her some lily-of-the-valley, another had written a poem for her and a third sniggered when he caught sight of her Lenin: 'You don't have to, you know! Why do you drink that dishwater?'

She brushed them all aside: 'I don't feel like larking about with you.'

Between two lectures, she went to the library. Nikolai Guerasimov was still working in the same corner; most of the students thought that he did not like Gemma because she did not hide her hostility to the régime, whereas he belonged to the Komsomol. She leaned over his table: 'Here's the Lenin you lent me. It bored me to death. Thanks all the same.'

He muttered something without looking up at her.

That night, it was Nikolai's turn not to sleep. He was the happy owner of a typewriter and it rattled on through the night, resting on a folded blanket to deaden the sound. Tomorrow, the first chapter of *The Russian Truth* would be distributed to the public. A week later it would have risen to an incalculable number of copies.

When the lectures were over, Gemma went to a telephone box and dialled a number.

'Viacheslav?'

'Yes.'

What luck! He was not out on a job.

'Could we go out sometime?'

'Tomorrow at Pushkino?'

'No. I'm busy tomorrow.'

'What a shame. We'll ring each other some other time.'

This was just a code: the meeting had been arranged for today, at six o'clock in the evening, in front of the statue of Peter the Great.

Viacheslav arrived first. He was wearing his usual smart little Italian leather jacket which made his bust even shorter and did not suit his truckdriver's shoulders. His fists on his hips and his head thrown back, he examined the monument.

'He was a heavyweight, too. Pushkin was right: if a machine like that starts to gallop behind you, you go mad. Hi, Gemma.'

'Hi. Are you leaving soon?'

'Tomorrow.'

Everything was working out perfectly.

'Do you want something to read for your journey?'

She handed him the parcel of *Ogonioks*. He pulled a face.

'Too bulky. If my cab is searched, they'll find it. Sorry old girl.'

'Viacheslav, but you've done it loads of times already.'

'Precisely.'

'Just this once, Viacheslav, please. You know it's for the love of freedom.'

'Freedom, freedom . . . I want to save my skin. It's not just our customs who go through my luggage with a tooth-comb as if they were looking for fleas, but the Poles, and the Germans. Have you ever been searched by a German? A page or two, O.K., but not your pal's complete works. Sorry!'

Gemma felt a flood of tears rise to her eyes.

'In a pocket? Under the seat? In the engine?'

He shrugged his shoulders: 'Out of the question, girl: they know all the tricks. Sometimes they even take out the spare wheels.'

'Then in the truck itself, in the container: it's so big!'

'The container? They put seals on it. They aren't taken off

until we get to Rome. That way I get through all the frontiers without bother.'

She turned aside so that he would not see her tears. He said, without looking at her: 'Unless . . . It's for the love of freedom, uh? I'm not a bad handyman . . .'

'Yes, Viacheslav?'

'It shouldn't be too difficult to make a pair of sealing pliers. They slap on the seals for me, I take them off, I stick your parcel between two ingots, I stick the seals back on—who's to know? I should have thought of that long ago.'

She, usually so careful with boys, flung her arms around his neck. Not that Viacheslav had renewed the advances he had made at their first meeting. Gemma was proud of the way she inculcated respect.

'The password will be *Armi, furore e morti*. Repeat.'

He repeated it several times, with his clumsy, laborious accent.

'When will you be in Rome?'

'I don't know. Perhaps Friday.'

'Do you know the Piazza Navona? The one that is oval at both ends. In front of the middle fountain. 1305 hours. If you arrive Saturday, same thing. You'll have the *Ogonioks* under your left arm.'

She telephoned 'Uncle Enzo'. She was at 'page 23' of the book that he had sent her; she found Petrarch difficult. As for history, she did not care very much for Prince Mikhail of Tver who had reigned about '1305'. 'On Wednesday or Thursday', she would go to the opera. Grucci noted it all down conscientiously, while pulling on his cigarette. He had no inkling of the importance of the item despatched, but, in any case, he was there to receive these things. He opened the 'breviary' at number 23: the meeting would take place in the Piazza Navona and the password would be taken once again from the libretto of *Norma*. Romantic? So what? With a less romantic network, he'd have had to pay. This time, he decided to go to the rendez-vous himself: he often sent one of his sons in his place, more out of laziness than cowardice.

Meanwhile Viacheslav also made a phone call.

'Parfionn Mitrofanich?'

'Yes?'

'Viatia here. I've got the parcel.'

'What is the rendez-vous?'

He gave it.

'What's the password?'

He gave it.

'Did you pretend to refuse at first?'

'Yes. Don't forget to send me the pliers.'

'You'll have them this evening with your envelope. Viacheslav?'

'Yes, Parfionn Mitrofanich?'

'Get to the rendez-vous early. Apart from that, proceed as usual.'

'Understood.'

Signor Grucci would have been surprised, but not embarrassed, to learn that part of the services of his 'romantic' network were paid for by the Committee of State Security. Being unable to stop the flood of samizdat material that was pouring outside the national frontiers, the second principal Directorate, at the suggestion of Directorate A and with the agreement of the first principal Directorate, had decided to transform this flow into a tidal wave. At all costs, a repetition of the Solzhenitsyn phenomenon had to be avoided and, to do that, the safest way was to encourage the massive export of mediocre texts, among which works of talent would stand more chance of passing unnoticed. When, at his first meeting with Gemma, Viacheslav had denounced the 'spy' to the Committee of Security, it had been suggested to him that he become a *seksot*. As a result, he made a nice little profit for himself by submitting for censorship the manuscripts that she gave him, before handing them over faithfully to the correspondents in Rome. Thanks to this ploy everyone was happy: the authors were published, Gemma triumphant, Viacheslav well rewarded, Grucci prosperous and, of course, Directorate A, who watched the prestige of the dissidents decline in the so-called free world day by day.

The network headed by 'Parfionn Mitrofanich' was working so well that General Pitman thought of using it to launch Operation Pskov. But as the substitution of recipient that he had arranged might arouse Gemma's suspicions, the added touch of the sealing pliers was included in the scenario: if Viacheslav had intended betraying her, why would he have expressed fears? Why would he have given himself the trouble of 'making' that tool, which he could show if need be? Good amateur that she was, Gemma would keep these arguments to herself and the network would continue to function.

Three days after Aleksandr had demanded his recall Ivan Ivanich asked to meet him in a brasserie at the Porte de Versailles.

'All is well, Aleksandr Dmitrich!'

'Come to the point, Ivan Ivanich.'

'Now don't get excited, Aleksandr Dmitrich! Look at you—who'd ever suspect that you were a second Sorge? But, one day, saving your reverence, we will stick your mug on letters in the form of stamps.'

'Oh come on, out with it!'

'Well, it's all agreed. Your resignation has been accepted. You can go home. But we have just one more little service to ask you.'

'And what's that?'

Ivan Ivanich leaned forward. He was misty-eyed.

'It's not even a service, Sasha. More like a little present . . . to crown your career! A real gem of a set-up!'

He bunched the finger-tips of his right hand and gave them a loud collective kiss.

'Well?'

Leaning backwards, Ivan Ivanich fluttered his ginger eyelids a few times, to add a touch of solemnity to the occasion: 'You've heard of Iron Mask?'

'I've read Dumas, like everybody else.'

'Dumas is about right. I'm referring to the Anonymous Prisoner, as they call him.'

Aleksandr immediately swooped on the game: 'The one that missed Leonid Ilich?'

Ivan Ivanich wriggled on his moleskin.

'That I don't know. "What does Russian Truth think?" That one. We must publish his book.'

'He's tied up with the Italians.'

'That can be arranged.'

'So our lot are taking an interest?'

'It would seem so.'

'But why? He's against us!'

'It's you, the know-alls of your Directorate, who are supposed to understand such things. We mere counter-espionage agents are small fry.'

With one exception—his target practice—Aleksandr had always played his masters' game with total loyalty. He would have regarded it as vulgar, quite unacceptable, to doubt them: such attitudes may be all right for the venal servants of a worm-eaten capitalism. If there was a reason for publishing *The Russian Truth*, it must be a very good one. But Colonel Psar wanted to know what it was.

'I'm not asking you to understand, blockhead; I'm asking you to explain.'

'It concerns the dissidents, Aleksandr Dmitrich. We're beginning to get a bit tired of these calumniators. Moreover, it has been noted that those who emigrate don't have as much authority as those who stay at home. So, imagine a genuine dissident, still living in Russia, who publishes a book—an anti-Soviet one, of course—that settles accounts with all those little Soljenitskins.'

'You mean we would write the book? Is that why all the fuss has been made about Iron Mask? To prepare the ground?'

Ivan Ivanich shrugged his shoulders.

'The book is already written. Who wrote it? No one knows. But in any case you will go to Rome to get it.'

'From under Grucci's nose?'

'It wouldn't be the first time that publishers filched dissidents' manuscripts from one another, as you well know.'

Ivan Ivanich gave details of the rendez-vous: Piazza Navona, Friday, 12.45, *Armi, furore e morti*, a parcel of *Ogoniok*s, 'a flaxen-haired fellow, about thirty, all legs'.

'And then don't hang about.'

'Grucci will be there too?'

'Twenty minutes later.'

They laughed together at the little trick they were going to play on the Italian publisher.

'You sign with Lux for the French translation, immediately.'

'When I have the manuscript?'

'No, before. They won't understand a thing in the manuscript. I'll bring you samples. You translate. Tell them you have the rest.'

'It's as urgent as that?'

'Better believe it.'

'And the Russian edition?'

'Out of the question, for the time being. External use only. Not to be swallowed on any account. Russian editions get back home.'

'I understand. Lux, you say. Supposing I tickle up another publisher?'

'No question of that either.'

Aleksandr could foresee no difficulty with Lux—or with any publisher for that matter. The press was intrigued by Iron Mask; whatever the interest of the book, it would sell.

'Do I keep the foreign rights?'

'You sell to the highest bidder—go for a big advance rather than for a good royalty.'

'That's what I always do: there's no way of checking sales abroad.'

'And you get it out before the Frankfurt fair.'

'Just a moment. It has to be translated. Is it long?'

'Four hundred tightly written pages. If the translation isn't too periphrastic, that should make three hundred and fifty printed pages.'

'You mean the manuscript isn't yet out in Russia and you've already done a word-count?'

A cunning but kindly smile spread over Ivan Ivanich's pock-marked face: 'Ah! You see—our young fellows don't sit on their hands!'

He took two crumpled envelopes out of his pocket.

'First, this. Let's have a receipt.'

The profits of the agency went, of course, to the Directorate; but the Directorate paid for *Oprichnik*'s services: half his pay was piling up in a Moscow bank, the other half was paid in cash. Aleksandr signed the receipt and slipped the envelope into his large black briefcase.

'And this is for you. Open it.'

The second envelope contained two photocopies of pages handwritten in Cyrillic characters. One was entitled *What Does Russian Truth Think of the Mass Media? Second Meditation*; and the other *What Does Russian Truth Think of Antisemitism?*

'This is by way of authentification,' Ivan Ivanich said. 'To prove to Lux that you have short-circuited Grucci.'

'You could have given me the lot without sending me to Rome.'

'It's more romantic like that. You'll be able to spin them a yarn about your rendez-vous. Give them the works! The KGB followed you through the galleries of the Coliseum! You hid behind the *Pietà* by someone or other! And the Grucci network is not smashed.'

'You mean it's been working for us all along?'

'I'm not saying that at all. Don't forget to get your plane fare paid for by Lux. First class, preferably.'

When Aleksandr got back to his office, he took out a sheet of thick, chalky paper from his desk and, in his light, firm, well-spaced handwriting, which he kept upright despite its natural inclination to slope to the right, he wrote:

Operation Iron Mask

He always found the planning of the tactics of an operation exhilarating. In writing out the names—they were always the same, since they were those of his sound-boxes—he felt the pleasure that staff officers feel when they draw blue and red arrows and circles on their maps.

This time, the last time, the operation would be particularly delectable: harnessing the capitalist publicity machine to a vehicle entirely set up by Dzerzhinsky Square! What a brilliant example of influence to add to the concrete cases studied in the appendix to the *Vademecum*!

Aleksandr had expected to be asked for 'one last little service' before being allowed to 'go home' and he was delighted to see that, as Ivan Ivanich pointed out, in the guise of a service he was being offered the finest opportunity of his career. He would show the Directorate what he could do.

Who knows? Before 'going home', he might have time to take another step up the ladder of promotion. And if he was fully integrated into the service—his ultimate ambition—what was to stop him one day becoming a member of the Supreme Consistory of Hidy-hats?

He called his secretary: 'Sit down, Marguerite.'

She brought up a chair and, as usual, sat at an angle to him, to show him that she understood that this privilege was subject to review on each occasion.

'Marguerite, we are going to launch a big operation. You've read the articles on Iron Mask? Well, I shall soon have his manuscript, *The Russian Truth*.'

'But, Monsieur, I thought that the Italian firm, The Seagull . . .'

'No longer, Marguerite.'

She caught her breath, open-mouthed, to show her admiration. He showed her the two photocopies.

'This is the real manuscript of the Anonymous Prisoner?'

'They are the photocopies of the original, which I shall go and get on Friday. You'll be so kind as to book the flight for me.'

'For . . . Moscow, Monsieur?'

'No, for Rome. A day return. And I must be there well before noon. O.K. Now look at this: *Operation Iron Mask*. Can you imagine what a commotion this will cause?'

He knew how to share his plans and passions with his employees.

'I shall have to pay you overtime, Marguerite.'

Her whole face lit up in a smile; her boss was joking, of course.

'It's always a pleasure, Monsieur.'

'We shall carry on as usual. Don't work on all the press in advance, but drop a few bits of well placed information first, to arouse jealousies. Get me an appointment with M. Fourveret as soon as possible.'

'Will you be going to Lux or will you invite M. Fourveret to lunch?'

'Just as he wishes, but leave him in no doubt that what we've got is dynamite. As for the press, here's what I've thought.'

He showed her the list that he had made:

Morning:	*Impartial*	J.-X. de Monthignies
Evening:	*Voix*	Jeanne Bouillon
Political magazine:	*Objectifs*	Ballandar
Popular magazine:	*Choix*	Mme Choustrewitz
Serious review:	*Objection*	M. Johannès-Graf

'Have you any suggestions?'

'Perhaps *Le Monde*? We've always got good reviews in it. Or *L'Express*?'

'Later, Marguerite, when the ball's in the air.'

'No one on television?' She used to say 'TV', but he asked her to stop doing so.

'When the book is out. Now we must gather together a team of translators. If we're going to publish before Frankfurt, even putting pressure on Lux's schedule, we must have handed in the translation by August at the latest. Try the people who worked on *The Anthology of Nineteenth-Century Russian Liberal Thinkers*. We'll need four or five of them. I'll supervise the translation myself. Then, what we'll do is this: make contact with the leading dissidents and ask them what they think of Iron Mask. Pruned down, that would make superb copy for the back cover.'

What pleasure he took in this call to Action Stations. Yes, Aleksandr could not wait to 'go home', to see Alla again and to meet Dmitri for the first time—but he could wait another three months.

M. Fourveret, ensconced behind his Louis XIII table (genuine antique), put his hand on his heart and raised his eyes heavenwards.

'God sees me. He knows that nothing brings me greater satisfaction than to serve Him, by helping the persecuted, by making their voices heard. All the same, to sign a contract without seeing the whole manuscript . . .'

'If this doesn't satisfy you . . .'

Aleksandr presented his translation of one of the two photocopied texts.

We Russians are regarded as anti-semitic, even though this cholera never reached among us the same proportions as it did among the Teutonic peoples. Our Old Order, in particular, has often been accused of encouraging pogroms. The statistics throw an interesting light on this accusation, since the Jews formed 4.1 per cent of the population of the Russian Empire, whereas, in 1959, they represented only 1.48 per cent of the Soviet population.

Be that as it may, Russian Truth thinks that anti-semitism is a monstrous misunderstanding.

If you had asked a nineteenth-century Russian why he hated the Jews, he would have replied: because they are usurers. The same sentiment was widespread in most European countries; the French writer Bernanos remarked as much. On the other hand, Italy is one of the least anti-semitic European countries; Mussolini's persecutions were as nothing compared with Hitler's. Why? Quite simply because in Italy, the Jews did not enjoy a monopoly in usury: the Lombards indulged in what I shall call an exorcising competition with them.

Let us see how little mother History arranged matters. 1. The Church decrees that usury is forbidden to Christians. 2. The Christians, who are absolutely determined to go into debt, force the Jews to become usurers, because the Jews do not depend upon the Church. 3. Transferring their hatred of the function on to the race or religion, the Christians begin to hate the Jews for practices that they have forced upon them.

Usury had to be forbidden, as I show elsewhere. But the debtor should have suffered the same stigma as the creditor.

The Jews are men like any others; usurers, whatever their origins, should be strangled.

That is what Russian Truth thinks of anti-semitism.

Fourveret was reading. Above the nobly poised head of the great liberal Catholic publisher, Aleksandr allowed his eyes to rest on the tops of the skeletal ashtrees in the courtyard, whose branches scraped against the office windows.

'Interesting,' said Fourveret. 'Interesting, if somewhat redolent of folklore. I can see what you like so much about this extract: it's the little sentence on the unjustly accused Old Order. You are, my dear Psar, an incorrigible reactionary. But that's no great matter, a little compassion will not revive a dead tyranny, and I'm the first to recognize that an intolerant left is hardly more acceptable than a dogmatic right. On the other hand, I'm always somewhat nervous when an author starts to talk about the Jews: unless all his Jews are saints, geniuses and heroes, there's always some little hair-splitting critic who will tie the bell of anti-semitism around his neck. God sees me: He knows how much my heart bleeds for the Jews, but, in a sense, the less said about them, the better. However, with a vocabulary like this one: cholera, monstrous, practices forced upon them . . . I think we'll get away with it.'

'If you have the slightest hesitation, my dear Fourveret . . . I was stopping in at the Presses after seeing you. Would you like me to offer *The Russian Truth* to Bernard? It would not in any way affect our excellent relations.'

'My dear Psar, I wouldn't dream of it! Tell me, by the way: is Jeanne Bouillon right in thinking that Iron Mask is Kurnosov, Brezhnev's would-be assassin? All right . . . poker-face! But admit that it would help sell the book!'

Fourveret's fine austere face lit up with mystical fire.

'I'll get someone to look through the old press-cuttings— there may have been some photographs of the attempt . . .'

Jean-Xavier de Monthignies asked Aleksandr to lunch at the *Tour d'Argent*. He arrived in a hurry, his jacket unbuttoned to reveal a respectable paunch; he looked something like a fat sparrow with clipped wings.

'I haven't brought Minquin, in spite of what you said, he's too young, he wouldn't appreciate it. You won't believe it, Aleksandr, but for me eating is a vice. And it really grieves me to think of the hunger in the world. Two people out of three are undernourished. It's scandalous, isn't it? And just think of the money we spend getting heartburn! Anyway, I like lunching here, because it's just as good as in the evening, but cheaper: that gives me a better conscience. You wanted to tell me about a new project?'

He was delighted with the news.

'Iron Mask! You know on which side your bread's buttered! Can I announce it? You won't give the news to anyone else?'

'Not in the morning papers. If you get it in tomorrow, you'll be the first.'

'And tell me . . . I must say I find this habit of numbering the ducks here particularly idiotic—they aren't limited editions, after all! Anyway, tell me: would Iron Mask be by any chance the fellow who shot Brezhnev? Just his luck—he'd have *really* brought him down, wouldn't he? It's almost as if he did, isn't it?'

'You may well be right, Jean-Xavier.'

'That would sell an extra 50,000 copies at least, uh? Can you imagine if Solzhenitsyn had knocked off Khrushchev?'

Ballandar was a middle-aged man in a cashmere sweater, trying to pass for a young sprout. Soft-spoken, his feet up on the desk (he worked for an American-type magazine), he promised a triumph.

'We'll be right behind you, Aleksandr Psar. *Objectifs* once had a rather left-wing reputation, but we're redressing the balance. It would never do to become a government organ— that would be too shaming! Personally, I'm . . . what am I? A poor lump who always tries to throw his weight on the lighter side of the scales. On the left when the wind comes from the right, on the right, or nearly, when the wind comes from the left. Get us a little extract: we'll put it in a holiday number, framed, with a run-down of what we know about this Iron Mask. What do you think? Do you think it's true?'

'What?'

'That, in fact, he did wound him, and that ever since Brezhnev has been ailing?'

As an extract, Aleksandr proposed the second meditation on the mass media.

You already know the story of how the bell was punished, broken and melted down into hundreds of sleighbells. Here's another story about a bell.

In the year 1667, Tsar Alexis Mikhailovich the Quiet, having decided to offer a present to the Savvino-Storozhevsky Monastery of Zvenigorod, ordered the master founder Aleksandr Grigoriev to make a bell of nearly forty tons. This fat lady had a remarkable voice and, throughout the centuries, many a musician went to hear her. There was no shortage of Rachmaninovs or Chaliapins among her visitors.

As chance would have it, the town in which the bell was to be found bore the predestined name of Zvenigorod ('Soundville'—A. Psar). Furthermore, in the bronze of the bell was engraved a cryptogram that took many years to decipher. At last the code was cracked and it turned out to be no more than the signature of the donor, but couched in terms of sublime conciseness: 'Tsar Alexis, serf of God'.

In 1941 the Germans threatened Zvenigorod and it was decided to evacuate the bell. It broke. The pieces were preserved in the museum of the sounding-town that no longer sounded. Bells should not flee before the enemy.

There is no better symbol of the Old Order than the Tsar-bell, which weighs two hundred tons, which fell from its scaffolding and which, with neither voice nor tower, rests, against nature, on the ground, silent among us, with a great wound in its side.

Do I need to explain my parable? Think on. Our modern bells are the mass media, which toll our knells and warn us of approaching danger. If they lie, may their tongues be cut out! But when they ring true, we should honour and revere them. However, even when they seem to ring true, it is just as well to decipher the signature of the donor.

That is what Russian Truth thinks of the mass media.

Above Ballandar's pale, bald head, Aleksandr observed the bushy, dusty chestnut-trees of the avenue.

'Don't you find that there is something hostile here to the freedom of the press?' asked the great critic when he had finished reading the passage.

'On the contrary. The broken bell, transformed into sleighbells, is the great bell of Pskov, the symbol of freedom that cannot be stifled. The bell of Zvenigorod is the free press, conscientious and "responsible" as they say—like *Objectifs*. The bell of Uglich, which must be punished, is the press that disseminates lies.'

'Perhaps one might put in a note to this effect. Anyway, you can count on me. I'll make the announcement next week; this summer, I'll lay the bait and, when the book comes out, we'll go to town on it. Any chance of some photographs?'

'What of?'

'It doesn't really matter. Of that special hospital, for example, with a window a bit different from the others, taken with a telephoto lens? We could call it his room.'

'I'll give you the address; send a photographer.'

Mme Choustrewitz received visitors in her drawing-room, which she called her boudoir. She received visitors in her dressing-gown, whatever the time of day. She liked to insinuate that in her youth she had been a prostitute in Vienna.

'Aleksandr, my dear! What can an old bag like me do for you? Ah! How well he kisses a lady's hands! Only the Russians can do it like that!'

But, of course, she would fight for Iron Mask—tooth and claw.

'What do you know about him? How old is he? Is he good-looking? Can I say that you got into this lunatic asylum via the drainpipe?'

Jeanne Bouillon already regarded Iron Mask as her own creature. Of course, the notion of coincidence had to be demystified; it was odd, all the same, that she had the idea for that article just when her friend Aleksandr was about to get his hands on the manuscript. She would head her article: 'A book that will (perhaps) change the history of the USSR.'

Aleksandr, sitting back in his armchair, counted the enormous insects—termites? preying mantis?—that were laying siege to the chandelier. The evening rush-hour traffic was relentlessly circling the Place de l'Alma.

'By the way, Jeanne, what are these rumours about Kurnosov and Iron Mask? Where did you get them from?'

She had a habit of covering her mouth when she laughed.

'You don't think I'm going to split on my informants, do you? It's just a whisper that's going round, that's all.'

For Aleksandr two things were clear: these rumours came from one of Pitman's other orchestras, and they were false. Kurnosov, the would-be assassin, must have been executed at the time, in the usual way. But was there really an anonymous prisoner in Cell ooo? Or did the nurse and huge psychiatrist go in merely to feed the campaign of disinformation that it was their task to carry out? Everything was possible in the kingdom of illusion. He thought of those delicious meals that were prepared in the knowledge perhaps that they were intended for a non-existent guest. Maybe the nurses took turns to eat them.

M. Johannès-Graf worked from tiny, windowless premises, down in a basement.

'Monsieur Psar, allow me to ask two questions. The first is, how shall I put it, factual and the other concerns, how shall I say, the substance.'

M. Johannès-Graf had a long face, composed entirely of verticals. He wore magisterial glasses. He had been a Protestant pastor, but had later turned to the murky world in which literature is political and politics literary. When taxed with this, he replied: 'I am not unaware of the fact: those circles are excessively corrupt. It is a good thing that there is one, how shall I put it, honest man among them.'

'Monsieur Psar, my first question is: do you actually have the manuscript? Have you read it? My second question is: can you guarantee that it is a sincere work? That its author, however labyrinthine his experiences and opinions may be, actually thinks what he says?'

'Monsieur, I have not met the Anonymous Prisoner and for very good reasons. But the tone of such a text cannot deceive. Whoever has read this work as I have, from beginning to end . . .' (In fact it had not yet left the Soviet Union)

165

'knows that it is as authentic as *The House of the Dead, My Prisons* or . . .' (M. Johannès-Graf was a Rousseauist) 'the *Confessions*.'

'You see, all this atmosphere of sensationalism that one is trying to create . . . We find all this somewhat disturbing. We are well aware that books have to be sold, but all the same, not just anything. However, I trust you. I suspect you of having published things that go against your deepest feelings, but you have allowed your, how shall I put it, your respect for justice, to keep the upper hand. As you know, we do not come out in the summer, but you can count on us for the autumn.' (The great puritanical jaws came together and parted again with monotonous regularity.) 'Anyway, without having read the book, what could we say? You know that, unlike certain others, we read before we criticize. Hence our audience among the political clubs, government circles, universities, civil servants, among, how shall I put it, readers who count.'

Every life has its peak. Aleksandr reached his at the age of forty-nine, one Friday, at 12.45, on the Piazza Navona in Rome.

In front of Bernini's fountain strutted a tall fellow decked out in a *signorino*'s jacket, a shiny orange-brown. Under his left arm he held a parcel of magazines; on the cover of the first, one could read in Cyrillic characters, *Ogoniok*.

Aleksandr approached, his hands clasped behind his back.

'I don't know,' he said in Russian, 'what oaf invented these ridiculous passwords, but today it's *Armi, furore e morti*.'

Viacheslav narrowed his eyes, as if they were being stung by tobacco smoke. 'Not an oaf—an oaffess.' He handed over the magazines cross-tied with thin string and made to go.

'Not so fast.'

Aleksandr parted the magazines, found the envelope, unstuck it with the tip of his finger-nail without pulling it out of the parcel and recognized the small handwriting on the almost transparent sheets of paper.

'Right—that's it.'

'One would almost think he was an officer,' thought

Viacheslav, as he moved off, whistling a tune, his hands stuck in the slanted pockets of his jacket.

Ten minutes later Signor Grucci arrived. He waited for his contact for half-an-hour. No one came. That meant that he would have to hang around again tomorrow, which was a Saturday. And he had been hoping to spend the day on the beach at Ostia! What a bore!

In his taxi, Aleksandr undid the thin Russian string, rolled it up and slipped it into his pocket. He did not know what to do with it, but it came from over there: he could not bring himself to throw it away. The magazines and envelope also came from over there, but, God knows why, he felt no such sentimental attachment to them. He left them on the seat.

The manuscript that he held in his hands—three hundred and ninety-nine sheets, with no margins, covered with that tiny, sloping, compressed writing in blue ink—was a treasure, but an ambiguous treasure: for the general public, it was the petrified cry of an idealist who had very nearly killed and been executed; for the Lux publishing house, it was a little gold mine; for the Directorate, the instrument of a new victory; for Aleksandr himself, the pledge of his new life. Aleksandr was not a dreamer and he seldom bothered to imagine what this new life would be like, but, from time to time, he had intuitions of it and this was the case now: in that Rome taxi, he thought with a touch of tender pride that he had a son to bring up, that he would bring him up well, with the passion to serve, which had quite disappeared in the West.

He leafed through the small pages with their unusual format. Mechanically, he checked the spelling: it was certainly modern Russian, whose simplistic spelling—one letter out of seven missed out, terminations of words contrary to philology—still irritated him; but the very fact that he had thought to check such matters betrayed a certain perplexity: the old-fashioned writing, the style inspired by fairy tales, none of this suggested an author who belonged to the Geebee.

Rome was disappearing around him, with its ochres beneath which one could always make out verdigris. Aleksandr did not see it. His thoughts were with the triumph that the publication of *The Russian Truth* would be. Translations in every language, considerable profits, the dissidents discredited.

He got on to his plane. He had promised himself not to begin reading before the plane took off.

It seemed to him that the journey lasted no more than a long minute. On landing, he knew why Ivan Ivanich had wanted the contract to be signed and to be sure of the support of his 'orchestra' before he read the manuscript.

The manuscript was quite simply unpublishable!

'Marguerite, will you get Mme Boïsse for me . . .'—'The telephone is ringing at Mme Boïsse's, Monsieur . . .'— 'We'll open a bottle of vodka this evening.'

And, that evening, he had another discussion with Ivan Ivanich.

'Who has concocted this mess? It's criminal! No, that's not what I'm asking: you don't know. But who decided to have it published? It can't be Pitman: he would have realized that it is quite impossible. Contract or no, Lux will never agree to it. Indeed, who would agree to it? I shall not leave any mention of my agency on the title page. If, for some crazy reason, this gibberish must appear, we will have to create a publishing house just for this book, or for any others of the same vein, if you happen to have a supply. Listen, Ivan Ivanich: the Hidy-hats may have gone completely mad, but Paris publishers haven't . . . yet. Or the journalists. If, by some aberration, some shady firm on the extreme right were bold enough to print such a text . . .'

'There'd be a scandal? But, Aleksandr Dmitrich of my heart, scandal pays!'

'You make me laugh with your cheap cynicism. There'd be no scandal. There'd be nothing. Silence. Not a ripple. People would talk about something else, as if someone had belched at the dinner table. You don't understand, Ivan Ivanich: we're living in a society in which the roles are handed out once and for all; one has to accept what one is given or be nothing at all. That's what the Westerners call freedom. For example, a Soviet dissident has to be a liberal: Marxist if he will, Nationalist possibly, but liberal. A nonliberal dissident is inconceivable. If I had got this manuscript through the post, do you know what I'd have done with it?'

Ivan Ivanich licked his finger and smoothed down the few ginger hairs that straggled across his scalp.

'You are intelligent enough to understand, Aleksandr Dmitrich, that that it is precisely why it wasn't sent to you through the post.'

'Ivan Ivanich, I know what disinformation is: it's my job. But there are limits. I can't be responsible for publishing sentences like . . . But it isn't a question of a few sentences—those could be cut. The whole book is imbued with the same mentality.'

'What mentality?'

Aleksandr read aloud a paragraph that he had crossed through with red pencil.

' "Whenever an organized Communist Party, lacking the clandestine support of the Soviet Union, has come up against a liberal, bourgeois, aristocratic, conservative or reactionary party, in an isolated nation, it has won. Whenever it has come up against a Fascist, and therefore reforming, equally organized party, it has lost." And he cites historical examples! You must see that such provocations are out of the question in a free society.'

'Even when confronted by a phenomenon like the new right?'

'Especially when confronted by a phenomenon like the new right. Fourveret has somewhat detached himself from the left in recent years, but it has been selling less well, the fact is well known; but, from that, to risk associating himself with a movement so diametrically opposed . . . The publication of *The Russian Truth* is out of the question. Why don't we re-issue *The Protocols of the Elders of Sion, Mein Kampf* and *Votre bel aujourd'hui*? No, sorry, I was wrong to put Maurras among that lot: a true monarchist can never be a Fascist. Let me tell you something: it was my Directorate that had the brilliant idea of treating Fascism as a right-wing tendency, whereas in fact it is rather more to the left than we are. Anyhow, I refuse to collaborate in this undertaking—it's doomed to failure. Are you sure there is no sabotage involved here? It would indeed be a master-stroke if someone could penetrate an enemy influence campaign and turn it to his own advantage!'

Ivan Ivanich assumed an expression of tenderness.

'This is very distressing, Sashenka. Very distressing. I have never seen you openly disobey an order.'

'Rubbish! I'm going to write a detailed report that you will send to Pitman by radio. You'll see that there's been a mistake.'

The answer to the report arrived the following day.

'This is to confirm the instructions that have been given to you orally. You will regard this message as a written order. It is imperative that the manuscript be published by the publisher originally proposed. In no circumstances must it be published by a right-wing publisher. You are also warned against any "toning down" that you might be tempted to make to the text in the course of translation. Any deviation of this kind will be regarded as a breach of discipline. If the publisher asks you for the translation piecemeal, refuse: the translation must be handed over complete. No new extract will be communicated to the press. Pursue and intensify your efforts to make the publication an international political event. Signed: Lieutenant-General Pitman.'

In a café at the Porte d'Auteuil—Ivan Ivanich was fond of cafés on the outskirts of the city, just one of those peculiarities by which second-rate agents finally get caught—Aleksandr read and re-read the typed sheets, bristling with statements like 'extremely urgent', 'absolutely secret', date and hour stamps, all the paraphernalia of official telegraphic communication.

Ivan Ivanich smiled sympathetically and held his hand out: the message had to be returned to him, of course.

On a corner of the table, Aleksandr scribbled his answer. He acknowledged receipt. He would carry out his orders. But he declined all responsibility: 'Neither Lux nor any other reputable firm will publish *The Russian Truth*. In the unlikely event of the work's being nevertheless published, the press will ignore it with disgust, and no event, international or even local, will take place. *Observations*: the author of the manuscript, whoever he is, must have gone far beyond the instructions given him. *Desiderata*: I would suggest that the text be re-read at the highest level.'

However the well-known dissidents approached by the Psar Agency had begun to react. Those who were still Marxists expressed their doubts as to the existence of a specifically Russian truth, but were delighted by the populist style of the Anonymous Prisoner and praised him for his reference to the bell of Pskov, the symbol of the ancient independence of the communes and consequently of the nation's Communist vocation. They were happy, of course, to associate themselves with a condemnation of usury that amounted to a condemnation of capitalism. One of them wrote a long article in which he demonstrated that the Anonymous Prisoner must have been influenced by his—the writer's—works; he expressed satisfaction at seeing that they had reached Cell 000 of the special hospital. Another already foresaw the conclusions that the author would surely draw from his observations: communism in itself is good; only its applications are generally catastrophic; one should continue with the experiments, not reject the doctrine.

An anti-Marxist novelist praised the style of the Anonymous Prisoner: 'It is like a good loaf, crusty on the outside, soft inside.' One critic commented: 'Our dissident chorus was getting a bit repetitive, but now a superb baritone is giving voice to a new, almost neo-Krylovian language.' A moralist openly expressed pleasure that the occupant of Cell 000 was not about to leave it: 'One should no doubt distinguish between the defectors who cannot wait to be safely abroad to yap against the régime and the prophets who have spoken like free men, whereas they were not yet free. But this is the first time that the indomitable song of freedom has risen from the depths of a *Psykhushka*.'

This last observation may have thrown some light on the unanimity with which the dissidents, usually so divided, applauded in advance the publication of *The Russian Truth*: some preferred not to see the Western cake cut up into too many slices; others understood that the situation of the prisoner elevated him above all the petty differences that existed between them. The bearded sage, whom many admired to the point of hating him, emerged from his barbed-wire-enclosed ivory tower to comment on the crypto-gram on the bell: 'Iron Mask has put his finger on a dazzling epitome of the monarchical myth at its most inimitably Russian. We await anxiously and hopefully what the gut truth, the crude, sacred truth of us Russians, whose motto was for centuries "We are Russians, God is with us", has inspired in this crusader of our time, the only one of us who has dared to take up arms to defend his faith.'

Aleksandr read all this with contempt. 'I hate turncoats, whatever the cut and material.' For him, these people were traitors, whatever their motives, a petty ambition unsatis-fied, a small, inadequate salary, a mean conscience not quite at peace.

Translators were commissioned. Aleksandr no longer wanted the best possible translation, completed at the earli-est possible date, but a translation that would remain secret for as long as possible. Instead of five translators, he chose only two: the risk of a leak would be less, and the work would be handed in later, so that Fourveret would have less oppor-tunity to go back on his contract. A rather prim old Russian lady who lived in an old people's home and a young Russian teacher who would be working during his holidays in Ireland were engaged, not for their talents, but because they would communicate neither between themselves nor with the Paris-ian intelligentsia. The other three took exception to being dismissed. Aleksandr already knew that Operation Iron Mask would scorch everything it touched: things were only just beginning to hot up. Fortunately the juxtaposition of fables from *The Russian Truth* lent itself to an incoherent division of labour: the teacher certainly found, on first reading, that the politics were hard to take, and the old lady that there were terms her dictionary described as 'fam.' or 'pop.' that she had seldom met before, but it was enough to hint to each of them that his or her portion, when illuminated by the other, would appear in a much better light for them to take it as said. Anyway, they were being paid, after all, and not too badly at that. Aleksandr was beginning to warm to this mission in which he still did not believe, as Ivan Deniso-vich warmed to his bricks.

July passed. The pages of the translation arrived through

the post. Aleksandr checked them, collated them, fumed with indignation and, finally, came to terms with his own indignation. He had been entrusted with an operation that was condemned in advance. He had come out and said as much, but now he was trying to carry it off all the same and would consider himself equally justified whether it failed, as he had foreseen, or succeeded, thanks to his efforts.

In order to bring the book out in September, Fourveret, leaning on his schedule, required the manuscript by the end of July. Aleksandr hung on until 10 August. He should have spent two weeks' holiday with Jessica and friends of hers, on their yacht; he excused himself. Jessica did not complain: 'I can do easily enough without a straw lover.' She took instead an attaché from one of the South American embassies. On the roads, the congestion reached record proportions this year. In Paris, Aleksandr's favourite restaurants were shut; he ate in bistros and was surprised how cheap they were. He needed only a quarter of the time to get from his apartment to the office. Two publishers wanted to bring out *The Russian Truth* in the original language. He refused. One of them tried to make discreet enquiries as to the identity of the translator. To no avail. The cinemas were showing nothing but old films. You could park your car wherever you pleased. Marguerite, who had intended going away in August, asked if it might not be better if she stayed, since an important book was coming out. Aleksandr thought the book would not come out. In any case, the circus, if there was going to be one, would not begin until September.

'No, no, Marguerite, you go and get a good rest. Where are you going, by the way?'

She was going to her mother's at Lisieux. Just a phone-call and she would come back. She went away. It was only after a few days that he began to miss her. He had got so used to that willing, deferential look in her eyes. He wondered absent-mindedly what colour her eyes were and had to admit that he did not know. 'For too long now my life has been a plod. All that will soon change.' The weather was unsettled; it was not very warm. 'This August is much less warm than June was, thirty years ago.' Aleksandr thought of revisiting the gallery of the Chimeras, but when ten coaches disgorged their cargo

173

of Teutons at the foot of Quasimodo's little staircase, just in front of him, he abandoned the idea. He wondered what the weather was like in Moscow or in Leningrad. 'If the Directorate has a branch in Leningrad, I'd like an apartment on the Fontanka . . .'

At last the translation was ready. In spite of Fourveret's harassment—'The printer is waiting! He's stayed open because of us!'—Aleksandr hung on for a few more days. He polished up a few passages, re-typed the messiest pages. In the end he had to take the thick white file tied with a red and white ribbon to the Lux offices. Aleksandr put down his bomb, was overwhelmed with thanks, and awaited the explosion.

The office of the managing director of the Lux publishing house was spacious and white and its entire furniture consisted of a table, three chairs and a glass case containing several Spanish crucifixes: objects of piety for some, a priceless collection for others. The table was placed with its back to the window, so that any visitor found himself in full light, whereas the severe but just face of the manging director floated in the shadow. Some believed that this was an accident, but one only had to see M. Fourveret at home in the evening to realize that his lamps were arranged in such a way as to create the same effect.

A handshake. Sit down. Fourveret sat ensconced behind his table, his hands joined, his eyes lowered. On his large ascetic face, he wore square-rimmed glasses, which he would whip off and put back in masterly fashion, to punctuate what he was saying.

Aleksandr waited. He was not a natural worrier, but having to defend a project that he did not approve of placed him in an awkward position.

Having given the matter due thought, M. Fourveret looked up, eloquently removed his glasses and pronounced with a fierce smile: 'So one must be on the right, because the good thief was crucified on the right of the carpenter from Nazareth!'

He paused for a few seconds and went on, more angrily: 'And when, in a profound movement of disgust, He rejected the gold coin presented to Him and declared that one must render to Caesar that which is Caesar's, what He meant, in fact, was that it is the task of the State and not of the banks to mint money! Tsarist Russia had seven times fewer policemen, proportionately, than Great Britain and five times fewer than France! Communism, that alien disease, took root in Russia rather like Asian 'flu, because the Old Order, in all innocence, had not secreted the necessary anti-bodies!'

Fourveret replaced his glasses and assumed an air of great gravity: 'Tell me, my dear Psar: who is kidding whom?'

Aleksandr had prepared something of an answer. He laid on the table the series of quotations that he had extracted from dissidents' letters. Though already favourable, these quotations had been further subjected to a skilful cutting and rearrangement: the final effect was dazzling.

'For the back of the cover!'

Fourveret glanced at the sheet of paper and pushed it away.

'They haven't read it. I, too, before I'd read it . . .'

He got up and walked up and down, his hands folded behind him, freeing them from time to time to make some vigorous, but noble gesture.

'My dear Psar, I thought that, despite the differences that separate us, we had a common denominator: total intellectual integrity. God sees me, but one doesn't have to be God: my reputation is sufficiently well known in the Paris marketplace. It is known that I am a publisher; it is also known that above everything else I have a conscience and that, to the utmost of my means, I have always tried to place this publishing house at the service of that conscience, not because it is mine, but because I believe that the consciences of all men of good will are tuned to the same key. I am a Christian, I have people in my office who are not; there may be Communists among them, almost certainly there are; but what does that matter, if, when we see a fine work or a fine deed we approve it with one heart, and if, when we see an ugly thing or a bad deed, we all condemn it. Other publishers, perhaps, have only one concern: lucre!' He spoke the word with a shudder, as if it was indecent, and made the obscene gesture of fingering banknotes. 'For me, lucre . . . if I had wanted my dear Psar, I could have been a rich man. But what matters to me is the great heart of bleeding humanity for which mine, too, bleeds and it is in that suffering for one another and in that of the artist for the community that I wish to see the true meaning of what we have tried to do here, at Lux: *Lux* equals light, of course.

'You have enjoyed my esteem, Psar.' He pronounced the name 'Psaaar'—as though he could not get the whole word out, and so much exoticism was becoming insulting. 'You have edited for me Genesis of Revolution and the White Books, to which no series published by any firm can be compared. I do not believe that your political opinions go beyond what is decent, for, after all, providing one is not an extremist, one can be an honourable man, even on the right, at least I imagine so. So I am asking you . . .' He stopped in his tracks and pulled off his glasses as if he was drawing a sabre from a scabbard. '. . . what has happened?'

Aleksandr looked at the publisher without concealing his amusement.

'What's come over you, Fourveret? Why are you getting on your high horse? So you don't agree with the Anonymous Prisoner's programme? Did I say I did? Are we such fanatics that we can publish only those theories we happen to subscribe to? According to you, does freedom of the press consist in providing a platform only for those who think as you do—or just a little further to the left?'

Fourveret went back to his table. He started to rub his glasses with his handkerchief to show that his patience was almost inexhaustible. He was no longer looking at Aleksandr. At certain moments he turned his back on him. Dropping his voice, he said:

'I am, as you may imagine, utterly perplexed by you. You may congratulate yourself that you have given me a sleepless night. I asked myself whether you have suddenly become blind, stupid, or—forgive the word, I have cause —venal? But, were the last to be the case, whom have you sold out to? Have you, perhaps, been in contact with some . . . neo-Fascist organization? Have they paid you to dishonour me? Yet you must have known that I would not go along with it! Anyway, what possible advantage would there be in it? *The Russian Truth* will not sell two thousand copies.

'I would like to confess to you that, in my perplexity, I

went to see José Ballandar, who is, as you know, an old friend. Under the seal of secrecy, I fed him a few extracts from this rubbish. "If I publish this," I said, "I know that I shall be doing wrong. But let us suppose I did, what, in that case, would you do?" You know Ballandar: he is a man of conscience. He said to me: "Out of consideration for you, and for your firm, I would turn a blind eye to it. I would act as if the book had never appeared." '

'If I understand you correctly, Fourveret, you're thinking of breaking our contract,' Aleksandr said, calmly.

This remark amused the publisher.

'I don't have to teach you, Psaaar, what a publishing contract is . . . I shall give you back your rights, to which, legally, you are not even entitled, since you have no contract with the author. That's all there is to it. But . . .' (He suddenly swung round, resting his back against the table as if it were a misericord) '. . . would you do me the honour of explaining how you have dared to offer me this heap of ignominious drivel?'

Aleksandr had the ability to stand fast, to deny the evidence, which had brought him considerable success in both his trades, the real and the apparent.

'Ignominious drivel? These aren't arguments, Fourveret. All I've heard from you for the last fifteen minutes is invective against a man who is rotting away in a psychiatric prison. To what end? To give a good conscience to a publisher who has always been regarded as the champion of intellectual honesty and who is going to break a contract because he knows very well that the Anonymous Prisoner will have no legal redress. What exactly is your complaint against *The Russian Truth*?'

'That is below the belt and unworthy of you, Psar,' said Fourveret, retreating behind his table. 'Either this text is publishable, and I am doing you no wrong in suggesting that you take it elsewhere, or it is not, and it is you who are doing me wrong by trying to force my hand.'

He sat down and replaced his glasses, rather like an English judge putting on his wig. He examined his notes.

'As far as one can see, given its incoherence, this work defends the following thesis:

1) The evil in the world today stems from capitalism.

2) That is why Communism must be destroyed (*sic*) and

3) Replaced by a theocratic monarchy, the principal aim of which will be to mint money. I'm making none of this up. What it all amounts to is an absurd denunciation of a supposedly world-wide plot, with historical illustrations like the following: Roosevelt was Stalin's agent, Stalin was himself Rockefeller's agent. And you're asking me what my complaint is against *The Russian Truth*. My heart bleeds for Russia, you know that. What I reproach *The Russian Truth* with is simply that it is neither Russian nor true.'

When Fourveret said 'my heart bleeds', he usually placed his left hand on that organ with the fingers spread wide, and kept it there for a second or two.

Aleksandr had no answer, but he persisted.

'It goes without saying that I associate myself in no way with the ideas of this madman, but I find his madness interesting, strange as it may seem, and I believe that with the support of the press . . .'

'Yes, my dear friend, but it will not have the support of the press. I told you what Ballandar said and you know what authority he has and how well disposed he has always been to this firm.'

Aleksandr got up and drew the manuscript towards him. Fourveret, still sitting in his chair, looked up at him. Then he took off his glasses, as one removes a mask: 'Psaaar, you have revealed yourself to me in a new light, and it may be wrong of me to go on trusting you. God sees me: He knows that I prefer to err on the side of excess, rather than of default.' When he said 'God sees me', he would lift his eyes to heaven, then, as they came down again, allow them to rest almost imperceptibly on the collection of crucifixes. 'If this thing is published by any other firm—but I will be very surprised if you find, even in this profession, anyone so despicable as to take the risk—I shall, to my sincere regret, be compelled to break off my association with you. On the other hand, if you understand to what extent you have been blinded by your Slav sensibility, if you drop this rubbish down the first drain you come to, then . . .'

He gave a broad smile. He was the father in transports

of joy, flinging his arms around the neck of the prodigal son.

'Then Genesis of Revolution and the White Books are still yours. We'll bury the hatchet and say no more about this little business. Obviously, with my programme in tatters I'll have lost quite a bit of money, but . . . what's money?'

He made a generous gesture with the hand which was still holding his glasses. Then, having put them back on, he led Aleksandr to the door. On the threshold he stopped him and took his hand. His noble face grew even more noble.

'I'm twenty years older than you, Psar. Allow me to give you a piece of advice.'

He closed his eyes and said, very quietly: 'Pray.'

He closed his left hand over his right and held Aleksandr's hand in the trap for a few moments.

Aleksandr had expected Fourveret's refusal: in fact, he approved of it. But that did not make it any easier to bear, especially when spiked with veiled threats and protective advice.

On the telephone, Ivan Ivanich hardly seemed surprised by the publisher's categorical no; he simply asked: 'Supposing the book comes out all the same, what would have to be done to make it a success?'

'If ever you find that secret, come over to the West: you'll be a millionaire.'

'Market research . . .'

'Useless where books are concerned. At least to begin with. We all know what makes a book more successful when it has already succeeded, but at the outset we just throw it out into the whirlpool of chance, or rather to the whim of Fortune. Most of them sink; a few rise to the surface; these we know how to pilot into open water, but the first jump is pure chance. Remember, there are pornographic crime novels that fail and truly great books that succeed.'

'All the same! The support of the press . . .'

'Makes little difference.'

'But it's not very often that the press all joins in crying up a book and nobody buys it.'

'Not very often.'

'And it seldom happens that a single dog barks in a village and the rest don't answer.'

'What are you getting at, Ivan Ivanich?'

'Who are the best barkers? Those who start the others off?'

'The best is Ballandar, and he's part of my orchestra, but I've just told you what he thinks—and quite rightly—of your piece of junk.'

'That's not the question. Will you find one or two voices to bark back?'

'As soon as the barking starts, of course. Three-quarters of the critics talk only about books mentioned by Ballandar, some to say the same thing as he, the rest to contradict him. But, I repeat, Fourveret will not publish us and even if he did, Ballandar would say nothing. I did warn you.'

'We have our methods! You may be sure that if those two musicians have been assigned to your orchestra, it is, as the French say, because they know how to sing.

'Don't be naïve, Ivan Ivanich, we're in Paris, in the last quarter of the twentieth century. No one has any guilty secrets any longer, since everything is permitted. If your wife learnt that you fancied Jessica, she might get after you with her rolling-pin, but that's because she doesn't belong to the trendy intelligentsia.'

Ivan Ivanich did not pick up on the insinuation. He fixed a rendez-vous for the following morning, in a café at the Porte d'Orléans.

From the Porte d'Orléans, clutching his big, black briefcase, Aleksandr went straight to the offices of Lux; it was 14 August and he found the doors locked. Fourveret must be at his house at Dourdan. Should he rush over there? The temptation was strong, but all that congestion on the roads . . . Anyway there was a certain pleasure to be derived from holding his fire . . . 'I'll go tomorrow.'

The next day, he arrived about half-past eleven in the morning at Le Chastelet, where he had often been a welcome guest. It was there that they had celebrated the success of the White Book on State Education with several professors from the Sorbonne, and that of the White Book on the Church in the company of a few prelates.

The white façade, Napoleon III in a very Louis XVI style, had been restored. The gravel on the drive, raked and watered, crunched deliciously under the tyres.

'They're all at mass, Monsieur Psar,' said Mme Emilienne. 'Would you like to wait in the drawing-room? Or shall I serve you a little apéritif in the garden?'

Usually Aleksandr preferred indoors, but on that day he felt the need to breathe fresh air. He sat down under a parasol. The gardens amounted to hardly more than a couple of acres, and the paths had been designed in the English style, in order to give an impression of distance and to vary the planes. Tall trees thrust their foliage to the sky. Birds were chirruping. An imperceptible mist filtered the light. Aleksandr had put his briefcase at his feet and, from time to time, touched it with the tip of his shoe. The ice tinkled in the crystal goblet.

Suddenly there was an explosion of noise and a swarm of children followed by a few adults emerged from one of the French windows.

'My dear Psaaar! What a surprise! You're staying for lunch, of course!'

Fourveret smiled with all his teeth; the eyes remained vigilant. He shook Aleksandr's hand, but his invitation was clearly one that it would be better to refuse.

'I don't know yet. I had to see you on an urgent matter. I'm terribly sorry to track you down here.'

'But not at all,' said Mme Fourveret, a tall, thin woman, with something frankly provincial in her bearing. 'We're delighted to see you. Do you know my daughter, Mme Faubert? And these are my grandchildren . . .'

The children had relatively simple names. They had been so well brought up that they were not even embarrassed at having been so. They pretended shyness to just the degree required. Aleksandr avoided asking them what they were doing at school, but he greeted them seriously, looking each one of them in the eyes, and they liked that. Perhaps he looked rather longer at Nicolas, a five-year-old boy, with short, fair hair.

'What do you want to be when you grow up, Nicolas?'

Nicolas still lisped.

'I want to be a thtock bwoker, like daddy.'

Aleksandr showed surprise: 'When I was your age, I wanted to command a submarine.'

Fourveret took him by the arm.

'Well, what is this urgent matter? I hope you have thought about what I said and are not going on with this . . .'

'Would you mind,' Aleksandr suggested, 'if we took a turn in the garden?'

He felt acute pleasure at the thought of what he was going to do and yet he was not too sure how to set about it. Not, thank God, because of any sense of charity, but rather because of a certain *savoir-vivre*, which had profoundly shaped his character. He was ashamed to put this man at his mercy; even dogs don't bite the jugular when it is offered.

They walked between mown lawns, a little yellowed by the summer. Bees were buzzing. On the terrace, Emilienne was laying the table. It would be a real family 15 August, with a mass, a grandpa, a granny, lunch out of doors, water coloured with wine for the older children, a few angry words during the dessert over a wasp that one of the boys would capture and want to guillotine with his knife.

Fourveret stopped to observe the scene over a lawn, a path, a dahlia bed and another path. The children were squabbling over who should sit where. 'No, I've already told you: if the gentleman is staying, everyone has to move down one.' A solemn little girl was helping Emilienne lay the table. Mme Fourveret and Mme Faubert, each holding a glass of port, were chatting animatedly.

'You can say what you like,' the mother insisted, 'I regret the passing of communion dresses. They did no harm to anyone and you can imagine how pretty Marie-Caroline would have looked in all that lace!'

Mme Fourveret spoke loudly, with the desperate authority of those who are not listened to. Mme Faubert chuckled.

'You'll never change, maman. Anyway, even if you did, I would be the first to regret it.'

M. Fourveret's austere face was illuminated by an inner glow.

'It's a beautiful thing,' he murmured, 'a Christian family.'

Aleksandr had found his way in.

'It's a beautiful thing. But it isn't always enough.'

'I'm not sure I understand you correctly.'

They spoke without looking at one another, their eyes still fixed on the graceful pastoral being played out under the parasols.

'Thirty years ago,' Aleksandr went on, 'a number of highly placed individuals, several of them with Christian families, got into a bit of trouble because they had taken part in what at the time were variously called the *ballets roses* and the *ballets bleus*—depending on the proclivities involved. Careers were ruined. There were a few suicides. For, you see, those gentlemen had been imprudent. Their young victims or young partners, call them what you will, were questioned; they recognized their clients and told everything: "That's the gentleman who did that to me, and that gentleman over there did such and such." '

'I remember,' said Fourveret, still smiling, his eyes fixed on the scene ahead of him.

'Shortly afterwards, a charitable institution was founded at Ville-d'Avray. Its aim was to give a good home and education to young orphans. Now, curiously enough, this private institution makes no appeal for contributions from charitable individuals, and yet when the orphans grow up, they are very nicely provided for when they leave the institution. Now it is true that these dear children do not remain entirely idle during their stay and that, moreover, they have one peculiarity that makes them even more precious to their protectors . . . Have you heard, Fourveret, of the Institution for Young Blind Orphans at Ville-d'Avray?'

Fourveret turned to Aleksandr. His voice betrayed anxiety, but he had forgotten to take the smile off his face, a smile full of nobility and humanity.

'Why are you telling me this appalling story? Those monsters, unspeakable as they no doubt are, are certainly invulnerable, since no one has ever seen them?'

'Ah! That's just it,' Aleksandr said lightly. 'I'm well aware that those gentlemen have pseudonyms that enable them to communicate with the management without compromising themselves, and keys to get into the house and even into a particular numbered room without being seen . . . But God, my dear Fourveret, God, as you are fond of saying, sees you at all times, and not only God. As you must know, cameras concealed in walls are to be found in places other than the movies.'

He snapped one of the clasps on his briefcase.

'Are you interested in dirty photographs, Fourveret? On one of them you can even see the little white walking stick at the foot of the bed.'

The affair of the blind orphans had been going on for the last fifteen years. Was the publication of *The Russian Truth* so important to the Department as to risk alerting those involved?

Fourveret looked back at his wife, his daughter, his grandchildren dancing their little ballet of the Assumption beyond the lawn and the dahlias.

'There's a wathp!' cried Nicolas brandishing the bread knife.

Fourveret's lips seemed frozen. With great difficulty he managed to bring out the words: 'The book will appear on the date agreed.'

'And you will do everything necessary for it to be a triumph,' said Aleksandr, stressing the words, 'otherwise, I can make no guarantees.'

'I shall do all I can.'

A smile crossed Aleksandr's bony face.

'In that case, it will give me great pleasure to accept your invitation to lunch with your family.'

That afternoon, Aleksandr, still playing his role of avenging angel, rang *Objectifs*. No answer. This growing habit of intellectual workers to take holidays exasperated him. 'Over there, at least they are forced to offer the Party Sundays of voluntary labour!' Was Ballandar at Ramatuelle or Port-Grimaud? Fourveret had seen him in Paris three days earlier. Anyway it was not like Ballandar to go away in August, out of snobbery and a taste for summer intrigue. Aleksandr rang him at home. 'But, of course, Aleksandr Psar, come along.' There was some reticence in his voice however: Ballandar had read *The Russian Truth* and feared that Aleksandr had gone over into the camp of those (contagious) untouchables, the extremists of the right.

Rue de Tournon. A seventeenth-century building, restored in the most aggressively impeccable taste. Exposed stonework on the staircase. Tapestries. Aleksandr disdained the lift: the exercise would do him no harm and, anyway, the tiny cabin gave him claustrophobia. He rang at a tall moulded oak door, a very good imitation of the original.

How many young authors must have stood trembling at this threshold! How many, published or not, had come here to play, sometimes sincerely, sometimes resentfully, the comedy of veneration. 'I admire you so much, Monsieur Ballandar!'—the swine, you didn't even put in a good word for me at Grasset—'Monsieur Ballandar, you're marvellous!'—I could kill him: he didn't even ask me. Ballandar was one of those men of whom it is said, wrongly, that they make or break literary reputations. In fact, the power enjoyed by Ballandar was limited. In order to preserve his authority, Ballandar had to censor himself at all times: 'One can't say this, that isn't done . . .' He had built up for himself a reputation for boldness, but he preferred to kick in open doors and never attacked anyone who could hit back; he kissed the feet of anyone who stood up to him. Apparently at the summit of his success, he lived in perpetual anxiety, fearing that X, married to Y's niece, or having some way of exerting pressure on Z, would take over his job, which, he felt, without wanting to admit it, would be easy enough, since he possessed no particular talent, nothing in fact but a signature. Moreover, while building up a reputation as a young intellectual well disposed towards those younger than himself (he had been young ever since he had ceased to be a child, that is to say, for a good forty years at least), he was careful to choose as protégés and neophytes those who were not overly endowed with talent either. He supported them at the appearance of their first book: then they sank from view, providing no competition to Ballandar, and became, or went back to being, insurance agents, starlets or teachers. It was better for everybody, for, just think, if Ballandar had lost his job, what would he have done? A failed novelist can still turn to criticism, but a critic? Besides, Ballandar was no more evil than good: he was simply prudent. An intellectual career is like water-skiing: the important thing is to hold on to the towrope handle as long as possible.

Having pressed the bell—the heart of a brass sun—with his index finger, Aleksandr thought how, he, too, at the time when he still considered himself to be a writer, might have presented himself here, sure that he had brought a masterpiece and that a leg up from M. José Ballandar would bring him fame and fortune. Fortunately he had escaped that particular string of humiliations. But he had lived through another. As a literary agent at the outset of his career, he had had to dance attendance on the great and powerful of the literary world: 'Read it, you won't regret it. Won't you at least glance at the first chapter? It will be a great success, I assure you. I'm telling you before anybody else. Did you know that the author burnt his first wife alive?' It was not disagreeable to turn up, fife in pocket, to charm one of those pontiffs of literature, one of those staff officers of the intelligentsia? A little tune and Ballandar would dance.

'Well, come in!'

Pleasant, pleasant with a hint of superiority and, of course, prudence. Does one come to discuss serious matters on a public holiday? It was no doubt to appeal against Fourveret's decision, but Fourveret was right: they must not touch *The Russian Truth*, not with rubber gloves, not even with tweezers.

Aleksandr came in. He could obtain satisfaction there, immediately; he could ask Ballandar to turn somersaults in front of him on the carpet, and Ballandar would do it. But he wanted more than somersaults: nothing less than a demonstration *ad absurdum*.

Aleksandr simply asked: 'What, in your opinion, is literature?'

Ballandar, in suitable open-necked shirt and silk scarf, his hips skilfully flattened by an American-style pair of white trousers, raised his blond eyebrows.

'Literature? Come now.' No physical contact, the Anglo-American tone. 'What can I offer you, a pawpaw juice? A batida? You aren't going to tell me you want a whisky, so common! Ah! I'd forgotten, vodka, of course, with orange juice, what the Americans call a screwdriver. No, not a screwdriver? Whisky, really? Not Glenfiddich at least: everybody has that. Old Mortality, perhaps? LLLLiterature, you were saying . . . My dear Aleksandr Psar, you embarrass me. Literature . . . is a snapshot of revolution, that's it: literature is revolutionary in its essence: Racine against Corneille, Hugo against Racine, Ancients against Moderns, I mean: Moderns against Ancients . . . Don't you think?'

'Hugo wasn't against Racine, nor were the Moderns against the Ancients. They were simply trying to do better.'

'Yeees . . . It all amounts to the same thing. Literature . . .' He had found the formula. '. . . is the creative act of a class or generation asserting itself against the preceding one.'

'Dialectical, then?'

'Not everything in Engels is bad either.'

'Dialectics are Engels' department.'

'Not everything in Engles is bad either.'

'Engels was a capitalist, who never accorded his wage-earners the slightest reform that would have made their lives more tolerable.'

'You find everything handy, don't you? If you want to shoot down Engels you're suddenly concerned about the well-being of wage-earners! Typical of you!'

They were sitting on either side of a small malachite table, in a room of indeterminate vocation: in Ballandar's apartment, all the rooms were drawing-rooms, smoking-rooms, libraries and all were stuffed with books: the review copies that he had the decency not to resell and for which he had had some splendid ebony shelves built.

Aleksandr looked around him. There was no doubt about it: he was in a temple, a monument, one of the rare points of reference in the world of contemporary literature. If a historian ever dealt with French criticism in the second half of the twentieth century, he could not fail to mention José Ballandar, whatever he decided to say about him. Ballandar lived largely by his golden pen (and by a few innocent dabblings on the stock exchange); Ballandar found every door open that mattered to him (or almost); other reviewers mentioned the name of Ballandar only with respect or horror, which amounts to the same thing; in the Republic of Letters

Ballandar had a quasi-official position: if a post of critic laureate—as the English have a poet laureate—had ever been set up, it would have been occupied by Ballandar. And everything in this temple suggested how Monseigneur must be pleased with himself: the Chinese screens and the pictures by minor Impressionist masters, the kakemonos and the invisible air conditioning, the indirect lighting controlled by dimmer-switches at the back of glass cases and the eighteenth-century English silver, the Caucasian rugs and the Jacob desk.

'You have a very beautiful apartment,' Aleksandr said.

'One has to bed down somewhere—providing it isn't too ghastly.'

Ballandar's eye fell on the wall that he had devoted to a tiny museum of contemporary art. The pictures had not cost him a great deal, but it was impossible to say what they would be worth in twenty years: that disturbed him. A fortune perhaps? If not, what a disappointment!

'So,' he said, to change the conversation, 'you're an August man too!'

'I have to be. I have this important book coming out in the autumn.'

'I thought Fourveret . . .?'

'He's changed his mind. He's going to pull out all the stops.'

Ballandar was worried. He was by profession a man not-to-miss-the-bus. Indeed he was in the habit of catching several buses simultaneously for different destinations, none of them too far from one another. He knew Fourveret: he was a cunning old fox and had taken up position in the same dug-out as himself. They both knew that to publish or praise a non-starter was suicide, but also that to miss an 'important' work was little better.

'Did Fourveret tell you that I had a look at it . . .? Just a glance, you understand.'

'He did tell me.'

'Listen, Aleksandr Psar, you must try to understand me. You and I like one another, but we don't come from the same background. I tend more and more to think that no one is responsible for his antecedents and I'm not blaming you for

188

yours; all the same one is conditioned. You come from a world with ties that I do not envy you for; I was born a revolutionary; I can't help it. My father was a banker, it's true, in a very small bank. But he was a Voltairean, an anti-clerical . . . At Le Vésinet he was known as the Red Banker! Well . . . One is as one is born, don't you think? In some cases, it is true, I may have attacked the excesses of the left—I did so recently—but when an author tried to demonstrate that the Russian revolution might have been prevented by Stolypin, that Hitler was a child compared to Lenin . . . With me, you see, it's physical . . .'

'Your heart bleeds?'

'My . . .? Oh, no! That's Fourveret. Publishers have their own imperatives: they have to sell. With me . . .'

'You see Red.'

Aleksandr could have opened his black briefcase, taken out the sheet of paper, placed it on the malachite and left. Instead he assumed a contrite air: 'In short, you really think, Ballandar, that we should leave it alone?'

'Fourveret knows what he's doing. He's run Lux for thirty years. He's been able to give it a certain tone, a certain dynamism . . . What's more, from a moral point of view, he is irreproachable. All the same I am surprised . . .'

'How does *The Russian Truth* strike you exactly—as subversive?'

'To begin with, if you'll excuse my saying so, after all, it is my field, it strikes me as . . . badly written. Yes, that's it: badly written. Mind you, that might be the translation. All those parables, those leitmotifs . . . Of course I'm overcome with sympathy for the poor fellow in his asylum, and if he really is the one who shot Brezhnev one has to admit that he has guts . . . But being some unfortunate wretch is one thing, having physical courage is another—and being a writer is something else again. No one has defended the dissidents more than I, but one has to admit that there are some notorious literary nonentities among them who have been acclaimed for the wrong reasons. If every Christian martyr had turned his troubles into a book, we'd have ended up with an anthology something like the complete works of all the Nobel prize-winners, don't you think?'

189

'So your advice would be . . .?'

'You're a friend. So is Fourveret. I honestly believe that the publication of a book of this kind . . . I know you have already incurred expenses, but if I were you . . . Unless Fourveret's flair . . .'

Aleksandr got up.

'Yes,' he said, 'you have a beautiful apartment. Do you know whom it belonged to before you?'

There was a moment of silence: an angel passed overhead, as the French say, or, as the more mundane Russians put it, a policeman was born.

'Not the slightest idea. I've lived here for so long . . .'

Aleksandr went to the window and observed the surrealistic perspective of the Rue de Tournon. He felt that he hated Ballandar. Why? Because he was a revolutionary? That would have been understandable, if paradoxical. But Ballandar was not a revolutionary. Because he was a bourgeois? That would have been doubly understandable. But Ballandar was not a true bourgeois either; not everyone who wishes to be is a bourgeois, even if he pretends he does not wish to be. However little inclined to introspection, Aleksandr was sure that he felt a need to explain to himself that upsurge of hatred that seemed to rise up into his oesophagus. 'I hate Ballandar because he is nothing.' That was true. This man who was considered to be a creator of opinion, had no opinion of his own. A Ghibelline among the Ghibellines and a Guelph among the Guelphs, he had been a collaborator under the Occupation and a member of the Resistance at the Liberation. He then joined the opposition, but only because in France, intellectuals have no choice: even if their friends are in power, they are obliged to vilify authority or be suspected of having sold out, and no one had bothered to buy Ballandar. 'No one,' he had once written, 'can doubt my courage. I have always defied the Great Beast.' And, indeed, no one doubted it. But he had never defied it: he had only teased it through the bars of its cage. In another country or at another time, Ballandar would have been the official supporter of any régime. 'He's not a man,' Aleksandr thought, 'he's a hollow in the continuum. And I'm like nature, in that I abhor a vacuum.' It was true: he felt no hostility towards anything that was constructed, anything that had substance, even if the construction or the substance was in the opposing camp. But Ballandar and his ilk were spineless, faithless, aimless, attached only to their own well-being, while conspiring nevertheless to jeopardize it, because it was fashionable to do so . . . 'I understand the selfishness of predatory barons, of exploiting industrialists, of colonists bleeding the natives; I can understand the revolt of the repressed, I see that they aspire only to one thing: to be oppressors in their turn; I accept Terror and Counter-Terror; I'm even capable of admiring those who choose on the contrary the defeat-victory of martydom, but the timid opportunism of the lowest mediocrities . . .'

Aleksandr came back to the malachite table, placed his briefcase on it and opened the clasps with a loud snap.

'On the subject of style, José Ballandar, I would like you to cast an eye on this sample of epistolary art. Tell me what you think of it?'

It was a photocopy of a handwritten letter.

Paris, 2 January 1942

Dear Sirs,

Desirous as I am of participating in the purification of the French nation, I wish to inform you that Aronson Léon, who has spread the rumour that he has left for America, is in fact hiding in one of the rooms of his immense apartment on the third floor, 218 Rue de Tournon. The entrance to this room is hidden by a large wardrobe. I know this because my father, who has just died, was the concierge in this building. I remain at your disposal for any additional information.

Yours faithfully,
Joseph Ballandar,
4 Rue Jean-Jaurès, Paris XX.

'It's a forgery!' Ballandar stammered.

Aleksandr had walked over and sat down next to him on his Directory sofa.

'Personally,' he said, 'I find the style rather low. But the spelling is already excellent and at least you had the decency to wait for your father to die.'

5
Something for a Rainy Day
(*Operation Pskov, Stage 2*)

There was a nip in the air; the birch trees rose up amid gilded
stretches of water; the maples flamed like torches. As a child,
Iakov had liked to pretend that the maples were the forerun-
ners, the heralds of Father Christmas, and later he had
identified their redness with that of the dictatorship of the
proletariat, a necessary transition between the chaos of
the past and the innocent radiance of the future. For him
winter was always welcome: he liked to see the angular,
anarchic shapes of reality disappear beneath the smooth
curves and swellings, the barely perceptible hollows, of
the snow.

'Will the snow come early this year, Potapich?'

The chauffeur, agreeably surprised by this opening from a
boss who was considered somewhat distant, decided to play
up to him: 'It will, Comrade General.'

In fact, he had no idea: he was a city child. But, for
Pitman, the people was the people and, like every good
Russian, he believed that the people possessed the truth.
'Good,' he thought, 'next month I shall take Sviatoslav out
on a troika.' Outings on a troika, with all the sleighbells
tinkling, over the powdered snow, the horses galloping along
and two or three of his children squeezed up against him, was
one of Pitman's great pleasures in life. 'Troika-Russia,' he
cried, like Gogol, 'nothing, no, nothing will stop thy onward
course!' Sviatoslav, the Benjamin of the family, the late-
comer, had not yet taken part in these escapades and, ever
since the thaw of the previous year, he had whined: 'Papa,
will there be snow tomorrow?'

Yes, thought Pitman, gazing at the crimson maples that
swept past in line, we'll have a very good winter.

But there was a painful reservation in his mind: Mohammed Mohammedovich would not be there to enjoy this good winter.

Volkovo. The sitting-room of the dacha was enormous: Abdulrakhmanov had knocked down two walls to have more breathing space. An atmosphere reminiscent of the Old Order reigned there, not in the sense of something heavy and pompous, but, on the contrary, in the sense of a clean disorder, a genuineness, the self-confidence of quality and contempt for any pretension. The furniture, of mixed styles, but precious both in the wood and in the craftsmanship, all dated from the last century; some of the items were upholstered, others not; the end of a chess game lay patiently on a table; glass-fronted bookcases contained some five hundred volumes, many of which were in languages that the master of the house did not know: this was not his personal library—which was to be found in the study that also served as his bedroom—but the trophies of his massacres, the harvest of a life devoted to influence and disinformation.

'Good morning, Your Excellency. Good morning. And how are you?'

Wearing a dressing-gown with a floral design and, on his head, a black octagonal *tubiteika*, with gold motifs, Abdulrakhmanov looked more than ever like a menhir. The contraction, the 'growth-downwards', which attacks so many old men, had not dared to touch him: he still held himself erect. But he was wasting away; his cheeks had almost disappeared and the cartilege of his larynx wobbled in the middle of his denuded neck like that of a condor. He coughed frequently, a dry, catarrh-cough; he often put his hand to the small of his back, though he was in no worse condition there than anywhere else; one felt that this great mechanism had had its day. However the intellectual faculties did not seem to be impaired, except that the old man would often recount, in detail, things that you knew perfectly well already and he knew that you knew: the fact was that he could no longer refuse himself the pleasure of story-telling.

'I've brought you a present, Mohammed Mohammedovich.'

'Open it, then.'

He did not want to show, perhaps, that, for some time, his fingers had become petrified.

Pitman untied the parcel. The white jacket represented, in section, a red and yellow Russian doll. In the title, the Rs of *Vérité* and *russe* were inverted. By way of author's name one read: 'Le Prisonnier anonyme'. Pitman took off the jacket. The book, in hardcovers, was heavy, compact, like a beautiful red paving stone.

'They've brought it out in two editions, a paperback and a hardback. Handsome, isn't it?'

Abdulrakhmanov stared at the object with tired eyes.

'Kenti, the samovar. And the liqueurs.'

He had taken to sipping liqueurs. People sent them to him from every country in the world. Above all he liked French Vieille Cure, which was almost impossible to find. 'For little old men, little pleasures,' he would remark ironically.

'Well, expound!'

Pitman began by admitting the sacrifices: the orphanage for blind children had been exploited and therefore of little further use. The denunciation of Aronson, found among ten thousand others in the archives of the Paris Kommandantur, brought back to Berlin, had had to be used.

'But these aren't sacrifices, my Iakov Moiseich, all-of-porcelain: it is an expenditure of ammunition. The gentlemen in espionage tend to accumulate intelligence for the sake of intelligence: for us, dirty little secrets are just a means to an end, no more. Carry on.'

The book had appeared in the bookshops. Ballandar had immediately declared that it was a masterpiece. *Oprichnik*'s orchestra, duly impressed, had followed as best it could. The review *Objection* had a long article, which, though hostile, was thorough: 'We detest this work,' wrote M. Johannès-Graf, 'but, when one is born a Jew and becomes a Protestant, as in my case, one has a reason not to take part in any systematic stifling of opinion, and a reason to overturn every bushel that might deprive us of any light whatever, even if it smells of sulphur.' Monthignies expressed himself with sincerity, but insisted on the importance of the work: 'The mere suspicion of a return of the labouring masses to serfdom at the hands of a so-called élite revolts our susceptibilities, offended as they are by all too unpleasant memories, by responsibilities that cannot be discharged; however it would be a token of bad faith to pretend that the Anonymous Prisoner is recommending this monstrous solution; in the Russia that he imagines, ownership and management would be synonymous. He does not seem to be hostile to workers' co-operatives being formed to take over a factory. Such co-operation may be redolent of folktales, but it stems from a conception that is humanist rather than totalitarian.' Jeanne Bouillon took over half a page to 'demystify the sort of theo-syndicalism advocated by Iron Mask. It is quite reasonable to wonder whether the appalling treatment that he has been subjected to in his *psykhushka* may not in the end have affected his brain. In which case, the Soviet régime has only its own excesses to blame for the intellectual teratology that is flourishing under its nose. Anyway, it is not inconceivable that the theories reaching us from cell Triple Zero, however mad they may be, are not inapplicable in the country of the *zemstvos* and *mirs*.' Mme Choustrewitz managed not to raise any political problems: what interested her was whether the author of the book was or was not the Kurnosov who had shot at Brezhnev.

'All this strikes me as quite excellent,' said Abdulrakhmanov. 'The target has been laid correctly. How did the dissidents react, whose support Psar solicited?'

In a clumsy gesture he turned the book over: on the back of the jacket the most famous names were preceded by enthusiastic comments. Pitman burst out laughing: 'We've certainly given the ant-hill a good kick, Mohammed Mohammedovich!'

Not wishing to reverse their judgement, but fearing that the Anonymous Prisoner's opinions might be attributed to them, the dissidents had launched into a mass of declarations, clarifications, communiqués and manifestos of various kinds. Some were so prolix that the newspapers were unable to publish their proclamations *in extenso*, which, of course, aroused new fits of anger and new professions of faith. The bearded magus partly associated himself with the Anonymous Prisoner; the Marxists took advantage of the opportunity to go for the bearded magus, tooth and claw; the professional slanderers had a field day; everyone accused everyone else of belonging to various 'organs'. Pitman amusingly described the ensuing confusion. Abdulrakhmanov laughed with pleasure.

'In short, our operation seems to be going very well. What did the rest of the press say?'

Apart from *Oprichnik*'s orchestra, the French press proved frankly hostile to the Anonymous Prisoner: even assuming that he was a hero and martyr, one had to avoid like the plague turning him into a touchstone of right-mindedness.

'How many columns do they take to say that?'

'A lot, Mohammed Mohammedovich.'

'Perfect. The independent spirits who are beginning to move to the right will slow the movement down. And we're only at Stage 1, my Iakov Moiseich all-of-vermeil.'

Voivode, one of the seven influence agents working in France, the one directly responsible for the press, had done a marvellous job: the sound boxes assigned to him set the tone for the other papers.

'Are you sure that no one has yet used the "obscene word"?'

'Don't worry, Mohammed Mohammedovich, we're keeping it for Stage 2, as you ordered.'

'The "corporation" has made a fool of itself as usual, I suppose?'

'As usual. *Fraternité* claims that the Anonymous Prisoner doesn't exist and that his manuscript is a forgery fabricated by Pinochet.'

Abdulrakhmanov smiled absent-mindedly. He hardly ever smoked now, but sometimes stuck his cigarette-holder in his mouth and inhaled the smell of all the cigarettes that had been smoked in it. This time, it produced a sucking noise that the old man did not seem to notice. Still staring into space, he said: '*Nnus* . . . There seems to be no reason, my Iakov Moiseich all-of-diamond, why we should not set Stage 2 in motion.'

'It's Stage 3 that bothers me, Mohammed Mohammedovich.'

It was a manner of speaking. Stage 3, that is to say, the running-down of the operation, troubled Iakov Pitman somewhat on moral grounds: if it had been left to him, he would have recalled Psar as soon as the operation was over, promoted him, given him an opportunity to have other children (young Dmitri had only to die in some imaginary accident). But that was not the nub of the matter: Pitman had an idea in his head, it seemed to him that the opportunity of realizing it was within his grasp, and he did not see why he should give it up.

'Stage 3, as it happens, will be child's play,' said Abdulrakhmanov. 'Kurnosov will stay where he is: he's hardly in a position to make trouble for us, to say the least. Zellman will get rid of Gaverin for us and himself fade into the background. That will leave Psar.'

'Precisely. It is he who . . .'

'Stage 1 corrodes him; Stage 2 discredits him. Stage 3 will disgrace him: he won't recover. What do you expect him to do? His citizenship has never been promulgated; it can be erased at the stroke of a pen. His rank? He can easily be stripped of it for anti-Soviet activities, if for no other reason, for the publication of that pseudo-*Russian Truth*. If he turns to the French, what will he look like, a reactionary manipulated by the Communists, or a Communist manipulated by the reactionaries? Besides, he still believes that we hold his wife and son: so it is unlikely that he will go over to the enemy. Even if he does, what will he be able to teach French-counter-espionage that French counter-espionage doesn't already know? No, my Iakov Moiseich all-of-Karelian-birch, you've nothing to worry about. Stage 3 will simply consist of discarding him like an old slipper. You change the telephone numbers, that's all. You remember Henry V? "I know thee not, old man." Obviously we'll have to send the case-officer outside France: that's the only precaution to be taken.'

'Should we leave the agency to Psar?'

'Of course: it will be completely discredited.'

Pitman had never understood Abdulrakhmanov's animosity towards his own 'protégé'. He had often wanted to ask him for the reason, but had never dared to. He might have done so now if he had not had this other project to put over. A fit of shyness made his heart pound, for all that he was a lieutenant-general.

'Mohammed Mohammedovich, supposing I had another suggestion?'

The old man pulled a face; his softened features lent themselves to it all too easily.

'What kind of suggestion?'

At once tender and obsequious, Pitman stammered out: 'You know, Operation Hard Sign, which you had the goodness to approve in principle and which the Consistory decided to apply as soon as all the conditions were met with . . .'

This plan was Iakov Pitman's own favourite brain-child and he regarded it as his future masterpiece: if it succeeded, he would enter the Olympia of the Hidy-hats. Directorate A and the first, second and fifth principal directorates had given their approval; the head of the Committee of State Security had counter-signed the proposal; the Party-General-Secretary-and-Prime-Minister had cast his alligator's somnolent but not disapproving eye over it. The plan would become operational as soon as the various elements had come together. And it now seemed to Pitman that he was confronted by an almost unhoped for combination of circumstances: the Psar-Kurnosov tandem, if one took the risk to create it, might bring about an operation beside which Operation Pskov itself would look like a drawing-room charade.

'I am well aware that according to the *Vademecum* operations must never overlap one another, but you yourself have taught me, Mohammed Mohammedovich, to distance myself from the *Vademecum*. Anyway, by introducing Iron Mask into the *Oprichnik* operation, which had remained until now absolutely aseptic . . . we are already departing from the rules. For an operation of the scope of Hard Sign . . .'

Pitman rambled on clumsily, intimidated by that pale eye that expressed merely haughty disapproval. Pitman was one of those sensitive flowers that need plenty of rain and sunlight. In the end Abdulrakhmanov interrupted him impatiently:

'Always trying to save your pawns, my Iakov Moiseich all-of-papier-mâché, always your short-term view. Psar and Kurnosov will never form a tandem. They'd be like two bits of soap stuck together, good enough for a bath, but to be thrown away afterwards. There isn't enough there to mount an operation like Hard Sign. Psar is what Sun Tzu calls a dead agent: put that in your pipe and smoke it. You should read Sun Tzu, you know.' (Pitman knew it almost by heart.) 'Sun Tzu distinguishes five classes of secret agent. He calls the fourth class, which refers to counter-espionage and specifically to the techniques of disinformation, "the dead agents". Yes, my Iakov Moiseich all-of-silver, "dead".

'I don't know if I've told you the story'—he told it four times a year and knew it—'of Chief of Staff Ts'ao. He was a real Chinese general, with drooping moustache and pigtail. He was waging war against the King of the Tanguts, who happened to have a prime minister of genius. *Nnus*, this is what Ts'ao did. He took a man condemned to death, pardoned him and dressed him up as a monk. Yes, Your Excellency, as a monk. And to do what? To draw attention to himself, for he spoke like a lay person. Before letting him go, he made him swallow a ball of wax. "When it comes out again," he told him, "you will take it to the prime minister of the king of the Tanguts." And he sent him away. The false monk arrived among the Tanguts, was quickly arrested and interrogated. He admitted that he was hiding on him, or rather inside him, a message for the prime minister. The ball of wax was recovered, opened and inside was a letter addressed to the prime minister alluding to secret agreements made between himself and Ts'ao. In fact, there had been no secret agreements, but the king of the Tanguts wasted no time in having the head of his prime minister cut off, together with that of the false monk. And that is how, my Iakov Moiseich all-of-gold, friend Ts'ao of the drooping moustache and long pigtail took possession of the kingdom of the Tanguts.

'I repeat, Psar has done his time and, in any case, he has never been anything other than a "dead agent", dead in advance. As soon as you consider that Stage 2 is complete, you will close the file, put it away and think no more about it. Obviously you will try to replace Psar, which will not be very easy, but, meanwhile, you will light the slow fuse and take to your heels. That's all I'm asking you to do.'

Pitman was not convinced, but he did not want to contradict his old master. He got up and took the two rough, heavy hands in his, which were supple and chubby.

'Mohammed Mohammedovich, you are no doubt right, as usual. What do you think we should do with Kurnosov?'

Abdulrakhmanov sucked on his empty cigarette-holder, producing a whistle.

'If we were still in the good old days, I would have replied, perhaps rather hastily: put him through the profit and loss account. Degenerates that we are, I think you'll be condemned to feeding him lavishly to the end of his days. And I beg you: don't skimp the *kulebiaka*, that wouldn't be kind. As for your Hard Sign, to set up an operation like that, you need fresh, clean agents.'

Abdulrakhmanov got up, repressing a groan.

'We'll put your little present here.' A Spanish book lay on a leather lectern. Abdulrakhmanov took it off and replaced it with *La Vérité russe*.

'The Mexican is very good, but I've seen enough of it. I always make a little exhibition for myself of the new books, as they come out of the oven, like bread-rolls and then, when the next one arrives, they all move down one, till the moment comes when it has to make room—in the direction of the libraries. It's a fine book, this one of yours, a good weighty volume; you can tell it's not rubbish, *The Russian Truth*! Personally, the part I liked best is Kurnosov's passage about the bells. It's both popular and learned: not easy to achieve! It's not for nothing that the review of that young whipper-snapper Herzen was called *The Bell*. You see, in olden times, bells were given all kinds of names. The commonest was Polielei. I don't know what it means: maybe it comes from *elei*, holy oil? One can imagine a bell being called The Myrrhific . . . But there was also Swan and Sheep, and even Goat.

'At Rostov, in the seventeenth century, there were two bells, called Swan and Polielei, the sounds of which formed a minor third, which gave great pleasure to Metropolitan Jonah, because he had just been disgraced by Tsar Alexis:

the chimes of his church soothed his sadness. Then, suddenly, the good man came into favour under Peter I! What was to be done? He ordered another bell, tuned to a fifth lower than Polielei. Instead of a minor chord, he now had a perfect major chord, but he had not changed the basic elements. What a lesson that is for us, my Iakov Moiseich all-of-bronze, all-of-brass. Imagine the people of Rostov condemned to melancholy for years and years, and then suddenly waking up one fine morning to the sound of a joyous concert! Imagine the effect produced on families, couples, workshops! The clowns found new jokes, lovers new caresses . . . Ah! I would like to have lived in Rostov in 1688, under good Metropolitan Jonah and under the man who was soon to become emperor of all the Russias. If they'd all been like Peter, we would not have had to have a Re . . .'

A fit of coughing interrupted and ended this tirade. It was so violent that tears were running down the man's enormous nose and his arms waved around like oars, pointing to the door. In the end, Pitman understood and left the room with the disagreeable impression of having been thrown out.

'The truth is,' he thought, 'he simply didn't want to be seen in that state: it's terrible to have been so strong and to become so weak. Fortunately I was not conceived on such a scale. It can't be very comfortable.'

He returned to Moscow, in thoughtful mood.

As long as his master was alive, he would not disobey him. He would bring Operation Pskov to completion, whatever he felt about it. A pity, though. It was not only his career that might suffer, it was also his appetite to serve, which had continued to grow with the years. It had become more and more entwined with his own ambition. What had happened to him is what happens to many men when they reach the top of the ladder: they are so close to their divinity that they begin to confuse themselves with it, not without reason: a prince serves himself by serving his kingdom. At the outset of his career, when Iakov used to think, 'It's my country, it's my Party', he felt that he belonged to them: now the possessive had imperceptibly changed sides, it was they who seemed almost to belong to him. At his position in the hierarchy to abandon an operation that he believed to be correct and even essential for the future of the Party was not only to sacrifice himself, it was an act of sabotage. Never mind! Abdulrakhmanov (Pitman generally used the term 'my benefactor' when he thought about him) deserved unswerving fidelity. If he died, it would be a different matter: death dissolves even marriage. In such an emancipation there would be some compensation for what would be the irreparable loss of such a master, but, for the moment, it was not fitting to think of such things.

The computer, questioned several times, had always come up with the name Gaverin and there could be no question of disobeying the computer. Nevertheless Pitman was apprehensive at meeting the man, for he knew that he had reached the ultimate stage of unhappiness, and Pitman hated unhappiness.

Arseni Egorich Gaverin was born just after the civil war, the posthumous son of an officer liquidated in the prisons of the régime. His mother had died of starvation when he was ten. Having joined the Red Army, he took the first opportunity to surrender to the Germans, determined to kill as many Bolsheviks as possible. In the grey-green uniform he had a distinguished career: at twenty he commanded a company. When defeat came Gaverin surrendered with his men to the British, because a colonel, with a stammer and an Oxford accent, promised them political asylum. The moustachioed Cossacks hesitated, but Gaverin told them: 'It's the promise of a king, my children, and kings keep their word.' Shortly afterwards, he was disarmed by the same British and handed over with the same men to Uncle Joe. He expected to be shot, and recognized that he could hardly expect anything else. He was condemned to twenty-five years forced labour and, with his courage still intact, he had tried to escape, which earned him fifteen years more. So, all of a sudden, this valiant man cracked. Hysterical at first, he was treated in the disciplinary cell. He then pestered camp commandants for jobs as an informer, quite ready to do anything to alleviate his situation. The good will that he put into his political re-education had brought him some improvement in conditions, but no reduction in penalty, and his health had not stood up to the life of the camps, even with the privileges he enjoyed. He was now fifty-nine, with four more years 'to do', but according to the doctors who, for what reason he did not know, had come to examine him, it was unlikely that he would serve the full term that he had so richly deserved: he would no doubt die before regaining his freedom.

From the very beginning of Operation Pskov, Gaverin had been taken out of his Siberian camp and thrown into the prison at Lefortovo. He expected to be used as a stool-pigeon again, but nothing of the kind was asked of him. For years he had believed in some miracle that would set him free: a new world war, a revolution in Russia, an invasion from Mars, anything; now he had exhausted all his hopes; he knew that the worst is always certain; when he was visited in his cell, he imagined that it was to be accused of some new attempt at escape. He clung to his bunk: 'I like it here. I won't leave.'

He had to be dragged by force to the curtained mini-bus that awaited him. A child dragged away from his mother could not have been more terrified than Gaverin as he left the lugubrious prison that had nets stretched between the storeys. The mirrors and gilt of Rostopchin House did not reassure him. In any case, he thought that the imagination of the Geebee was quite capable of exceeding his own where horror was concerned.

'You speak French, I think, Monsieur Gaverin?' Pitman asked him, in that language, no doubt in order to set up between that man, who had been deprived of his humanity, and himself, who had remained so human, a useful barrier to their mutual shyness.

'Certainly I speak French.'

His mother had taught him French while he was still a child, 'in case things ever get back to what they used to be.' In his camp, anonymous donors had sent him books. He had taught French to several prisoners and to the family of one of his commandants. He rolled his 'rs' in the old way, whereas Pitman did not, but his pronunciation was almost perfect.

'Monsieur Gaverin, I have asked you to come and see me,' Pitman continued slowly—it was rather he who had lost the practice of the spoken language—'because we may be able to help one another. You have committed serious crimes, you have repented of them and have almost completed your expiation: you have only four more years' punishment left. I think that, if you agreed to help us out, we might well be able to settle this matter with the Ministry of Justice. But I think I ought to warn you that we will be appealing to your intelligence and to your devotion to your Soviet fatherland.'

Instead of the miracle in which he no longer believed, Gaverin suspected a trap.

'I'm at the service of the fatherland, but I have no complaints to make. If it's about the last hunger strike, I was against it. Everybody will tell you that.'

'Monsieur Gaverin, have I reproached you with anything? It's simply that, on the one hand, your knowledge of French and, on the other, a certain interest that you have shown for reactionary political ideas . . .'

'Comrade, that was forty years ago. I'm a reformed character. I am now a convinced Marxist-Leninist.'

It was odd, these two Russians conversing in bookish, rather stilted French beneath the chandeliers of Rostopchin House.

Pitman became even more conciliatory.

'I know, Monsieur Gaverin, but you see, during the years you spent in the Nazi army, you had an opportunity of reading, of making contacts with . . .'

'But I've paid for all that!' cried the prisoner, thrusting back his usually bowed shoulders and rising to his full Don Quixote height. 'I have paid for that! Thirty-six years of my life! Have pity on me!'

Pitman suddenly slipped into Russian. The prisoner's terror was beginning to affect him.

'Calm yourself, calm yourself, Arseni Egorich. Nobody's talking about the past. All I'm asking you to do is to help me to shorten the time still left to you to suffer. If you accept my proposition you won't even go back to Lefortovo.'

'I wasn't badly off there,' Gaverin whimpered. 'And don't make out I'm saying what I'm not saying. I wasn't badly off at the camp either. Send me back to the camp. Four years are soon over. I know I signed an appeal for clemency. It was stupid of me. One must know how to pardon stupidity.'

So Russian, so unSoviet, that word 'pardon'.

'But we did pardon you, Arseni Egorich, long ago. It's just this devilish legal system. If we can't show that you're employed by us, do you know what awaits you at the end of your term? Deportation to some Kirghizistan or other. No medical treatment, and you're a sick man! How would you earn your living . . .?'

He kept his sympathetic eyes on Gaverin and allowed these new terrors to penetrate his intelligence.

'Of course, if you prefer to run the risks of such an exile, you are free . . . I mean: free to choose them. What I had in mind for you was rather . . . It may seem incredible to you, but I swear to you that I have the power to keep my promises . . . It was rather the French Riviera, a little villa at Nice, the sea, the sun . . . You no longer have any family ties in the Soviet Union, I think? And, as you know, the French are very hospitable people. I know them. They are full of *joie de vivre*. Anyway, there are a lot of émigrés over there and quite a few even from what is called the first emigration. You would feel quite at home. Especially at Nice: they're all princes, counts . . .'

Pitman had not mentioned money—on purpose. What could figures mean to a man who had probably not spent a hundred roubles in his life?

Lev Aronovich Zellman, a small man afflicted by a slight harelip, had spent fifteen years in what is now called the Gulag, or, put more simply, forced labour, for anti-Soviet propaganda. 'I criticized the penal system; I was given the opportunity to check my ideas: it's understandable,' he said, with a contemplative smile. He felt hardly any bitterness; in fact, he was grateful to the régime for releasing him on such easy terms. He reasoned thus:

'After all, human life has become longer, if not gayer. With a little luck, fifteen years is only one-fifth of the time allocated to me by the Supreme Praesidium, I don't mean the earthly one, but the other, if it exists. What is a fifth? Less than five hours a day and again, in the camp, I slept my full eight hours: it would not be fair therefore to subtract those five hours from my waking time. A third of that fifth must be counted as sleep. Out of my conscious life, therefore, I would have lost only three and a half hours a day. And the twenty years still left to me to live are no longer mortgaged, since I have paid my debt in advance! Really I would be very ungrateful to complain.'

This humility and this humour—is it not significant that the two words seem to have the same root?—had saved him. He had come through hell scorched, but not burnt. However, when the possibility of emigrating was offered him, he had decided to take advantage of it. 'It is not,' he said, 'that I do not love Russia. I do love it, and I can't see myself sweating my guts out in a kibbutz: I have got too used to the climate of Vorkuta. But if I stay here, how will I ever be sure that one fine day they won't send me back to Vorkuta? Well, thank you very much, but I can do without that. Fifteen years is instructive, but it's quite enough.'

He had asked for exit visas for himself and his wife, who had waited for him for fifteen years. Three years had already gone by. There was always some bit of paper missing. The ill-will of the authorities was flagrant; Lev Aronovich insisted, gently and obstinately, convinced that one day he would wear down the official resistance, 'as a mouse nibbles at a cable,' said this modest, but stubborn little man.

He was wrong. The cable had not been laid inadvertently or as a matter of routine, and it would hold until the day when Directorate A gave the order to remove it: it would then disappear as if by magic.

One autumn day, Lev Aronovich was summoned to an address 'which he had not yet attended'. Strange: he thought he had queued up in every administrative department that had the remotest connection with his problem. Stranger still, this time there was no queue. An orderly led him into an office like the ones to be seen in historical films: rugs, chandeliers, mouldings. Of course, the inevitable portrait hung on the wall. Zellman joked with himself: 'After all the time he's been hanging everywhere, they still haven't managed to strangle him!' And he added: 'So I'm in a service dependent on the Geebee. Be careful, Lev Aronovich, don't put your foot in it.'

A man of Zellman's age, about fifty-five, plump and

benevolent-seeming behind his small spectacles, smiled from behind a minister's table. A short round nose gave this Pickwickian face an even more innocent, almost childish expression.

'Lev Aronovich Zellman?'

'Present, Comrade General!'

Zellman managed to hold himself in a pose somewhere between standing to attention and being about to kneel. He had no idea of the rank of this dignitary: he judged his seniority by his desk. The dignitary became even more affable.

'Let's not be so official, Lev Aronovich. I am called simply Iakov Moiseich, and I have the very pleasant duty to inform you that your request for emigration has been granted.'

Zellman wanted to express his gratitude while concealing his unbounded joy. He began to splutter. The dignitary saved him from embarrassment by gently cutting him short.

'I didn't want to keep you on tenterhooks, Lev Aronovich: that's why I told you the most important thing first. Still we must have a little talk. Do sit down in that chair . . . The country you have put down under the heading "Destination" is Israel. But, between you and me, I don't think that's where you really intend to go: the climate wouldn't suit you at all.' (Zellman was seized with panic: 'My little joke! Who repeated it?') 'Anyway, you don't speak Hebrew and, at our age, learning a new language . . . is difficult. But you speak French. France would be an excellent refuge for you.'

Out of prudence, Zellman did not answer. It was indeed in France that he hoped to end up.

'And you want your wife, Lizaveta Grigorievna, to go with you, of course? Well! There we do have a bit of a problem. Her visa has not yet been granted.'

Zellman had concealed his joy; he now tried to conceal his despair. If Lizaveta could not go, he would stay.

'However,' continued the good general (supposing that he were a general and good), 'I'm sure with a little understanding on both sides we can arrange that. You're a free man, Lev Aronovich, and it would be absurd to keep you by force in a country of which you must have bad memories. You might be tempted to fall back into your old ways and consequently expose yourself to the same unpleasantnesses. No, no, we can't have a repetition of those misunderstandings.'

Zellman now tried to conceal the terror that was taking hold of him: the threat was clear.

'I give you my word of honour, Lev Aronovich,' the dignitary went on, still smiling, 'in a year at most, and more likely within three months, you will be reunited with Lizaveta Grigorievna in a small, but comfortable apartment under the roofs of Paris.'

Half-an-hour later, Lev Aronovich was shaking Iakov Moiseich's hand with immense relief. He was really not being asked for very much: to tell the truth on one precise point without exposing anyone to serious punishment, in such a way as to be of service both to Russia, that he really did love, and to France, whose hospitality he hoped to solicit.

Lizaveta Grigorievna did not disapprove of the deal that her husband had made with the Geebee, but she was worried at first at the idea of his leaving alone: 'And what if they keep me here?'

He stroked her hair, her pepper-and-salt hair, which she dyed red: 'Who would need you, old woman? You know very well that I'm the only one who loves you.'

He kissed her tenderly. She packed his small suitcase and next day, as if by a wave of a magic wand, he landed in Paris.

'Monsieur,' said Marguerite, in her steady voice, 'a M. Kurnosov would like to speak to you.'

'Is this some sort of joke?'

'I don't know, Monsieur.'

Marguerite tended to take things literally.

For the past two weeks, since *The Russian Truth* had come out, all kinds of people had made calls to the literary agent who had brought off the masterly coup of getting Iron Mask's entire manuscript out of the Leningrad Special Hospital. Grucci had telephoned from Rome, beside himself with fury, accusing him of patent theft. Some authorities were anxious to know what contacts enabled M. Psar to make the USSR look so ridiculous. There were specialists who were very interested in the network of exfiltration: could it be used again? Foreign publishers bandied figures around. Journalists demanded details concerning the 'human' side of the adventure. Old émigrés took up positions. Dissidents protested against the use of their names on the jacket. Lawyers offered their services. Madmen made threats. Sceptics thought they had fathomed the mystery: 'Monsieur Psar, take off your mask, which is not made of iron; admit that you are the true author of *The Russian Truth*.' The name of the unfortunate assassin Kurnosov was, of course, on everyone's lips. On the whole the Parisian intelligentsia had decreed that the author of the book and the author of the assassination attempt could not be the same person for the simple reason that the intelligentsia would have felt dishonoured if it had thought like everybody else and, on the contrary, everybody else believed that Kurnosov was Iron Mask, just as Ian Fleming was James Bond.

'Put him through.'

'May I speak to Aleksandr Dmitrich Psar?' Kurnosov spoke in French, with a Russian accent.

'Speaking.'

'It's me, Kurnosov. I'm at the airport.'

'What Kurnosov? Which airport?'

'Mikhail Leontich. Who do you think? The very same. Airport? Are there several then?'

'Where have you come from?'

'From our mother Moscow.'

'It'll be Roissy, then. Are you at Roissy?'

'I'm in an office of . . .' someone must have whispered to him. 'Of the airport police.'

'I'll come at once.'

As he left, he said to Marguerite: 'I don't know what this story is all about. I'll rely on your complete discretion, of course.'

'Oh, Monsieur!'

From a café he rang a number that had been given him for extreme emergencies.

'Get me Ivan.'

'He isn't here,' said a prudent voice. 'Who is it?'

'*Kobel.*'

This was Aleksandr's code name, as opposed to his pseudonym, which he did not even know.

'He has left a message for you: "Everything is in order." '

'Tell him I want to see him, this evening at the usual place.'

The Omega sped towards Roissy. It was drizzling; the tyres hissed over the damp surface.

'Monsieur Psar? This way, please.'

There were two men in a small office: the policeman, with humourless eyes, wearing a three-piece suit and a toothbrush moustache, and the Russian, a tall, tubercular crow, unshaven, in a bright blue suit, which hung on him as if he were a coatstand.

'I don't think I've ever seen such a scrawny man,' thought Psar.

He looked with intense curiosity at the large ashen face, the almost exposed bones, the hair plastered down with brilliantine, which did not keep it down, but petrified it in its disorder. He wanted to ask at once: 'Are you really the author?' The real Kurnosov, he was convinced, had been pushing up the daisies for ten years. He introduced himself.

'Psar.'

'And I . . . I'm Kurnosov,' said the other man.

'Monsieur Kurnosov says he's the author of *The Russian Truth,* which you published,' said the policeman. 'Would you confirm that?'

According to Ivan Ivanich, 'everything was in order.'

'I've never met M. Kurnosov. Would you allow me to ask him a few questions?'

'Yes, but in French, if you don't mind.'

'So you are Kurnosov?'

'Yes I am. Monsieur has my passport.'

The policeman held out the small brownish-red book. Aleksandr had an almost identical one in the embassy safe: he had got someone to show it to him.

Mikhail Leontich Kurnosov. Soviet citizen of Russian nationality, born at Kostroma (R.S.F.S.R.) 4 June 1926 . . . The photograph was certainly that of the man with the sunken cheeks, hollow temples and haggard eyes.

'This passport was delivered yesterday.'

'Yes,' said Kurnosov. 'They gave it to me yesterday. If you'll allow me?'

There was a stamp on one of the pages. It said, in Russian: 'Passport delivered to serve as international identification; valid to leave the territory of the USSR; not valid to return to the territory of the USSR.'

'You've been stripped of your nationality.'

'Not yet. It's just that I can't go back.'

'Well, then, so you're the author of the book?'

Kurnosov smiled timidly, like someone who had forgotten how to smile. His mouth opened like that of a pike, to reveal a frightful set of teeth, blackened, decayed, with several gaps and metal fillings. 'It's odd how little his name suits him!' thought Aleksandr. *Kurnosov* means: 'with a turned up nose.'

'That's me.'

For Aleksandr, the author of *The Russian Truth* could only be an officer of the Geebee.

'But you are also . . .'

'The Anonymous Prisoner of Cell Triple Zero, Iron Mask, all that, yes. I've seen the papers. They showed them to me before . . .'—he stumbled on the word—'expelling me.'

'They expelled you? Why?'

'They said I wasn't worthy to breathe the Soviet air.'

Aleksandr, remembering that he was 'a man of the right', smiled ironically.

'They like their big words, don't they? It's a Jacobin vice—and therefore a Bolshevik one. All right. I'm very glad to meet you. You know, I suppose, that you're a rich man, or nearly?'

He shook the hand of the consumptive skeleton. Was this man a comrade or an enemy? As if he were answering that very question, Kurnosov said:

'In fact I'm a completely confused man, I've just spent ten years in a lunatic asylum, and I'm not quite certain whether they haven't managed to drive me mad. Besides I don't know how you manage to live here in the West. It seems you're free. That must be like standing on top of a skyscraper, without a parapet.'

'You'll soon get used to it. Do you intend to ask for political asylum?'

'Monsieur Kurnosov has already asked for it,' the policeman interrupted. 'I've rung through to headquarters. I don't foresee any particular difficulties, but it might take a little time. Meanwhile, we're quite ready to give M. Kurnosov a tourist visa. We just wanted to be sure that it wasn't a case of mistaken identity. A writer of M. Kurnosov's importance'—he made a bow—'is most welcome to our country.'

'France and Russia are the only countries in the world where a writer is an important man,' said Psar.

'Monsieur Psar,' said the policeman, 'you are well known: we know where we can get hold of you. May I consider that you are responsible for Monsieur Kurnosov until the situation is regularized?'

'Of course. Have you any luggage, Mikhail Leontich?'

'Just this old bag, nothing more.'

They had no sooner left the office than Aleksandr asked the other question that he had been dying to ask all along: 'And the Brezhnev business? Is it true? Did you really shoot at him?'

After some hesitation, as if the admission were true, but difficult to make, he said: 'I tried.'

Aleksandr's interest in shooting was aroused:

'What with?'

'An AK-47.'

'What's that?'

'A Kalashnikov: haven't you heard of it?'

'Of course. What calibre is it?'

'7.62. Effective range: 400 metres.'

'How many in the magazine?'

'Thirty. And you can fire six hundred rounds a minute.'

Aleksandr did not repress a whistle of admiration.

The next two hours were very strange. Aleksandr had no way of knowing whether this man was Kurnosov, the tyrannicide, Iron Mask, author of *The Russian Truth*, an agent of the Geebee, whether he was all of those things at once or something else. When questioned about it, he spoke intelligently about 'his book' and of the ideas expressed in it; he had no difficulty in admitting that the officers who had taken him from his cell and pushed him on to a plane had also advised him to contact Psar as soon as he arrived in the West; he did not seem to want to talk about it. His main concern was to understand how he was to live in a free country.

'One lives as one lives.'

'No. Explain to me how one lives.'

He had quite erroneous ideas concerning the functioning of capitalism and of the three powers. He was sorry to learn that most well-off people in the West were no longer, so to speak, served: 'But, you, you have at least a manservant?'

'No. The caretaker's wife comes and does the cleaning once a week.'

When he realized that there were often strikes in France, even by those in public service, he was scandalized: 'If you shot one out of ten of them—not the leaders, just at random! —it would calm the others down,' he said.

He was surprised to see children in the streets: 'They ought to be at school. And why don't they wear uniform?'

He wanted to visit a big store. Aleksandr took him to the Galeries Lafayette. Red patches lit up on the sickly man's cheeks: 'All that's to trick everyone, isn't it? You can't buy anything, can you?'

To prove the contrary, Aleksandr immediately bought him a fine fox fur hat: 'If you don't have a fur hat the French will never believe you've come from Moscow.'

Kurnosov was not impressed.

'Yes, we've got plenty of that rubbish, I can assure you.'

'But it isn't rubbish.'

'I wasn't born yesterday. If it was good fur, it wouldn't be on open sale.'

Aleksandr took him to Hermès, but he couldn't get him to drop that tone of superiority. It was worse at the Plaza-Athénée, where they had lunch. Kurnosov did not have the slightest idea how to behave at table, and he spoke to the *maîtres d'hôtel* in the tone of General Durakin speaking to his serfs. As for the décor: 'Not bad, not bad,' he declared, leaning back in his armchair. 'It's a bit like our Metro.'

Yet he came back again and again to the same question: how does one live here? He went into greater detail: do people own their own house? Do they work for a boss? How many hours do they work? How much do they earn? How much does he earn? What does a piece of bacon cost? And a pair of woollen underpants?

He was astonished at the crime figures.

'And you don't guillotine all those good-for-nothings?'

'The death penalty was abolished recently.'

Kurnosov sniggered, stuffing into his mouth a triangle of cheese impaled on his knife.

'In our country, they shoot people for economic crimes. If you make too much profit, then you get twelve bullets in your hide.'

Aleksandr who, deep down, could see no objection to getting rid of criminals of any kind, was nevertheless irritated by so much self-satisfaction.

'You seem to think everything is fine in the Soviet Union. All you have to do is repent of your errors and they might take you back. You could publish a second book, *The Russian Krivda*.'

Fourveret, steadfast in the face of adversity, who found *The Russian Truth* less shocking since it was selling so well, gave its author his accolade.

'I am happy to welcome you to our country, my dear Sir. We have worked well on your behalf: I hope you will be pleased. Our friend Psaaar has defended your interests valiantly. Unfortunately, when we got some particularly good news, some favourable article, praise from some important person, we thought of you, the source of all this triumph, locked up in your psychiatric cell, and our hearts bled for you. Now that you are here, free, our joy is complete.'

'How much will I make on this book?' Kurnosov asked.

And when he was told the figure, he asked: 'How much is that in roubles? What can you do with that amount of money? Where is it deposited in my name? What rate of interest do you get? What is the advance? Why is it so small?'

That evening, Aleksandr took him to Suresnes. A press conference was to take place the next day and it was vital that no journalist should get hold of Kurnosov before then.

Iron Mask found the apartment comfortable, though the ceilings a bit low. On the other hand, the electronic chess game seemed to hypnotize him. Aleksandr left him with the game, a bottle of 'single malt' whisky and a fine cut-glass tumbler.

'Did they let you drink in your hospital? If not, be careful: you'll make yourself ill. You don't look as well-fed as they said, and when the organism is weakened, whisky can have a terrible effect.'

Kurnosov was surprised.

'Just one bottle? Over there, Aleksandr Dmitrich, we drink pure alcohol and we're all the better for it.'

Jessica was as dark as an Indian. She had taken pills to tan more quickly on the yacht and now she was keeping up her tan under lamps.

'One day you'll have skin cancer, my fair lady,' Aleksandr said to her.

Ivan Ivanich had already arrived.

'So you've got the package? What do you think of the son-of-a-bitch?'

'If you Soviets are all like him, I'm staying here.'

They sat down side by side on the black and white striped sofa.

'Now: who is he?'

'Kurnosov.'

'The man who shot at Brezhnev?'

'The same.'

'And it's really he who wrote *The Russian Truth*?'

'Who else?'

'Why wasn't I warned of his arrival?'

'So that you really would look surprised. And, anyway, you know, for some time now, you've been criticising the orders you've been given . . . So I suppose Comrade Pitman wanted to present you with a *fait accompli*.'

'And we've really expelled this Kurnosov?'

'It would seem so.'

'What for?'

'To give the dissidents a good scorching.'

'Have you got any new instructions for me?'

'Yes. You must do whatever Kurnosov wants.'

'And you want me to believe that he's not a colleague?'

Ivan Ivanich laughed.

'He, a colleague? I don't think we've any colleagues as scrawny as him, Sashenka!'

'So you're still claiming that *The Russian Truth* was not cooked up by us?'

'Of course not! Shall I tell you the whole story? When Kurnosov shot at Brezhnev and was caught, he was interrogated. He seemed a bit cracked. So he was packed off to the psychiatrists. The psychiatrists didn't find that he was too round the bend, except that he had reactionary ideas and a whole non-Marxist political culture. So what was to be done? Shoot him in Red Square? That would have upset tender-hearted Westerners. Stick him in a camp? That didn't seem commensurate with his crime. So Comrade Stalagmite, of your Directorate, came on the scene: "If you don't want him, give him to me. I'll find some use for him sooner or later. I won't hurt him. I'll just put him away, for a rainy day, as you might say." Kurnosov didn't seem dangerous, he was quiet, he simply asked for a pen, ink and paper. And he began to scribble away like mad. He imagined that by writing one page on top of another, with observations of no interest whatsoever on top, he could hide what was underneath. And he hid them inside his television set. But you can imagine that the cell was stuffed with cameras. Stalagmite had sensed genius in that fellow and he was meaning to exploit it to the full. Just think: a failed assassin with reactionary ideas! It's worth its weight in gold. A conquering doctrine like ours needs opposition to feed on, to make progress. And at home, you know, we are not noted for opposition—Ilich and Visarionovich saw to that. So they watched Kurnosov like the apple of their eye. He was given two nurses: they were both, of course, colleagues. At night, one of them took him out for exercise in the yard and, while they counted the stars together, the other one photocopied the contents of the television set. Then a specialist recopied the new pages, imitating the prisoner's handwriting, and an officer of your Directorate, passing himself off as one of the nurses, exfiltrated selected passages.'

'Why?'

'To prepare for what we are doing today.'

'And what are we doing today?'

'I've already told you: wringing the necks of the dissidents, one and all.'

'But, wait a minute: now Kurnosov knows that it was the Geebee that exfiltrated pages from his book. He knows that he took no one in . . .'

'Of course; we told him that when we showed him the papers. Up till then, he didn't know that his book had come out. He still imagined that there was only one copy hidden in his television set. But there's no point in telling him that. The last thing he wants is to be suspected of complicity with us. Even involuntary complicity. And remember: for him, you're a Westerner like any other, which means that he won't trust you.'

'How long have you known all this?'

'I was given his curriculars yesterday when I was told that he was going to be freed.'

'Wouldn't it have been simpler to send one of our officers? Once Kurnosov's been given political asylum, we'll no longer be able to manipulate him.'

Ivan Ivanich sighed.

'What a pain you are! And you're the one that belongs to the Directorate of the subtle and ingenious? We don't need to manipulate him. We know his ideas better than he does himself. We know by heart what he's going to say. If we'd sent one of our own officers, how would we have got him back afterwards? Why, he's the genuine article. He inspires confidence. Later we'll simply dump him. What risk is there? All we want from him is to be sincere, to tell the truth, his truth. And there's something else, Aleksandr Dmitrich, which perhaps I shouldn't mention to you: it has been known for one of our officers to change sides. If only for religious reasons, like the prototype of that Popov whose story you showed me. Suppose our comrade declared: I am Major Such-and-Such, I never fired at Brezhnev, I did not write *The Russian Truth*, but I'll now write my memoirs as an officer of the Geebee. We'd look pretty silly, wouldn't we? Kurnosov can't turn against us: he's already against us and that's why he's useful to us.'

Aleksandr was not entirely convinced. It seemed to him that there was a flaw in Ivan Ivanich's argument. And, anyway, did the confusion into which the dissidents had been thrown justify so complicated an operation and the use of a man who, according to Ivan Ivanich himself, 'was worth his weight in gold'? But there was nothing more to be got out of the case-officer.

'I'm warning you that he'll be getting his royalties. I can't stop it.'

'Don't.'

Curious. Usually the Geebee made it a point of honour to grab any money paid to its agents. But after all, Kurnosov was not an agent; perhaps the Directorate had decided that he deserved to keep what he had earned by his talent. The system had a certain respect for legality. Aleksandr left after writing out an official complaint: he should have been warned of Kurnosov's arrival in time and even consulted on the matter; if he went on being treated as a subordinate officer, he disclaimed all responsibility for the consequences of actions in which he was called upon to take part.

Next day, a hundred or so Parisian and provincial journalists were gathered together between the elegantly faded gilt panelled walls of the Lux publishing house. A television cameraman tramped around carrying his apparatus on his shoulder like a bazooka. Sweating photographers dragged their paraphernalia around, getting their straps tangled and swearing with an alarming lack of imagination. The flood-lamps went on and off, transforming colours and perspectives. There were not enough chairs: some journalists had to stand, leaning against the wall; others sat on the floor, crossed legged or American-style, legs streched out, and cursed the photographers who trod on their ankles. A thicket of microphones bristled around the small table, behind which the Anonymous Prisoner would sit. 'What do you think he looks like, Iron Mask?'—'Was it really him who shot at Brezhnev?'

They came in: first Fourveret, austere and smiling at once, followed by Psar, with a concentrated, thoughtful look, containing his ebullience, and lastly the man everyone had come to see, the Prisoner without name, in his new blue Soviet suit, with the tie that Aleksandr had chosen for him, not perhaps without irony, at Hermès.

Everyone got up together—for a better view, but also out

of respect. The man had spent ten years in one of those psychiatric prisons the mere mention of which sends shudders down one's spine. What injections of sulphur, what mysterious treatments had he been subjected to? Was he still in his right mind? And earlier, in the first hours after the assassination attempt (assuming it was Kurnosov), what nights he must have spent in the cellars of the Lubianka? Even if he had not been tortured, were not ten years of solitary confinement horrifying enough? We no longer know how to respect a noble deed, but we still bow before suffering. The applause broke out, rose in volume and intensity and went on and on. In the end Fourveret called for silence by raising his arms in a gesture almost reminiscent of de Gaulle.

'Ladies and gentlemen, friends, sisters, brothers, comrades, yes, I feel that we are all comrades today . . . I have the honour . . . Yes, honour . . . to present to you the author of *The Russian Truth*, the Anonymous Prisoner, though he will not remain anonymous for long. The pleasant task of revealing his name I shall leave to that great discoverer of genius, whose friendship I have the honour to enjoy . . . My dear Psaaar, can you get through? Mind people's hands—mind that charming young lady—I'm afraid I don't remember your name. Ah, yes! Denise Esclaffier, of *L'Alsacien patriote*. There are so many of us here, it gives me great joy to see so many people of good will and intelligence gathered here together against hypocrisy and persecution, it is such a pleasure, in such cases, to have too little room . . .' (He babbled on with great skill.) 'Ladies and gentlemen: Aleksandr Psaaaaar!'

Aleksandr knew how to address an audience. He knew how to stand motionless for a few moments, gradually fill himself with what he was going to say; his eyes would remain vacant, then suddenly focus on the audience, and on a few faces in particular; slowly he would turn his head, like the turret of a battleship; then, finally, he would inhale deeply so that the rhythm of his breathing might prepare for the moment when the first sentence would burst out. In a rather low voice he said:

'Let me present . . .' Then he pretended to reject one after another a number of qualifications, terms of praise, dithyrambs, periphrases, perhaps restrictions and, opting in the end for simplicity, which alone was worthy of such a subject, he stretched out his arm and cried: 'Mikhail . . . Leontich . . . KURNOSOV!'

At the first name of Mikhail a ripple of expectation had already run through the audience, at the patronymic (not that it was recognized, but under the effect created by Psar's voice) the murmur grew in volume, then, at the surname the noise became a roar. This author of a violently controversial book really had held an offensive weapon in his hands, had really shot at the most powerful man in the world. That certainly was copy!

Before this explosion, Aleksandr smiled and made a rather charming gesture of powerlessness, as if to say, 'What can I tell you? You know most of it already.' He withdrew modestly.

Kurnosov remained there, confronting the applause and shouts, his arms hanging rather loose from his body, his head rather bowed, tall, but emaciated, his chest as tubercular, his complexion as green, his cheeks as haggard as could be wished. One sensed that he was not intimidated, but that he wanted to seem a little so, out of politeness: the Soviets are used to public meetings. Lastly, he moved sideways towards the table, and that was enough to silence the room.

'I should like to share with you a few thoughts.'

This took people by surprise. They thought they were there to ask him questions and here he was, pulling out of his inside pocket a bundle of notes, thin sheets of paper covered with thin, blue, sloping handwriting.

Kurnosov launched into a savage attack on the Soviet Union, the camps, the prisons, the standard of living. Such a régime was doomed to collapse in the near future. Solzhenitsyn was a god and the late lamented Amalrik a prophet.

Aleksandr listened to the precise, old-fashioned voice chant in a minor key the French of Dmitri Aleksandrovich and the men of his generation, a French taught by governesses educated in the best convent schools in France, then reshaped by a society that bound itself within this foreign language as it did within corsets, stiff collars and moustache-trainers. 'At least they might have warned me that he'd been allowed to bring out notes.' For some time now the Directorate had not shown him proper consideration and he felt each fresh neglect like a *banderilla*. He did not know that his (administrative) execution had already begun.

When he had finished denigrating the Soviet régime, Kurnosov turned on the West: heedlessness, egoism, corruption, everything displeased him. Once more he quoted Solzhenitsyn and threw in Bukovsky. The days of the West were numbered. 'For you, ladies and gentlemen, it is one minute to midnight.'

The audience was beginning to weary of him: they had heard all this already and one must be very careful not to repeat anything to Parisians that they have not understood first time round; if they have understood it, that is different: they have a weakness for refrains.

Kurnosov went on reading apparently unaware of the disappointment; there was strength in that very obliviousness. Aleksandr stood nervously consulting his watch the whole time. Fourveret had let his fine head roll on to his right shoulder as if to say both 'I'm undergoing martyrdom' and 'Who was right?' A journalist got up.

'Excuse me interrupting you, Monsieur Kurnosov, but it seems to me that you are contradicting yourself: you say that the USSR is about to collapse and that the West is rotten. How do you reconcile the two?'

Kurnosov raised an impatient hand—one does not interrupt the orator—and went on imperturbably. But, three minutes later, without his having changed his tone, the ballpoint-pens were unclipped and back at work, scribbling notes.

'However,' Kurnosov read, 'I have to recognize that, however just the ideas of the dissidents whom I have quoted, those men themselves are corrupt, as much as, if not more than their acolytes and rivals, those who scorn them and those who flatter them.'

Everyone in that audience had heard some gossip about one or another of the dissidents, but no one had ever witnessed a mass execution like the one that followed; not a single well-known name escaped the massacre. Not a single cellist, dancer, singer, sculptor, chess player, not to mention, of course, poets, novelists, trade unionists, logicians, or those whose sole exploit consisted in providing the model for some character in a novel. Neither the dissidents within the USSR, nor the survivors of the early emigration were spared.

A, recited Kurnosov, falsified his name and patronymic, he claimed to be Orthodox, but he married his god-daughter. The notoriety of B serves as a snare to the dissidents who gather around him and are therefore immediately picked up by the 'organs'; this trick has been going on for so long that one wonders whether the principal actor concerned is not simply on the payroll. C set up a support fund for the victims of the régime, off which his closest collaborators live very comfortably. D's career has been built on a series of denunciations and he finally chose exile only because, despite all his work for the régime, he did not get the chair he coveted. E spent so many years in a camp because he criticized Stalin for excessive moderation. The life of F has been marked by suicides: three of his associates so far have hanged themselves on his account. G is a pornographer, H an alcoholic, I a lesbian, J a stoolpigeon, K speculates in icons, L deals in dubious manuscripts. Impenitent Marxists were no better treated: M is an informer, N a homosexual. Taken separately none of these accusations would have shocked this ultra-blasé audience. But the accumulation created a distinct sense of unease.

It lasted for three-quarters of an hour. Kurnosov read slowly, like a meticulous teacher, so that everybody had time to take down notes. And he provided names, first names, patronymics, lists of the facts imputed, dates. Aleksandr began to understand: of course, the cry would go up that he was an agent of the KGB, a wolf in the sheep-fold! But the damage would be done, the public always has a good memory for dirt. Some journalists went out, perhaps to telephone, perhaps because they had had enough; but most of them stayed, and asked for more.

Kurnosov went on: 'Most of these men and women are in agreement on one point: they recognize that democracy pure and simple is impossible in the Soviet Union. But among the dissidents, note, there is not a single true democrat. They are all Marxists or reactionaries. And the interesting thing is that they are absolutely right!'

His way of speaking was totally unrhetorical, which gave his observations all the more eloquence.

He lauched into an exposition of the system that he advocated. It was the one already to be found implicitly in *The Russian Truth*: an acknowledged dictator; a system representative not of geographical regions, but of professions; a basic bureaucratic structure:

'One should not be afraid of the word *apparat*': yes, the *apparat* and the *apparatchiks* are necessary, but they must be in thrall to the nation, whereas the Party is in thrall to an ideology.'

Kurnosov was against universal suffrage; he recommended on the contrary a system of co-option which gave the élites their place in the sun. Freedom of the press was an outdated bourgeois notion. (The ballpoint-pens scribbled faster.) Freedom of thought was a relative concept since, in any case, most citizens let television think for them. Freedom of association had to be controlled: association for the good of the community, yes, but for the good of the sub-community, no. Human rights, maybe, but man's duties were even more important: the individual, he declared, using a formula that few of the journalists jotted down, may be regarded either as the more or less fortuitous fruit of a more or less random coitus—in which case why should one speak of rights?—or as the product of a society that guaranteed his livelihood, his security, his education and towards which he had obvious obligations.

The end of the speech came as a complete surprise—he had used none of the usual oratorical tricks to lead up to it. Kurnosov quite simply turned over the last sheet of paper and announced: 'That's it, I've finished.'

He added in Russian, as he folded up his papers: 'I'm not answering questions.'

Aleksandr leaned towards him: 'You can't do that here. You have to answer.'

Kurnosov calmly shook his head.

'Answer, for God's sake! What's come over you?'

Kurnosov got up. What could he do? Aleksandr turned to the audience: 'Monsieur Kurnosov is exhausted. With all he's been through . . . He asks you to excuse him.'

'I'm not exhausted at all, but I won't answer questions,' said Kurnosov, making his way to the exit under a barrage of flashbulbs. He stumbled, with an air of disgust over the outstretched legs of young women journalists in blue jeans and muttered: 'What decadence!'

In the small reception room, where drinks awaited the organizers, Aleksandr seized Kurnosov by the elbow: 'Where did you get all that vicious gossip? Did they bring it to you in your madhouse?'

Kurnosov looked at him in surprise: 'Do you imagine that they let me out for nothing?'

Aleksandr was beginning to see the operation more and more clearly. All the same! To sacrifice someone like Iron Mask in order to spread a few calumnies!

'Who are you working for?' he asked. 'Us or them?'

But who were 'us' and who 'them'?

Fourveret put a hand on his fore-arm.

'Don't bully my friend Kurnosov. When I think of all he's been through . . .'

He put a hand on his left breast.

When he opened his papers next morning, Aleksandr recognized at once that a quite different orchestra than his own had joined the dance, and he was relieved to see with what brio and ensemble they played. Apparently the Directorate still knew what it was doing. All that had happened so far had merely been a setting up of the target. Now the order to shoot had been given. It did not bother Aleksandr in the least to find himself in the firing line. He was a soldier, after all, and quite capable of heroically drawing the fire on to himself to save an encircled post. He also knew that in order to capsize a boat it has to be rocked from side to side. 'I don't know who my counterpart is, but he certainly knows his job,' he thought.

Etienne Depensier's article, which looked to Aleksandr like the work, if not of an influence agent, at least of a methodically-used sound box, set the tone of the symphony.

The article by the great journalist, whom the intelligentsia was pleased to regard as 'humanitarian and moderate', bore the title: 'We've got what we deserve.' The article went on:

M. Kurnosov's press conference came as a great surprise, but one wonders whether this surprise, which I shared, is not the result of the naïvety proper to liberal régimes, of the hypocrisy that characterises bourgeois society. In my own case, I will plead rather a certain lack of democratic vigilance.

No one of course can accuse me of indulgence towards the Stalinist and post-Stalinist régimes: this makes it all the easier for me to remark that our attachment to democratic values is on the decline. The pseudo-teaching of the pseudo-new pseudo-philosophers has invaded the columns of our newspapers and the windows of our bookshops; a reactionary splinter-group dares to call itself the New Right, and it is not countered by the spontaneous creation of a people's court to judge and condemn the gangsters who have grown like parasites on the indolent body of our intelligentsia; and we welcome with open arms men who, instead of taking part in the greatest revolution, that is to say, in the greatest hope of modern times, even if it entails putting it back on the democratic path when it strays off it, come and weep on our shoulders for the suffering they have endured. Well, gentlemen, one does not make an omelette without breaking eggs.

In essence, M. Kurnosov is saying this: We dissidents are all[and it was here that *Voivode* had at last authorized 'the obscene word' that, following Abdulrakhmanov's instructions, had been kept back until now] Fascists. Curiously, the indignation raised by this declaration was moderate. Some of my colleagues, for whose integrity and talent I have had regard, not only praised the book, but listened to the speech to the very end. This brings us to some rather severe thoughts. Let us be quite clear about it, however much it costs our fundamentally Republican, but nevertheless, middle-class conscience.

We have all preferred the glitter of the varied to the pure brightness of the certain.

I'm thinking in particular of a certain literary agent whose links with the extreme right are well known; of a certain publishing house which, after building up for itself a reputation in the defence of liberalism, has sunk into the commercial exploitation of reaction; of a certain critic, once an independent, estimable mind, and of the publication in which he has denatured himself and whose objectivity no longer seems to be the essential preoccupation, even if the word is still to be found on that publication's banner. I am also thinking of a certain voice that lays claim to impartiality, but which, nostalgic perhaps for a time of privilege, seems to base heaven knows what horrible hopes on the obscure forces of a still latent Fascism.

The *Quousque tandem Catilina* that we had to recite on the school bench is still valid, and I make this solemn warning to those who seem to find democracy indigestible: we demand tolerance, but not for the enemies of tolerance, freedom, but not for the enemies of freedom. The death penalty has been abolished for the sons of the people; for the enemies of the people, who, indeed, are such fierce advocates of it, the penalty might in all conscience be restored. I don't mean the odious death penalty decreed by eloquent judges in red robes, but the expeditious penalty decided on the spot by citizens with their sleeves rolled up.

M. Kurnosov admits that he is an assassin—a clumsy assassin, but an assassin all the same. He also admits that he has been in a psychiatric hospital—and no one has ever claimed that the Soviets keep in such institutions only men of sound mind. If M. Kurnosov is rabid, do we have to allow ourselves to be contaminated?

I appeal to public opinion. Let us carry out, my friends, a radical purging of our society and, above all, of that intelligentsia to which we are so proud to belong. Otherwise we shall fall once more into the most shameless Fascism.

And it will be our own fault.

The consequences of this article, supported by a dozen others in similar vein, were not slow in coming.

The board of directors of Lux held an emergency meeting and voted unanimously to retire M. Fourveret—though on generous terms. The editor of *Objectifs* asked M. José Ballandar, yes, the legendary Ballandar, to sell his prose elsewhere. Inevitable reductions in staff forced *L'Impartial* to deprive itself of the services of M. de Monthignies. This call to toe the line was obeyed. Almost all the Paris newspapers published editorials that would earn them certificates of civic sense from M. Etienne Depensier.

Aleksandr was witnessing, with some perplexity, the dismantling of his orchestra. 'And yet the Directorate seemed pleased enough with my sound-boxes. I suppose it must have others up its sleeve, other Ballandars, Fourverets, and de Montignies. In any case, one has to admit that the operation came off: those heads that have not yet rolled are retreating into their shoulders.'

Denunciation spread, became fashionable; everyone beat his breast—or rather his neighbour's. It became all the easier to denounce when no one died as a result. The Kurnosov incident allowed innumerable jealousies, innumerable stinking envies, to creep out from under the stone. At first only those who had a good word for *The Russian Truth* were suspect; soon even those who failed to speak ill of it also became so; and to be suspect in a Jacobin period was to be guilty. Into the places left vacant by the condemned, *Voivode*, of course, pushed his own sound-boxes like so many pawns.

Aleksandr then began to realize that the object of the operation was much wider than he had been led to believe, and also why he had been kept in the dark about its strategy: it was feared that he would hesitate to destroy his own work and his own reputation. 'They underestimate me,' he thought bitterly. But, after all, what did it matter? Soon, in a few weeks, he would be 'home'.

None of this bothered Kurnosov in the least.

'I want,' he said, 'to buy a house.'

Most of the dissidents want to buy a house. Aleksandr had

orders to keep Kurnosov happy, and the two men spent several days on the road, calling on provincial estate agents, for Iron Mask did not intend settling in Paris.

'I want a house with solid walls and railings all around it.'

'Haven't you spent enough time behind bars?'

'I want bars to defend me, not bars to keep me in.'

'What are you afraid of? They let you out. You've been given asylum.'

'You don't know them. They let me out to spread a whole lot of filth on the dissidents, but if I'm no longer useful to them, they could just as easily liquidate me. I don't want to make it any easier for them than I can. Anyway, the dissidents have it in for me too.'

'Doesn't your conscience trouble you, Mikhail Leontich, for speaking ill of the good in order to please the bad?'

'The good, the good! Have you noticed that all the dissidents come from the privileged class of Communist society? Most of them are frustrated oppressors. And not one of them has done what I have done—taken up arms against the régime!'

During these outings, Aleksandr tried to draw out Kurnosov about his past: 'Now you ought to write your autobiography.' Kurnosov replied: 'I'm a one-book man.' Or: 'My life isn't interesting.' Or: 'I'd like to spend what little time is left to me forgetting.' He had consulted doctors, who had found him to be in poor health, but not beyond recovery. He did not believe them: 'I'm a wounded old wolf.' It proved quite impossible to learn anything from him about his assassination attempt, about his youth, about the causes that had turned him into a rebel. He had a certain knowledge of politics that merely deepened his pessimism. 'Yet there is a programme in *The Russian Truth* and therefore a hope.' '*The Truth* is a book and I'm a man. Let's talk about money, shall we? Money is good: it's nourishing.'

And he began once again to calculate the mortgage he would have to take out to pay for his house, the interest he would get on his investments, the share of his income that would go in tax, how he would compensate for the effects of inflation.

These subjects interested Aleksandr very little, and he stared more and more at the landscape.

At the outset he was under the impression that the wounded old wolf wanted to set up house on the Côte d'Azur. 'No, there are too many people there. I don't want to see a single house from my windows.'

'You'll be more at risk,' Aleksandr objected.

'I'll have my hunting gun.'

Then they went off together exploring the Quercy, the Périgord, the Limousin. Aleksandr did not know France well. Gradually, he was getting more sensitive to the delicate variety of the landscape. He remembered Machado's words: God was young when he painted Spain, he was getting on when he modelled France. He was struck by the unchanging nature of the French mystery. The network of churches had been laid down on a pagan land, the network of roads had been stretched over a mosaic of forests and valleys and despite these superimposed abstractions, the soul of the country eluded the traveller.

He also noticed, as someone who had spent more time in museums than in the countryside, that the landscapes he saw belonged to various periods. It might be a stretch of pasture land in the late afternoon, shaded by majestic trees, with white cows standing motionless beneath a dappled sky pierced by the visible rays of an invisible sun: seventeenth century. Or it might be a stream in the morning, two hedges bordering a triangular field, a watermill, a light mist, an old, moss-covered wall, a roof garlanded with ampelopsis, perhaps the pink face of a child peeping over a wooden fence: eighteenth century. Or it might be a restored castle, washed by rain, the groins of its arches gleaming in the sunlight, the sides of its battlements shining like mirrors, ornamental gardens, orchards, sloping vineyards lying at its feet in rectilinear claws, beanpoles arranged in lines, over the whole scene a sky of deep, cold blue, and Aleksandr, not so much because of the castle, but rather because of the straightness and angularity of the furrows and poles, felt transported to the Middle Ages. Autumnal foliage rising behind the tops of a stone wall, with, at the end of a path overgrown with grass, a stone vase covered with verdigris, standing on a balustrade in need of repair, gave him the poignant feeling of the romantic period to which he had always been particularly attached, perhaps because that period was Russia's golden age, perhaps for more personal reasons: we contain within ourselves all the centuries that have preceded us, but we have more affinities with some than with others.

He was surprised by the beauty of the houses he visited and by the state they were in: some had little more than walls and chimneys; others, on the contrary, had been entirely restored—complete with wall-to-wall carpeting, loggias and deep-freezes—but had lost their souls. Until now he had not known that houses have souls. Moreover, he realized that he knew very few real houses: a few small country houses, a few 'second homes' and above all apartments. He thought he had learnt something important when he discovered that in the middle of the twentieth century not all the French lived in an ant-hill.

'I'd better get back or I'll be tempted to buy a house myself.'

His thoughts began to dwell on balconies, log fires, dogs under the table, chicken runs, dovecotes and horses. Perhaps he was rebuilding his grandfather's estate that his father had told him about: 'We used to pull out the feathers from a cockerel, stick them in our heads and play at Indians. We picked cucumbers in the beds and we tied our girl cousins to the torture stake . . .'

Kurnosov found only one house entirely surrounded by railings, but it was enormous and situated in the middle of a park-jungle that he would not have known what to do with. And he was in a hurry. So he contented himself with a small fortress, with a small garden, surrounded by a brick wall. 'I'll set broken glass on top,' said Kurnosov. He made enquiries concerning the possibility of reinforcing the door and shutters. He was disappointed to learn that he could not have possession at once, and signed the contract the same day. That evening, he took Aleksandr out to dinner in the best restaurant in Limoges and insisted on ordering whatever happened to be the most expensive items on the menu and wine list. This produced a rather surprising mixture of freshly-made foies-gras, Clos-de-Vougeot and lobster, but the Anonymous Prisoner derived great satisfaction from regaling his guide in this style.

'I'm sorry I didn't think of bringing you a present,' he said. 'Perhaps an old icon. If I'd asked for one, surely they'd have let me bring out an icon.'

In Paris, a new movement was beginning.

The small section of opinion that was not hostile to Kurnosov was regrouping. This was easy enough, since they were nonconformists of the so-called extreme right who already knew one another quite well. They were joined by a few free spirits, shocked by the Jacobin phariseeism of the majority. After all, what did their criticism of Kurnosov amount to? That he was anti-Soviet? What else could one expect of a dissident? Of not being particularly fond of his fellow dissidents? Was it not well known that they were divided into almost as many sects as they were individuals? And that was in itself neither incomprehensible nor reprehensible: they were discovering freedom of thought and were keen to make use of it. The only serious accusation was that he was a—'the obscene word'—Fascist. We had got to it at last! But what did the word mean? The dictionary defined it as: 'Advocate of an authoritarian régime.' Kurnosov himself was imposing no régime on anybody. Indeed was anyone able to demonstrate that Russia was ready for democracy? And was every authoritarian régime bad by definition? Whereupon everyone mounted his hobbyhorse: the Tiger (Clemenceau), the General (de Gaulle), the Marshal (Pétain), the princes of the Quattrocento or 'the forty kings who over a thousand years made France'. Result: innumerable requests for interviews, especially as *The Russian Truth*, which was no longer displayed in bookshop windows, continued nevertheless to sell briskly.

'I don't give interviews,' said Kurnosov.

Aleksandr alerted Ivan Ivanich.

'Insist.'

Aleksandr was adept at persuasion.

'You want to pay for that house and get out of debt. You'll need money to live on, you know. Each interview sells several copies. Those people aren't the most important, but they are well disposed towards you: don't spit on them. Don't you understand that, if you insist on rejecting every interview, people will begin to wonder whether you are anything more than a front-man for someone else? You may be able to recite passages of *The Russian Truth* by heart, but what·does that prove? There have been insinuations in the press: some people think you're being manipulated by the Geebee and, as far as your treatment of the dissidents goes, you are. The more you refuse to meet journalists, the more suspect you'll become.'

'All right. I'll meet them.'

The interviews were not particularly interesting: more than anything else the journalists wanted details about the assassination attempt, and Kurnosov preferred to talk about the Eurasian vocation of the Russian empire. However one brave bookseller, confident in his public, asked Iron Mask to come and sign copies of *The Russian Truth* in his shop. Pressed by Aleksandr, Kurnosov did not back out.

The bookshop was in a pedestrian walk near the Pompidou Centre. Aleksandr only knew it by repute; in it were to be found the works of all the authors on the black list and the owner, a big fellow with a Tolstoyan beard and a gentle voice, added, when introducing himself: 'This is the most right-wing bookshop in Paris.' The extreme right gave Aleksandr the sense of disgust one feels when confronted by a sick animal—and sometimes a sick person: 'Hurry up and die!' It was not without some feelings of unease that he entered this place, which he imagined to be populated by landowners, tramps or parachutists. But the swarm that buzzed between the La Varendes and the Griparis seemed no more unusual than that to be found in a less esoteric bookshop. Besides, Kurnosov had created such a scandal that he had become 'a personality', and some fearless members of the *Tout-Paris* had come to join the usual clientèle of the place, which consisted of students, shopkeepers, practitioners of the liberal professions, looking no different to ordinary members of the public. Perhaps the social range was somewhat wider here than in a typical bookshop in Saint-German-des-Prés: there were more women in mink, more wild-haired starvelings, more soldiers in mufti, more beak-nosed provincials, more archivists and anarchists, but no particular miasma seemed to pollute the atmosphere.

Kurnosov had already arrived. He went out only at irregular times and changed his hotel every day. 'Has he really anything to fear?' Aleksandr asked Ivan Ivanich. 'I swear to you that we wish him no ill!' the case-officer had replied, his eyes brimming over with tenderness and sincerity. And as sincerity is a dangerous slope, he had added: 'Of course, if there was blood in the air, no one would tell me about it. But, frankly, I'd be surprised if there were: department V have acquired delicate stomachs.'

Among the men swarming around Kurnosov, trying no doubt to provoke him into revelations, Aleksandr recognized a former minister, the editor of a much vaunted and much derided review, a small publisher who had been involved in enough scandals to have some hope of making a name for himself: his beringed hand was constantly darting into his inside pocket, as if to touch his chequebook. No doubt he was making improper advances to Lux's golden goose: it was all part of the publishing war and Aleksandr, who was already feeling quite remote from what Divo called 'the Paris duckpond', had no reason to intervene.

Kurnosov had bought some new clothes; he was wearing a heavy, dark, pin-striped suit that looked very warm and very luxurious. Sitting at a small table, he was signing copy after copy. For once, it was a signing-session that paid.

'Monsieur Kurnosov, is it correct to say that you're a Fascist?'

The small young woman with tinted glasses and dirty hair had her pencil poised over her pad.

Kurnosov looked around him anxiously. Yet Aleksandr had explained to him beforehand the mentality that he would find in the bookshop. 'Provided those people haven't got it in for you, they're more liberal and less puritanical than the other lot: they can listen to anything!'

'I am a Fascist to the extent that Solzhenitsyn and Bukovsky are Fascists, in so far as Fascism alone has any chance of overcoming Communism.'

A lady, with a small dog under her arm—she seemed to think she was at the Pen Club—looked scandalized: 'But,

Monsieur Kurnosov, Fascism was swept from the face of the earth at the end of the Second World War.'

'Fascism is an eternal tendency in human society. Julius Caesar was a Fascist. So was Napoleon.'

'So you are hoping for a rebirth of Fascism?' asked a smartly dressed young man, wearing an expensive eau-de-cologne and holding a gold pen in his hand.

'I have said in my book everything I have to say,' Kurnosov replied stiffly. 'Next. Madame, would you mind writing your name on this sheet of paper; I wouldn't like to mis-spell a name: it would be very impolite.'

He went on signing. The bookseller and his employees kept bringing in more and more copies of *The Russian Truth*.

'We'll have to go and fetch some more copies from Lux,' said the bookseller.

A crowd had gathered outside the shop; inside, photographers jostled everybody with their satchels.

'If you don't mind, Monsieur Kurnosov? A little smile, perhaps? Come now, don't look so fierce! D'you always look so constipated?'

The flash bulbs exploded.

A small man in a threadbare overcoat that was too long for him pushed his way to the front. He had square, bi-focal glasses and a slight hairlip. He stayed there, his hands in his pockets, buying nothing, his eyes fixed on Kurnosov's long, fleshless cranium. Perhaps he wanted to say something and dared not speak up; perhaps some scruple prevented him from speaking; perhaps he did not have enough money to buy a copy of the book.

'Next. Would you care to write your name on . . .'

Kurnosov had already looked up; his eyes caught the small, humble, careworn face.

Then, despite all the people around, something took place between those two pairs of eyes, between the dark, morbid, tubercular eyes of the one man and the tender, terrorized eyes of the other.

'I knew it,' said Kurnosov, in Russian.

'You're Gaverin,' said the other man, in French.

'I'm Kurnosov,' Kurnosov replied, also in French, but

without much conviction, rather like a bull charging for the last time after being stabbed.

'You are not Kurnosov. You are Arseni Egorich Gaverin and I am Lev Aronovich Zellman, and we slept in the same double-bunk at Vorkuta. You were in the bottom one, I on top. You called me "little monkey" because I would climb up. *Obezianka*.'

Zellman's quiet voice had silenced everybody. The bookseller, still leaning over his last pile, appeared between an astrakhan coat and a pair of blue jeans. A journalist had already reached out towards the telephone.

'Did *they* send you?' Gaverin asked, reverting to Russian. Zellman did not answer. He stared at Gaverin with intense pity.

A very fair-haired student, with a notebook, asked very courteously: 'Monsieur, do you accept this gentleman's allegations?'

'I can prove them. I have photos,' said Zellman, his gentle eyes fixed on Gaverin as if to spare him a lie and at the same time to beg his forgiveness.

Gaverin lowered his cadaverous eyelids and dropped his large, new fountain pen.

'I accept them.'

Aleksandr dashed out to the café next door to telephone. He called the emergency number and started speaking at once: 'This is *Kobel* here. I want . . .'

A well-oiled voice was already reciting: 'The number that you have dialled does not exist. Please consult your telephone directory.'

6
The Turn of the Screw

That day Pitman closed for the last time the pale pink file, which had grown paler with the years and on which, thirty years earlier, he had written in his straight, rounded, well-spaced handwriting, in cheap black ink that had turned with time into a sort of iridescent violet in places, the single word *Oprichnik*.

He shut the pink file and, before handing it to his secretary, Major Beloshveiski, his mind dwelled for some time on that long period, marked by so many successes. It seemed like only yesterday that he was standing up there on the gallery that connected the two towers of Notre-Dame, and now the earth had turned thirty times around the sun and he was approaching old age step by step and winding up the business that he had set in motion. The same hands, the same cardboard. 'How I've changed! Have I changed all that much? No, in fact I've changed very little.' Anyway, there were still files to be opened, vast adventures to undertake. It was not the end yet, far from it, and yet the light of his present life was so coloured only because its decline, as yet still imperceptible, had begun. He thought of the imprecision of the notion of summit: in a way, it is the moment before one reaches the summit that is the most exquisite, but, in another way, it is the moment after, when one can sit back and regard its accomplishment as being behind one and one can enjoy its pleasure to the full. The middle of the night is not midnight, but later, and what the French call *le démon de midi*, or middle-age love, turns up at about two o'clock.

The manipulation of *Oprichnik* had been one of the most profitable in Pitman's career. But he shut the file without regret. Perhaps, deep down, he resented the fact that Aleksandr Psar had been so successful, whereas he, Pitman, had predicted no more than a modest success for him. His diagnosis had been: not red, not a 'radiator'. Not a 'radiator'? Psar had made up for his coldness (natural or acquired) by such determination, such an ability to bewitch people—to deflect their eyes, as one says in Russian—that his winter sunshine had ripened more fruit than the facile, superficial summer heat of apparently more promising agents. But red? Psar had given every proof of fidelity, and yet he remained outside a certain ethic, a certain aesthetic perhaps.

On the other hand, Pitman deplored Abdulrakhmanov's stubbornness in preventing him from rewarding Psar in accordance with his merits, forcing him on the contrary to reward his exceptional services only with ingratitude and desertion.

Again, too, he regretted that he was unable to use *Oprichnik* one last time, but he would like to have done so in a more traditional way, in an operation of disinformation more in accordance with the letter of counter-espionage, the Hard Sign operation on which he had placed such hopes and in which Aleksandr Psar would have acted supremely well. Yes, sadly, he had to recognize that Abdulrakhmanov was losing his touch as happens to many old artists, especially cooks. What a shame it was to drop *Oprichnik* when he could still be of service! What a pity he had to persist in carrying out the third stage of Pskov when he could be initiating the first stage of Hard Sign!

Not that the third stage of Pskov was to afford him no satisfaction. The denunciation of Gaverin by Zellman would enable *Voivode* to trigger off a campaign the theme of which had already been handed to him, in a sealed envelope, the week before: 'The dissidents are systematically manipulated by the KGB.' A lot of people had already suggested as much, of course, especially the dissidents themselves, each pretending to believe that all the others were secret agents, but now it had been proved: the man whom everybody had taken to be the author of *The Russian Truth*, a second Solzhenitzyn, almost the new leading dissident, was in reality an (unmasked) tool of the Soviet government. To go on to believe that most of the other dissidents, or at least some of them, were (as yet unmasked) tools of the same government . . . The dissidents had already lost some of their popularity: stage 2 of Pskov had disguised them as Fascists: stage 3 would show that those Fascists were working for the Communists: that really would deprive them of any credit and we would have a bit of peace for half a dozen years or so. For one could not deny that the world-wide uproar that the dissidents organized at every end and turn to defend this hooligan or that parasite was irritating in the extreme. But on their own they could do nothing: if, as soon as they appeared here or there, one yelled out 'Fascism will not pass' or 'Communist murderers', they would be forced to keep quiet.

Yes, this third stage would function of its own accord, like those toy drinking-birds that Pitman had seen in Paris, which you had only to flick for them to oscillate backwards and forwards forever. Having exhausted its possibilities it would break up of its own accord, with the French courts finding themselves in an impossible position over Gaverin (whose only identity papers said that he was Kurnosov), the Lux publishing house swept by contradictory waves like a rowing-boat caught in the wake of a ship, Psar under suspicion of having consciously or unconsciously served the Soviet régime (without anyone ever being able to know the extent to which those suspicions were well-founded). The inveterate chauvinism of the French would come into play: cultured journalists would reproach the émigrés, whoever they were, with Stavisky, Gorguloff and the Russian loan. A young critic would write a *roman à clef* in which Ballandar would be presented as a Communist agent, since he seemed to have moved slightly to the right lately. The balance sheet: Besides the decisive blow delivered to the swarm of dissidents, intellectual terrorism, which had been on the decline, would be re-established in France, an influence operation that had lasted for twenty-five years would be teased out in masterly fashion ('the ultimate stroke,' Abdulrakhmanov used to say to his disciples, 'is to make your set-ups biodegradable') and a new dynamism would be given to the *Voivode* orchestra.

And yet . . . was this not a rather short-sighted way of seeing things? Having saved a great political thinker, the real

Mikhail Kurnosov, from the execution squad, solely in order to biodegrade Aleksandr Psar, to disperse the mosquitos of dissidence and to sow terror (which is easy enough) in the ranks of the Western intelligentsia? . . .

Pitman sighed.

'Are we closing the file, Comrade General?'

'Yes, Beloshveiski; put it in the archives.' Unlike the other Directorates, which tended to destroy all trace of their activity, Directorate A was building up a body of doctrine for itself. 'Recall the case-officer before he has time to make his farewells. His family can follow in a few days. Give the case-officer two weeks' exceptional leave at Sochi, all expenses paid. Ask him if he wants his family to join him there or whether he'd prefer to meet them here on his return: his wife can always be told that he's on duty.'

'What's to be done with co-opted Colonel Psar? Is he to be struck off? Promoted? Be given the right to retire? And what are we to do with the sums deposited in the bank in his name?'

Pitman hesitated. Abdulrakhmanov, whom he loved, was extremely ill . . .

'On all these points, we shall wait a bit before reaching a decision.'

'Very well, Comrade General. The influence post held at present by *Oprichnik* has been allotted to *Khorunzhi*. What are your orders on that matter? Should we place him at the head of his orchestra as from now? Will he be using the same cover? Who will be his case-officer?'

'On that, too, we shall wait. *Khorunzhi* is a sleeper, don't let's wake him up yet. He'll take his place quietly. He has time: he is already assistant editor of the French *Ogoniok* . . . We have six other orchestras working in France . . . There's no need to make *Khorunzhi* operational just yet. As for the Agency . . . no. We've earned twenty times more money that it has cost us: leave it to Psar. It will be our parting gift. If he is still able to get anything out of it after the scandal of Stage 3, he'll richly deserve it. Anyway, who knows, we might still need him, and in that case . . .'

Pitman never stopped thinking about Hard Sign, sleeping there in his safe.

'So his salary will not be paid, Comrade General? I mean neither his salary in France nor his salary in roubles?'

'Stop all that until further notice, but don't dispose of the money. Leave it to accumulate. We shall see later what we'll do with it.'

'Very good, Comrade General.'

Beloshveiski went to the door. He was a pleasant, rather anaemic young man, with a loop of fair hair over his forehead; he was very proud of his English suit and, since he had been wearing it, he had avoided making regulation aboutturns. That did not bother Pitman: he had never been particularly careful of about-turns himself. Just before leaving, Beloshveiski swung gracefully around on his heels:

'One more thing, Comrade General. What is to be done with Alla Kuznetsova? She's been putting in requests for the last three years. We are keeping her busy doing office work that's well below her capabilities. She claims that we are ruining her career.'

'Thank you for reminding me of that aspect of the question.'

Pitman was playing with a propelling pencil.

'Where does she come from, originally?'

'The Second Principal Directorate. Seventh Department, Second Section. She has done a course in the manipulation of French-speaking intellectual tourists.'

'Well . . .'

This business of the wife and child had always disgusted Pitman. Abdulrakhmanov had told him time and time again that the whole man was engaged in intelligence work, 'with his physical, cosmic and spiritual bodies', but Pitman could not help thinking that it was wrong to abuse family ties, those for which he himself felt most sympathy. Psar had a daughter: why deprive him of her? By what right had they imposed a son on him that was not his? It was with relief that Pitman decided to put an end, at least as far as possible, to the immoral imposture devised by Abdulrakhmanov, that great man who believed himself to be above good and evil.

'You will put Captain Kuznetosva at the disposal of her original directorate. Propose her for promotion and send for my car, Beloshveiski: I must go to Volkovo.'

Snow had fallen, but there was not enough to go sledging, and it probably would not last. Sviatoslav would have to wait until January. In January, Pitman's eldest daughter, Svetochka, would marry a lieutenant in the Ministry of the Interior whose dream it was to be transferred to the Committee of Security. Pitman would help him, but without putting his own prestige in the balance; the recruitment service preferred boys who had everything to gain from their own abilities, not well-connected sons-in-law. Anyway this lieutenant . . . Pitman was not overjoyed at his daughter's choice: there was in Valerik a disconcerting Slav brutality. Would he be affectionate enough? Svetochka needed so much affection and she had never lacked it from her parents. Valerik thought only about parallel bars and rings; he could not enter a drawing-room without doing acrobatics on the arm of a chair. Were acrobatics an indispensable element in a happy marriage? What kind of a father would Valerik be? Pitman feared that he would stifle any tenderness in his children, that he would inculcate in them a simplistic careerism passing itself off as Bolshevism that amounted to little more than: 'Grab what goes—but mind your toes.'

Pitman sighed. He often sighed nowadays. His father, the little tailor, may not have been averse to an ethic of this kind, but he never inspired in his son anything but rudimentary filial affection and it was towards another than Iakov had turned when he had need of a father to venerate and imitate. The little tailor had died modestly, silently, ten years earlier, and now the other father, the colossus, was going to die in turn. A whole epoch was coming to an end. That file had now been closed, and soon that prodigious life was also going to come to an end, like some book in its monumental binding, with its bands jutting out, its thick, illuminated pages, its gilt edges, a book that would be closed with the sigh of all its pages sliding over one another and the final slam.

The dacha was perched behind its snow-covered hill, as on a postcard. A layer of ice, as thin as a sheet of cellophane, covered the lake, giving off a cold dampness.

The great man was lying in the old style, on a leather sofa, surrounded by his books and rugs, his Arab pistols and powder horns, which mottled the walls with splashes of copper and silver. It was in a room of this kind that most of the wealthy men of the Old Order had lived and died. The matrimonial bed-chamber belongs as little to Russia as the dining-room does to France. Is there any meaning in these differences in furniture and houses? For his part, Pitman would never have wanted to sleep far from his warm Elichka.

The old man's lair was plunged in darkness, shutters and doors closed, but in a corner, opposite the door, shone a small red lamp reflected in a silver plaque: this plaque was an icon and the lamp a *lampadka*, a sanctuary lamp. Pitman, who had never seen these objects at Abdulrakhmanov's house, wondered whether his adoptive father had not gone mad.

On the sofa there was a pile of blankets, furs and pillows that he could only just make out in the dark. From the midst of this mausoleum came a muffled voice, a voice still strong, but cracked, collapsing from time to time into an involuntary whisper. The diction was still the same: precise, musical, urbane.

'Ah, there you are, Your Excellency!'

Hearing the voice, so distinct, but so obviously marked by the catastrophe that would not be long in coming, Pitman was reminded of those logs that, though consumed from within, still glow, preserving every detail of their surface, their fibres, their nervures, the bumps and cracks on their bark, then suddenly—one has only to brush them with the poker—collapse without a sound into colourless cinders.

'How are you, Mohammed Mohammedovich?'

The dying man did not answer. There could be no lies between these two men. For a long time they said nothing, each happy to warm himself in the presence of the other, to feed himself for the last time on the friendship that united them.

'*Nnus*,' Abdulrakhmanov said at last, still the same academic or senatorial *nnus*, 'and how is my protégé?'

Pitman's eyes had become used to the darkness. He could now make out the enormous head stuck between the swellings of the pillow. A strange nightcap extended the cranium still further into a sugarloaf. Half sitting, rather than lying down, Abdulrakhmanov had placed his hands on the sheet and, from time to time, they crumpled it a little, as if they had a will of their own. A sign of imminent death, apparently.

'Mohammed Mohammedovich, I've always wanted to ask you . . . but I've never dared to . . . and yet it was you who . . . You still don't want him to come home, do you? It would be neater if he did. All the loose ends would be tied up. And, after all, he has served us well.'

A bellow began somewhere in Abdulrakhmanov's guts, wound its way through his huge body and expired on his lips. He then sank back into a sort of sleep, a suspension rather between consciousness and unconsciousness, a private limbo from which it was impossible to call him back.

Pitman stayed there for over an hour, his hands clasped between his knees. Then he went back into the dining-room. Innokenti was laying the table: one setting. He had already put a camp bed in one corner: he was expecting Pitman to spend the night at the dacha. That didn't suit Pitman at all; he would much rather spend the evening at home and come back the following day.

'Look,' he began.

The dumb man turned his head and on that rough, bloated, wrinkled face, with its big red nose and mop of unkempt hair, Pitman saw two damp, gleaming furrows, like those left by snails on walls. He said: 'All right, I'll stay.'

He rang home. Elichka did not sound too pleased.

'Elichka, without him we should be nothing. And he's only got a few hours left.'

He went back to the dying man. Abdulrakhmanov's eyes were shining in the darkness.

'The liqueur!' he ordered.

He thought Pitman was Innokenti, but when Pitman came up with the green bottle and the small glass on a tray he smiled: 'Oh, it's you. Put it down there, my son.'

His lips moved, but no sound came out and his hands fiddled with the sheet.

'Draw back the curtains.'

Pitman went and drew back the heavy, floral-patterned curtains. Through the double-glazed windows the landscape could be seen powdered with snow crystals, under an indigo sky, dotted with the crystals of stars. Abdulrakhmanov looked out greedily, as if to feast his eyes on this last vision. He muttered two phrases that Pitman did not understand:

'The slave of the one through whom pardon arrives has no business to be merciful. The son of the one through whom pardon arrives has no business to be merciful.'

He seemed to hesitate: which version should he choose?

The superstitious little lamp was still burning before the silver plaque, which was also red.

'Haven't you noticed?' said Abdulrakhmanov. 'One almost always dies at the other end of the year. I was born in June. I always knew I would die in the autumn.'

Pitman bent down and kissed the old man's hand, that tiny hand at the end of that giant's arm.

'Go,' said Abdulrakhmanov. 'Go and eat. Innokenti must have made cabbage soup for you. I think I can smell it. But I might well be mistaken, for my nose has long since been on strike.'

There was cabbage soup and even smoked herring and vodka. Pitman ate this muzhik's meal, trying to hold back the sobs that were preventing him from swallowing. 'I'm too sensitive,' he told himself. 'After all, it's quite normal for an eighty-one-year-old man to die.'

He wiped his mouth and went back to his friend. Abdulrakhmanov had dozed off. From time to time the half-darkness altered: it was Innokenti, who had come to stand for a few moments by the half-opened door.

'Nnus,' the dying man said suddenly, in a strong voice, without raising his eyelids, which sat like huge shells over his eyes, 'we must just wait. Like in some rather delicate operation. Wait and above all do nothing. Wait while it sets. That's what he does, up there, the Great Contriver: he waits.'

'Who?' Pitman asked, afraid that he understood only too well.

'He of the greatest set-up of all. Isn't that how you see the creation, my son? And yet that's what it is. And we, you and I, are merely cut-outs. It is no use regarding ourselves as sources of radiation, as conductors of orchestras . . . We are, my Iakov Moiseich all-of-plastic, merely sound-boxes. You know what they say in the Book. The angels rebelled. There was war. Mankind is merely a disinformation operation to trick the Shaytan, the serpent . . . As you know, the serpent was the Word disguised. The prohibition, that was disinformation. Because men had to be forced to interest themselves in good and evil. Otherwise the war against the Nazi Lucifer was lost. And the best way to make men do something . . . Oh, it's you, Kenti? You're the muzhik of muzhiks, Kenti, but you've taken good care of your general. Your general thanks you, Kenti. Do you hear? Your general thanks you . . . It's as in Sun Tzu. One day, my son, you must read Sun Tzu. He tells how the prefect Hsiang waged war on two rebels. I don't recall their names. He'd inflicted a few defeats on them and seized some loot. Then his soldiers no longer wanted to return to the fray, lest they lost what they'd won. Do you know what Hsiang did? He sent them out hunting and set fire to the camp. When the soldiers came back, there was no loot. They wept. Sun Tzu says quite explicitly that they wept. Then the prefect spoke to them: "Gentlemen, what you have lost is nothing as compared with what the rebels still possess." The soldiers themselves asked to attack the rebels. Hsiang, says Sun Tzu, ordered that the horses be fed and that everyone ate his meal in bed. Why in bed, I don't know. Anyway, the next morning the rebels were annihilated. That is how the Great Contriver works.'

Pitman, fearing that his master was about to bring shame upon himself, but wishing nonetheless to be quite clear on the matter, asked: 'Mohammed Mohammedovich, what do you mean? That you believe in God?'

There was no answer: Abdulrakhmanov had once again withdrawn from the world.

Pitman looked at the small red lamp. What did it mean? A bit later, Abdulrakhmanov came to himself again.

'You know,' he said in his most normal voice, as if he were not even ill, 'I'm not displeased with my life. I may have given History a little push in the right direction and once or twice I've given the Shaytan a good kick up the backside, and often I've got him to work for me.'

Pitman knew what the right direction was, but did his master still know it?

'What is the right direction, Mohammed Mohammedovich?'

He was trembling. If Abdulrakhmanov replied: 'The direction laid down by Marx and the other fathers of the Revolution,' he was still there; if not, that great body was no more than an appearance. Abdulrakhmanov did not answer, or at least Pitman thought that he was changing the subject.

'Have you read Dostoievsky?'

'A little.'

Reading Dostoievsky was not encouraged in those circles.

'He painted my portrait, you know.'

Pitman closed his eyes in pain. He would so much have wanted his benefactor to die lucid, as a Bolshevik should. Perhaps the doctors might have arranged that, but Abdulrakhmanov had declared that if a doctor were sent to him he would receive him with pistol shots: 'I'm too old to get better and he wouldn't like to die in my place, so what is the point?'

'Mohammed Mohammedovich, who is this Shaytan you keep talking about?'

'The Shaytan, my son, is the Great Dismantler. When I was young, there were camels all around. I used to ride them. There were camels and dervishes. And carpets more beautiful than women's bodies.'

'You're an Uzbek, Mohammed Mohammedovich. That's why there were camels.'

'No, my Iakov Moiseich all-of-brass, I'm no more an Uzbek than you are a Jew. We are Russians, my Iakov Moiseich all-of-gold. The rest, as you know perfectly well, is disinformation. We are true Russians, the only true Russians, with our swarthy faces, you who spring from the loins of Shem and I from God knows where: have you really looked at me? The others, the Great Russians, they were there simply to hold the stirrup for us. Look at their history: they began by begging the Vikings to rule over them. Then we crushed them. After that, the Poles. Then they went to look for lords in Germany . . . Russia has never managed to govern itself, my son, has never been able to give itself a stable capital. Its only effective boss since the Revolution was a Georgian. The others are just amateurs. That's how it has to be. The Russian Empire! There's nothing wrong with the word. It's the only modern colonial empire that has succeeded—and do you know why? Yes, there was no sea to cross, of course, but also because the Russians have always practised integration. Give us your women and we will make little Russians together. Do you remember that book that *Oprichnik* got published? Nothing but statistics? The author demonstrated that the empire would break up. That reassured the West. Very good, *Oprichnik*! But the author forgot one thing: that the Uzbeks are more Russian than the Russians. The true Russians are at death's door. They drink so much they're becoming impotent. Their wives are rebelling. Have you seen the birthrates? You have a family: you are the Russian of the future. And how many bastards have I got? I have sown Uzbeks in the wombs of Great Russian and Little Russian women, White Russian, Circassian, Jewish and Lapp women . . . I don't know them, I don't want to know them, but I've worked for the cause. Have you ever heard of the myth of the third Rome? It is quite correct in that the emperors, apart from the very first ones, were not Romans and the emperors of the Russia of the future, my Iakov Moiseich all-of-diamond, will be you and I. Augustus and Caesar . . . The greatest Tsar we ever had was a cousin of mine—Boris. The English are quite right: scratch a Russian and you'll find a Tartar. But also a Jew, a Latvian, a Pole. And Russia has not finished scratching itself yet, as long as the mixture is not homogeneous, but when it is . . .'

Abdulrakhmanov withdrew again and Pitman sat there, summoning up the moral strength—or was it weakness—to resign himself to the great man's decline. 'It wasn't only his intelligence I loved; it was the whole man; so I shall go on loving him as long as a spark of life remains in him.' He sat down on the bed, in order to get a closer look at the large face. It seemed so dark, against the pillows, as to be black. The breathing quickened, slowed down, stopped for a moment, resumed, like an engine running erratically. 'He won't see morning,' Pitman thought.

When Abdulrakhmanov opened his eyes, looked around him with an expression of surprise and then, having stared at the red icon, parted his lips to smile, Pitman still found the courage to ask him, very gently, sensing that he would be capable of listening to the most absurd, the most degrading answer: 'Why do you have that there?'

'Ah, that's what's been bothering you! I thought so. Well, to begin with, it's his feast day today: I thought he'd like that.'

'Whose feast day?'

'Matvei's. And, anyway, when I was young he was always there and there was an old maid with a pair of tweezers which . . . you know . . . the wicks.'

'But, Mohammed Mohammedovich, you're of Muslim origin. Muslims don't have icons.'

'Origin, origin, you make me laugh with your origins. Origin, yes. But I was baptised, and probably my father, too. I'm called Matvei Matveich.'

'But you told me . . .'

'Disinformation, my Iakov Moiseich all-of-chocolate, dis-in-for-ma-tion. At that point, it was better not to be a Christian.'

'You mean that . . . you belong to the Christian religion?'

'My son,' said Abdulrakhmanov, 'there is only one religion.'

He gave a sigh that seemed to raise his entire body.

'Bear in mind, this Matvei isn't the Evangelist; it's our own, Pechersky, the Russian Matthew. Ah! I'll have loved Russia very much, my son, and I'll have eaten a lot of it.'

His eyes wandered around, as if looking for something.

'Do you want your liqueur, Comrade General?'

Pitman no longer dared to say either Matvei or Mohammed.

'I think I have drunk my last on this earth, my son. My body could absorb nothing more.'

His eyes found the icon again, clung there and seemed pacified.

Abdulrakhmanov withdrew again, this time with his eyes open. When he came back to himself, Pitman asked him if he was in pain. He answered: 'I don't know any more.'

He went rapidly downhill, without trying to cling to bits of jutting rock, but from time to time he seemed to climb back again, like a balloon into which a little hot air has suddenly been blown. It was at one of these moments, very close to drunkenness, that he revealed to Pitman the secret of the Hidy-hats.

'You must be beginning to understand what we are doing? They've been giving you a glimpse of things, haven't they?'

'Yes, I think I can guess . . .'

'That's it, that's exactly it. Do you remember what happened in the case of Bukovsky? It was we who thought of exchanging him for some Chilean number, to show the world that we were no more evil or dangerous than Chile. Leonid Ilich didn't agree. So we got him to believe that Bukovsky was mad. When he realized that he wasn't, it was too late. He didn't suspect anything. He was furious, of course, but he thought we'd been wrongly informed. It will take them some years before they realize . . . Yes, if they'd wanted to go on with their ideology, they shouldn't have created the Directorate. While ever we were just a small department with specific duties . . . Now we have plans stretching over twenty or thirty years . . . You can't employ professional liars without giving them a monopoly of the truth. We in the Consistory are a truth factory. For external and internal use. We have got so far with our techniques . . . all images come from us. They may shoot us, but they can do nothing any longer against the images that we have created. We have planned the twenty-first century, my son. Everything is moving into gear, everything is under control. Even without us, they cannot help but follow the tracks that we have laid down, for they will never know what is the ultimate lie. They will not escape from our labyrinth. Meanwhile, my Iakov Moiseich all-of- . . . all-of . . .' His imagination let him down. 'Meanwhile we are leading mankind towards happiness, that is to say, the good: all that . . . is . . . the same thing. As for the Russians, they have held the stirrup for us. That was very good, but now . . . The Russians . . . they're no longer needed.'

Pitman did not know to what extent his master was the dupe of the monstrous megalomania of certain dying men and to what extent, on the contrary, he was telling the truth. He had himself already glimpsed a secret of this order: those who have the keys to disinformation must also have the keys to information, and the keys to information are the keys to the world.

'I'm cold,' said Abdulrakhmanov suddenly.

'Kenti! Another blanket.'

'No,' said Abdulrakhmanov. 'A rug.'

Pitman chose what seemed to him to be the most beautiful one: a near-square rectangle, ultramarine blue and dried blood in colour, with lozenge-shaped motifs. He covered his master's body with it as with a flag, leaving only the face visible. The material of the rug was so dry and rough that it did not look as if it would keep in any heat. But, maybe it was not a physical heat that the old man was asking for. Under this stiff, hieratic thing, he no longer looked like a man, but more like a reclining figure on the lid of a sarcophagus.

'Is that better?'

Abdulrakhmanov did not answer. His eyes had turned to glass.

Innokenti let out a yelp of pain and Pitman did not know what to do, what gesture to make. This death suddenly seemed to him like a monstrous incongruity, as if his benefactor had been lacking in a certain decorum to die there, in front of them.

The embarrassment was short-lived. He fell on to his knees at the foot of the bed, his face buried in the old blue Bokhara, and wept. Kneeling beside him, Innokenti had reverted to the habits of his childhood, making broad signs of the cross over himself, pressing his fingers against his forehead, shoulders and breast, as if he could express his love and piety through the pressure exerted.

Colonel-General Abdulrakhmanov, Mohammed Mohammedovich, twice Hero of the Soviet Union, twice recipient of the Order of Lenin, decorated with the Order of the Red Flag of Combat and the Order of the Patriotic War, bearer of the insignia of an honorary member of the Cheka, was given an official funeral. It was attended obsequiously by members of the diplomatic corps who had no idea who this important man was, of whom they had never heard. Several speeches were made and Lieutenant-General Pitman, in whom many recognized the dead man's favourite disciple and, as it were, spiritual heir, spoke for half-an-hour of his absolute loyalty, a loyalty that had inspired this exemplary soldier to carry out his superhuman duties. No details were given concerning the superhuman duties. As for the loyalty, Pitman did not know what to think of it. Yes, Abdulrakhmanov had served the country and the Party better than anyone. But on his death-bed had he not hinted that the country and the Party had been for him no more than means to an end? But means to what end? To good? To happiness? But was not the Party the supreme judge of the good, of happiness? . . .

When the funeral was over, there was, of course, a funeral lunch, from which many of the guests emerged in so tottering a state of sadness that they had to be driven home by their chauffeurs, even though the day's work was far from over. This was not the case with Pitman: he hardly touched the strong liquor. He was driven to Rostopchin House and shut himself up in his office. When a great man dies, his followers cannot wait to set aside his last wishes: that is precisely what happened to those of Comrade Abdulrakhmanov.

With his hands clasped behind his back, Pitman paced up and down for a while on his own rugs, which were merely imitations of old ones, since Elichka did not approve of extravagance. Sometimes he swung to the right, sometimes to the left; on the whole, despite his sadness, he felt rather elated. He had suffered an irreparable loss, but there was no point in dwelling on it. Abdulrakhmanov's disappearance had opened a great breech in the Consistory, in the Director-ate, in the Committee of State Security as a whole; all sorts of staff movements would take place in the near future, and Pitman certainly expected to benefit from them. Was that not what Abdulrakhmanov would have wished?

After pacing up and down for a quarter of an hour, sometimes with a tear in his eye, sometimes with the shadow of a smile on his lips, Pitman finally stopped in front of his safe and opened it. He took out a cardboard box on which was written, in addition to the headings of the service and of Directorate A, the words 'Absolutely secret'. He carried the box over to his table, sat down and untied the sky-blue cord that held the lid in place.

Inside was a pale green folder, on which in dark green was written not a title or even a word, but a sign; the hard sign, a very rare letter in the Russian alphabet, unpronounceable in itself, which simply indicates the velarization of the consonant that precedes it. It had given Pitman great pleasure to give his cherished plan a name that no one could refer to in speech without periphrasis. One could hardly go further along the way of the impalpable, which is the daily bread of the special services. Besides, Hard Sign was very much in the spirit of the Directorate: this letter, commonly used under the Old Order, also suggested what was most intransigent about Bolshevism. In Russian there is a soft sign, but no one would ever have dreamt of calling an operation 'soft sign'.

Pitman opened the folder and, his mouth watering like any author reading his own prose, fixed his small spectacles on the first page.

Since the defeat, which may be regarded as definitive, of what we refer to by the vague but convenient term 'Fascism', and which would be more accurately described as national socialism (*Nationalsozialismus*), two forces are confronting one another in the world: one, energetic, constructive, aggressive, animated by great faith in itself, namely Marxism-Leninism, and the other, apathetic, conservative, peace-loving, lacking in any ideal or inspiration, namely capitalism. Providing this equilibrium, or rather this disequilibrium, of forces remains unchanged, it is now possible to wager on the victory of Marxism-Leninism, whether it triumphs of its own accord, or whether non-nationalist socialism plays for it the role that the Trojan horse played for the Greeks.

However we must not allow ourselves to be duped by exaggerated optimism. If one takes as an example a Western country like France, it would seem on the contrary that a certain intellectual ferment is taking place there that might in the end lead to the creation of a third movement of ideas, though it is impossible at present to predict its chances of success. Appearing in a given country, such a movement might spread rapidly, in view of present-day means of communication, to the whole of the West, and we should then find ourselves faced with the need to engage in open conflict, instead of allowing ourselves to sit back and wait for the adversary to collapse of his own accord and for the reward to fall into our hands.

Let us be quite clear: not only is such a movement possible, but it is well nigh inconceivable, the rules of the dialectic being what they are, that an agitation of this kind should fail to arise and upset the realization of our plans. Whether this movement will be based on reactionary or progressive, religious or humanitarian values, whether it will spring from the people or from the élites, whether it will have any serious chance of causing difficulties for us, whether it would be followed in those nations that already benefit from a Communist structure, we do not know, but we can reasonably count on a manifestation of this kind. From this point of view the present tendency of Great Britain, Federal Germany, Australia, Sweden and above all the United States is in no way contradicted by the tendency that seems to have been dominant at the time of the French elections: one has only to remember that the French are peculiar in that they put into opposition whatever faction they have most sympathy with, because their temperament finds all authority repugnant.

Unless capitalism pure and simple gets a second wind, we may therefore regard as probable the creation of a world-wide Third Party, which will be as hostile theoretically to bourgeois capitalism as to proletarian Communism, but, in so far as it will have the freedom to operate only in the capitalist countries, one may predict that it may be particularly sensitive to the threat of Communism, which will alone remain capable of annihilating it. Enjoying greater vitality than capitalism, this Third Party will be able, at least for a time, to impede our march towards a radiant future.

The violent destruction of this group, once it has been formed, will present a number of problems and would not be entirely compatible with the spirit in which the security organs of the Soviet State are in the habit of operating. On the other hand, the infiltration of this Party might in no way prove embarrassing for our country, and would turn this weapon directed against us into one of our most satisfactory tools. One may therefore deduce from what I have said that, in the event of such a party taking some time to form, it would be good strategy to provide it with the necessary catalysts, in such a way as to agglomerate around a secure base all the elements likely to adhere to this kind of activity. In other words we have an interest in throwing into the West a magnet that, while belonging to us, would attract to itself the iron filings of new ideas and their promoters. Quite obviously, the present Directorate would be better placed than any other to carry out such an action.

Let us remember that operations of this kind, though on a smaller scale, have already enjoyed some success: the *Trust* network enabled us not only to drain off a considerable fraction of the White émigrés, but also to subsidize a number of our own operations at the expense of the United States, which believed that it was financing a counter-revolutionary group; and the Young Russians Party, directed by one of our penetration agents, made it possible to fragment the émigrés into hostile generations while absorbing and sterilizing all the talents that might have been attracted by Fascism in the strict sense.

But the international situation has greatly altered. In particular the Russian emigration, which was entirely isolated in the twenties and thirties, is now playing a role in the world: its representatives, whatever lack of qualifications they may have, are received by heads of state, their declarations are published in the press, one sees them on television and they have an effect on public opinion. What we are envisaging within the framework of Operation Hard Sign is to use this penetration of the Western world by our dissidents in order to penetrate it in turn. If we wish, this Third Party, whose creation seems to us inevitable, might be encouraged to crystallize around those dissidents, because they are *a priori* well regarded in liberal circles.

When consulted on the decision to take concerning A. I. Solzhenitsyn, the Directorate recommended expulsion pure and simple, in the hope, one will remember, of seeing him provide the nucleus of an extreme right-wing magma consisting not so much of émigrés as of Westerners: indeed, any concentration of the adversary in a defined space makes him a better target, psychologically as well as physically (cf. *The Vademecum of the Influence Agent*, p. 47: 'Each blow delivered must replace the red ball and the opposing white ball in a position that makes it possible to cannon them again.') This operation did not produce the expected results because the subject immediately upset even those Westerners who were well-disposed towards him. This was because we had omitted to infiltrate around him a manipulator employed by us, and the subject found himself abandoned to his own intransigence.

On the other hand, within the territory of the Union, when subjects remain in our hands, operations of this kind are conducted successfully with the collaboration of the Second Principal Directorate (see references attached).

In other words the secret of success for an operation such as Hard Sign lies in an appropriate manipulation of the catalyst by an influence agent, unless, as in the Young-Russians operation, already mentioned, the execution is entrusted directly to the influence agent under the supervision of a case-officer. However, in the case under consideration, this simplified solution is not, it seems, to be recommended and for two reasons:

—the catalyst is sure to arouse the suspicion of the adverse organs and his legend, if there is one, will be dismantled piece by piece; if the slightest flaw is detected the operation will become impossible;

—disinformation and influence may be carried out, as we know, only through multiplicatory relays whose increasing ignorance and distance from the source make their falsified information credible.

It seems to us to be essential, therefore, that the catalyst chosen should be his own dupe, but that he should be duplicated by an influence agent of proven ability . . .

When he reached this point, Pitman stopped reading. The late Abdulrakhmanov had always insisted on carefully written reports:

'You aren't some militiaman sent out to keep the traffic moving! You're a political thinker and, don't forget, style is the mould of thought.'

Everything was going well so far, but now he had to insert a paragraph, perhaps a whole section, the plan of which immediately occurred to Pitman's alert mind:

1) Point out

a) that a subject and a manipulator of the type required are not easy to find;

b) that, as it happens, the Directorate has at present two individuals capable of forming the constellation in question.

2) Draw attention once again to

a) *Oprichnik*'s career and show why he would be the ideal manipulator;

b) the qualifications of the author of the attempt against Brezhnev, who had been given the pseudonym *Diak*; show why he would be the best possible catalyst.

3) Draw up a balance-sheet

a) of the expenditure agreed to maintain *Diak* and of the services rendered by him, the latter being disproportionate to the former;

b) of *Oprichnik*'s activity, pointing out that there was no reason to stop using an experienced agent in full possession of his faculties. Add this note perhaps: '*Oprichnik* has asked to terminate his duties, but this does not appear to have anything to do with exhaustion or risk of detection. He is simply basing his request on a promise given him thirty years ago—there seems to be no reason why this promise should not be fulfilled, but, equally, it could be delayed a little longer—and on a desire, no doubt legitimate, but which could hardly be urgent, to make the acquaintance of his mother country.'

For thirty years, Aleksandr had been guided, sustained, watched over, protected. Suddenly he found himself alone like an orphan in the vast world. He had been pushed overboard and he could not swim.

His first intuition was correct: 'They've abandoned me.' But he quickly took control of himself again, that is to say, he learnt to swim and to lie to himself. No, they had not abandoned him; certain events, all too easy to imagine, had taken place: the French police were on to the affair and, in the interests of general security, for some hours or some days, he would have to avoid any contact with his controllers. He now remembered that this situation had been anticipated in the instructions that he had learnt by heart during his apprenticeship in Brooklyn: if contacts through the usual channels no longer operate, go on to the emergency channel; if the emergency channel is blocked, wait: it is up to the Centre to renew the connection. He then reproached himself for his momentary panic. He was an officer, he should know how to keep himself in hand. There was nothing surprising in the fact that Gaverin's imposture had made him, Psar, suspect—after all, he had been the guarantor of the false Kurnosov. The Directorate would naturally have to wait until counter-espionage deployed its paraphernalia—bugging, shadowing, acts of provocation—and, in Aleksandr's own interest, arrangements were being made so that all this would lead nowhere.

Considerably reassured, Aleksandr asked himself the obvious question: had Zellman been sent by the Directorate? The Geebee must have known that Gaverin was not Kurnosov. Was it imaginable that they had been so imprudent as to free Zellman by mistake? Or, on the contrary, was it all part of an operation, and had Gaverin been presented as Kurnosov only in order to unmask him? There were two arguments in favour of the second hypothesis: the Directorate's usual efficiency and one important fact: the emergency telephone had been cut before and not after the public denunciation.

There, again, Aleksandr resented his not having been warned. It was now he who had to face the storm, and the least they might have done was to give him instructions, supposing that the storm had been triggered off to order. He tried to console himself; perhaps he was already being treated like a member of the hierarchy and not as an agent; perhaps that was why he was being left free to take the initiative for the good of the service.

He was summoned to Special Branch headquarters; he was visited by an inspector in general intelligence. No one saw M. Psar as an agent, but they did wonder to what extent he himself had been manipulated. They wanted information on the line that ended in Rome. Politely, but firmly, he refused to answer: 'I'm a literary agent, I just do my job, I was taken in by the identity papers that I was shown, I am not involved in politics . . .'

Gaverin had tried to disappear, then turned up at the Agency: 'I want to talk.' *The Russian Truth* was now on the best-seller list and requests for interviews were pouring in. Gaverin agreed to all of them and never told the same story twice. Sometimes he was the real Kurnosov, whose mental health had been shattered by his stay at the Special Hospital; sometimes he had been sent on a mission to sabotage the book; sometimes he directed an anti-Communist network that had members even in the Supreme Praesidium; sometimes he was a colonel in the CIA who had deserted. Two things really did bother him: 'Will I be expelled? Will they take my money back?' For he had arranged to receive, apart from his advance, a substantial loan and a mortgage to buy his house.

Psar remembered the last orders that he had been given and which had never been countermanded: 'Do whatever Kurnosov wants.'

'What did you tell the police? You must have been questioned about your identity since you admitted that you weren't Kurnosov.'

'I said I didn't know any more. The sulphur injections have ruined my memory.'

'And what's the truth?'

Gaverin's suffering eyes took on a mad look: 'The truth is that it was the cold packs.'

Aleksandr shrugged his shoulders. He had no idea what game this man was playing and was not too concerned about it: he knew his job well enough to accept that there were some things it would be better for him not to know.

'Everything will depend on Zellman.'

Zellman had told the truth to everybody. As a result nobody had believed him. 'A story repeated so many times, at the first request and without the slightest variation, quite evidently learnt by heart right down to the slightest details, cannot *but* be a fabrication,' wrote Jeanne Bouillon in *La Voix*. 'The Zellman case must be demystified.' But there was nothing to demystify: 'They promised me an exit visa for my wife and me if I denounced an impostor.' The poor fellow was embarrassed: 'I'm not a stooly. I thought there was no harm in telling the truth. And you don't realize, she waited for me all the time I was in the camp. Any other woman would have married again.' This pitiable tone might have moved people's hearts: in fact, it provoked hostility. No one wanted to believe in so much innocence. The two photographs that Zellman had brought back from the camp were published; in both he was seen next to Gaverin—one in a group of twenty prisoners, the other at the foot of their bunk. It was hinted, however, that they were fakes.

The situation remained in suspense. Gaverin wrote for *Objectifs* an article entitled 'How I missed Brezhnev', in which there were four errors of fact. Psar spent three days at Frankfurt and sold the foreign rights in *The Russian Truth* to nine countries. The advances were considerable. Gaverin demanded his share: after all, he had a passport proving his identity. While awaiting new orders, Aleksandr played for time.

During this whole period, he got closer to Marguerite. She knew nothing of his true fear, but she read the articles in which he was variously described as a sinister Fascist, a dupe of the KGB, a prehistoric White Guard or a run-of-the-mill, well-intentioned liberal—and her devotion increased accordingly.

It was she who answered the letters from lawyers threatening libel suits against M. Gurverin-Karnosov sent 'care of' M. Psar. It was she who saw journalists of every shade and plumage who came to interview her boss with a hostility calculated to make him hit the ceiling. She understood that, in the dissidents' view, M. Psar was responsible for Gaverin because he belonged to the French literary establishment; similarly that the French held him responsible because he was himself of Russian origin. Above all she sensed that the small world over which he used to reign had vanished into thin air: she no longer knew who to telephone at *L'Impartial* or at *Objectifs*; the new editorial director at Lux, M. Baronet, gradually severed his connection with the Agency; the publication of the White Books, even the demystification of God, had been suspended, and for all too obvious a reason: Baronet was looking for a less compromising editor.

Throughout these trials, Marguerite remained herself, attentive, receptive, smiling only in response to a smile, staying in the office after working hours without totting up her overtime. Aleksandr even noticed that she had the bluest eyes and jet-black hair, a piquant contrast. But all he ever saw was, fleetingly, a pair of grey eyes.

In his childhood, he had so often heard, 'We'll be home for Christmas' . . . 'Don't let's be too optimistic: let's say Easter at the latest.' But, as in the song, Easter came, then Trinity . . . but still no homecoming. Now Christmas was approaching. Where was Alla? Where was Dmitri? Without Ivan Ivanich there was no way of communicating with them.

'Mme Boïsse on the line, Monsieur.'

'Jessica?'

'How are you, you sinister, Fascist liberal, dupe of the KGB? Would you be free this evening?'

'Of course.'

'I'll have vodka.'

He thought that they should change the password. He had no doubt that his conversations were being recorded. But how happy he was, ah! how happy he was that the prodigal father was taking him back once again to his bosom!

Jessica opened the door: 'It seems that you are notorious. My friends advise me to drop you. I'd be quite willing to tell them that I've never held you . . .'

A man of about forty, swarthy, with a triangular head, wearing a charcoal three-piece suit, was sitting on the striped sofa. His white shirt cuffs set off the darkness of his skin. The nipped in waistcoat under the unbuttoned jacket emphasised his slimness.

'Who's he?' asked Aleksandr.

'The new one.'

'Oh! Ivan V. What did they do with the other one? Stuff him?'

'My name if Piotr,' said the visitor in Russian.

His eyes had a natural tendency to shift about, but he had trained them to stay as steady as pearls sewn on for buttons.

Aleksandr thought that he looked like a little snake and took an instant dislike to him. Was this because he had replaced the excellent Ivan Ivanich, because he did not stand up to be introduced, because he spoke in that sententious, typically Soviet tone that members of the first emigration find so trying, whatever their political opinions may be?

'As far as I'm concerned,' said Aleksandr, 'you will be Ivan, but don't bank on being terrible: you're one number behind.'

The two men looked at one another with an antipathy that they did not bother to hide. Jessica was full of sparkle as she observed them. Piotr crossed his legs and pointed to an armchair.

'Please sit down,' he said, patiently, as one might speak to a child whose rudeness will be overlooked only for the moment.

The Geebee is a family. As he climbed the stairs, Aleksandr had thought, for a moment that he would find his own people again, find himself again, find some compensation for the hostility in which he had lived for the last few weeks. Instead he had come up against an even more dense and completely undeserved hostility.

'What's your rank?'

'I'm a lieutenant-colonel, I'm not co-opted and I'm your new case-officer.'

For a moment, Jessica thought that Aleksandr was about to pull Piotr up by the tie, treat him to all the wealth of insult that the Russian language is capable of and throw him out of the window. Aleksandr smiled ironically. Walking over to the table laid at the other end of the room, he poured himself a tot of vodka with a firm hand—the carafe was opaque with condensation, as he always insisted—drained it in one gulp and bit into a gherkin, which crunched between his teeth.

Piotr observed him with the pitying look of someone who

is holding all the good cards. He waited for a few moments for Psar to pretend to be more receptive, then, seeing that he went on chewing and held out his hand to the carafe, said: 'I've bad news for you, Psar.'

He took an envelope from his inside pocket. Aleksandr had to cross the room to take it. Jessica, who had not been dismissed, was leaning against the wall and observed the scene, drawing on a cigarette: it was time, she thought, that Aleksandr was put in his place.

Aleksandr walked over to the standard lamp to read the letter:

> 'My dear Aleksandr Dmitrich, I don't know how to tell you of the disaster that has struck you so close to home. Be a man and bear this trial as befits a man, an officer, a Bolshevik. You are not unaware that our roads are dangerous. A drunken truck-driver and, in an instant, two innocent lives go up in smoke. Your wife and son did not suffer: let that be some consolation for you.
>
> 'You are still young and nothing is ever lost for a man who enjoys health, energy and a faith, as you do. On your return to our beloved country, you will start, I am sure a true Russian family, a true Soviet family.
>
> 'This return must already seem less urgent to you; action is the best distraction for souls of your temperament; and I believe that I am anticipating your wishes in asking you to undertake on our behalf an important operation from which the country and the Party expect much.
>
> 'Cordial salutations.
>
> 'Sincerely, Iakov Pitman.'

'Hand it back!' Piotr commanded, holding out his hand.

Aleksandr could no longer hear—or see. 'Dmitri! Son! . . . Alla! Allochka.' He took a deep breath—and another. He filled himself with air. There was something inside him that was about to explode. Nothing did explode. He saw again Alla's grey eyes and the gaiety with which she used to leap into their bed. He tried to move his jaw up and down— he did not know why. He felt ill. He no longer knew for how long he had felt ill. 'My little boy . . .' He hardly found enough voice to ask: 'And the driver?'

Pitman had foreseen the question. Piotr replied: 'Dead too. The truck caught fire. Hand back the paper.'

A suspicion crossed Aleksandr's heavy heart: 'Supposing it was the Bolsheviks who killed them?' But there was no reason why they should kill that woman and that child that they had given him.

Absent-mindedly, Aleksandr walked a few steps, handed back the letter to Piotr, who was still sitting, and wandered around the drawing-room. His arms swung loose. He was trying to get back to a normal rhythm of breathing. He went through the motions of swallowing, but had nothing to swallow. Jessica looked at him, curious, frightened, but not displeased. She did not know what was in that letter, but she had caught the words 'Dead, too.' That was enough. So there was someone in the world whom that icicle Psar had loved?

Piotr's expression veered to boredom. Aleksandr went and placed his forehead against the window, looked out into the street, saw nothing, looked at his watch without knowing that he was doing so.

'Come on. Get a grip on yourself,' said Piotr.

Aleksandr looked at him, without understanding.

'I've a few orders to give you. Our contact procedures remain the same, except that you will no longer mention vodka: if you ask to see Jessica or if she asks to see you, that will be enough. The emergency number has been changed. It will now be . . .'

He gave it. Aleksandr made a mechanical movement to take out his diary, then remembered in time that this kind of number has to be learnt by heart.

'Repeat, please.'

Piotr repeated, without concealing a touch of impatience.

'If you need me, you ask for Piotr. Avoid any contact that isn't indispensable.'

'I've been practising this trade for thirty years,' Aleksandr said quietly.

He wanted to weep, not because he had lost his wife and son—that pain was above tears—but because this man was bullying him.

'For the moment your duties will consist in demanding and getting your orchestra to demand . . .'

'I don't have an orchestra any more. You sabotaged it.'

'. . . the freeing of Mikhail Kurnosov, the real author of *The Russian Truth*.'

'I don't have an orchestra any more.'

'Pick up the pieces. Other orchestras will be demanding the same thing. It's a concerted operation. *Concertante*. But your voice must be heard first. It will be the best way of shifting any blame from you in the eyes of French opinion. Once you start, you'll get support. At our next contact, I'll give you the rest of your instructions.'

Piotr got up: small, vigorous, agile.

'An asp!' Aleksandr thought.

The other man held out his hand. Numb with pain, Aleksandr took it.

'Do something to get over it,' said Piotr with a trace of pity. 'Take a few politico-cultural measures.'

He indicated with his chin the well furnished table and Jessica.

'You have all you need.'

He looked at Jessica coldly.

'And you,' he said to her in Russian—and he added, a coarse little word—'I've got my eye on you.'

He strode to the door with a springy step. His charcoal suit—two slits on the sides—had been cut this side of the Oder-Neisse line.

It occurred to Aleksandr to follow Piotr's advice. He would no doubt have done so if Piotr had not inspired such horror in him: it was hate at first sight. He contented himself with drinking two nips of vodka, because he was thirsty, as if alcohol could have slaked his thirst. Then he left, without a glance in Jessica's direction.

He walked in the streets. It was cold; the dampness clung to his skin, seeped in, reached his bones and arteries. In a *pâtisserie* that was still open, a parallelepiped of light in the night, he saw a group of children. He hated their parents.

What hurt him most was that broken lineage, that unused

tenderness . . . And by what right had they taken that unique being from him, a being who could never be repeated, whom he had not even known? 'Ah! If only I'd known him, it would have been easier.' He was wrong, of course. The words 'by what right!' constantly came back into his mind. He had been treated with the ultimate injustice. He was forty-nine, he would still have sons, but he could never have that one, that Dmitri. Usually, he thought in no particular language, rather in abstractions. This evening, however, his thoughts followed one another in such incoherence that he felt the need to pour them into words, and he spoke to himself with French words linked together by Russian grammar: 'If I *shall* never have a son, why have I lived?'

Less deeply, he also suffered from Alla's death, heartbroken at the thought that a particular moment of intimacy, of trust, a particular transfiguration of the flesh that they had brought about together, a particular dimple that appeared in Alla's right cheek—or was it the left?—when she smiled, a particular darkening of her grey eyes when she gave up all self-control, were irrecoverable. How many such smiles had there been? So many. Not one more. And there would never be any more.

These two pains formed the *basso continuo* underlying an even more acute pain: on the surface, where pain emerges without reference to any order of causes, he was devastated by the trials of recent days, by the insolence of journalists like the one to whom he had shown the door when he would have been more willing (and able) to throw him out of the window, the sense of his powerlessness before the calumnies piling up against him, his humiliation at the idea that they hurt him, even though in a sense calumny was his business. These vexations tormented him like a corn on the foot or an ulcer in the mouth, and yet they did not distract him from his mourning as physical discomfort might have done. He felt he was getting spiteful, something he had never been, for he had always regarded spite as a weakness.

He crossed Paris, from La Muette to the Luxembourg and found himself ringing at Ballandar's door. A short young man with black hair, a white shirt opened down the front revealing a chest of refined delicacy, looked him up and down.

'José isn't in.'

'That depends,' Aleksandr replied, moving forward.

He would have been delighted if the young man had tried to stop him: he would have thrown him down the stairs head first. As it was the youth ran off waving his arms like a butterfly beating its wings: 'José, José, there's a Turk here wants to speak to you.'

With his mane of wavy light brown hair, his veiled brown eyes, his pink and white complexion, Aleksandr looked nothing like a Turk. But he gave, especially at that moment, an impression of brute strength that almost justified the designation.

Ballandar, in shirt sleeves, was taking down one of the more saleable paintings from his collection of contemporary art. When he saw Aleksandr his expression changed.

Aleksandr smiled.

'You don't seem very pleased to see me.'

Choosing his words and being careful not to look at the young man, Ballandar said slowly: 'That paper I did out of friendship for you, Aleksandr Psar, cost me my career. That's enough, don't you think?'

'José Ballandar, I'm very well aware of your friendship, especially as I propose to invoke it a second time.'

The raised hands that were still holding the painting against the wall began to shake. Aleksandr noticed this with satisfaction.

'Don't get worked up like that. You'll drop that daub of yours. You write, I think in a little rag for impotent, left-wing intellectuals called *Bulldozer*.'

'That revolutionary and honorable publication is called *Le Soc*.'

The young man stood, mouth agape with horror. Aleksandr nearly said something offensive to him, but contained himself.

'Well, I'm going to make a present to *Le Soc*. If you know how to use it, you'll get certain advantages from it that might take you far. It might even hoist you back on to your pedestal. Tomorrow you'll launch a campaign for the freeing of the real Kurnosov. The press will follow you, I promise.'

This time it was Ballandar's turn to smile.

'You promise me, *you*? You don't seem to realize that if I'm in the gutter, you're in the sewer!'

'It's up to you, my dear Ballandar. Either you become the instigator of this campaign and reap the rewards . . .'

Aleksandr remembered that, on the first occasion, he felt a certain embarrassment at blackmailing Fourveret and Ballandar. But that was all over now: today, he was in a mood for shooting captives.

'Or we shall do a little *explication de texte* in public and, as a little rehearsal, we might do it in front of your young friend here.'

He put his hand into his inside pocket.

'One day,' said Ballandar, in a tone of resignation, 'I'll find a way of getting rid of you.'

Aleksandr gave a brief, insulting laugh that sounded false and turned on his heels.

Two days later, *Le Soc* published the following text inside a black frame:

Whom are they trying to fool?

The publication of a book that we have to dare to call by its name, *The Russian Truth*, and on the value of which the best minds are far from being in agreement, has exceeded, has far-exceeded the limits ascribed to a purely literary event. [The phrase was not a very happy one, but the author wanted to show that he was moved.]

Some time ago, the USSR sent us a pirate who presented himself at first as the author of this book, then confessed to his imposture, then denied his confession . . . We no longer know where he stands. Could it be that he is on a war footing?

We would prefer not to think so.

The only way to clear the matter up, the only way to re-establish the truth, is to free the real author of this controversial book and also, if he is not in fact the same person, the author of the attempted assassination of Brezhnev, Mikhail Kurnosov.

I throw down the challenge: I am offering an opportunity to the leaders of the Soviet Union. Gentlemen or Comrades, as you please, establish your good faith once and for all!

Having dared to write these lines Ballandar went to ground. He now expected to lose his job at *Le Soc*, but hardly had twenty-four hours passed than Aleksandr's prediction came true. The great Etienne Depensier himself, performing a volte-face, made his cultured, liberal castrato voice heard: 'Our friend Ballandar, from the depths of a retreat that has moved all those that admire his immeasurable talent (I intend no slight to his new pulpit!), has set us an example of an anguish that we should all share, of a demand that we should all give voice to loud and clear. We have had enough! The Kremlin must not go on playing with French public opinion, like a cat with a mouse. Let them free and present to us the real Kurnosov!'

Paris is capable of getting excited about anything, from the yoyo to the guillotine, but these crazes are not always as spontaneous as one might like to think. Seven orchestras producing the same music at the same time tended to result in thousands of perfectly sincere fiddles and bagpipes taking up the tune. With these relays of relays infecting their own relays, at the end of the week nothing could be heard in Paris except a single clamour: 'Free Kurnosov!'

Since one of the orchestras was perched in the civil service, the press seemed almost immediately to have scored points. Certain officially unofficial voices let it be known that the government was examining the possibility of asking the leaders of a certain country to throw light on a particular problem, which might lead to the freeing of a particular person whose name was on all lips . . .

Public opinion (or what is called public opinion, as if the public had already grown so stupid as to have only one opinion for fifty million individuals) hurled itself into the fray. Generally speaking, those who get worked up about the freedom of others without themselves taking too many risks prefer to attack Greek colonels or Chilean generals who are quite unable to come and ask them why they are bawling their heads off; with the Communists one never knows—it might after all take very little for scores to be settled in blood. But, for once, the idea prevailed that one might get away with giving the tiger's tail just a tweak: after all, it was more amusing than pulling the tail of a mere cat! First, since there were Communists in the government, it was the reflex of every self-respecting Frenchman to distance himself from the extreme left; and, anyway, had not Ballandar set the example? There couldn't be much danger in it then. So everyone went and courageously demonstrated before the Soviet embassy and the ambassador's residence.

It was one of the gayest fashions in Paris. Every organization issued its slogans and the carnival began. Only the bad weather of that late autumn intervened several times in favour of the USSR; but when one has humanitarian convictions, one can risk a headcold. Anyway, why not combine business and pleasure? Whether one lived in the sixteenth or the seventh arrondissement, whether one had a dog or a bicycle or was an adept of that Western yoga known as jogging, there was nothing to prevent one demonstrating for freedom in the world while taking care of one's own—or Fido's—health.

In the Rue de Grenelle, everything was done within reasonable and—almost—decent limits: a few dog-owners stopped ostentatiously in front of no. 79, but it was the dogs rather than their masters who expressed their opinions; at those times when particularly boring law or literature professors were lecturing, there were even young champions marching up and down in front of the *porte cochère* yelling in unison: 'Give us Kurnosov! Give us Kurnosov!'—but that was as nothing compared with the circus going on at the other end of Paris, in front of the palace-blockhouse whose privileges of extra-territoriality have transformed a couple of acres of the sixteenth arrondissement into a little piece of proletarian paradise.

Here there was an endless round. 'Walk around it, clock-wise!' the tribunes of freedom had ordered. So they walked around it clockwise. Gentlemen wearing hats swapped yarns about their war experiences or their youthful escapades. Schoolboys practised their thousand metres. Little girls in navy-blue uniforms brought their terrier along, ladies in furs, their afghans. Some, it was said, sent their Portuguese maids to walk round the embassy three times at the standard hourly rate. Members of the Racing Club turned up in smart coloured riding breeches and trotted round the building, timing themselves abreast of the red flag. There were fanatical cyclists and lazier two-wheelers on mopeds. They went round and round. It was used as a rendez-vous: 'Taking a turn this evening?' The noun 'turn' signified for some ten days or so 'a turn from left to right around the Soviet Embassy'. Comedians told stories: 'Here I am "taking a turn" yesterday and here's this guy next to me, big paunch, cigar, typical capitalist, he's also taking a turn. So, to pass the time, what with I'm getting bored like, I says to him "I'm a comedian," I says, "and you?" "I'm in cognito," he says. "Well," I says, "I guess it's a living." "Don't you believe it," he says. "An ambassador's salary," he says, "an ambassador's salary's chicken-feed." D'you know what . . . I was impressed. "You mean to say you're . . ." "Yes," he says, "I'm an ambassador," he says, "but don't let that change nothing between us." "Well," I says, "you wouldn't mind my asking what country you represent?" "The USSR, see," he says. "You don't think I'd have bothered to turn out if I didn't have my orfice right here?" "Now half a mo'," I says. "If you're the ambassador of the USSR, what you doing taking a turn with us?" "Weeell," he says, "It's just I ain't no snob. It's good for the health," he says, "and I like doing the same as everyone else." I ain't half shocked! "Listen," I says, "let me give you a piece of advice. If you want to take a turn, go ahead, but if you do it from left to right, you might get into trouble with your bosses. You ought at least to do it from right to left." "Why, thank you very much," he says, "I never thought of that." Well, you can go and see for yourselves. If you see a guy turning in the opposite direction to everyone else, you know what—you'd better address him as Your Excellency.'

Most of the dervishes, as *Le Dindon déchaîné* nicknamed them, considered that they had done enough by taking part in these circumductions, but many also sported pennants that fluttered over their bicycles or with the poles stuck into their belts, so that they rode or walked around surmounted by slogans of varying inventiveness: 'Freedom for Kurnosov', 'No to the Soviet Imposture', 'Free the Anonymous Prisoner', 'Unmask him or unmask yourselves', 'Would exchange Marchais for Kurnosov', 'Free Kurnosov, treat Brezhnev', 'Down with the psykushkas', 'You are worse than the Tsars', etc.

Many of these ingenious declarations had been translated into Russian by well-meaning Russian-speakers and then lots of individuals, who had never seen Cyrillic characters in their lives, spent the whole night copying them out, as best they could, on pieces of paper, cardboard, bits of sheet, squares of plywood, anything from the ragbag and even (obviously those with nostalgic feelings about Action française) on old underpants, which fluttered proudly at the end of their broomsticks.

Police were deployed to keep the demonstrators away from immediate proximity to the embassy, but the entire sixteenth arrondissement could not be declared out of bounds to the supporters of Kurnosov and, under the blasé eye of the *gardes républicains*, the circumambulation continued at some distance, tirelessly. Local insomniacs came and performed, about two in the morning, one or two revolutions around the haughty edifice. A famous cartoonist showed two men in elegant tailor-made dressing-gowns trotting the circuit shoulder to shoulder: 'This is the first time in my life,' said one of them, 'that I have felt revolutionary.' The National Assembly began to stir. One deputy walked round the embassy, wearing his scarf as a sash. Without knowing it he had launched a sub-fashion. Mayors appeared, with their tricolour sashes slung round their bellies. Those who had been awarded decorations, began to flaunt their medals; before long it became *de rigueur* to wear them, suspended from their appropriate ribbons. There were decoration competitions, which were reported in the papers: those of Albert the Bear, St Julian of the Peartree, the Upturned Dragon, the Polar Star, African Redemption were the most commented upon. For two days, ladies appeared wearing the most incredible hats, brought back from Rio or New Orleans, found in attics or old trunks. Heavens! How amusing it was to attack the Soviet Union, especially when there was a

Socialist government! The accessory was king. Kurnosov's freedom was demanded in Hotchkisses and Studebakers, on De Dion et Bouton motor-tricycles, on roller skates, on skateboards, on bicycles. Assaults were launched with cigarette-holders and sword-sticks. The first prize went to a Belgian princess who, for two years, had owned and run a thoroughbred that she had called Iron Mask. When she turned up in front of the Soviet Embassy, riding her bay like an Amazon and accompanied by an entire cavalcade unfurling a banner that simply proposed the following exchange: 'Mine for yours', a tremor of delight ran through Paris. The lefties and the princess in the service of the same cause! There were moments of epic fraternization: latter-day hippies joined Knights of Malta to chant slogans. A unique snobbery convulsed every layer of Paris society; nothing of the kind had been seen since the advent of scoobidoo.

Aleksandr Psar, the discoverer of *The Russian Truth*, found himself the uncrowned, unchallenged king of this carnival. He was photographed kissing the Belgian princess's hand, he was interviewed by the newspapers, cross-examined by the state radio and more deferentially questioned by the free radio stations. He appeared on television in a discussion in which Ballandar took part; the two men made a great show of friendship. 'What do you think of Gaverin? Who is the true Iron Mask? What aim is being pursued in this affair by the Soviet Union? Was she not, in fact, beginning to look ridiculous?' Psar gave voice only to suppositions, preferably contradictory ones. That people could regard the foremost military power in the world as ridiculous struck him as an unfathomable stupidity.

Without seeing Piotr again, Aleksandr threw himself furiously into the fray. Speaking here, answering questions there, collecting secret sympathizers and noisy supporters, alerting the professionals of conscience and the specialists in public opinion, he demonstrated to his masters that, though deprived by them of most of his orchestra, he was still capable of directing an operation. All this activity helped to numb his pain; he suffered less. Marguerite, of course, worked as much as, even more than, him, and did not conceal how delighted she was to see the Agency, which had been decried for a time, acquire more and more authority. Manuscripts piled up, the telephone never stopped ringing. Aleksandr's diary was filled weeks in advance.

'You aren't taking too much on, are you, Marguerite? Would you like me to take on a temp?'

'Oh, no Monsieur, by no means! Unless you find my work isn't up to scratch.'

The blue eyes under the dark hair shone with devotion.

Aleksandr mistrusted official invitations, but the summons from the Quai d'Orsay was couched in the most flattering terms and the *chef de cabinet* who received M. Psar in a Louis Seize office with hardly faded hangings received him in the most fulsome way. From the two tall windows one could see the early twilight falling over the Seine and a lilac-tinted mist rising up to meet it.

'My dear sir,' said Edme de Malmaison, putting the fingers of both hands together to form a late-Gothic arch, 'I have news for you that is not entirely bad.'

His hair was turning silver; his eyebrows, in the shape of circumflex accents, had remained very black.

'I realize that you possess no legal power to enable you to represent M. Kurnosov, but your talents and, if I may say so, your courage—excuse me for using such a coarse word— have brought you to the forefront of this imbroglio, in which, for our part, we can play only an intermediary role, though one that has been traditionally ours, as the minister pointed out to me. I would even go so far as to say—or rather he himself said—that it is our vocation.

'This is more or less what the Soviets are saying: "You say that we have created an embarrassing situation for French intellectual circles by throwing at your feet, so to speak" '— M. de Malmaison smiled saucily—' "a false dissident, a false assassin, a false author of a false *Russian Truth*. All this," declare the Soviets, "is quite untrue. We owe you no explanations, but we are willing to give them all the same. We simply granted an exit visa to a certain M. Kurnosov, who, for reasons unknown to us, then decided to claim authorship of a work that we do not know either, which one of your publishers has published under his own responsibility and which they attribute, God may know why, but Marx does not, to a certain "Anonymous Prisoner", which "Anonymous Prisoner", also known as "Iron Mask", has been confused by your press with a poor mental patient who, some ten years ago, provided a demonstration of his mental state by firing on the First Secretary of the Party, and who is also called Kurnosov, which is hardly surprising in a country of Great Russian noses. Of course this confusion has nothing to do with us. So, what is it all about? You have on your hands a campaign we find rather irritating, but one that must be especially humiliating for you, since you have shown yourselves incapable of protecting us, your guests, against the clowns performing their routines under our windows." I am still speaking for the Soviets, my dear sir, as you will appreciate. "Well, we'll treat you more than fair—and we intend to pull this thorn out of your foot for you. If those hysterics want our madman, they can have him: the more fools together, the better the fun, as your proverb truly puts it. Of course, we cannot guarantee that it was that particular madman who wrote the book in question: if he did write it, if he did send it into the West, if he did publish it, it was without our knowledge. On the other hand, what we can assure you of is that the Kurnosov whom we shall send to you carriage paid will be the same one who thought fit to fire on M. Brezhnev. It will be said once again that we are giving in to the pressure of world opinion: let it be said! After all, it is a fact that a truly democratic government is sensitive to the opinion of the peoples. In exchange for this good act, we would ask you only one thing: do not send us back the other Kurnosov, the one who claimed at a certain moment to be called Gaverin and who must also be mad: we would not know what to do with him. If we shut him up somewhere, you might take it into your heads to demand him back after two weeks, saying: 'No, he's the right one.' So, please keep both of them, even if you put them together in a padded cell." That, my dear sir, is what the Soviets are saying to us.

'I shan't try to persuade you that our government is overjoyed about this affair. One Kurnosov may be acceptable; two becomes rather tiring. But what can we do? Public opinion has certainly risen, or should I say has been raised?'

The left circumflex accent became sharper. 'Anyway the indications appear to be that our Soviet colleagues really are influenced by it. In short, the Prime Minister is not against. However, the less our respective high spheres are seen to have taken part in this performance the better it will be, and my minister thought that you might head a sort of . . . reception committee made up of artistic and literary personalities, which might stress the private rather than the public character of the negotiations.

'Ah! One last thing. The Soviet government seems rather irritated by the attitude of Kurnosov-Gaverin who, I understand, seems to fear an attack against his person, changes his hotel in the middle of the night and is having an electronic fortress built for himself . . . It would be better if M. Kurnosov no. 2 did not give himself such fantastic airs. We have been assured—not formally, of course, but apparently to our satisfaction, at least that is what my minister believes —that no ill will befall him from the Soviets, so will he please refrain from playing hide and seek . . .'

The other eyebrow imitated the Eiffel Tower.

Aleksandr went back to the office. Mme Boïsse had telephoned: she would be at the Bar Anglais of the Plaza at 7.30 that evening.

She was there. She had brought a message from Piotr: 'Tomorrow at 2.30 p.m. in the Louvre, in front of the Egyptian mastaba. If impossible, the day after tomorrow half-an-hour earlier, in the Opéra Museum.' Aleksandr repressed a grimace. He had had case-officers who liked to meet in the busiest place possible, others who felt at ease only in some deserted spot at midnight. The new Ivan was subtler: he wanted a crowd, but the smallest one possible.

'Piotr reminds you,' said Jessica, 'to take the necessary precautions.'

Aleksandr changed métro twice, passed through a store with two entrances, and found his way into the Louvre through the entrance on the *Cour carée*. Piotr, small, slim, supple as a viper, wearing a smart suit, black with a hint of blue, was walking up and down, his hands behind his back. Aleksandr remembered the procedure for these rendez-vous and went and planted himself in front of the mastaba. A voice behind him said: 'Psar, if I'm not mistaken?'

'You aren't mistaken, Ivan.'

'Piotr.'

'I thought you were Ivan.'

'I'm Piotr.'

'Last time you were Ivan.'

Piotr shrugged his shoulders. He started to walk, pretending to admire the vases and sarcophagi.

'What precautions have you taken?'

'Sufficient precautions.'

'What time did you set out?'

'From the office? 12.30. I stopped for lunch.'

'When I say "precautions" I mean "precautions". I left home at seven this morning and I've been changing routes ever since.'

'That's what one has to do when one hasn't much talent.'

'Psar, don't force me to take disciplinary measures.'

'Ivan, I advise you to consult my file. I was still young and tender when they sent me just such a busybody as you. Consult the year-book and you'll see where he's busying himself now.'

They stopped in front of the crouching scribe with the strange encrusted eyes.

'I have orders to give you,' said Piotr patiently.

'Apparently there have been bureaucrats in every civilization,' said Aleksandr, pretending to compare the scribe's stare with Piotr's.

'I observe that you have borrowed from the French a certain flippancy of tone that I would advise you to drop at once. I have already informed Comrade Pitman of our differences, and suggested that he appoint some other influence agent than yourself for the extremely important operation that I have been entrusted with. He replied that you were to remain at your post, and he simply added: "You have only to tighten the screw." Is that clear, Psar?'

'Clear enough.'

'The operation will consist . . .' Piotr had learnt his text by heart so as not to have to carry compromising documents on his person. '. . . in setting up, first in France and then throughout the world, a universal Party, right-wing in tendency, authoritarian, corporatist, that could offer a credible third solution to those who approve neither of the Communist system nor of the capitalist system. France has been chosen on account of its universalist tradition: besides, the choice of a more powerful country, such as the United States, might have produced a negative effect on certain individuals. The catalyst of this party will be a dissident who will have suitably demonstrated his hostility to Communism, and whose works are evidence of his hostility to capitalism, the man chosen for this task is Mikhail Leontich Kurnosov, born at Kostroma on 12 July 1926, the author of an assassination attempt against Leonid Ilich Brezhnev and of the work entitled *The Russian Truth.*'

They had left the Egyptians, walked through the Assyrians, followed a long corridor bordered with white wall panels and arrived at the Greeks. The rooms were being rearranged and redecorated: the gods retreating before the invasion of ladders and scaffolding suggested the advent of some ultimate chaos. 'All those sublime bodies, all that civilization, what is the point of it all?' thought Aleksandr. 'I have no son, and the state that I have served for thirty years is setting up a Fascist party. The Barbarians have won. The Barbarians always win.' He felt uncomfortable in the dreary light that reigned around those great masses of living stone.

'Kurnosov,' Piotr went on, in his didactic tone, 'is enthusiastic about the idea of creating a party of the type I have just described. Obviously he does not suspect and must not suspect that his party will be radio-controlled by the Committee of State Security. In these circumstances, since it is impossible to attach him to an ordinary case-officer, he will be placed under the aegis of influence agent Aleksandr Dmitrich Psar.'

They arrived at the grand staircase. Influence agent Aleksandr Dmitrich Psar stopped in front of the Victory of Samothrace. 'To conquer: there is nothing more beautiful. But who conquers whom? Marathon, Salamis, all right. And what then? Rome or Greece? What does it all mean?' At the same time, he felt a prodigious ambition stirring within him: to be the *éminence grise* (the Mephistopheles?) of a party of that importance, and to hand it one day on a platter to his masters . . . He was wrong to believe that he was not appreciated. The Directorate had chosen him for the most magnificent mission imaginable. For a moment, his mind went back to the gallery of the Chimeras and to the two figures caught in the rigging of that vessel. Then he thought of a story by Jules Verne in which the traitor conceals an iron ingot near the compass and alters the course of the ship by shifting not the helm but the north itself.

'Psar's first objective,' Piotr continued in his expressionless voice, 'will be to gain Kurnosov's complete confidence. Kurnosov will be "primed" in such a way that he can't take a single step without Psar. Kurnosov seems anxious to spread his doctrine, but he will have to be taught to present it in a more articulate way, one more accessible to Westerners than in his book. He will also have to be guided in the choice of a management committee to be taken from the following list.'

Piotr recited a list of thirty-seven names of men and women of various nationalities, all intellectuals, all fairly well known, who would be only too pleased to be better known, all belonging to the moderate right, which it was the purpose of the operation to compromise. A good haul, if they could all be caught.

All this suddenly struck Aleksandr as enormously complicated, utterly wearisome. Yes, he was flattered, he was capable of carrying out the operation, but, in a way, it no longer interested him. In a way, he was through with it all. He no longer had any wish other than the one that had been the axis and mainspring of his life. 'I shan't go home. Alek, you will go in my place.' And that finger stretched out to his cheek and unable to reach it. Today, Aleksandr had no more strength than that finger.

'I'm tired,' he said, 'and the handbook says that one should never push a tired agent too far. My main wish, as you know, is to go home. If, when Pitman offered me this ambush, I accepted it, it was because I already wanted to go home, with my head high.'

He had difficulty standing or speaking distinctly. Rather than mount the steps, he turned back.

'Supposing I agree to infiltrate your new party. It would mean ten years more work. At fifty-nine, one should no longer have children. Children don't care for senile parents.'

Piotr followed him, observing him ironically.

'I still think Pitman is wrong about you, Psar. He imagines that you are one of the glories of his celebrated Directorate. In fact, you aren't even capable of losing a woman you saw for two weeks and a kid you've never seen at all without working yourself up against the whole world. That shows either that your nerves are in a very bad state or that you have an imagination that is quite unacceptable in our profession. They tell me that you were something of a man-of-letters once. Obviously, you still haven't got over it.'

Reprimanded by his junior, Aleksandr just managed to contain his anger.

'You may be right,' he said. 'Yes, you may well be right.'

'It isn't up to me to be right or wrong. I have orders to pass on: I pass them on; a screw to tighten, I tighten it.'

'You're taking your wishes for reality, Ivanchik. How do you think you're going to tighten this screw? You haven't even got a Bulgarian umbrella under your arm.'

'Psar, the phenomenon is well known: you're going off the rails. If you want to apply for leave, I shall back up your request. But if you refuse to carry out my orders . . . No, no, we won't put curare in your chocolate. On the other hand, you must realize that our people can do without undisciplined freaks.'

They paused for some time in front of the Vénus de Milo.

'Fine female,' Piotr commented.

There were a few tourists there, three reactionary nuns in winged coifs, two giggling schoolboys.

'I prefer the Aphrodite with Eros,' Aleksandr replied, pointing to a fine classical Venus flanked by a later Cupid. 'So, if I refuse, I too shall rot at Sainte-Geneviève?'

Piotr shrugged his narrow, neatly tailored shoulders.

'What does it matter which worms one feeds?'

'Well, to me, it does matter. I have a definite preference for my own hereditary worms. I have no desire to be eaten by maggots fed on French petty bourgeois.'

'It's up to you.'

Piotr walked off, an asp wriggling its tortuous way between the gods.

Aleksandr caught up with him: 'How long, this time?'

'Five years. Three if we find you a stand-in.'

Aleksandr shut his eyes. 'I shan't go home. Alek you will go in my place.'

'I'll take on the operation, Ivan.'

'Piotr.'

'I'll take on the operation, Piotr.'

7
Hard Sign

A frozen, porous crust covered the desert of Roissy when the special plane landed. Gaverin, 'dead' or 'biodegradable' agent, had been sent to France by the back door. Kurnosov, whom France was so stridently demanding, was officially handed over by representatives of the Ministry of the Interior in their green uniforms with red epaulettes.

The reception committee were shivering behind a window and observed the little man striding towards them, his short, pyramidal nose sticking out under his steel-rimmed spectacles, his body bundled up in a new sheepskin coat, torrents of steam emerging from his mouth.

'Who'll supply the caption to put into the balloon?' asked Monthignies.

Though out of work, he was one of the lucky ones: he had decided to learn German and, consequently, received from the state 110 per cent of what he had earned when working.

The other members of the reception committee presided over by Aleksandr Psar might be divided into two categories: the amateurs, consisting of a drunken Albanian dramatist, an insidious Bulgarian bishop, an American-Jewish countess, all, of course, more Parisian than the Parisians; and the professionals: M. Baronet, managing director of the Lux publishing house, M. Fourveret, who had retired, but probably not for long, M. Ballandar, still a reviewer for *Le Soc* and temporarily occasional contributor to *Objectifs*, Mme Choustrewitz, who wanted to know whether the Soviets kissed ladies' hands as well as the émigrés, and Monthignies, already mentioned. Aleksandr had systematically eliminated from the committee anyone who might be too conspicuous or who might belong to another orchestra, or who quite simply was capable of saying two words in Russian. Indeed, he intended to keep Kurnosov on as tight a rein as possible, and the Directorate, accommodating as ever, had given him the means to do so: Gaverin, who was never to be anything but a false Kurnosov, had been secretly assisted in his study of French; the true Kurnosov, on the other hand, had been given all the books he wanted, but never any oral teaching, so that he pronounced the French word *oiseau*, for example, as 'oh heess eh ah hu' and the English word *church* as 'skhiurskh'. For a time, this pronunciation would protect him from the indiscreet as surely as the bars of the Leningrad Special Hospital.

'Mikhail Leontich?'

'Yes. You are who?'

'Psar, Aleksandr Dmitrich.'

'Ivan the Terrible's Psar?'

'Precisely.'

'You're from the first emigration, then?'

'My father was an officer in the White Army.'

'Let's get acquainted: I'm not prejudiced.'

Journalists were swarming around. Flash bulbs flashed. Kurnosov stopped in the middle of the circle, majestic despite his short stature and his over-long sheepskin coat. He stood very erect, holding under his arm a parcel of handwritten notes.

'I have luggage. Have someone take care of it.'

He was bombarded with questions from every side.

'What do they want to know?'

'Mikhail Leontich, you have a press conference this evening. I think it might be better to make no pronouncement now—keep your powder dry.'

Kurnosov nodded gravely, then turned to the journalists and declared distinctly: '*Viv lia Fran-ss.*'

He stressed his words with a quick movement of the chin.

'You have my book? They only showed me the press cuttings.'

Psar showed him both editions, the paperback and the hardback.

'Not too bad,' said Kurnosov, with good grace. 'Though the margins are a bit mean. Where's the car?'

This time the press conference took place at the Palais des Congrès. There were at least a thousand people there. The 'dervishes' came to applaud their victory, having snatched the unfortunate Anonymous Prisoner from the clutches of repressive psychiatrists. There was a babble of journalists; even the internationals had turned up. International Communism may triumph in Angola, Abyssinia, Nicaragua, El Salvador, Poland . . . but the Soviet Union had just shown that it trembled before public opinion. That was something to be proud of.

Backstage, Aleksandr met Divo, who asked him at once, with one of his slanted smiles: 'Is it the right one, this time?'

'I hope so.'

'Very different from the other?'

'Yes and no.'

Aleksandr was surprised to hear himself add: '*Homo sovieticus* always remains *homo sovieticus*.'

'I'm talking to Divo almost with fellow-feeling, almost with complicity,' he thought. 'What's happening? In a way he is closer to me than *they* are.'

He went on: '*Homo sovieticus* believes that everything is his due because nothing will be given him: as a result, he is willing to get anything by any means. You know, one thing surprises me. When I go out to meet someone who has been in the camps, I expect to find a hungry, stunned, degraded individual, one of the living-dead, as it were. After all, if they are sent into those institutions, it's not, as we do with our common-law criminals, to slap them on the back and treat them to film-shows every week. But those I go to meet seem quite full of themselves, more concerned with making demands than with survival. Gaverin was constantly asking me for money. This one had no sooner set foot on French soil than he was calling for his car. Why do you think that is?'

Divo listened, observing with an ironic eye the minks and squirrels, the cashmeres and alpacas that seethed around them. 'What have we here?' he muttered. 'The World? The Underworld? The Third World? It must be the Global Duckpond.' He reverted to Aleksandr's observation: 'I think it's a question of natural selection. To survive in a camp, to make oneself heard by international opinion, to find, once one has got out of the hole, the energy to emigrate and to go on struggling, one has to possess certain qualities and certain defects. The man you describe is necessarily *homo sovieticus militans*, and you define the species very well. I would have said quite simply that he has an incredible cheek. But, don't you see, without cheek Solzhenitsyn would still be teaching physics at Riazan, at best. I should even bet that it took him sheer cheek to overcome his cancer.'

He was still smiling his slanted smile.

This man of irony, yet utterly lacking in bitterness, this intellectual to whom no one could reproach a single base action, this kind of poet whose speciality was surgical lucidity, would, Aleksandr thought, be a choice recruit for the Universal Party. It would be delightful to get this so purely reactionary (in the best sense of the term, that is, in reaction against) mind working on a subversive enterprise. The most delicious thing about the theory of relays is that the relays never know what they are doing. Subversion, thought Aleksandr, operates like a gigantic electronic machine: with semi-conductors. Divo would be an excellent semi-conductor. Of course, he would have to keep him out of Kurnosov's way and not allow him any say in the direction of events: he might tangle up the divine skein.

Aleksandr took his place on the platform of the Palais des Congrès with deliberate slowness and assurance. Not so long ago he was presenting the false Kurnosov to the press; now it had fallen to him to present the real one, while launching upon the world an undertaking of the greatest scope. Meanwhile, he had been cut to the quick: the deaths of his wife and son were lodged inside him like those bullets in the body that cannot be removed without a risk to the life of the wounded man. The feeling that his Directorate and Pitman himself no longer had as much confidence in him as before had wounded him at least as deeply. His life, up till now, had been marked by no great pain, except for the death of his father; he had been, so to speak, a virgin to pain, and now these trials had brought him closer to other men and, at the same time, given him a weight, an authority, that he had lacked before. He had never been as 'radiant' as he was that evening.

As he opened his mouth, he suddenly remembered that

sun-drenched moment last summer, in front of the Bernini fountain, when he had taken from that man in the orange jacket the parcel of *Oggi*s containing *The Russian Truth*. He did not say to himself: 'How happy I was then!', but 'How young I was then!' And it was true: for some days his light-brown hair had begun to take on a new sheen. If he lived long enough he would have a magnificent shock of silver hair. For the moment, he felt at the peak of maturity.

He began by summing up the situation. Soviet treachery no longer had to be demonstrated, but here one saw a new example of it: seized with panic at the interest shown by the free world in *The Russian Truth*, the Soviet Union had rushed into freeing a false Kurnosov, who had taken everyone in, beginning with him, Aleksandr Psar: he craved forgiveness for this lack of discrimination. Fortunately, the pressure of public indignation had forced 'the fathers of lies' to let go: like Jonah snatched from the whale, the true author of that book, whose importance could not be overestimated (200,000 copies sold in two months!), was there to give hope to the democratic countries and oppressed peoples. Unfortunately Mikhail Leontich did not speak French, but, through Psar, he was willing to answer whatever questions people wanted to ask him: the truth had nothing to fear from indiscretion, on the contrary. The initial declaration by the prisoner who was no longer anonymous could be summed up in a few words: Mikhail Leontich Kurnosov, expelled from the USSR, hoped to devote his life to the setting up and organization of an independent group that would be called the Confraternity of the Truth of the Peoples.

Next day, *L'Impartial*, where Hugues Minquin had taken the comfortable place of his friend and retired protector, published 'long extracts' from the press conference. With guarded approval, Minquin wrote: 'Some of Kurnosov's views may seem to run counter to common sense, but their singularity in no way diminishes their charisma. Here are some of the exchanges between this non-conformist guest of France and the men and women of good will who questioned him.'

Question—Monsieur Kurnosov, you are no doubt aware of our confusion concerning your identity. Would you please confirm that you are the man who tried to assassinate M. Brezhnev?

Answer—I confirm it.

Q.—How did you set about it?

A.—I had a brother-in-law in the militia who tended to drink too much. I took his uniform and his sub-machine-gun. It cost me 2,000 grams of vodka. My brother-in-law was far gone. (Laughter)

Q.—May we ask what motive you had in committing this attempt?

A.—You may. I thought it would be enough to take away the keystone of the Soviet cathedral to bring it all down in a heap.

Q.—You don't think so any more?

A.—No. Communism is a cancer that would immediately have seized on the wound.

Q.—What made you change your mind?

A.—I became more intelligent. After my assassination attempt, I was regarded as mad and put in a psychiatric asylum, where I was given all the books I wanted. That enabled me to complete my political education and to see things a little more clearly. If you know *Boris Godunov*, you know that in Russia it's a tradition: only the mad can see clearly.

Q.—How did you manage to get your writing into the West, first in the form of fragments, then the whole manuscript?

A.—The naïvety of that question is matched only by its impertinence.

Q.—You were well treated on the whole. How do you explain that?

A.—At first, the régime found it advantageous to show that only a madman could have tried to assassinate Public Benefactor Number One. Then the Geebee realized that I had a certain political education and helped me to improve it, rather as doctors grow bacilli. Marxism regards itself as a scientific doctrine. Marxists think that when certain circumstances are brought together, the consequences are always the same. For them, my capture was a godsend. It enabled them to study *in vivo* how a counter-revolutionary mind functions.

Q.—Your guards knew that fragments of your book were reaching the West. Didn't they keep a closer watch on you?

A.—Of course. They put wiring across my windows, questioned my nurses and the other patients, searched my cell . . . They never found anything.

Q.—Doesn't this inefficiency strike you as suspect?

A.—In the Soviet Union, inefficiency is never suspect.

Q.—What made you a militant anti-Communist?

A.—Communism, of course. But also an event in my life that I will not speak about in public.

Q.—Monsieur Kurnosov, what do you think of the West?

A.—The West is only a fraction of the world, and the world turns round and round like a squirrel in its wheel. This is the wheel: democracy is stronger than Fascism, Fascism is stronger than Communism, Communism is stronger than democracy. I think we must get out of the wheel.

Q.—You seem to be unaware that it was the Communists who defeated the Nazis.

A.—Untrue. It was the Russians who defeated the Germans. I detect in your voice Communist sympathies, and I would advise you to re-read Stalin's speech of 9 May 1945.

Q.—Monsieur Kurnosov, what do you think of Socialism?

A.—I might answer with Vladimir Bukovsky: 'If you want to transform your country into an enormous cemetery then join the Socialists.' But I would also like to quote Pushkin. Do you know our Pushkin? He wrote a tale that began something like this:

'Three girls were sitting in the window, spinning late into the evening. "If I were the Tsarina," said one of the girls, "I would prepare a banquet for the whole of Christendom." "If I were the Tsarina," said her sister,

"I would weave cloth for the whole world." These two girls later turned out to be utter bitches: they had no compunction about betraying the Tsar who became their brother-in-law, and murdering their sister the Tsarina and their nephew, the Tsarevich.' This passage is comparable to the temptations in the desert, as interpreted by Dostoievsky in the legend of the Grand Inquisitor. That's what the Russian Truth and I think of Socialism.

Q.—I'm not sure I understand you, Monsieur Kurnosov. What did the third sister want to do?

A.—The third sister said: 'If I were Tsarina I would give the Tsar a hero for a son.' You see the difference. This Cordelia wants to do something possible, natural, useful. Something within her capabilities. The other two, the Socialists, dream. And they dream about material things that are not even worth dreaming about.

Q.—Monsieur Kurnosov, the impostor who presented himself under your name has said some very negative things about the dissidents. What do *you* think of them?

A.—They are different from us. They come from the Soviet élite and consequently they are not really representative of the Russian people. But there are some good individuals among them.

Q.—What do you mean by 'us'? Are you not a dissident yourself?

A.—No. Your Diderot said, 'Persecuted dissidents will become persecutors themselves when they are the stronger.' I am not a potential persecutor. In Russian, dissident means 'one who thinks differently'. I don't think differently. I think like everyone of common sense. I am not a dissident: I am a Russian who is trying to draw the organic consequences of being Russian. To be Russian, to be French, is not an ideology, but a concrete fact.

Q.—Do you identify yourself with the Russian nationalists?

A.—I'm aware that, in the West, the word 'nationalist' has a pejorative connotation. You're very good at giving pejorative connotations to words whose true meaning is not pejorative. 'Nationalist', 'Negro', 'Jew' . . . This reveals a regrettable linguistic devaluation. The suffix *ist* is hardly applicable to so concrete a reality as a nation. Any ideology, whether of right or of left, that involves the violation of a reality, is essentially Luciferian.

Q.—What do you mean by Luciferian?

A.—The revolt of Lucifer is not the revolt of evil against good, but of the good against being.

Q.—To get back to earth . . . are you a Fascist?

A.—Fascism is a form of Socialism; Fascism is an abstraction: those are two reasons why I cannot be a Fascist.

Q.—We have heard that there are monarchist movements in Russia, for example, the Ogurtsov movement. Are you a monarchist?

A.—It's not I who am a monarchist: it's Russia that is, has always been and probably will be a monarchy for a long time to come. I think the only means of containing Soviet ideological expansionism is to recognize the imperial Russian fact, which has a territorial and therefore limited aspect.

Q.—In your book, you refer to a sort of theocracy. Could you say more about that?

A.—The government of men proceeds from two principles: legitimacy and practical necessity. We have to have a policeman at the crossroads—that's a practical necessity. But this policeman wears a uniform—that's legitimacy. Legitimacy is always irrational: divine right, heredity, universal suffrage, picking names out of a hat are not founded in reason and that is why they are founders of legitimacy. We know very well that the son of a genius may be an idiot; we know very well that there are more fools in the world than intelligent men; but this is quite unimportant, because intelligence has nothing to do with it. Republican legitimacy is based on incoherence, just as monarchical legitimacy is based on the absurd. Practical necessity may be argued point by point, it evolves one notch at a time, it adapts; legitimacy, on the other hand, can only be grasped as a whole: yes or no. Being a Christian, I think it is good that the irrational foundation of legitimacy should be a Christian irrationality. That doesn't mean that Christians should organize the earthly city as if it were the heavenly Jerusalem. Practical necessity remains. The expression 'a Christian prince' is a contradiction in terms, but that is no reason for rejecting it.

Q.—Dostoievsky was also in favour of theocracy. Didn't theocracy rather come a cropper in your country?

A.—Russia has a Christic vocation. Look what happened in the case of Christ. His apostles believed that he would restore the kingdom of Israel. The pharisees believed it, too, and, fearing that they would have no place in it, they crucified the king. But it was because he was crucified that he was able to create his true kingdom, which the pharisees were incapable of conceiving. It is no longer a question of *felix culpa*, but of *felix error*. Similarly, Dostoievsky thought that Russia would save the world through theocracy, but she will save it through martyrdom.

Q.—Who, in your opinion, are the pharisees?

A.—So it's true! The West is still not aware of what has been explained to them so clearly by such men as Knupfer and Chesterton!

Q.—What did they explain?

A.—That the Usurers are the pharisees of our time. That Western capitalism and Soviet Communism are like beaters driving the game into the open where it can be shot at.

Q.—Who is the game?

A.—You.

Q.—And the hunters?

A.—I see you haven't read my book with much attention—allow me to recall its main point.

'Everything begins with credit, that is to say, usury. It is not for nothing that the medieval Church condemned lending with interest. I am aware that this is what built modern society, by making the industrial revolution possible, but I'm not sure that that is anything to be proud of.

'Whenever there has been credit, there have been banks. Everything was all right as long as the banks were only agencies for exchange and loan. Unfortunately they were soon allowed to issue money, not by minting coins, or by printing banknotes, but by lending sums that they in fact did not possess. Make no mistake: the cheque from the bank that represents your loan is 80 per cent at least without real funds behind it. This is no longer banking, but conjuring. But the banks go further: not only do they usurp the privilege of the state by creating money, but they lend this non-existent money, this wind, to the State, thus putting the nation itself in thrall. Did you know that, some years ago, Great Britain had not yet paid back to the Rothschild bank the sums she had borrowed to wage war on Napoleon?

'I shall no doubt shock you cynics when I say that the banking system is quite simply immoral. Think for example of your limited companies, which in French you rightly call "anonymous". You know that they deal with sums ten, twenty times more than their capital. If they make a profit, all well and good; but if they go bankrupt, who pays? The creditors. As for the shareholders, they are not even consulted about the adventures into which their board of directors throws them. As long as they get their dividends, they don't worry, but is it moral to renounce one's responsibilities to such a degree? My money is still I. What connection is there between a shareholder who sells or buys one millionth of a copper mine as if he were putting on or taking off his slippers, and the black miner who breaks his back crawling through that mine, pick in hand?

'By the way, don't attribute views to me that I do not hold. I think it quite permissible to own a mine providing one started it oneself, or runs it oneself, but I think it is immoral to gamble with men's labour as you gamble on your . . . what do you call it? [M. Psar provided the word: sweepstake.]

'To return to the banks. They are in the hands of men whom I shall call the Usurers. There is, in the accumulation of their profits, a *hubris* and perhaps a fatality: they have begun to swell, they can no longer stop. You know better than I how they have established an almost absolute grip on Europe and North America; how they have encouraged the process of decolonization, because inexperienced young nations, possessing under-exploited mineral wealth, guaranteed them higher profits than those they could obtain from the same territories through more organized nations, which took some of the profits for themselves on the way. I will show you what happened in Russia.

'Imperial Russia was an embarrassment to the Usurers for several reasons, but first because she depended on them much less than did the other European countries. In 1908, the national debt stood at the index 288 per inhabitant in France, but only at 58.7 in Russia. In 1914, 83 per cent of that debt had been paid off, thanks to the state railways. In 1912, taxation stood at the index 3.11 in Russia, as against 12.35 in France and 26.75 in Great Britain. In 1913 the Russian gold reserves stood at 1,550 million roubles, whereas only 1,494 million paper roubles were in circulation. At the same time, the French franc was covered by only about 50 per cent. With all that, the growth of the Russian economy was such that a French economist said in 1914: "Around the middle of the century, Russia will dominate Europe politically, economically and financially." Industrial production per inhabitant increased by 3.5 per cent per year, as against 2.5 per cent in the United States and only 1 per cent in Great Britain. So you see, the Usurers had every reason to be worried. One should add that in 1912 the president of the United States, Taft, remarked that the social legislation of the Russian empire was "closer to perfection" than any legislation in any democratic country. If it were proved that a country attached to a non-democratic form of government, what you call, I suppose, a theocracy, was capable of resolving problems against which the Usurers were stumbling, the control that they exercise over the economy was condemned.

'What followed was not unexpected. It is generally known that the banker Warburg made considerable subsidies to Lenin. What is not so well known is that this same Warburg had a brother who founded the American Federal Reserve system, which also subsidized the Russian revolutionaries, with the help of American bankers, Ruhn, Loeb, and Schiff. At the same time Trotsky openly admitted that he had received a large loan from a financier who belonged to the British Liberal Party.

'Result: the Russian empire was put out of action and the Soviet Union became a client of the West. Ford built the first Soviet car factory (though the Russian Empire was already producing its own cars), and Campbell was Stalin's adviser on collectivization. I am not even speaking of what is happening at the present time: a popular tag invites children to drink Coca-Cola rather than go to school. Meanwhile the State is emptying the country's gold reserves trying to feed the people. But that is only the least odious aspect of the complicity that binds the capitalist Usurers and their Soviet counterparts. Suppose for a moment that the USSR became a country like other countries, you can imagine the extent to which the Usurers would lose their hold on the Western world. You are so afraid of the Soviets (and you are right to be afraid of them) that you rush into the arms of the Usurers, crying, Granny! But it isn't your grandmother: it's the wicked wolf, sharpening his teeth, all the better to eat you with, my dear.

'Does all that strike you as fantastic? See how the United States, which are entirely in the hands of the Usurers, treated their greatest enemy during and since the Second World War.

'Whereas they ought to have waited for the defeat of the USSR before swooping down on an exhausted Germany, the Americans intervened just in time to save the Communist régime, which was on the point of collapse. It is, I repeat, the Russian soldier who fought the

293

German soldier, but it was American equipment that saved the Marxist system. When Molotov, in exchange for this equipment, proposed certain liberalizations, Roosevelt replied that he did not see any need for them.

'Churchill wanted the Allied landing in the Mediterranean to take place in Greece, but America insisted on attacking Italy. As a result, Romania, Bulgaria, Czechoslovakia, Hungary, Albania and Poland, over which the West is now shedding crocodile tears, were handed over to the Soviets. And what about Germany! Don't you find it significant, the partition of Germany, that hen that lays golden eggs, between the two godfathers? A thigh for you, a thigh for me. You know, too, how thousands of Russians who had fled the régime were piled into trains and trucks with rifle butts in their behinds and sent back to the Soviets. And by whom? By the Americans and British.

'There is no tragedy without comedy: the Soviet butchers sat beside the Western judges at the Nuremberg circus-trial.

'China, whom the Americans might have helped in her desperate struggle against Communism, was handed over to it.

'Hungary was urged on to revolt by the CIA, with the result that the free forces fermenting in that country were crushed by the Soviets.

'And remember, with what ensemble—two threatening voices at either end of the world—Moscow and Washington have prevented you from sorting out the Arab world!

'Cuba, of course, is the most shameless case. How could any country tolerate that pistol pointing at its belly? But it was with the connivance of the Americans that Castro seized power, that is to say, the pistol was loaded (with blanks, of course). The Americans then pretended to support the émigrés and deliberately sabotaged the invasion at the Bay of Pigs. Yes, deliberately; remember that it was on the personal orders of President Kennedy that air support was withdrawn. When the Soviets, who tried from time to time to shake off the yoke of the Usurers, loaded the pistol with real bullets, then the same Kennedy sent them back with their tail between their legs. You see, Khrushchev, for all his faults, was a real Russian, who wanted above all the independence of his country. But it only needed Rockefeller to spend his holidays—holidays, my God! —on the Black Sea and Khrushchev was dismissed!

'Do you or do you not know that Roosevelt declared that Indo-China, after the war, should not return to France in any circumstances? Look who Indo-China belongs to now. As for the war that the Americans claimed to have waged there, they made quite sure that they did not win it by accident. They even invented for that purpose a remarkable procedure: *escalation*.

'Which are the two great nuclear powers in the world today? Which gave the bomb to the other? Oh! Secretly, of course, through spies, whom America took pleasure in sending to the electric chair, but the fact remains: if America alone had had the bomb, who would have played the werewolves to the Usurers' advantage?

'Who, quite recently, divided up the world at Helsinki? And what were the results of this division for the peoples of the Soviet Union? Redoubled repression, because those agreements meant simply this: "Everything is fine, you're playing your part, carry on."

'What is happening in Afghanistan? One of the two cronies is doing his work with gas and napalm; the other forbids its athletes from taking part in the Moscow Olympics.

'I'll go further. I do not find very convincing the way in which Reagan pretends to show his teeth and Brezhnev to show his claws in Poland. All the Soviet Union asks for is a pretext not to invade; all that the United States is asking for is an opportunity of re-establishing her prestige. This cat and this dog have a perfect understanding, like pickpockets at a fair . . .'

These surprising declarations [Hugues Minquin continued] were met with various stirrings in the hall, but one has to admit that M. Kurnosov had a surprise up his sleeve that he pulled off to masterly effect. Seeing the incredulity of part of his audience, he cried good-humouredly: 'You don't want to believe me? Well, I shall now prove to you that the United States is helping the Soviets maintain the Russian people in slavery, all for the greater profit of the arms dealers, the Usurers' cousins.'

He then took something out of his pocket.

'This morning,' he said, 'I left the Soviet Union. As long as the plane was flying over national territory, I was forced to keep my handcuffs on. I had them taken off as soon as I learnt that we had left Soviet air space, and as I am something of a pickpocket, I managed to keep them as a souvenir . . .'

He turned to Mme Choustrewitz, of *Choix*, and held out to her what he had in his hand.

'Madame, would you be so kind as to read the mark stamped on this object?'

Madame Choustrewitz brandished the object at arm's length: it was a pair of handcuffs. And she read the stamp in a loud, intelligible voice: 'Smith and Wesson. Made in USA.'

After the press conference, M. Baronet, who liked small, discreet restaurants where the food was good but did not bear too heavily on his expense-account, took Fourveret, Psar and Kurnosov off for dinner *chez Tiburce*.

'Aren't you tired? Wouldn't you prefer to rest?' Aleksandr asked Kurnosov.

'Tired? I've done nothing but talk.'

'But this morning you were . . .'

'I've been preparing myself for this trip for the last ten years.'

'You knew? . . .'

'I knew that if they'd kept me alive it was to export me sometime or other.'

Kurnosov behaved much better at table than Gaverin.

'I've read a great deal,' he explained in all simplicity, 'and, among other things, I've read books on etiquette. I'm convinced that knowledge is one, and that one shouldn't use the wrong fork if one is a good Christian.'

M. Baronet, a self-important young man with chubby cheeks, a pink complexion, fair hair, and anxious eyes behind gold-rimmed spectacles, wanted to know why the movement that Kurnosov wished to launch was to be known as the Confraternity of the Truth of the Peoples.

Kurnosov, with short white hair, his pyramidal nose, his sententious glasses, his methodical hands, with his fingers all of equal length, or almost, with that air of a chief accountant suddenly gone mad, replied:

'The Confraternity of the Truth of the Peoples is so called in honour of the Confraternity of the Russian Truth, whose members were arrested and brought to trial during the post-Leninist terror. Instead of humiliating themselves, prostrating themselves, accusing themselves of every crime, as did the Communist riff-raff who appeared before the same court, the Brothers of the Russian Truth replied to every question that was asked them by singing in chorus: "God save the Tsar." One may not share their opinions, but one cannot but admire the way they went to their deaths.'

Aleksandr hated this autodidact's self-assurance, even the logic of that insanity, and yet he felt that, inside that little carcass, bundled up in that black roll-neck sweater, inside that small, square, obtuse head, surmounted by that hedgehog of hair, so straight and stiff that it almost seemed electrified, there was a great passion that, in other circumstances, he might well have shared.

'Translate them this. I trust you. Up to a point, at least.'

The tiny, hard eyes darted over Aleksandr's impassive face.

'The Russian people really is the truth-carrying people, as I have said in my book. Even the Catholics have known, since the apparition of Fatima, that we have a special destiny. The so-called Russian revolution is a non-Russian attempt to scotch that destiny.

'Russia has a mystical heart whose true name is the Monastery of the Trinity—St. Sergius. The place was rebaptized Zagorsk in honour of an obscure revolutionary whose pseudonym was Zagorski and whose real name was Krachman. Is that not symbolic?

'Do you know the names of the assassins who murdered

the Tsar, Tsarina, Tsarevich, Tsarevas and four of their faithful followers in the cellar at Ekaterinburg, on 17 July 1918, at 1.15 a.m? Three are Russian, but listen to the other seven: Iurovski, Horvat, Fischer, Edelstein, Fekete, Nagy, Grünfeld, Vergazy. Trotsky's real name was Bronstein; Zinoviev's Apfelbaum; Kamenev's Rosenfeld. It is not important that some of these names are Jewish. Dzerzhinsky was Polish, Stalin Georgian, Beria Mingrelian, Lenin a little Swedish mixed with a great deal of Tartar. So one should not cry anti-semitism, as do the Usurers, whenever one observes that the Russian Revolution was in reality an anti-Russian Revolution.

'Anyway, by their fruit shall ye know them. Fourteen republics of the Union live better than the fifteenth—Russia —as everyone knows. Each of these republics is supposed to be sovereign, which in theory gives the R.S.F.S.R. (140 million inhabitants) as much weight as Estonia (1 million), but in reality the R.S.F.S.R. is the only one of the fifteen not to have a Communist Party of its own.'

'What?' Aleksandr expostulated.

'Ah, yes. There is a pan-Soviet Communist Party, but there is no Russian Communist Party, any more than there is a Russian Academy of Sciences, whereas all the other republics have their Academy and Party.'

'Isn't this the effect of what some people call Greater Russian colonialism?'

'No. A Russian scientist must begin his career by going into exile, by working among the Uzbeks or the Kirghiz, before he can prove himself at Moscow or Leningrad. And a sincere, devoted Russian Communist cannot serve his people and his country: he is attached directly to the federation. There are more serious aspects to this. The alcoholism maintained by the State is transforming the Russians into eunuchs: you have only to see the growth rates of the population. In a few decades from now the Communist State will have literally destroyed the Russian people. Only then will the so-called Revolution have achieved its aim, and the Usurers-pharisees will be able to rub their hands, hands that let fall a shower of gold by a natural process of desquamation.'

'What's happening? What's he saying?' Baronet asked, seeing that Kurnosov was getting heated.

Psar hesitated to translate. Russian messianism would be the yeast of the Confraternity, but too much yeast kills the dough.

'M. Kurnosov,' he said, 'is a great patriot, and he was anxious to make me see that.'

'What a beautiful language Russian is!' said Fourveret, raising his eyes heavenwards. 'But Molière would have said that as far as conciseness was concerned, it was quite the opposite of Turkish.'

The dinner had been a postscript to the press conference. There was still a postscript to the dinner.

Kurnosov wanted some exercise and Aleksandr accompanied him to his hotel on foot. Frozen mud sprayed off the tyres of passing cars, their headlamps haloed by the damp air. Kurnosov walked with a firm step, his thick shoes treading the snow and slush. Aleksandr, who was a good half-head taller than him, looked at him out of the corner of his eye with mingled curiosity, fear and amusement. This man was a force, but he would be led to serve a greater force than his own. He would be an unconscious relay in the propagation of what he hated most, and it was this very hate that would make him an effective relay. 'Influence,' said the *Vademecum*, 'is able to make use of Archimedes' principle. In the final analysis, Nero and Diocletian served Christianity.' The words of a psalm that Aleksandr had learnt by heart as a child came back to him: 'Against thee, thee only, have I sinned, and done this evil in thy sight: that thou mightest be justified when Thou speakest and be clear when Thou art judged.' He wondered if that too was an instance of the relay. And Judas, to whom Jesus had held out a piece of bread, which pointed him out as the traitor (not denounced him, but pointed him out, as one points out a man for fatigue duty), was he not the relay without whom Operation Salvation-of-the-World would have been impossible? And could not the words 'Forgive them, for they know not what they do' also be applied to unconscious relays? The icy wind cut into one's lips; both men tightened their scarves around their necks:

Kurnosov his grey woollen one, Aleksandr his white vicuña one.

'Mikhail Leontich, what has made you what you are?'

'My parents, for a start—they never gave me false ideas. Discreet of them, wasn't it? They did not give me any because they had very few ideas themselves. They were fundamentally truthful people and in a society like ours, which is based on lies, they saved themselves by humble labour, simple language and the passivity, the conscious stolidity of the colonized. They went to demonstrations when they had to. They signed petitions and protests when they could not do otherwise, but all that filth washed over them without leaving its mark. They believed in God and in Russia, but they had too much common sense or too much purity to believe in an abstract idea, whatever it was. To make an idea, which is an object of comprehension, into an object of faith is perhaps the celebrated sin against the Holy Ghost, and they were certainly incapable of that. All this gave me a foundation of intellectual integrity and above all the feeling that whatever is abstract (except in mathematics, of course) is necessarily adulterated and adulterine. That is why I did not write a thesis, but a collection of tales. The essence of truth is to be ineffable: it has to be snared. Hence the parables in Scripture. Then I went to war, I was taken prisoner and I met this man . . .'

'This is your hotel. Would you like a drink at the bar?'

Kurnosov read the sign.

'Ah! You've put me up at the S-khoï-sayool [Choiseul], the man who acquired Lorraine and Corsica. Or was that the other one? The one who killed his wife? One of the *causes célèbres* of the nineteenth . . . No, I'd rather walk around a bit longer. Or let's go to a real bistrot, where there are French people, real ones. They fascinate me, you know. One has such a strong sense that, collectively, they know nothing of unhappiness, they have only petty cares, and even those cares are only there to make them look serious.'

They entered a café that smelled of frying.

'The smell of freedom!' Kurnosov declared.

'You mustn't be content with the smell,' said Aleksandr. They ordered a bag of chips and two *demis* of beer.

Kurnosov considered the waiter who brought them with a sort of clear-sighted tenderness.

'*Merci, monn-see-ayoor!*' he said, gravely.

When the waiter had gone he added: 'I know it isn't correct to say *mon-see-ayoor*. One must say *moossioo*. But I prefer *monn-see-ayoor*. It's a word that shows that there is something to respect in the worst good-for-nothing.'

'Tell me how you ended up in a psychiatric hospital.'

'You mean at the madhouse? Thanks to a man—I don't know his name—a mountain of a man, from the Geebee, of course, but with a decent haircut, nothing to remind one of the guillotine . . . He spoke like a professor from St Petersburg University. He said to me: "Admit that you're mad and you'll have nothing more to worry about. You'll live better locked up than if you were at liberty. You will eat, you will drink; you will read, you will write. If you need a woman from time to time, we'll arrange it. Otherwise, I'll have to hand you over to those nincumpoops in Justice, and you'll end up in the salt mines, which would be a pity with your intelligence. *Nnus*"—he said *nnus* like in the olden days—"what's your decision?" A good man, I think, and very dangerous: he's done more evil than the wicked.'

'In that deal you made with the Geebee,' Aleksandr asked lightly, 'what did you have to offer them?'

Kurnosov replied without hesitation: 'The truth. Those people imagine that they can harness truth and make it work for them. But the truth is a mare that cannot be broken in. Do you know our Russian folk tales, Aleksandr Dmitrich? Do you remember the stick-that-beat-on-its-own, you only had to take it out of the sack? And the tablecloth-that-laid-itself, you only had to unfold it and you had the most gargantuan meal in front of you? Those are icons of the truth: the truth that justifies itself, the truth that liberates. The truth alone is both essence and function. I said that to that Elbruz of a man, that Sviatogor of a man, I smiled at him and told him, in that box in which they stuck me, stripped naked after searching me inside out. I told him: "I'm stronger than you." '

'And it's because of your intelligence that the Geebee

decided to turn you into a focus of counter-revolutionary infection?'

'Not entirely. Thanks to that meeting in Germany, I had a non-Marxist political education, unique among the 250 million inhabitants of the Union. My intelligence had not been contaminated by the microbe of the dialectic, or at least I had got used to reasoning without restricting myself to using only one method—and a pretty simplistic one at that! For the Geebee, Aleksandr Dmitrich, I was a priceless catch. I jotted down my thoughts. I submitted them freely to the man-mountain. He chose the pages that suited him best and gave them to one of his agents. The agent passed himself off as one of my nurses and handed them over to a network. The network exported them in all innocence . . . What an organization, Aleksandr Dmitrich! An organization of which the man-mountain believed himself to be the head, when in fact he was only a cog working for me! Of course, I told a different story to the journalists: one has to know how to lie in order to be believed.'

Kurnosov wiped the beer froth around his lips with a handkerchief. He devoured his greasy chips without remorse for the excellent dinner he had just eaten. Aleksandr ordered him another *demi*.

'Don't you want to tell me about that meeting?'

'Certainly. I told you I was taken prisoner, I think. We surrendered at the first engagement, the whole division, and why? "*A propos de bottes*", as I believe one says in French. Because we had no boots, and because the USSR had just sold hundreds of thousands of boots to the Germans. We felt that we had been sold along with the boots. It was the outbreak of war and the Germans did not treat us too badly. They shot our political commissars, but that hardly bothered us: we never felt that they were really with us. Do you know what finally forged the people and the Party together? War. After all, one has to admit that the Party led the people to victory. We got to Germany in our cattle trucks and were dispersed to various farms. Some kept themselves busy enough: the peasant away in the army, his wife alone in the house, etc. I wasn't one of them. I wasn't twenty yet. I'd never had a woman, and for me the farmer's wife was more like my mother. She buttered my bread for me, not like a Russian woman, it's true, but like a German woman: with one side of the knife she spread the butter on the bread, with the other she scraped off whatever had not sunk in. But, for all that, she was a good woman. Sometimes she hid that bread and butter in the dustbins that other prisoners had to empty: I mean later, when the Germans had captured so many of us that they didn't have enough food to feed us . . . I began to work on the land. My father was a bookbinder, imagine! But once you've accepted her rough ways, mother earth is generous, she isn't too hard on you. She rewards you, even foreign earth. I hoed and scythed. I enjoyed it. I felt regenerated by contact with real things: if you plant, things grow; if you don't hoe, they are smothered; if you harvest, you are rewarded; if you leave it too late, the crops rot. There's no Marxism-Leninism there.

'Our farm—what am I saying, *our* farm!—was situated on the edge of a forest. On the other side of the forest, there were other farms where French prisoners had been distributed. Both of us depended on the same village. One day I went to the village to get ten bags of chemical fertilizer—the Germans go in a lot for chemical fertilizer—and I met these Frenchmen. One of them gave me a funny look and said to me, in Russian: "Hey, you, are you from over there?" I could hardly believe my ears: I had heard of White émigrés, but they'd told us they were all princes and counts, depraved drug addicts. And there was this fellow, not much older than me, with a broad back, big hands and small ears, saying to me: "Are you from over there?" For me, how can I explain to you? . . . It was as if I'd met the ghost of Old Russia. We weren't supposed to talk to one another; we were supervised by invalids, though not too strictly. We managed to arrange to meet on Sunday, at three o'clock, in the forest under a double oak tree that we both knew.

'The first time, my comrades came with me to see this rare bird, the Russian from France, the gentleman's son, but their curiosity soon turned to disgust. "He's a White Guard. He wants to put the Tsars on our backs again. And who says the Tsars won't keep the commissars? And we'll go on sweating under both of them!" In short, they preferred to stay with their farmers' wives. I went back under the great double oak tree every Sunday.

'Now, I can see all that in perspective. Nicolai Vladimirovich was a member of Young Russia, and I get the impression that that party was being manipulated by our Geebee. When I began to suspect this, I was overcome with despair. I felt encircled. Then I thought about it and concluded that it didn't really matter, that the truth is a dangerous explosive to handle, and that it may blow off the noses of those who want to use it to back up their lies. Anyway, under my oak tree, I stopped asking these questions: I just listened to my émigré talk to me about Russia, and I drank in his words, I sucked them dry of all the truth I could find in them, as one does with the bones of a partridge . . . or a crayfish. Ever since, the smell of mushrooms and moss has remained for me the smell of the truth.

'Nicolai Vladimirovich taught me by heart a whole programme of studies, put me through exams . . . I learnt, I swatted, I questioned, I recited, he put questions to me, gave me marks, prompted me when I dried up. Our feet were frozen, our noses were frozen, we had only one ink-pencil between us; on weekdays we worked like slaves, if we'd got caught, we'd have been in for it, but we didn't care: I was growing up thanks to him and he—but that, I only understood this later—he was growing up thanks to me. He passed on to me what he believed. He breathed on me, and I, ignorant beast that I was, began to stir. Through me, through the ideas that he filled me with, he went home, do you understand that? He "went home". Not only home to his own country, but home to his childhood, even to his mother's breast . . .

'His ideas were a confused ragbag. *Polit-grammata*, he called them. It was a Monarcho-Socialo-Fascist doctrine. "We need a Tsar to reign over us and a leader to govern." Personally, it seemed to me that a Tsar was enough. One needs bosses, of course, but the fewer the better. He'd get heated, we'd argue. At last spring came and I passed my final examinations. Then I was allowed to take the oath.'

'The oath?'

'The oath of allegiance. To the Tsar.'

Kurnosov's metallic eyes did not mist over; they became quenched, rather as steel is quenched—with pride. His lips moved, silently mouthing the sacred phrase that could certainly not be spoken aloud in that bistrot while munching chips.

'Yes,' said Kurnosov, 'I was twenty years old and I spoke those words, syllable by syllable, and I have never betrayed them. Those people wanted to know why I fired on Brezhnev . . . It was to make room, Aleksandr Dmitrich.'

Aleksandr's mouth twisted into a smile of derision and perhaps of envy: 'Room for whom? For the present pretender?'

Kurnosov wiped his lips with his handkerchief again.

'Up to a certain point in History, Aleksandr Dmitrich, it is the princes who make the thrones; then one crosses the ridge and it is the thrones that make the princes.'

He got up.

'Shall we walk a little more?'

The ex-prisoner of cell 000 was indefatigable.

The organization of the Confraternity began. There were three main points: the programme, the budget and recruitment.

The basic idea of the programme was a universal declaration of the duties of man. Kurnosov wrote:

'Every social theory based on the rights of the individual and not on his responsibilities to other individuals will necessarily be tantamount to placing the cart before the horse. The Slavophiles already repudiated bourgeois democracy because it is based on an absolute liberalism that can only lead to the exploitation, however mitigated, of the weak by the strong. Liberty can be based only on responsibility; as for equality, there is only one, the sacred equality of death. Indeed, every egalitarian system necessarily leads to death, whether it fails in its struggle against nature and sets about amputating it in order to get it into its artificial framework (which we call Terror), or whether it succeeds and eliminates the difference in potential that is indispensable to the passing of any vital current (which we call Socialism). Responsibility, on the other hand, provides a solid foundation for the establishment of a just society. This responsibility engages man in his concrete relations, firstly with other men—the producer and the consumer, the artisan and the customer, the superior and the subordinate—and, secondly, with the natural communities to which he belongs, family, trade, people, mankind, the most immediate duties to one's neighbour always claiming priority . . .'

A text written by Kurnosov, revised by Psar and revised again by Kurnosov, was then secretly submitted to Piotr, at some rendez-vous at the Cluny or the Carnavalet museums. This led to certain conflicts, because Aleksandr was used to working independently and Piotr's ham-fistedly didactic attitude constantly irritated him. 'Your programme isn't educative enough,' said his case-officer, by way of criticism. 'You should work out an anti-Marxism that will be false by definition, since Marxism is true. We must teach our enemies to think inside out, nothing more.'

'I don't know from which directorate you come,' the agent replied, 'but you have obviously understood nothing of the operation that you are supposed to be directing. What is happening is that we have at last recognized the obvious: Marxism is itself only one stage of the dialectic, and there is a risk that a synthesis that has digested it but is hostile to it will take the place of the antithesis that it represents. So we have decided to trick History, as one tricks certain insects by giving them artificial eggs that they use to fertilize to no purpose. This is the trick that we intend playing on the Western intelligentsias, and we hope that using our pseudo-synthesis, into which we will have put our hands, as if into a glove-puppet, we shall be able to mesh into a thesis that will be favourable to us once again.'

Having extracted some concessions out of Piotr, Aleksandr went back to see Kurnosov and tried to impose on him the revisions that Piotr had not given in on. Of course Aleksandr had to present them as if they were his own, whereas in fact he disapproved of them totally.

'Aleksandr Dmitrich,' Kurnosov said to him indulgently, 'you're the most changeable man I've ever known.'

The budget presented other problems. To save money, Kurnosov had left the *Choiseul* by the second day and had settled into a small hotel in the 15th arrondissement, where he had taken a room without a bath. 'I'll go to the baths on Saturday. Do you know that in Leningrad that was one of my privileges? The secret was well kept, but every Saturday, I left my cell, handcuffs on my wrists, American ones of course, and my escort took me to an establishment reserved for the Geebee. My guards threw the hot water over my back and beat me with birch branches. Sometimes I did the same to them. We had a good time.' When Kurnosov discovered that there were no Russian baths in Paris, he was scandalized. 'What are you thinking of, you émigrés? You've been here for sixty years and you've no Russian baths!' Nevertheless he contented himself with a Turkish bath and refused to budge from his cheap hotel. Besides he hardly ever ate except when invited out: 'I stuffed myself enough in prison; it's time I fasted a bit.' Most of the money paid to him every month by Lux until such time as they had forced Gaverin, whom they were suing, to cough up the money already paid him, went therefore into the coffers of the Confraternity.

However, these sums were not enough to set up a world-wide movement, even on the most modest basis. The Psar Agency would devote some of its profits to the common enterprise; this would enable Aleksandr to exercise some control over the Confraternity, even if, for whatever reason, his relations with Kurnosov turned sour. But, since these profits necessarily went through Piotr, the case-officer gave himself the right to pore over the Confraternity's accounts. He walked up and down the parquet floor of the salons of the Hôtel Biron (his shoes squeaking odiously), stopped in front of the model of the Gates of Hell, and demanded justifications for every stamp and every métro ticket.

'You're an obsessive cheese-parer!' Aleksandr snapped.

Piotr replied with a slight smile of self-satisfaction: 'I'm a professional.'

When it came to recruitment, there were further difficulties. Kurnosov was after quantity: 'We need a critical volume, if we are to win over the élites. Let's accept everybody, with a deep bow, *à la russe*.'

'Out of the question, Mikhail Leontich. Suppose the whole of the French Fascist ghetto decides to join en masse:

307

no one else will want to work with us. Do you know that in France there are four royalist circles, all at loggerheads. You don't want us to be colonized by the Trotskyites, or the Bonapartists, do you? Or by the fashionable, or by the anarchists? You don't want us to provide the Gaullists with the doctrine that they have been looking for for the last thirty years? You don't want us to rehabilitate the left-wing intellectuals, those *nouveaux riches* in power? We are creating an absolutely new body and we must be careful that no group already in existence takes us over.'

Piotr wanted to confer membership as a privilege, make candidates fill up six-page forms, check their antecedents, start a file on each of them. Trained as he was in counter-espionage, he was obsessed by the fear of infiltration. Aleksandr became more and more irritated: 'Who do you think will infiltrate us? We know in advance that our supporters will be anti-Communists.'

'Precisely. Suppose some good French Commie infiltrates the Confraternity and discovers that it's manipulated by us. Just think what a short-circuit that would be!'

Squashed in this way, Aleksandr felt an unhealthy fatigue building up within him, but he flattered himself that it prevented him from succumbing to self-pity, which he feared and detested above all else.

To this internal, deleterious lassitude was added the superficial exhaustion induced by his public life. Kurnosov was constantly being invited to appear in the provinces and even abroad: in Belgium and in Great Britain. Aleksandr played the interpreter and mentor at his side.

One morning, very early, he was on his way back from Monte Carlo. Kurnosov had dozed off; his head was thrown back and his mouth was slightly open; despite that, one sensed that his masseter muscles were still contracted. Aleksandr looked at the profile with a mixture of feelings which he did not try to analyse.

'So that's Iron Mask!' he thought. 'That's the failed Harmodius who attacked Brezhnev! That's the disciple of Nicolai Vladimirovich! That's a sixty-year-old man whom I suspect of being a virgin! That's the little boy of a humble bookbinder who never gave him any false ideas! That's the madman who spent ten years in a psychiatric asylum, not to be cured, but in order to treat, that is to say develop, his madness . . .'

He opened the first edition of *L'Impartial*. It carried news of Gaverin's death.

The postman, who had brought a new pile of bills and various summonses, to the fortified house in the Limousin, noticed that the letterbox had obviously not been visited for several days. He reported this fact to the police. The police found the owner in his kitchen, hanging from one of those exposed beams that estate agents are so proud of. The corpse was dressed in a blue suit of foreign manufacture and was swinging from the end of a silk tie bearing the Hermès label.

So the fear that had possessed Gaverin since he had arrived in France had been justified after all? Aleksandr requested a rendez-vous for that evening. He found Piotr already sitting on the end of Jessica's striped sofa, his lip adorned with an adolescent moustache. This detail made him all the more odious in Aleksandr's eyes: an asp with a moustache, that was really too much!

'Did we do it?'

Piotr calmly read the crumpled cutting that Aleksandr had thrown on to the sofa.

'No.'

'I showed the paper to Kurnosov. He said: "That might simplify the procedure for recovering our money." Not bad for a Christian! Ah, you're all the same!'

'Who do you mean by "you"?'

Aleksandr made an effort and controlled himself.

'You're right. If Gaverin was in the way, he had to be liquidated. I was thinking of the man's wretched fate, rather than of the good of the cause.'

He added proudly: 'I plead guilty.'

Piotr accepted the apology with good grace.

'And now, why did you want to see me?'

Aleksandr realized the extent of his error. He did not want to deny anything: again, out of pride.

'For that.'

Piotr sighed very gently under his tiny moustache (still too new for twisting).

'You mean to say that you, a co-opted colonel, have taken, and got me to take, all the risks inherent in an emergency rendez-vous all because of the death of an agent who has long since been expendable? Take care, Psar: at our level, incompetence is but a short step from sabotage.'

Next day Aleksandr had to lunch with Emmanuel Blun. Their relationship had somewhat deteriorated ever since Blun, while still writing the same mediocre, but reasonably successful novels on the theme of the 'faithful friend', had discovered that it was easy enough to get them published without having to pay the Psar Agency a commission. But for all that, he was not ungrateful and, in the press receptions where they met, he made a point of putting a protective arm around the shoulders of his ex-agent and declaring: 'He's the best one in Paris, you know. It was he who pulled me out of the mire.'

His telephone call—'Invite me out to lunch. Shall we meet at the *Pont-Royal*?'—had taken Aleksandr by surprise. What could this man, who had made a fortune in defending the wretched of the earth, want with him?

They arrived at the same time and went together to the cloakroom to leave their coats. Blun's was in black cashmere, with a velvet collar. Having placed it on a hanger, which he carefully selected from several other strictly identical ones, Blun appeared in a three-piece suit with a watch chain, the waistcoat perfectly adjusted to reveal a still youthful but nonetheless prosperous paunch.

'Shall we have a drink here and then go up? I've booked a table.'

Aleksandr nodded. He appreciated the comfort, the chiaroscuro, the quietly efficient service of this bar, but he did not really like it: one met too many writers here, and deep down he was convinced that writers were not exactly his kind of people. He allowed himself to be guided by the elbow towards one of the brown armchairs.

'I like this cellar,' remarked Blun with a contented sigh.

'It's like a shrine.' They gossiped as they drank. In the first pause Blun observed: 'I'm just back from Russia.'

But Aleksandr did not notice the perch being held out to him. There was nothing surprising in a man of letters coming back from the USSR, where he had been given a prize. So the literary agent went on talking about literature, while scrutinizing the smooth, puffy, pasty face of this petty bourgeois who possessed a little talent, but of such a common variety that there would have been more honour in his having none at all. Where was the Emmanuel Blun with the dirty fingernails and a head full of ideologies that Psar had pulled out of anonymity to make him one of his cut-outs? Now his nails enjoyed the regular attentions of a manicurist, and the ideologies had been scattered to the wind by his swollen bank account.

'I think my table must be ready,' said Blun.

They politely stepped back for one another in front of the semi-concealed door that led into the entrails of the hotel.

It was only after ordering the meal with meticulous care and exploring the various possibilities on offer in the wine list with the head waiter that Blun embarked on the subject that had occasioned this meeting. He again felt the need to make a preamble, followed by a desultory exposition.

'Last year, it was simple: you were quite safe with Bouzy. But that's already beginning to look archaic. I hope you will like the Cahors. After all, it's the communion wine of you Orthodox. By the way, how's the Confraternity getting on?'

'Well. We've just enthroned a big American film director: the one who made *The Moose Hunter*.'

Blun was playing with his bread.

'What do you do to join your . . . club? Is it a party you join, a rotary that invites you, or a Church that initiates you?'

'Something of all three.'

'I won't conceal from you the fact that I'm interested.'

'You, Emmanuel Blun? But most of the members are resolutely anti-Communist. We have . . .'

Aleksandr mentioned some very well known names. Blun fluttered his eyelids.

'Good, very good. Could you get me in?'

'Blun, I don't understand you. You're an official prize-winner of the USSR!'

'I'm banking on that to get myself in. After all it ought to please all you reactionaries to see me turn up in sackcloth and ashes.'

It was impossible not to think of infiltration, the thing that Piotr most feared.

'But why would you turn up in sackcloth and ashes?'

'I've nothing more to lose, Psar. I've broken with the left and I need a public.'

'Broken with the left? How come?'

'It's a long story.'

'Monsieur,' said Aleksandr to the head waiter, 'another bottle.'

Blun was only too delighted to tell his story; all the same he wanted to be asked to do so; the full-blooded Cahors would do the rest.

For some time his books had no longer been reprinted in the Soviet Union. He wondered why and had accepted an invitation that was not in itself particularly flattering, but which would allow him to go and see what was happening on the spot.

'Some years ago, they put out the red carpet for me, all expenses paid, caviar by the ladleful. This time they were much more stingy. I wanted to clear the whole matter up. After all, I'm still quite capable of paying for a room at their *Ukraina* myself, and even a suite with a grand piano if I want to.'

From the moment he arrived, Blun had been made unwelcome. He was kept waiting when he had appointments, he was not invited to receptions. He spent two evenings alone in his hotel. On the third evening, at the bar, he met one of those women who manage to combine brains with beauty. She was staying at the same hotel. He went and joined her in her room, via the service staircase, 'so as not to be seen by the old hag of a floor attendant'. Next day, he went back to his Soviet publisher, 'Well, Gennadi, what's going on? Why don't you bring out my books any more? Is it something in my political line? Of course I have a conscience, but . . . if it's a matter of reconsidering certain details . . .' 'You must go and see Seriozha,' said Gennadi.

'Seriozha? I'd never met Seriozha. I thought he might be some super-publisher. Not at all. The address told me enough. Seriozha, who was about as cheerful an individual as an undertaker on strike, received me in a sinister office, with the portrait of some ascetic madman, in the manner of El Greco, on the wall. And he put the deal to me: either you work for us and you'll be paid 25,000 copies a year, whether or not they sell, or we'll ditch you. Well, that was really too much. Not me. No, thank you. To begin with, I'm a Frenchman and a good Frenchman at that and, secondly, espionage is a matter of finding oneself in the Saint-Martin canal or the moat at Vincennes. "Sorry, Seriozha, I'd love to, but I really can't see in what way I could help you." "Yes, yes," he said, "you can provide us with information about the prevailing climate of opinion and you can reach people who would not agree to speak to us." "But I know only writers." "To begin with writers are not as useless as people say, and anyway you know a number of politicians who are now in the government. Secretary of State Polipier is a personal friend of yours . . ." "No, really, I'm really very sorry," I said, "espionage isn't my department." At first Seriozha had been very polite. Even exaggeratedly so, a common ideal, etc., etc., but he got less and less polite and began to swell up like the frog who wanted to be as big as an ox. "Listen to me," he said at last, "we have tried to make things easy for you. It is always pleasanter when people work for us out of idealism, but self-interest is not a bad motive either. However, you mustn't think that we don't have other motives on offer. Would you like us to send a set of these to Mme Blun?"

'And he opened a drawer and took out a file, opened the file, took out a folder, opened the folder, took out an envelope, opened the envelope—just like Russian dolls— and spread out in front of me a dozen photographs. If you want to publish a new edition of Aretino, you might use them as illustrations. They were, as you have guessed, the doll in the hotel and your humble servant caught *in flagrante delicto*.

'However what this Seriozha did not know—and, in this the Russians disappointed me: apparently they are not in-fallible—was that Mme Blun and I have felt that the joke has gone on quite long enough and, just before I left, we had started divorce proceedings. So I laughed quietly to myself. Seriozha could huff and puff to his heart's content, and I said to him: "That's a clever move. It might give my lady wife some new ideas. Teaching by pictures, love without tears, that sort of thing: you'll pull off in one go what I haven't been able to do in twenty years. Look, to save you the postage, I'll take your educational snapshots to her myself." With that I grabbed the photographs and left Seriozha looking like something the cat brought in.

'I must say, I was searched from top to toe at the frontier, it took two hours. But I'm no fool, I'd already passed the photographs on to one of my friends who works at the embassy: and they arrived here by diplomatic bag, and no one the wiser. I'm telling you all this in order to explain to you that I'm through with the Soviets, and that you'd better make the best of me while it still looks as if I'm the one who's broken it off. Otherwise, I promise you that in two weeks there'll be an article in the *Literaturka* declaring that Blun is a filthy viper devoid not only of genius, but above all of class consciousness. Mind you, I have some merit. I admit that I did hesitate. Seriozha hinted that, if I went along with the deal, my case-officer would be the floozy I had spent the night with. And I'm telling you, as case-officers go, she's a case of all right—the skin of a baby. The snag is, though, I'm still more interested in my own skin than in hers.'

Blun was on his second Armagnac when Aleksandr, who was not madly interested in this kind of pictography, but whose professional curiosity was aroused—or was he listening to the call of destiny?—asked off-handedly: 'Have you got them on you, the photos?'

Blun chuckled: 'Why d'you think I asked for a corner table?'

He had some difficulty locating his inside pocket, but when he finally did so he quickly took out a set of photographs, which he kept hidden in his hand.

'Shut your eyes.'

Aleksandr shut his eyes.

Blun, still chuckling, arranged the twelve photographs on the yellow tablecloth.

'Open.'

Aleksandr looked at them for a quarter of a minute, pushed back his chair, got up and made for the door. The head waiter stood back to let him pass. Blun half stood up: 'Psar . . .'

Psar left.

Blun fell back into his chair. For the first time in years he was left to pay the bill.

8
The Pearl

It was the same noble mansion, the same staircase whose stone steps seemed practically softened with wear, the same Trianon-grey panelling, the same medallions and the same ova, the same Marguerite already standing: 'M. Lewitzki has phoned again. He's threatening to take his idea on Dostoievsky somewhere else if he doesn't get an answer in three days.'

But it was not the same Aleksandr Psar. A man who prided himself on his self-control had changed out of all recognition. His face was white, his veiled eyes wore a haggard expression. And he arrived without his camel-hair coat or gloves—he had left them in the cloakroom of the *Pont-Royal*.

'I shall have to be away for a few days.'

The words did not flow easily and he had obviously not heard what she had said to him.

'Shall I make reservations?'

The gangue in which he had lived for thirty years, the whole of his adult life, was cracking around him. He would have to learn a new way of breathing. At forty-nine, it can be frightening.

'No, no reservations. Or rather, yes. A plane for . . . New York.'

'When for, Monsieur?'

'As soon as possible.'

'While she telephoned, he went and put his forehead against the window. At first he thought he could not see anything that was happening in the street, but after a while he noticed the same fellow with the scarf walking up and down.

The image of Gaverin, hanging from his beam, came back into his mind.

'Book me a compartment on a *wagon-lits*, too.'

'Where for, Monsieur?'

'Rome.'

'When for?'

'As soon as possible.'

He thought that he ought to have arranged one of these alternatives through Marguerite and seen to the other himself. But he felt too exhausted to stand in a queue in one of those shoddy travel agent's and to talk over a counter to one of those idiotic girls with a perm who could not read a time-table.

Barring a few mistakes, he had reconstituted the events of the last few years as he drove around Paris without even knowing that he was driving, crossing the Seine in order to escape from the left bank, then recrossing it to get nearer to the office, stopping automatically at the red lights, moving off at the green, going round in circles, consulting his watch, without seeing anything on the dial—and he a man who had always been so intensely aware of everything he did!

Alla had never been anything other than just another case-officer, who had been attached to him to give him the illusion that he would be allowed to 'go home'. After she had carried out her mission, she had been given others, of a similar type. There was no lack of women in the service, but there could not be so very many women officers capable both of seducing a man and of continuing to manipulate him: such women would occasionally have to be put to repeated use. In the Second Principal Directorate Alla must have been trained in the manipulation of French-speaking, literary intellectuals; it was not at all improbable that she had had to deal with two who knew one another: there was always that risk. The Geebee had accepted that risk, out of an exaggerated concern with economy, and that hurt Aleksandr in so far as he identified with his service and he found any kind of meanness repugnant. On top of that, he was hurt that he did not merit a case-officer of his own. Wounds to vanity are by no means the least painful. Far from it.

He had never believed that Alla LOVED him, the way the petty bourgeois of the post-romantic era talk of 'lurv', and he was not disappointed to learn that she was on duty when she opened her arms to him; in fact, he had always known as much, and he had congratulated himself on having a relationship with her based not on the contact of two skins or the exchange of two fantasies, but, rather, on the certainty of being able to build together an edifice that was much greater than the builders. He did not feel betrayed in love; that at least he was spared.

On the other hand, he found no compensation, no comfort, as a more ordinary lover would, in the fact that Alla, whom he had believed dead, was alive, and the loss of his son had become even more painful to him with the idea that he in fact had never had one. Just as, when we discover that we are no longer loved, we find a certain appeasement in the idea that we have been, Aleksandr preferred his earlier bereavement to the new feeling of ignominious emptiness that now gripped him. He did not pause for an instant to entertain the idea that his son, after all, might actually exist; he was too certain that a woman on duty would have had an abortion; and he never guessed that he had a daughter somewhere, which would have been some compensation. 'I never had a child. I don't even know if I'm capable of having one.'

This subterranean current of love that, for five years, had flowed from him was imaginary, since it had no object. But is it not monstrous to love what does not exist? He had devoted himself, evidently, to a sort of ghastly onanism of the heart. All that gentle internal scolding, that certainty of loving that was so acute that it had sometimes made him shut his eyes as if they hurt, that hand placed on the future: 'My son will be . . . My son will . . .', that feeling of no longer being alone in the world, yes, of having broken the shell of ontological solitude to which birth condemns us and from which having children delivers us, all that had been merely a mirage, then? And the photographs! How he had secretly drooled over the photographs! He had sought (and found!) resemblances— how absurd! How proud he had been to recognize in this offspring of God knows whom an heir to his line! It had given him such deep satisfaction to give that child his father's Christian name, according to the tradition! 'Forgive me, papa.' It was, a hundredfold, the embarrassment one feels when one introduces to respected friends some acquaintance who disgraces one.

He had been tricked. By whom? By those whom he had agreed to serve at the price of disloyalty, the paternal disloyalty that he had ratified. To be tricked by one's subordinates is bad enough; it was not playing the game, but it was still a game. But to be tricked by one's superiors was the end; it was what had made the Son of Man cry out *'lama sabacthani'*.

He had been tricked. Why? Had he failed to fulfil some commitment? Had he demanded some reward incommensurate with his services? He suspected that the deal made thirty years earlier had been fraudulent, that his masters had never had the slightest intention of letting him 'go home'. Even his rank, which he clung to with the childishness typical of certain soldiers, had been merely one more decoy. As he climbed, from year to year, a ladder of imaginary ranks, his masters must have been laughing at him, in that illusion factory that his Directorate was. It was hardly surprising, in the circumstances, that Piotr treated him like a vulgar agent; it was not at all a question of 'tightening the screw', as he put it, on an officer who had proved to be rather too independent, but simply a question of getting him through the stick period in the binary system of the stick-and-carrot that is applied so profitably to low-level agents.

'Monsieur,' said Marguerite, without irony, 'you're leaving for Rome this evening and for New York tomorrow noon.'

He went through into his office and, unusually, did not shut the door. He had been very fond of the panelling that had surrounded him with the pink flesh of its bare wood. His eyes alighted on the kanjars: he would leave them here so as not to arouse Marguerite's suspicions. Of course, she must suspect that he was leaving for a third destination, but she could hardly know that he did not know himself whether he would ever be coming back. Then he caught sight of the icon: 'You, too, would make fun of me, if You knew how to.'

He went behind his desk. There was mail. He tried to read it and realized that he could take nothing in.

'So? Were they right, after all? Perhaps I am just a poor footslogger incapable of subjecting myself to my own discipline.'

The necessary lucidity returned. He scribbled a few notes on a piece of paper, for the replies. He could not get the thought of Gaverin out of his head.

'I don't want the same thing to happen to me.'

He had not yet managed to come to any decision. All he knew was that he needed a few days away from it all, and that, during that time, he had to escape the surveillance of the Directorate. Would he come back tamed? Would he try to disappear? Would he lay down conditions for resuming his service? He did not know. But, in any case, he had to get away.

'Marguerite.'

He had never called out to her in this way, through the open door.

'Marguerite, I have to go away for a few days.'

The same sentence, like on a record. But he already knew that he could flee only if he made arrangements to organize his absence. He owed that to himself.

'Yes, Monsieur.'

Normally, she would have asked him if she could communicate with him by telephone, but that day she asked nothing. She stood there, pen and notebook in hand, her head slightly to one side. She was wearing a navy blue dress with a large collar and white cuffs on three-quarter length sleeves. Framed in black by her hair, her deep blue eyes were all attention.

'You will say that I have had to pop over to New York to negotiate a contract and that I'll probably be back next week.'

As he spoke, he scribbled a note of apology in Russian for Kurnosov.

'Post this. By express delivery, please. If Mme Boïsse rings, tell her I'll be ringing her shortly.'

Of course, he had no right to go away without telling Piotr how to contact him.

He felt he had resumed command of his boat.

'You were saying . . . Ah, yes, M. Lewitzki. It's true,

320

we've treated him rather badly, what with all these Kurnosovs. Tell him I'd be grateful if he could wait another fortnight, but that I'll understand if he wants to try somewhere else.'

'He has certainly already done that, Monsieur,' said Marguerite rather stiffly.

'All the same, present my apologies to him. One mustn't allow oneself to get too far behind. I've left a draft for a letter to M. Baronet, who asks me to resume my editorship of the White Books. I'm not aware that I was ever relieved of it: that ass must be made to realize it.'

It was the first time that he had ever expressed his opinion of an equal in front of a subordinate. Marguerite was ashamed on his behalf.

He looked at his watch.

As he talked, he went on asking himself whether he would take his car—the registration number, especially on a rare make, might give him away—or whether he should rent one. For the moment, he did not want to have to seem to be covering over his traces. But he had had several opportunities of seeing the extent to which the Geebee was well informed and equipped. How easy they had found it to bring Ballandar and Fourveret to heel. Escaping the surveillance of the Geebee struck him as a task beyond the capacities of an ordinary man. Yet that was what he was going to try to do, at least for a few days. The best way would be to borrow a car. But from whom? He realized that he did not know anyone well enough to ask.

'I wasn't listening. I'm sorry.'

Marguerite repeated: 'Couldn't I come with you?'

She was blushing under her make-up.

'I'm sorry if I'm being indiscreet. I thought you might need me.'

'No, I won't need anyone, thank you.'

And then something snapped inside him. He was used to living alone, not to feeling alone. For thirty years, Pitman's hand had weighed impalpably on him, a familiar, protecting hand. Soon he would be alone at the wheel of the Omega, or of some unknown rented car. That isolation terrified him. Perhaps the presence of someone as understanding, as uninsistent as Marguerite would help him live through these few days. He would not, of course, discuss his dilemma with her, but the warmth of her attentiveness, her desire to see him succeed at all times, might help him to come to the best decision. 'Would I be exposing her to too many risks if I took her with me?' he wondered, and the picture of Gaverin, with his protruding eyes and tongue, came back to him. 'On the contrary, I would be limiting my own risk.' He did not remember much about his apprenticeship in Brooklyn, but one thing came back to him: 'To attempt a blood-letting against two individuals is not twice, but ten times as dangerous as against a single person.'

Almost overcome with shyness, Marguerite made a last attempt: 'There's nothing that can't wait for a day or two. Anyway it's Christmas the day after tomorrow and we have the answering machine . . .'

Aleksandr still hesitated. Marguerite had certainly guessed that he was going neither to Rome nor to New York. She would sooner be cut into a thousand pieces, as they say, than reveal that to anyone. But what if they really did get the knives out? Even without resorting to physical violence, there are very rewarding methods of intimidation. And if he rented that car, it would be clever to rent it in the name of Mme Thérien.

'Very well. You'll buy a toothbrush en route.'

'What should I put on the answering machine, Monsieur?'

'I'll record it myself.'

One had to avoid suspicion as far as possible.

'This is Aleksandr Psar speaking. Thank you for your call. Unfortunately I have to be away from the office for a few hours and, my secretary, Mme Thérien, is off sick. Would you be so kind as to record your message? I shall be glad to ring you back. Please speak after the signal.'

If, after 'a few hours', they set out to look for him, they would try the New York track first; when they realized that he had not taken the plane, they would then try Rome.

As he went out he picked up his big black briefcase. In the other office, he helped Marguerite on with her grey coat, the one with the fox fur collar. A pleasant smell assailed his nostrils: 'What scent are you wearing, Marguerite?'

'*Jolie Madame*, Monsieur. You gave it to me for my birthday.'

'It was a good choice.'

With a half smile he asked forgiveness for being so absent-minded.

In the courtyard, Aleksandr clambered into the Omega and opened the passenger-door from the inside. First, he said to himself, the sinews of war. He stopped at his bank in the Boulevard Saint-Germain.

'I'll double park the car. If the police make a fuss, charm them.'

It was the first time he had allowed himself to make such a personal suggestion to Marguerite.

He drew out all his available money in cash. When he came out of the bank, he saw that Marguerite had moved the car, but had got back into the passenger seat. She explained: 'We were in the way.'

He remembered something: the monitor at Brooklyn had recommended anyone who wanted to pass unrecognized to 'desilhouette' himself. But how did one 'desilhouette' one-self? In one of Paul Bourget's novels, a schoolteacher bought new clothes at *Old England* before daring to turn up at a tailor's.

'I'll do the opposite.'

Aleksandr crossed from the left bank once again and found a lucky parking place near the Opéra.

'Marguerite, the district is full of car-hire agencies. Will you rent a car in your name? I'll reimburse you, of course. You have a credit card?'

'Yes, Monsieur. When for?'

'As soon as possible.'

'Shall I have it delivered?'

She must not be found and followed.

'No. We'll drop in and pick it up at the garage. Meet me here in half-an-hour.'

She hesitated.

'If you're worried about the Omega, Monsieur, would you like us to take my little Renault 5? It's blue,' she added, as if that mattered.

Marguerite's car might be on the file.

'No, thank you. Get something more comfortable for a long journey.'

He had no idea where they were going.

Without his overcoat Aleksandr was cold, but he remembered that he had not yet taken any precautions to put a possible shadow off his scent. So before making his purchases, he carried out a few crude manoeuvres at the Galeries Lafayette. The guy with the scarf had not reappeared; no other suspect had shown himself. Aleksandr left. Above the street, garlands of fairylights glinted in the gathering dusk. Long live the profiteers' Christmas!

At *Old England*, Aleksandr bought a warm, reversible raincoat, a tweed cap, an umbrella and gloves. He had never carried an umbrella or worn a hat and he felt very stupid in his new outfit.

Marguerite was already waiting for him near the Omega. She considered it polite not to conceal her surprise entirely.

'Very English, Monsieur.'

'Sherlock Holmes in person. All I need now is the pipe. Well?'

'We have to go and collect the Peugeot, in the Avenue de la Grande-Armée.'

'You collect it. Pick me up at the Gare Saint-Lazare. I'll be in front of the Cour du Havre, so that you won't have to park.'

Marguerite walked off towards the taxi rank. She walked well; her grey coat hardly touched her hips. It began to snow and a few flakes landed on her black hair. She opened a small blue umbrella. There was no taxi at the rank, but she soon flagged one down nearby. Aleksandr had followed her for a good distance. She had not turned back a single time. She got into the taxi without anyone appearing to follow her or to dash into a café to make a telephone call. It was reasonable to suppose that all was well in that department.

Aleksandr caught the métro. Clutching the slippery white bar, his eyes staring into space, he said to himself: 'I shouldn't have left Blun so suddenly, he might suspect something. After all, how do I know that he in fact did refuse to collaborate?'

Perhaps there was a subtler plan there than he had

thought? Perhaps it was not a mistake, the Directorate being merely petty; perhaps it was a parallel set-up? Perhaps they had chosen this way of telling him that he had been hood-winked. But why? The Confraternity Operation was going extremely well and the Geebee could have no advantage in discouraging Psar or in pushing him over to the French. Of course, he would never betray them; but could they know that? No, it didn't stand up. From the station, Aleksandr telephoned Blun: 'I'm terribly sorry, I could tell you a lie, but I would rather you knew the truth: I had a terrible attack of colic.'

Blun did not dare to ask for the bill to be reimbursed. Aleksandr hung up, smiling.

He started to pace up and down the pavement. The cold was freezing his nose, his cheekbones, his ears and was beginning to petrify his toes.

'One doesn't have to fill up forms in hotels any more. But the receptionists are all informers. We'll have to give false names. That will surprise Marguerite. What shall I tell her?'

He could put all the blame on the Geebee: Gaverin's death would be sufficient excuse: 'they hanged Gaverin, so I'm now going into hiding with you.'

He remembered how carefully Marguerite had double-locked the three locks on the office door: a good housewife, sure of coming back, wanting to find everything in its place.

False names. 'My name is Jean Dupont!'

'Well, I'd have sworn that you were . . . What was his name now? Aleksandr Psar. Really, you just look like him. Amazing. He was on the box, last Friday, with Iron Mask.'

'Yes, I'm not yet "desilhouetted" enough. And I haven't even got a beard I could shave off! Very thoughtless of me! Glasses! But I wouldn't know how to go into an optician's and ask for glasses with clear glass. Tell him it's for a play? No, that might seem suspicious. What about a wig? Marguerite seeing me with a wig or a false moustache? And supposing I get caught, and they snatch off that moustache, that wig, those glasses . . .' He bought slightly tinted sung-lasses, but they bothered him: he did not wear them.

Marguerite arrived with a black Peugeot; she gave up the driving seat to him. The Peugeot felt quite different to drive from the Omega; one sensed that the power was distributed quite differently; there was something more aggressive about it: Latin instead of Anglo-Saxon.

Aleksandr gunned the engine, taking pleasure in finding it so responsive, capable of keeping up the pace, of finding extra, sustained power when called upon to do so: 'My battleship!' It occurred to him that he had never driven a Russian car. 'When I go home . . .' But would he ever go home? He was beginning to doubt it. He stroked the controls with his hand and looked fondly at the dashboard, taking possession of the bridge, as his father would have said. Marguerite looked at him, in an expressionless way, her chin stuck down into her fox fur, her lipstick marrying precisely her broad, firm mouth.

The Peugeot joined the metallic flux. Aleksandr went through the gears, enjoying the fact that he was doing something that meant nothing. A gloomy Paris was slowly bubbling around them; ill-tempered people were running after one another without knowing why; newspaper vendors were turning blue in their kiosks; a chestnut seller introduced a nostalgic note into a scene that might have been one of Dickensian good humour, but instead was dreary and sour.

Marguerite was staring straight ahead of her.

'What a terrible thing!' she said. 'That poor M. Gaverin.'

What association of ideas had been at work?

It was only after he had left Paris, heading north-west, that Aleksandr realized where he was going. It would only be one stage, of course, but a necessary one, in their journey. He found it strange, for he had always calculated his actions with such care, to see himself thus taken over by the spontaneous initiatives of his unconscious, like a ship on automatic pilot. Did Gaverin ever buy his hunting gun? Did he hang himself out of sheer despair? A hunting gun is no protection against despair. But yes, it is in some cases. Aleksandr came from a family where, for centuries, the possession of a weapon had been regarded as necessary, not so much for man's security, as for his dignity. Poor Dmitri Alexandrovich had hoped all his life to own a gun, if only a carbine. How often he had tried to save a few francs to buy one, not because it would be of any practical use to him, but because, in a sense, it was indispensable! And then what little he had saved had gone on a meal for a friend, some roses for his wife or a second-hand Latin dictionary for his son. A weapon is not just a weapon: it's a decision, a matter of pride; it's an opportunity to show courage, a way of banking on oneself, of looking one's fate in the eyes.

'Yes,' said Aleksandr, after a quarter of an hour of silence, 'it's a terrible thing, that Gaverin business.'

He thought of that man alone, one evening, in his barricaded house. Used, worn out. Perhaps liquidated, by way of tidying up, tying up the loose ends, removing the scaffolding; perhaps abandoned, because it was known that he would be driven to liquidate himself. Liquidate: how telling is the wrong meaning given to this word! Deprived of his solidity, merged in a general collapse, disintegrated in the septic tank. How had Gaverin been 'liquidated'? Had a team been sent to him from Department V or did he have, within himself, his own liquidation team, cells or globules, like tiny gnomes which, one day, had methodically climbed up into his brain and set about the task of liquefying it? In a sense, it did not matter. He had been classified as out of service, or he had classified himself as out of service, and the Hermès tie, decorated with stirrups and bits, the beautiful silky tie, itself sliding like liquid, had tightened over the larynx, the pharynx, God knows what, and he was dead. How long had he suffered? Can time, in such circumstances, be measured like ours? Had he reached out with his foot to find the stool that he had kicked away? Alone, alone. Or perhaps not alone, if the specialists of Department V had helped him, but alone all the same with the physical pain and that final blurring . . . Wiped out, wiped out. Can one throw away a man as one throws away a tool that doesn't work any more?

'I gave him that tie,' said Aleksandr.

Was that a sign? Was it a signal? Were they trying to convey something to him in the choice of tie? Marguerite placed her gloved hand on Aleksandr's gloved hand.

'It isn't your fault: he'd have found something else.'

She imagined that he felt remorse. Was she entirely wrong?

'Or do you think,' she added, 'that it was . . . them?'

He concentrated on driving.

'If I'd kept the Omega,' he said to himself, 'they might have sabotaged it. But, for the time being at least, they have no way of knowing that I am driving this Peugeot. Tomorrow, or the day after, they will think of checking Marguerite's movements, but for the moment we're safe. Unless they had my office bugged all along!' Men who had been 'we' a few hours before had suddenly become 'they'! 'In that case, they know I left with Marguerite, but they don't know that we left by car, still less in a rented one. Nevertheless, they've got their contacts in car-hire firms, and they must have . . .'

He tried to take a grip on himself. 'Am I getting like Gaverin?' he mused.

Gaverin hanging from a necktie. Perhaps he hadn't been as paranoid as people thought. And Ballandar had been revisited by a past forty years old. And Fourveret had been impaled on his own shame and been told to go on smiling. All that in the twinkling of an eye.

They reached Pontoise.

'Marguerite, I have a call to make. Will you wait for me in this café?'

He took his briefcase.

The fat little colonel was delighted to see M. Alexandre.

'Long time no see! But first could you clear up something? It was you, wasn't it, I saw on television the other day, or have you got a double? The thing is, I always thought you spelt your name R-sar, and they said P-sar.'

Aleksandr felt the tiny refuge of identity that he had constructed around himself here collapse. Suddenly he had an idea: 'Yes, it was me. But you see, I'm of Russian origin and in our alphabet the Ps are Rs.'

'You don't say!'

The colonel thought it would be impolite to pursue the matter, but the cogs in his brain went on turning. Before long he would ask point-blank, 'What's your official name, then? The one you have on your driving licence, for example?' He had not got there yet.

'A little practice with the air-gun, followed by the real thing, as usual?'

'Only the air-gun, I think. I've a touch of rheumatism. I'm afraid of the recoil.'

He himself had no idea why he did not want to shoot real bullets.

His three cartons were bad. He did not manage to achieve that synthesis of breathing, vision and relaxation that concentrates the shots on the bull's-eye. But when he left, he took with him in his briefcase his Smith and Wesson, and the box of .357 magnum cartridges with the hollow-point bullets. He had no fire-arms licence. 'What I'm doing is quite illegal,' he said to himself, with morose satisfaction. What were the chances of the police stopping and searching him? And the extra weight of his big briefcase reassured him. 'For a few hours, for a few days, I'm a lone wolf. What happens after that, we'll see.'

He no longer depended on anyone and, once he had got over the initial anxiety, he found this sensation exhilarating. He looked at his watch: 'Poor Marguerite will be waiting for me . . .' But, having parked the Peugeot, he took time to open the sacramental box and replace the .38s that usually filled its cylinder with six big, long, heavy evil .357s, deriving special pleasure in saying to himself that their open mouths would cause, if necessary, much more damage than the pointed ones.

Marguerite was waiting patiently in front of a cup of hot chocolate. For the first time in her life, no doubt, she did not stand up when her boss came in, but contented herself with a smile, in order not to embarrass him. He noticed that she had only taken off her right-hand glove, and that she had astonishingly small hands for a woman so solidly built. He looked at his watch, for he had already forgotten the time. For a few minutes, he felt rejuvenated, more supple.

'Chocolate? You still like that? I haven't had any for forty years. I used to like it. After all, why not? Monsieur, a cup of hot chocolate, please.'

The bitter, sickening taste brought back his childhood with painful sharpness.

'When I got home from the lycée, my father wasn't back

329

yet, but he used to leave on the stove a small enamel saucepan, all streaked with white and blue, with a bit of enamel missing on the rim, which made a black mark. I'd turn on the gas, make myself some chocolate and write an epic or two while it boiled.'

'Didn't you have a mother?'

'My mother died when I was two.'

'So you don't remember her.'

'No. Sometimes I imagine . . . A pink shape, blue sky . . . It must be an illusion.'

'Did your father talk to you about her?'

'Never. And I've just realized something . . . It's funny.'

He was really perplexed. She waited for a long time, then, gently, dared to ask: 'What's funny?'

The veiled eyes were looking at things she could not see.

'My father had taught me to say my prayers: the Our Father, the Hail Mary, and a prayer for the living and for the dead. I prayed for him, for my grandparents, for others. Never for my mother. It didn't seem strange at the time: I thought my mother was a saint and one didn't pray for saints. I'd have prayed to her, rather. But why did my father . . .?'

She smiled sadly. He felt obliged to ask her: 'Are both your parents alive, Marguerite?'

'My mother is. My father was killed during the war in Indo-China. My mother lives in Lisieux. That's why I go there for my holidays.'

He was no longer listening to her. He was thinking of that great void that surrounded him and of the Russian expression that meant that one has lost one's father and mother: 'a round orphan'. He really felt like a round orphan: whichever way he turned, he was confronted by the void. He clung to the idea of that revolver he still possessed, like a tramp to his dog.

'Let's go,' he said, getting up.

'Where?'

Since he did not know what to answer, he said: 'For dinner.'

On the banks of the Seine he knew one of those 'country inns' where businessmen take their secretaries and doctors their assistants. Fourveret had once thought fit to take him out to lunch there. Night had already fallen when he parked the Peugeot between a Jaguar and a Porsche, in the courtyard flanked by modern buildings with half-timbering stuck on. It was freezing. The muddy snow was laboriously turning to ice. As Marguerite had nearly slipped, Aleksandr led her by the arm to the brightly lit entrance.

'Has Monsieur booked?'

'Should I have done?'

'It's the day before Christmas Eve, Monsieur.'

'You'll find us something.'

Sighs. Eyes raised to heaven. Ah, these customers! How lovely it would be without them!

'This way, Monsieur.'

Aleksandr could not cure himself of the feeling that there should always be a table reserved for him in every restaurant and, in fact, he was seldom turned away. When this did happen, he was furious. If that happened to him now, in front of Marguerite . . . But no, everything was all right. Suddenly he wanted to—at first he could not find the word—'treat' Marguerite. She put more than competence into her work; she deserved more than a mere salary.

'Cloakroom, Monsieur?'

He insisted on helping Marguerite off with her coat himself, as if he was jealous of the privilege, then he turned his back to the head waiter to be helped off with his Burberry. Nothing irritated him more than the vulgar 'service' that consisted in helping the ladies off with their coats and pushing their chairs forward, while leaving the pigs who foot the bill to fend for themselves.

'Shall I take your briefcase, Monsieur?'

'Yes . . . Er, no. I'll keep it with me.'

He placed it beside his chairleg. Fortunately it was heavy enough in itself, with its leather and locks, for the weight of the revolver not to be noticeable; all the same, one had to be careful. Aleksandr's imagination began to run wild again: in a French prison would he be protected from his friends?

Marguerite asked for a port and was given a fifty-year-old one. Aleksandr had a single malt whisky with very little ice. The symphony in black and white of the waiters and of the table-cloths crinkling with starch, the fire roaring in the false medieval fireplace contrasted deliciously with the freezing cold and wet outside.

'You were saying a little while ago . . . Perhaps I misunderstood you . . . That you used to write poems?'

'Dozens! I thought I was a poet.'

'Don't you write any more now? It's a pity. Obviously you haven't got the time.'

Did she imagine that one wrote because one had the time?

'It's not time, but talent, I need, Marguerite. I think I'm a fairly good'—he stumbled over the word 'literary'—'literary agent, but a writer? No. You have to be quite shameless, quite lacking in self-respect to be a writer . . .'

He pulled a face.

'It really isn't a very . . . how shall I put it . . . nice profession. Especially since the romantics: spitting into one's handkerchief and sticking it under people's noses in the hope that there will be blood on it? Not likely!'

The menus were bound in leather, with pseudo-coats-of-arms stamped on the outside.

'What will you begin with, Marguerite?'

She hesitated, embarrassed by the absence of prices.

'A soup, perhaps . . .'

He guessed that she was trying to cost him as little as possible.

'Would you like me to order for you?'

He composed a princely menu, ordered a Dom Pérignon for the foie gras, a Clos de la Pucelle for the crab, a Grands-Echezeaux for the pheasant. He forced Marguerite to have cheese, when she could hardly eat another thing and inflicted on her a passion-fruit sorbet to conclude. He himself ate voraciously. Yes, he had never had a son; yes, he had been betrayed by his own people, yes, he had fought France, and France was now serving him of her best. An aggressive mood was taking hold of him.

'Tell me about yourself, Marguerite. It's quite ridiculous: we've been working together for twenty years and I know nothing about you. Have you any brothers or sisters?'

She told him the story of her life. Father an NCO, killed in battle; mother a typing teacher; she herself an only child;

good sound education; showed talent for law; mother ill, need to work, willingly accepted; only two jobs before being taken on by the Agence Psar.

Aleksandr looked at her more than he listened to her. He liked the way her fingers, with their carefully rounded and polished nails closed over the glass of white Burgundy. This girl may have come from a petty-bourgeois background, but she had style. She dressed very well, she held herself very well, she almost spoke well. She was not dazzled by this restaurant and, above all, she did not put on a show of being so. He interrupted her in the middle of a sentence:

'And you've never thought of getting married?'

She had loved someone. A long time ago. He was married, with children. 'I wouldn't like to have to say to myself that I'd stolen anything from anyone!' And then, smiling, she added: 'I'm happy as I am.'

And then, more quietly: 'I'm happy working for you.'

'I don't know'—he knew very well—'whether I've ever told you how much the Agency owes you Marguerite. We'd never have made a go of it without you.'

'Oh! Of course you would!'

'No, no. We'd have gone under more than once.'

What did that royal 'we', from which, apparently, Marguerite was excluded, mean? She resumed, gaily refusing to be so excluded: 'Yes, we had some hard times. Once or twice it was a near thing, but we always came through in the end, and you'd have done so by yourself. Or with somebody else.'

After two cups of coffee he paid in cash, so as not to leave any trace of his passage. Outside it was also a symphony in black and white; the sky was black and the earth white. And the timbering formed black and white stripes. Without knowing why Aleksandr drove southwards. They drove for a long time without saying anything.

'Why south?' Aleksandr asked himself. 'Because the map is larger on that side, or because I got into the habit of going in that direction with Gaverin, or because I'm drawn by the smell of his corpse, like the murderer who is drawn back to the scene of the crime?'

As the small dark cell launched itself into the cold like a space-ship into the cosmos, the heat from the engine, the heat that Aleksandr and Marguerite shared, gradually dissolved some of the barriers between them.

'You haven't even asked me where we're going,' said Aleksandr.

She was looking straight ahead, her chin stuck into her fur.

'I don't mind,' she said.

He thought of that hot chocolate they had had earlier and of all the memories that had then come flooding back to him. The small enamel saucepan. Later, in the evening, his father's key in the lock. The last few weeks before he went into hospital, the key groping for a long time before finding the hole, and the smell of stale, cheap wine emanating from Dmitri Aleksandrovich's mouth when his son got up to kiss him. All that formed, in his memory, an epic constellation, together with holes in his shoes, the colds that resulted from them, the discovery of the masterly rhythm of the Russian hexameter, the profile of a woman seen against the light through a window on the other side of the street, and the enticing mystery that already surrounded his periodical meetings with Iakov Moiseich. He suddenly remembered the test that the warm-hearted, but ironic Iakov Moiseich had imposed on him: never to be top of the class and to get himself placed as near the top as possible. He thought of it with a great sense of self-disgust. Those exercises, justified as the ascesis of an order of knighthood, now looked like petty bullying. Bullying endured for nothing.

That word 'nothing' struck him. For thirty years, he had lived for something in which he believed, but whose existence suddenly seemed to him extremely dubious. Russia? The Russia of his father, because he came from it; the Russia of his son, if he had had one, because he had been born there, yes. And even if he had known that a little girl with brown hair, the fruit of his loins, had learnt that very day the first verses of some doggerel in honour of Lenin ('When Lenin was but a little man / His felt boots were all stuffed with bran'), he would have gone on believing in Russia, not because of Vladimir Ilich, who meant nothing to him, of course, but because of that incarnate History. Imagining himself to be sterile, it seemed to him that the whole of Russia was merely a blood-soaked myth. Who could prove to him that Piotr and all the Ivans and all the Kurnosovs really did come from that kingdom beyond forty kingdoms? Piotr was not called Piotr nor Ivan Ivan, nor some of the Kurnosovs Kurnosov. Russia, one-seventh of the land surface of the earth, may not be land surface at all: a tidal wave had covered it over, with its silver birches and its grey wolves, its golden onion-domes and its endless plains, and the men for whom he worked came from elsewhere, from another planet. Or that madman Kurnosov had been right all along, and the agents of the Geebee were in the final analysis merely sub-agents of the universal conspiracy of Usurers. The KGB a cover!

What was happening to Aleksandr was more or less what happens to a youth who has always believed in God because he has seen churches, holy images, crucifixes, sacraments, and who discovers that all these things prove nothing, because they may all add up to nothing but a great stage-setting. People had talked to him about a Russia that was supposed to have existed somewhere in the world and he had deduced from this that another, eternal, essential Russia was shining somewhere in the world. But what did he know about it? And, if that was the case, in what sense did he belong to it? In what way were they united?

A horrible thought struck him. What are we? We are what we eat. That's why the Christians eat Christ: to become Christ. And, apart from a few litres of vodka, a little caviar, what had he ever eaten that was a product of his ancestral land? He had never felt that he was a Frenchman, but all the molecules that made up his body had come from this humus here. No, not all. There had been, at the base, two gametes that had merged together and which had come from elsewhere. And the rest? That original cell, supposing that it still existed in some way, was exiled in Aleksandr's great body, a body fed on French wheat and French meat.

Of course, there was the language, the civilization, certain ways of thinking, the heritage, you might say, and the fidelity. But fidelity for itself?

He then understood, in a flash, the paradoxical ideogram of his destiny.

He was born a traitor.

He was the traitor-exemplary, the traitor without motive. He had betrayed Russia by being born in France; he had betrayed her again by eating in France; he was betraying the France that he was eating by dreaming of Russia.

By putting himself at the service of the Bolsheviks Aleksandr and his father before him had denied the spirit of a whole civilization and of the caste that had moulded him (not class, no: deep down Aleksandr had always rejected that word, so typical of the bearded pedant who launched it); but this caste, this civilization had had their day, and the widower who remarries is not an adulterer: that betrayal, if it were betrayal, was merely accidental, expedient, superficial, of no consequence. The other betrayal—being born somewhere else—did not depend on choice, went beyond temptation or allegiance, and was in no sense mitigated by the fact that Aleksandr had thought that he had based his life on fidelity.

Fidelity, first of all to a hope: to 'go home' to that paradise from which he believed he had come, a fidelity imposing innumerable humiliations and affording only inward satisfactions. Then fidelity to an imaginary memory: that civilization, long since dead and buried, which Aleksandr himself had not known, but which he would have regarded as shameful to disown—an even more gratuitous fidelity, therefore, the glorious, but sterile immolation of a living being in the name of the beautiful, but dead beloved. Lastly, beyond repudiation, fidelity to an anticipated future; a fidelity less disinterested than the preceding ones, this, but one that is expressed in a similar way: isolation, contraction over a painfully contained fecundity, deliberate exile. In this way he had become, so to speak, the negative of himself.

'I don't know what it means to live like a fish in water.'

And what was the point of it all?

'I suppose I wanted to give God a lesson in fidelity.'

God, like many princes, is well known for abandoning his faithful followers. The White armies attacked with prayers, banners unfurled, and they were mowed down by the machine-guns of blasphemers. Where were the legions of angels and archangels who should have come to the help of the soldiers of Christ? An old story: Christ himself was left unaided.

Ever since Aleksandr had put his hand into the hand of the enemies of God, he had felt supported, sustained. Pitman had told him, with a smile: 'You will see, Aleksandr Dmitrich, you know your Latin: *KGB, patria nostra.*' When he had to put pressure on Fourveret, or Ballandar, he had been given the means. The same thing when he had decided to turn Blun into a success: on innumerable occasions, when he had asked for help, effective help had come, indeed, to startling effect when the need arose. So what had happened now? Had they only pretended to accept him into that body, or did the devil too abandon his own?

Aleksandr drove slowly, convincing himself that he was doing so out of caution, because the road was slippery; in fact it was because he did not know where he was going. Similarly, instead of taking the *autoroute*, he had chosen the smaller *route nationale*, so as to allow more time for his destination to mature inside him. The dashboard clock shone in the darkness—it was past three. Aleksandr told himself that he was sleepy and wondered what he was going to do. Suddenly he remembered the woman sitting next to him.

His first reaction was one of irritation. He had enough worries without her. Then he told himself that it was Marguerite, that she had always smoothed his way for him. Marguerite was leaning back on the headrest and her closed eyelids, delicately hemmed in blue—she had made up for the evening at the inn—were confronting the night outside with their own shadow. Her breathing was gentle and regular.

'Poor girl,' thought Aleksandr, surprised at his own tenderness.

He thought with gratitude of those twenty years of attentiveness, not a gratuitous, but a fruitful attentiveness, which was better, of all that continuous friction with reality, of all those intelligent efforts devoted apparently to the prosperity of the Agence Psar—in reality to the success of the Geebee: Marguerite had merely been one more relay.

Very carefully, wheel by wheel, he drove the car on to the side of the road. Marguerite opened her eyes.

'We'll sleep here for a bit,' said Aleksandr quietly. 'It would be silly to go on. I'll adjust your seat-back.'

She let him operate the levers and found herself reclining

without having changed position. The engine would stay on, because they would need the heat. Aleksandr switched off the headlamps, pulled his briefcase towards him and half opened it. Then he tipped back his own seat, placed the briefcase on his lap, put his hand in and gripped the squared wooden butt. It amused him to play the adventurer. 'You *will* wage war,' Pitman had said to him, so long ago. But he had not waged the war he dreamed of. He shut his eyes and sank into sleep. The last image to pass in front of his mind was that of the electronic chess game that he had left in operation that morning. He wondered whether the computer would have played the castle or the knight.

Despite the purring of the heater, Aleksandr was awoken by the cold. He noticed with surprise that his antelope-gloved hand was holding Marguerite's tiny kid-gloved hand. He could not remember committing this incongruous act—taking hold of his secretary's hand.

But he had committed a greater one. To sleep beside some one, however chastely, presented incalculable cosmic risks. To all appearances each individual withdraws into his own dreams where he cloisters himself as long as sleep lasts, a prisoner in his own fortress, the guard of his own prison. But how do we know what occult influences two parallel sleepers exert upon one another? What mutual infiltrations of fantasies might take place between them? And above all, when one sleeps, how can one be sure that the other does not give one the most indiscreet looks, indiscreet because we cannot return them? To sleep next to someone is really to place oneself at his mercy and, without ever asking himself why, Aleksandr had always felt repelled at the idea of sleeping next to his occasional mistresses. Usually, whatever it cost him, he had got up and gone home; on the few occasions when he had had women in his apartment, he had gone and slept on the sofa in the drawing-room and had locked the bedroom door, so that his visitor could not enjoy the spectacle of his sleeping face: 'How could I tolerate someone else seeing me as I have never seen myself?' Only with Alla had he abandoned such precautions.

The fact of having taken this risk with Marguerite might have humiliated or irritated him. Marguerite meant nothing to him. She had seen him careworn, puzzled, tired, triumphant, and he might have resented the fact that he had shared with her these hours of oblivion as well. But no, this increased intimacy did not weigh on him. He locked his briefcase and righted his seat.

The windscreen was covered with snow. The wipers shuddered, but refused to function. Aleksandr unlocked, then opened his door, and put a foot outside. It sank into the snow up to his ankle.

He was delighted with the landscape. Inveterate Parisian that he was, he had never seen such a sight. Snowy undulations, swellings and hollows. Black, leafless trees, like men drawn by children: one line for the trunk, two for the branches. An astonishing silence. Bushes by the roadside with leaves weighed down by snow. Across the immensity of a field, the diagonal, cuneiform flight of a rabbit.

Aleksandr took a deep breath.

In the distance, he discovered the capital A of a clock tower, dominating a few dwellings set in lower case.

Marguerite was in the car, invisible as under a tent.

Aleksandr walked a few steps. He was cold. He began to slap himself on the back with both hands as, it seems coachmen used to do: left arm over, right arm under, then vice-versa. His father had taught him these gymnastics. Gradually Aleksandr increased the pace. The blood began to circulate through his limbs. A clump of snow came away from a branch and fell on his nose. It made him laugh almost out loud.

'Where am I? I've no idea. It would be too bad if *they* knew.'

He had never felt free before.

'This is the first time.'

He rubbed his face with snow, spontaneously rediscovering ancestral gestures. He ate some snow—and drank it.

He opened the door. Marguerite was rubbing her eyelids.

'Good morning, Marguerite.'

'Where are we?'

He laughed: 'Not the faintest idea.'

She sat up and turned the rear-view mirror towards her: 'What a fright!'

'Didn't notice. But if you want to freshen up, rub yourself with snow. I've just done it, there's nothing like it.'

She ventured outside with an uncertain step. When she came back, her cheeks were glowing. She had washed in snow. She was laughing, a little bashfully, with a touch of coquettishness.

Aleksandr removed the snow from the windscreen with the side of his hand. He had taken off his gloves on purpose in order to feel the prickling of the cold. He turned on the de-froster. The windscreen wipers went to work.

'Marguerite,' he said, when they were sitting side by side again, 'all this must strike you as ridiculous in the extreme, you who are so . . . level-headed. The truth . . . The truth is I can't tell you the truth. But I'm sure you don't want me to run the same risks as Gaverin. That's why we're playing gypsies for a bit. In a day or two I'll see things more clearly. Now, if you like, I can take you to a railway station . . .'

'But, Monsieur, I'm enjoying it,' she said, her cheeks rubicund and her nose shining.

Was this the first time in her life she had used that word? Anyway she laughed heartily, surprised to see herself in so unusual a situation, and even more surprised to find it funny.

'Good. Let's go and get some breakfast. We don't have much petrol left. I hope we can find a petrol station so that the car can have breakfast too.'

Yesterday the adventure had been tragic; now it seemed more like an escapade. The world of the Geebee, at once real and mythical, was fading into the background. Sometimes we dream that some misfortune has befallen us and then we wake up. That was more or less Aleksandr's state of mind. His nightmare had lasted thirty years.

They found a village where the petrol pump was operated by an early-morning witch, who also ran the local café.

'Coffee, m'sieu-dame?'

'Have you any chocolate?' Marguerite asked.

And Aleksandr also wanted chocolate, without knowing why.

When they had got back into the car and resumed their

journey southwards, destination unknown, Aleksandr began to talk about his childhood, as if he were continuing some interrupted meditation.

'It was strange to grow up like a bird in water, like a fish in air. If that strangeness had come only from my schoolfriends . . . but the entire world seemed to me to be twisted. When I was small—it was no longer like that in your day, Marguerite —all the lessons in the textbooks ended with a summary that had to be learnt by heart. The geography lessons especially. "England is an island that produces a lot of coal . . ." I can't remember much else. But I remember the summary for Russia, because I learnt it by heart and refused to recite it: "Russia is a vast plain, rich in wheat, inhabited by a barbarous people." You don't believe me? But it's true. It was important for me to have good marks, but I felt I couldn't repeat those words. I read the summary, in a low voice, to my father. He said: "If you recite that, you'll dishonour yourself." I was . . . what? Seven? It was too soon to dishonour oneself. I said to the teacher: "What the book says isn't true." She didn't understand: this little boy who was always so polite, so studious? Was he getting rebellious? I was punished, more harshly than the dunces. I suffered from that punishment, but gritted my teeth proudly. I saw myself as a martyr. In a sense, I was one. I wasn't top of the class that month, but I hadn't said that my family consisted of barbarians.

'And the torture of the Larousse! I had been taught that Russia had more great men than other countries. I was quite willing to recognize that this might be an exaggeration, but I demanded at least some. And that marvellous Larousse, which, on every other subject, provided me with so much delicious information—I remember the biographies of Archias, Damocles, Bonchamps, Aster . . .—do you know what it said about Russia?'

Aleksandr was driving, without knowing where he was going, he thought, and bits of sentences that had eaten into his heart forty years earlier surfaced intact in his mind.

'Kutuzov, for instance. For us, he was a demi-god and surely they had to recognize that he'd trounced Napoleon. Well, Larousse certainly put paid to him with a minimum of words: "Kutuzov (Michael), Russian general, defeated at the Moskova." That was all. And Suvorov, whom the Larousse persisted in calling Suvarov! All his great exploits were summed up in the words "defeated by Masséna at Zurich". And Mussorgsky, who carried the incredible Christian name "Petrovich"! And Alexander! Do you know what remarkable deed he performed? He "fought against Napoleon, who defeated him at Austerlitz"! How do you think a small boy in exile could bear that, when greeted every day by his schoolfellows with: "Dirty Russky! Go back to where you came from!" '

Marguerite listened, without a word of comment, but torn, one could guess, between pity and indignation. Monsieur, her Monsieur, had had to endure such indignities? Aleksandr was gradually blossoming in the warmth of this deferential sympathy.

But destiny may also govern the roads and, after driving past innumerable signposts that meant nothing to him, nothing at any rate that he was aware of, he arrived at last before a saint's name that did remind him of something: St Yrieix. Aleksandr had no idea what Yrieix had done to become a saint, but he remembered passing through two months earlier with Gaverin and an estate agent. Quite near there was the *château* surrounded by railings, that Gaverin had nearly bought and which had even made Aleksandr envious. He did not yet know it, but the shadow of a plan was already forming in his mind. For the moment, he wanted only to see the house again.

'Would you mind if we made a detour, Marguerite?' he asked.

As if one could make a detour when one was not going anywhere in particular.

He was not used to orientating himself in the country. Besides, the snow had altered whatever landmarks there might have been. But he managed all the same to find the village he was looking for; a high street, a Romanesque church, clumsily restored in the nineteenth century, a telephone box on a small square, everything covered with snow and, apparently, deserted. Since the introduction of television, village houses were, it seemed, closed to the outside

342

world, and passers-by had disappeared. The *château* must be on the right, or maybe on the left, but not very far.

Aleksandr drove another two kilometres. On the right an avenue of tall majestic trees appeared. Here the snow was entirely virginal.

He turned up the avenue, its smooth surface marred by the crests of a few ruts of black, frozen earth. The rusty gates hung between two stone piers, which, though not particularly elegant, had a certain dignity. The key had been lost or the lock no longer worked, for the gates were fastened together with a chain and padlock. Aleksandr remembered that the estate agent had had some difficulty opening the padlock.

'Have you got friends who live here, Monsieur?'

He shook his head. He had forgotten the padlock. The gates were ten feet high, extending above the piers, and each of its bars ended in a spearhead. Aleksandr got out of the car. The house—towers, gables, pinnacle turrets—rose beyond an oval lawn overgrown with weeds and shrubs, all frozen and covered with snow, reminding one, with its stripes and hatchings, of a sketch in white on black paper. A cold, persistent wind was blowing. From time to time a heavy clump of snow detached itself from a high branch and fell to the ground slowly and silently, like in a film in slow motion with the soundtrack turned off. Ten minutes earlier, Aleksandr could have done without seeing this house again, but now, no: an old gate was not going to stop him! The obstinacy that had brought him success in business came into action.

First he tried his bunch of keys on the old, rusty padlock, which dirtied his gloves. No use. Marguerite was already bringing hers.

'Don't stay in the snow Marguerite: you'll get your feet wet.'

The apartment keys were obviously not suitable. He looked for a stone under the snow and, guessing what he wanted, Marguerite set about helping him. She found a large, pointed stone. He set to work on the chain, but to no effect. He was about to swear, but controlled himself. In the end he brought the stone down with all his might on his thumb and had to stop himself from crying out.

343

'Perhaps,' suggested Marguerite, 'you could see the house another time, when the owners are there.'

'I've already seen it. It's you I wanted to show it to. I really don't know why, but I won't be stopped by a confounded gate . . .'

He knew he was being childish, but that did not bother him. Better to be childish to the end, than retreat before a difficulty.

He noticed that the lower left-hand hinge was broken, so he tried to push the gate from that side. The compact snow resisted. He then set about removing the snow with his hands, and Marguerite helped, crouching beside him. When he had dug a large enough furrow, he slightly raised the gate and pushed it forward, getting it away from the pier, so that Marguerite managed to slip into the grounds on all fours. She now held the gate open and Aleksandr, dragging behind him his precious briefcase, followed her.

Marguerite, having let go of the gate, laughed gaily. He tried to brush her down: she was covered in snow and rust.

'Never mind. My coat only needs a visit to the cleaners. But you, heavens!'

She was caught between horror at the motif printed on her boss's new overcoat and amusement at the image presented before her mind's eye, which in the end she dared to give voice to: 'You look as if you've had a grilling, Monsieur.'

The *château* was an ugly nineteenth-century building, with false crenellations, false machicolations, and yet it had about it a strength and solidity which carried conviction. One felt that the society that had laid this big angular egg believed in itself, in the permanence of its institutions and acquired characteristics. It was, of course, a masterpiece of Bovaryism, but Bovaryism, thought Aleksandr, is not all bad: it has the elegance of a certain nostalgia, a certain regret for a vanished past.

A broad flight of about ten steps led, between two heavy square balustrades, to the carved stone doorway. The wind had piled up a mountain of snow in the left-hand corner. The right-hand corner was almost clear. The door, obviously, was locked.

'Wait for me here.'

With snow up to his knees, Aleksandr walked round the house, trying to climb up to a window or to force open a side door, and failing. He felt more hopeful when he came to the terrace that ran along the back of the house, with four pairs of French windows; he would have broken a pane, and even, if necessary, the frames holding the panes: he felt he was in conquered territory. But he was put off by the inside shutters. He turned his back to the house and looked out over the frozen pond, which was a muddy white, over the snow raked by the wind, a most vigorous gardener, and over the impenetrable thickets of trees and shrubs which had grown up and out into a disorderly mess: the primitive jungle was resuming possession of this place which, in spite of its clumsiness and borrowed grace, had nevertheless been dedicated to a certain order, and therefore to thought.

The ground was sloping, so that the back of the house had a floor more than the front. On one of the sides, Aleksandr found a door that led to the basement thus formed. He gave a little push and entered a vast, rectangular room with a stone-flagged floor; it was badly lit by three windows, each in the form of a semi-circle. This must have been the old orangery. He walked in the dust and half light and, on the right, he found a wooden staircase which he ascended, holding a banister that consisted simply of a pole supported by three uprights. This brought him to a small balcony overlooking the organgery. A door led into a room. He went in: light coming through green bottles arranged in alternating rows told him that he was in the wine cellar. He picked up several bottles: they were all empty. He was beginning to remember this place. Gaverin had thought that these empty bottles were being sold to him as full ones and that therefore he was entitled to get the price reduced. Aleksandr went back on to the inside balcony. After the almost pitch-dark of the cellar, the orangery seemed quite light. Spiders' webs were draped over the windows, floated over the lampshades shaped like upturned saucers, and filled the nooks and crannies. He found a lightswitch, pressed it down, but no light came.

He went down again, crossing the orangery from end to end. In a dark corner he found another staircase, this time of stone, that began under a semi-circular arch. He began to climb, step by step, knowing that he had nothing to fear, but all the same with his right hand in his briefcase, which he held in his left. In the end he gave up this 'precaution', took the revolver out of the briefcase and pointed it around him, like a boy playing at soldiers.

He emerged into the ground floor, which was composed of vast corridors, vestibules and inter-communicating drawing-rooms. It must have been very pleasant to receive one's guests here. Aleksandr imagined the well-educated *nouveaux riches* who must have had this house built; they would invite the nobility of the district, but also, to make up the numbers, delighted, but anxious bourgeois. As they sipped their host's Madeira, the gentlemen must have made fun of him or exchanged confidential information concerning the dowries of the bourgeois women. The parquet floors squeaked, the doors groaned, the panelling led on to more panelling. All in all, Aleksandr liked this bourgeois gigant-ism dating from a period when the nobility had lost its touch and only the bourgeois was still capable of conceiving things on a large scale. Both were now desperate and discomfited. So much the worse for them: the man who does not believe in himself deserves to perish.

Before visiting the first floor, Aleksandr put his revolver back into his briefcase and went to look for Marguerite, who had also walked round the house but had stopped in front of the orangery door. He took her hand to guide her through this labyrinth, first through the cellars and boiler-rooms, then to the ground floor, opening the shutters, letting in cracks of light here and expanses of light there, then to the first floor, moving from room to room, rummaging in the cupboards, finding crumpled photographs and livery but-tons, exclaiming with surprise at the sight of metal bathtubs standing on their leonine paws, and lastly to the attic, sneezing with every step, wiping away the spiders' webs that stuck to their hair.

'I've never seen a house like this,' said Marguerite.

Aleksandr turned on a tap. Nothing came out but the smell of rust.

An idea was germinating in him. Why not spend the two or

three days of retreat he needed here, where no one would come looking for him? What risk was there that an estate agent would come to show this building to a client in the middle of winter? And even if, by some unimaginable chance, a buyer did turn up, well, a few words of excuse and a small payment would settle the business. And what a marvellous game it would be to settle in here like Robinson Crusoe on his island!

What would they do for water? There was the snow. Fire? There was a park full of dead wood. Food? Limoges was twenty kilometres away.

He had one doubt, however. Whenever, as a child, he had tried to involve a friend in some mad exploit, he had been let down: it was too dangerous, it would never work, it was a bore, what would papa say? Yet, beyond a certain point solitary games are no longer enough: one needs complicity. Could Marguerite be that indispensable companion? Or would she soon be clamouring for central heating and spare stockings? On the other hand, would he not be dropping his role as boss by suggesting this absurd escapade? No, he told himself, he would not be dropping it. For heaven's sake, he was not a bourgeois, he was permitted to have his caprices; he even flattered himself that if Marguerite had served him so well, it was precisely because he had always seen things from a superior viewpoint, with that lightness of touch that came only with a certain grace of heart.

'Marguerite, we'll spend the weekend here.'

She clapped her hands, obviously pleased, but without an exaggerated show of enthusiasm.

'Really, you agree?'

He was happy in his unhappiness.

'Ah! In that case, we'll need provisions, matches . . . Can you cook on a wood fire?'

They lunched quickly in Limoges, before setting out on their raid of the shops, as if they were preparing for a siege. Aleksandr was delighted to find a playmate at last. Marguerite soon took charge of the operation; she made a list of everything they might need, with, of course, innumerable hesitations; she saved Aleksandr's money as much as possible and she could hardly bring herself to buy a coffee pot: 'I know you'll be able to keep it. And the sleeping bags too.'

'We won't keep anything,' said Aleksandr. 'We'll leave everything there for the unknown owners whose house we have borrowed.'

As soon as the shops re-opened after lunch, they set about filling the Peugeot with their purchases: an axe, a saw, crockery, sleeping bags, candles, candlesticks (Aleksandr insisted on candlesticks), a frying pan, rat traps (Marguerite might be afraid of rats), wine, preserved goose, corned beef, bread, steaks (too much canned food was unhealthy), champagne (we'll keep it in the snow), whisky, cognac (but you like port, Marguerite, we must get some—Aleksandr was discovering that he was able to think of someone other than himself), Irish linen napkins, an electric torch, crystal glasses, paper towels, blankets, two big sweaters, a plastic bowl (no, Marguerite, no paraffin, a pair of bellows on the other hand, yes, that's a good idea), salt, oh, and toothbrushes and a razor . . . Aleksandr paid in cash, so as not to leave any trace, but also because he liked fingering the thick bundle of notes in his inside pocket—they did not seem to have diminished noticeably.

They went back to the house and unloaded their booty in a small panelled drawing-room, which Marguerite had chosen in preference to the large stone-floored drawing-room that Aleksandr had wanted: a smaller area would be easier to heat. While she was settling in, the best literary agent in Paris went out into the park and, armed with saw and axe, set about cutting wood. He worked like mad, sawing and splitting, grazing his hands, dropping logs on to his toes, breathing heavily, losing his temper, sweating in the cold, using all the muscles that he had so patiently kept fit in his gymnasium, finding a deep primitive pleasure in brandishing at the end of his axe the heavy stump of wood that he would split against a sawn log.

Night was falling, tingeing the white ground with blue, setting off the bare trunks against a sky that seemed to lighten as the earth grew dark. Greyish-brown snow clouds dropped lower and lower, like gigantic zeppelins, and shredded themselves on the crests of the trees. Aleksandr, the warrior-woodcutter, gave a few last blows with his axe, delighting in the sound, which was getting ever duller as the twilight thickened around him and the snow began to fall once more.

He took back his supply of wood in five journeys, his torso thrown back, his forearms serving as a tray for ever heavier loads, delighted by Marguerite's flattering exclamations: 'That's too heavy, you ought to be careful . . .'

'No, no, the old man isn't finished yet,' he simpered, dropping armfuls of fresh-smelling newly-cut logs on to the wooden floor.

When he had brought his last load in, he went and shut the orangery door—'we want to be undisturbed'—and even barricaded it with an old rickety table. Then he walked round, closing all the shutters that he had left open. The pond reflected the last whiteness of the day; the vases that bordered it on either side projected their obese outlines against the sky. Through the vast empty rooms—with scarcely the flicker of a shadow in a mirror losing its silvering —he walked, feeling the chill of the evening seeping in through the cracks in the windows; he wandered around a little through the maze of corridors and rooms that led back to the small drawing-room where Marguerite awaited him.

She was tactful enough not to work on the intricate structure of twigs, branches of graded thickness, and logs without which a wood fire cannot be built according to the rules. So Aleksandr tackled it, but since this was the first time, it took him a good hour, and the help of the bellows, before the flames finally attacked his wooden cathedral. At first the fire drew badly until, when the snow that blocked the chimney had melted, it suddenly flared up, everything crackled, and an alternation of yellow and black ghosts ran around the walls as on a theatre cyclorama. The fire panted and puffed, the red cinders organized themselves into Peruvian ruins, then bleached into catacombs; it needed just a blow from the bellows for them to burst into flame and activity once again.

'Your whisky, Monsieur.'

Their hands touched and, over the cut glass, their faces, red on one side and black on the other, smiled at one another.

The dinner was both sumptuous and extravagant. Aleksandr threw the corks into the fire and watched them turn into glowing embers. He began again to recount childhood memories, which always revolved around the same theme: the lack of understanding that had always bedevilled his father and himself.

'Yet Foch said: "If France was not erased from the map of Europe, we have Russia to thank above all." And fifteen years later, in 1929, Joffre said: "I take every opportunity to pay homage to the Russian armies and to express to them my profound gratitude . . . I shall never forget the terrible sacrifices heroically and consciously endured by the Russian army, which, at that cost, drew the enemy's fire on itself." And Mangin said: "The Allies must never forget the service that Russia has rendered them." And Naylor said: "The battle of the Marne was won by the Cossacks." And Paléologue said: "We never had a better, more loyal friend than the Emperor Nicholas II." '

All these poor quotations that his father had learnt by heart came back to him and he recited them in a voice of thunder, letting the bile that had accumulated within him flow out at last.

'Joffre should have known, shouldn't he? And all they could talk about to my father was the Russian loan!'

The flames lit up his glass of Bungundy. Marguerite, who had put on one of the two big white sweaters and folded her legs under her, listened to him, responding only with small, plaintive sounds.

Aleksandr went on drinking. Other images came back to him.

'Psar! They called me Tsar, of course—resentfully! But, after all . . . the Tsars? Who could have made a better job of it? My family is not a very old one. You've heard of Ivan the Terrible? He set up a guard and a territory separated from the rest of the country, a crown domain in which this guard—the *oprichnina*—lived. And it had a whipper-in, a dog keeper, whom everybody called Psar, because *psar* means "whipper-in", and because he was known by no other name. He was one of the fiercest, most faithful of the *oprichniks*. He travelled the length and breadth of Russia, with the symbolic dog's head and broom tied to the pommel of his saddle: the dog's head for vigilance, the broom against treason. We have them both in our coat-of-arms. The old families made fun of us: "They've nothing to put on their coat-of-arms, so they stick on the badge of their trade." On the other hand, a proverb was invented about us: "I'm in favour with the *Tsar*, but not with the *Psar*." In other words, the Tsar likes me, but if Psar is against me, it won't get me very far. That's what the old boyars, bundled up in their pelisses, their hands crossed over their bellies, whispered to one another. We were new men, yes. In a sense, Bolsheviks.'

Marguerite listened, her cheek tanned by the intermittent, brutal heat of the wood fire. From time to time, Aleksandr unceremoniously flung a log into the embers, delighting in the sight of the sparks flying up.

Dmitri Alexandrovich constantly cropped up in his rambling memories.

'How he must have suffered! And for nothing! He would have been better off getting himself killed fighting the Reds.'

'Then you wouldn't have been born,' Marguerite murmured.

He told the pitiful story of the French peasant provoked by his father to fight a duel.

'And you . . . you never even had a mother.'

He did not know how, but he had taken Marguerite in his arms. He found himself pressing his mouth against hers, which smelled of smoke and burned like fire. This sensation brought him back to himself. He was horrified at the thought of abusing this woman's devotion and compassion. He pulled away: 'I'm terribly sorry. I didn't know what I was doing.'

She, however, resting all her weight on the arm that he had put around her shoulders, replied: 'But *I* love you, Monsieur.'

Over their heads, the ceiling was still red long after the deliciously dry heat of the fire had stopped gnawing at their naked skin. Aleksandr fell asleep, with the thought that he had held a French woman in his arms for the first time and was surprised at finding her so tender. French women were sensual, sentimental, yes. But tender? Those painted women who slap their children? He had always believed that tenderness was an appurtenance of Slav women. He melted into sleep, delighted to have been proved wrong.

Marguerite struggled against falling asleep, sometimes by pinching herself, sometimes by sinking the nails of her right hand under those of her left.

When she sensed that Aleksandr was perfectly relaxed, unwound, as one is only in deep sleep, she slowly dressed, without taking her eyes off him. She put another log on the fire and, being careful not to make the floor creak, she picked up the torch and went out into the corridor. Following the yellow circle that she projected in front of her, she went down to the orangery, removed Aleksandr's barricade and went out. Her feet were immediately wet through and her legs scratched by the brambles. She went through the gate, pushing it back and wedging it with a stone so that she could get back again. She could have taken the car keys; she knew in what pocket Aleksandr kept them, but she was afraid that the noise of the engine would awaken him. So she set off for the village on foot. Fortunately she had never cared much for high heels, but even her town shoes were very uncomfortable for walking in the snow. It took her forty minutes to walk two kilometres.

The village slept as in a fairy tale.

She found the telephone box, slipped a five-franc piece into the slot and dialled a number. It rang for a long time. Where? In an office? In a bedroom? She did not know.

The ringing stopped, but no voice answered. She said: '*Laika* here. I haven't got much change and I'm in a phone-box.'

'Keep calm,' said a man's voice. 'I'm recording.'

She gave a summary of the events of the last thirty-six hours. She mentioned the briefcase. 'He never lets it out of his sight. At the moment he's using it for a pillow.' She gave the car registration number, the name of the village, described the location of the house, explained how to get into it.

'I'm sorry I had to resort to emergency steps. But I'm only following orders. He's at the end of his tether. He needed this break to get his confidence back.'

'Well, carry on as you are doing,' said the man and rang off.

Marguerite went back to the *château*, stepping into her own footprints to avoid sinking into the snow. She felt she had caught a bad cold. But what did it matter? In a way she had lived twenty-two years for this moment.

Twenty-two years before, she had been a law student, active in research groups, at UNEF, courting all the Communists she met. She could not forgive her father for getting himself killed. Her ambition was to join the Party. One day, a new comrade, older than the others, took her to one side: 'Do you really want to do some serious work? Not just chit-chat? In the corporation you'd have to choose between being a butcher or a cart-horse. You're worth more than that.' He sucked on his cigarette-end and looked down at her. She trusted this little curly-haired man with green eyes, broke off all contact with the far left, dropped out of the law faculty, took a secretarial course, got a little experience; then she was given a case-officer and a mission: to keep a watch on Psar, that tool of reaction. Every week, she had made a report on the activities of the Agency and of her boss, drawing up a list of the appointments, enclosing copies of letters, mentioning telephone conversations, missing nothing out. From time to time she began to worry: 'He doesn't seem as right-wing as all that. In any case, he's not doing anything secret, honestly. Are you sure you're not making a mistake? I wouldn't like to be wasting my time or the training you've given me.'

Sometimes she was ticked off: mind your own business. Sometimes she was reassured: the man is not all that he seems to be. You'll understand one day. The publication of *The Russian Truth* and the organization of the Confraternity had at last set Marguerite's mind at rest: yes, Psar was anti-Communist, he wanted to hurt the Soviet Union, which she had visited twice and where she had been so well received. She was far from imagining that, as a mere secretary, she would have any right to such a reception, but the USSR certainly knew how to recognize the deserts of its vassals, whereas France had done nothing in particular for Quartermaster Sergeant Thérien, who had gone and got himself killed at the other end of the world for her. She had adored her father and she now hated him; she hated him in order to punish him for being dead.

She went back into the *château*. Psar had not moved. She looked at him for a few seconds, as he lay on one side, his mouth half open, his face flushed by the fire, his cheek crushed against the leather of his briefcase. Seen from above, he lost the arrogance of his handsome looks and, asleep, the radiation of his intelligence. He was merely a gentleman of a certain age, lying like a hunting dog, like a child. He might have inspired pity, but Marguerite had no pity for him. He was a class enemy—she had been sufficiently indoctrinated —and it would have been indecent to pity a class enemy. She had served him in such exemplary fashion only because she believed that by doing so she was compassing his fall. He was a White Guard, a counter-revolutionary. Marguerite's father had never been anything more than an NCO—second-class travel, no access to the officers' mess—but he too had been a counter-revolutionary. And yet, in a people's army, he would have been a colonel at least.

As she rubbed her feet with whisky, she wondered whether she hated her boss. No, she had enjoyed working for him, being indispensable to him, but because of the Agency, not because of the man; it was the work she liked. And that was why, a few hours before, she had enjoyed being in his arms, but only because of the pleasure itself. She did not particularly like the man who had given her that pleasure, but she did not dislike him either: he was a class enemy, that was all there was to it.

Shivering, she slipped under the covers and snuggled up close to him: stealing heat from a class enemy was not a bad idea.

9
'Going Home'

'Sorry to wake you up, Petiusha, but I think "yours" has taken off.'

Nikitin, a quiet young man with fair hair, had rung at Piotr's door at three in the morning.

'Come in. Sit down. Shoot.'

Piotr put on a Japanese dressing-gown, black with gold flower patterns, over his brown and salmon-pink striped pyjamas.

Nikitin, Marguerite Thérien's case-officer, sat down, crossed his legs and lit a cigarette.

' "Mine" has rung me.'

He gave an account of what he had learnt, punctuating each part with a few smoke rings.

Piotr was not very surprised. He had already sensed that *Oprichnik* was working loose. That was why, apart from obeying Pitman's orders, he had carried out that harsh reassertion of authority. Apparently it had not had the desired effect—far from it. These things happen.

What worried Piotr was this business of the briefcase. He was sure that he, personally, had never left any documents in *Oprichnik*'s hands. But his predecessors may not have been so careful. And even without documents . . . if *Oprichnik* had been taking notes during the past thirty years—notes that he had evidently been keeping in a bank safe at Pontoise—and if he went and took them to the French, it would create a bit of a furore. And it was clear that Piotr, whether or not it had been his fault, would pay for it. His head would surely roll—metaphorically, of course, but it would be a pity all the same. Just the thought of it brought back his familiar heartburn.

He thanked Nikitin and dismissed him: 'Keep me informed.'

'If I've got your boy sized up right,' said Nikitin, 'even if you do get him back, you'll have to get him a new secretary. He doesn't seem the type to fondle his staff.'

'We'll sort it out.'

Nikitin left. Piotr took some pills for his heartburn.

It couldn't be helped: he would have to ring Mozhukin, the 'resident', his immediate boss. Mozhukin was as famous as a man could be in a secret service. 'Illegal' for twenty years—that is to say, living under a false name, passing himself off as a Frenchman—he was finally uncovered, was able to escape in time and, unique in the annals of the Geebee, managed to have a second career as a 'legal'. He was a bachelor, drank his 1500 grams a day, mended his own socks using a *brioche* as a darning mushroom and, when he had finished, ate it. Piotr would rather have gone boar hunting with a spear or bear hunting with a knife than wake Mozhukin at three in the morning.

'Comrade Colonel, can I come and see you?'

'You've been working for those smart Alecks. I don't know you any more.'

'Comrade Colonel, I was seconded to them against my will. I would have preferred to remain under your command, you know that very well.'

'Go to hell. Ring Moscow and let me sleep.'

Piotr dressed hastily, jumped into his Volvo, crossed Paris, entered the mastaba of La Muette, got to his office and, on his scrambler telephone rang Moscow.

The call was automatically transferred from Rostopchin House to Pitman's private apartment.

'The sun isn't even up yet. You know very well I won't be able to get back to sleep. You've no concern for my health,' grumbled the gentle Elichka, who was growing peevish with age.

Pitman paid no attention to her; he was listening to the worried voice speaking to him from Paris. Flight . . . briefcase . . . not my fault, Comrade General. If *Hard Sign* is exposed to the French, the entire Consistory would be a laughing-stock. Pitman had enemies among the Hidy-hats:

to start with, they were all anti-semites who would be only too pleased to see his set-up turn turtle. One good thing, however: the secretary, who had cost so much and who, for twenty years, had sent admirable reports that were of not the slightest use, was earning her keep at last. Another good thing: if Psar was hiding in that *château*, there was still time to finger his collar. Had the case-officer lost his touch? Or had he, Iakov, been wrong to tighten the reins on *Oprichnik*? He was always ready to accuse himself of possible mistakes, but, in this precise case, he still thought that Operation *Hard Sign* was too important, too dangerous, to be left to the initiative of a mere influence agent, whatever his qualities might be. At no point did the notion cross the lieutenant-general's mind, which was perhaps too closely focused on detail, that the handing back of Alla Kuznetsova to her original directorate had anything to do with this matter.

What was to be done now? Perhaps it was a false alarm: *Oprichnik* had a secret rendez-vous with some member of the Confraternity, or had simply opted for a rather unusual holiday with his secretary. In which case, all he could be reproached with was his failure to advise Piotr of his movements. In any case, the whole business must be treated with extreme care, as when one defuses a bomb. If only Elichka would stop grumbling into her pile of pillows, Pitman might be able to think more clearly.

'This is what you will do. You will shoot over to the *château* this instant and you will tell *Oprichnik* that you have good news for him. You'll bring him back to Paris and keep me in touch, hour by hour, with the psychological situation. If you think a meeting with me might be beneficial—after all, I recruited *Oprichnik* myself, we are old friends—don't hesitate to say so. And if you think the announcement of a promotion might help . . .' Pitman hesitated: he was not lavish with promotions, or expenses, but he decided, for once, to make a splash. 'Tell him we're very pleased with the way the set-up is progressing, that, for someone directing an operation of such magnitude a general officer's rank . . . and that . . .' He hesitated all the same over the words, if not over the thing. 'A good surprise awaits him.'

'Yes, Comrade General.' Pitman would have preferred to

have been called by his first name and patronymic as Moham-med Mohammedovich used to be, but, for some time now, the 'Moiseich' had not gone down very well . . . 'Comrade General, how shall I explain to *Oprichnik* that I've discovered his hiding place? Shall I blow the secretary's cover?'

'Thank you for raising the problem . . . No, don't blow her cover. We'll find an explanation in time. For the mo-ment, play on our reputation as omniscient golden cockerels. Be vague. And don't forget there is one imperative more important than any of the others: get your hands on *Oprich-nik*, stop him going over to the French if he intends doing so. At any price.'

Superiors like to use phrases like 'at any price'. They are sufficiently vague and dramatic to provide a screen behind which they can shelter in the event of an accident, of whatever kind.

'Comrade General?'

'Well?'

'Should I . . . go armed?'

Piotr spoke the word with some embarrassment. The smart Alecks in Directorate A regarded weapons with mis-trust and contempt. But the only way to check what 'at any price' meant was to ask whether one should take what might be needed to pay the highest price.

Pitman sighed.

'Yes, I suppose so . . . But for the love of heaven, try not to use it. Proceed gently, use your head . . .' Elichka was already snoring; Iakov Moiseich would not go back to sleep. *Hard Sign*, the greatest operation in his life, was at risk. He got up, moved across the room on tiptoe, got dressed and had himself driven to the office. In that way, if there were any more telephone calls, they would be put through there. Elichka could have a lie-in and he would be there, on the spot, to take any necessary decisions.

Part of the Directorate had been moved to new premises, on the ring road, but Pitman had kept the same office which was both more intimate and more elegant, with its fringed and tasselled curtains, its old-fashioned furniture, its order-lies who had taken on the style of the building and always had a samovar bubbling.

Iakov Moiseich walked up and down his imitations of old rugs in his thick army shoes that cost him nothing, almost regretting that he belonged to the Hidy-hats, that is to say, that he no longer had the right to pop over to Paris. 'If I could see Aleksandr Dmitrich myself, I who knew him when he was just a boy, whom I seduced on the towers of Notre-Dame, I would soon make him see reason.' He began to play with the idea of getting him over to Moscow on a lightning trip, Moscow our dear mother of a thousand gilded heads . . . 'That would flatter his imagination: a special plane! Mohammed Mohammedovich would have been against it, but for mystical rather than professional reasons. I would be given a hero's welcome, we'd dress him up in his uniform, find him a woman . . . Yes, from time to time, one has to make a splash to raise the morale of the troops.'

Pitman dreamed on and still Piotr did not telephone from France.

Thick snow lay on Dzerzhinsky Square. This time, yes, they would be able to go out on the troika with Sviatoslav.

Aleksandr awoke with a fever, but happier to be alive than he had been for a long time. He lay there, looking at the white window and saying to himself that he would go and cut more wood, that it was a pleasant occupation.

It was only a little later that he felt the presence of Marguerite next to him and remembered what had happened. 'I love you, Monsieur.' How long had she loved him? And he had noticed nothing! The situation would become impossible if he decided to go on with the game and keep the agency. 'I'm a swine, I took advantage of the situation. And if she only knew who I work for!' He would have to look for another secretary: one can't have one's correspondence typed by one's mistress. He would give Marguerite all the recommendations she deserved. If need be, he would make use of Fourveret to get her a job worthy of her. Meanwhile . . . Meanwhile, he took her once again in his arms, not without a degree of unworthy calculation: 'I've made a mistake, I may as well make the most of it.'

Then he went out to get some snow in the plastic bowl and wash as best he could. His hands were trembling with fever and he cut himself several times as he shaved. Then he brought some snow back to Marguerite and went out again to cut wood. The fever kept him warm. When he came back, Marguerite had already relit the fire with some cardboard packaging; she made coffee, which was awful because it tasted smoky, but delicious because it was their own smoke.

Marguerite stretched. 'We're like a real lord and lady of the manor.'

A church bell could be heard in the distance. Its sound, a bit like that of a cracked gong, floated slowly through the snow-saturated air, but, after a long journey, it arrived all the same, one stroke after another, striking against the windows of the house. For how many centuries had that bell rung out? 'It's the voice of France calling me,' Aleksandr thought.

The confidences he had shared the night before with Marguerite had, in a sense, emancipated him.

'If we're the lord and lady of the manor,' he said, 'we ought to go to mass.'

Never had he allowed himself to be ruled by his instinct—or destiny—in this way, but today he felt at peace, quite unwound. The idea of going to mass made Marguerite laugh. But why not? After all, it was Christmas, and they were already in the middle of a fairy tale.

Her shoes, which she had left beside the fire, were ruined, hardened, but almost dry. She coughed and sneezed and smiled at this new flight of lunacy, as she allowed herself to be driven to mass, the first she had attended since her father's death.

The church was freezing, enormous, empty. No, not entirely empty. There were about thirty worshippers, as many men as women, huddling together in the front pews. A red lamp provided the one warm spot in the grey expanse of the stone, the brown of the pews, the drab colours of the hair and clothes. The bell had just stopped its monotonous tolling. The silence was enhanced by coughs, whispers, the scraping of a chair on the stone floor.

The procession came in. Behind the cross came a line of children in fancy dress. It took Aleksandr a few moments to realize that they were the characters from the crib: a little girl with a bit of red material over her head and a doll in her arms, a little boy with a cotton-wool beard, another boy whose face was blackened up under a cardboard crown covered with gold paper, another with a jewel box in his hands, yet another swinging a censer, then a boy and a girl carrying staffs, and wearing sheepskins on their backs, leading a lamb: since the lamb refused to budge, the boy gave it a kick in the belly.

Behind the children, in a white and green chasuble, the priest waddled along: a grey face, thin grey hair, sticking up like wings, small prying eyes that seemed to be counting the number of worshippers. The poor fellow looked exhausted: he probably had to look after ten parishes and was now saying his fifth Christmas mass. Everyone was bawling a jolly carol full of 'angels from on high' and so on.

When the children reached their papier-mâché cave and the little girl had laid her doll on a straw bed, the priest, clasping and unclasping his hands, made a plaintive little speech.

'My friends, let me ask you one thing. It may seem odd, but I'm sure you can do it for the Good Lord—or for me, if you prefer. I know you love your children, and I love them too. You will get them back again at the end of the mass. Then, of course . . . feel free—but here in church, even those of you who have gone to the expense of buying flash bulbs . . . The children understand the solemnity of what they are doing. You must not tempt their vanity. So . . . I would ask you, it's difficult, I know, but . . . please—no photos.'

A few already loaded cameras disappeared, and Aleksandr felt a certain regard for this priest who refused to accept every compromise, who tried to preserve in his church some semblance, however small, of the sacred.

The mass began. It was a disturbingly paltry thing, the vulgarity of what passed for music merely stressing the platitude of the words. Aleksandr, who remembered the austere magnificence of the Gregorian rite and sometimes visited Orthodox churches where 'the Lord is clothed in splendour', could make nothing of this parody of a Protestant service with its numbered hymns and its readings in trivial, not to say common, language.

'It's inconceivable,' he said to himself, 'that the Directorate has not had a hand in this. The Church could never of her own free will have given up the beauty of a service that gave men on earth some idea of the Kingdom of Heaven. *Quos vult perdere Directoratus dementat.* Yet I seem to remember that their Master had expressed a clear preference for Mary over Martha.'

In spite of everything, something eventually happened, though he could not define what it was. Perhaps the Holy Spirit was less fastidious than Aleksandr, perhaps He had decided to endure the blasphemy of systematic ugliness out of humility, perhaps some unbreakable mystery was contained in the gestures and words. When, after a rather uninspired sermon, the grey priest began to busy himself around the altar, Aleksandr was first moved, then overwhelmed. What was taking place here, this domestic scene, with the tableware, the bread and wine, a child carrying water in his little hands, all that possessed a crucial meaning, despite the banality of the rest. People had come for *this*. The priest was here for *this*. *This* had not changed, or very little, in two thousand years. What was beginning to take place in Aleksandr was a great reconciliation with his destiny, and he was not sorry that it had taken place under the sign of a supernatural reality which, however debased, was proving ultimately to be unbreakable.

He had always reproached God for abandoning his own, but here God seemed to be abandoning himself and yet finding himself, in a properly miraculous way, all the more recognizable for being dishonoured. Was there some deeper meaning here that Aleksandr had hitherto only suspected? When the wheels of God grind down his faithful, is it to make something like God's flour? Was Christ, by definition, he who endures, and could one not be linked to him simply by enduring martyrdom, abandonment, loss of everything one possesses, and even stupidity? Was that what he had come to this village church to learn, among these bumpkins, who were given the same lessons in bad taste every Sunday by their priest?

'Perhaps this purification is necessary,' he thought. 'Perhaps there have been too many cardinals in all their regalia, too many monsignori in purple hose, too much sublime, but profane music rising in garlands around the Church, too much of a deviation in one direction that made this one necessary, by way of compensation . . . Perhaps the Church is a sailing boat like any other and has to tack to windward . . .' But he did not like it all the same; he wanted mitred bishops, crozier in hand, reminding men that they were not of this world, that they had a kingdom elsewhere, that when they finally made up their mind to 'go home' their celestial fatherland would be waiting for them.

'And what about me?' he wondered, 'do I still want to "go home"?'

But when one comes from nowhere, where does one go home to?

After the mass, followed by the curious looks of the locals, Aleksandr and Marguerite went back to the *château*. Marguerite declared that she was going to do the cooking.

'Bring me some snow, please.'

She no longed called him Monsier, she did not yet call him Aleksandr, she almost gave him orders. He took the bowl, but did not forget to take his big briefcase with him. She dared not ask him why he would never let it out of his sight. He did not know himself why he did not want her to know that he was armed. Perhaps quite simply he was afraid that it might make him look ridiculous, or did not want to show her the extent to which he had stepped outside the law.

They were about to take their places at the table, as they said, which amounted to sitting on the floor in front of two steaks that had a charred taste, when Aleksandr, whose hearing was very sharp, heard the squeak of metal against metal. He leapt to the window. A small man in a navy blue trenchcoat, tightly pulled in at the waist, was tugging at the gate in order to get into the park. At the end of the drive he could just make out a car, which must have been left there in order not to attract attention with the noise from the engine.

'What is it?' Marguerite asked, without moving.

Aleksandr had just said that he liked pepper and she was peppering his steak a second time.

The little man had managed to slip under the gate. He stood up, dusted himself down with his bare hands, which were covered with rust, and looked around. His eyes rested on the footprints in the snow and, following them, he walked around the house, from time to time shaking his feet in a rather comic manner, in order to shake off the snow that was stuck to his shoes.

'Wait for me.'

Aleksandr seized the briefcase and dashed out into the corridor. As he ran, he realized that he had already made his defence plan, probably the night before, while chopping wood. He ran down the stone stairs four at a time. As he was crossing the orangery, he sensed a shadow pass in front of one of the semi-circular windows. He went back up the wooden steps that led to the wine cellar and stood on the small balcony, in the doorway, which gave him a commanding view of the orangery from end to end.

The man was opening the outside door, pushing back the barricade. One could see his busy outline, bending and stretching.

Without making a sound Aleksandr undid the clasp of his briefcase, put it at his feet, took out the revolver and, protected by the darkness and his high position, waited. His heart was pounding, his throat contracted, but his hands were no longer trembling.

The man came in. He was ten metres away from Aleksandr and three metres below him. If he had turned to the right, he would have seen the first steps of the wooden staircase, but he did not seem to be looking in that direction. He knew where he was going. He moved towards the stone steps, which were nevertheless invisible.

Aleksandr moved his lips. No sound came out. He took a deep breath. The man was already half-way across the orangery. Another four metres and he would have reached the staircase.

Aleksandr spoke. 'Piotr.'

The man froze. Then, slowly, he turned. His eyes tried to pierce the darkness, to discover where the voice was coming from.

'Where are you?'

His triangular face was struck diagonally by the pale light falling from the dirty windows, hung with spiders' webs. The ends of his little moustache were turned up.

'An asp with a moustache,' Aleksandr thought with disgust.

He cocked the gun; that made two distinct sounds: the cylinder revolving and the hammer clicking home.

'Where are you?' the asp with the moustache repeated nervously.

It occurred to Aleksandr that he ought to ask Piotr how he had found him. But, after all, they had found Gaverin easily enough. Well, Psar was not going to let himself be taken like a Gaverin.

He lined up the bead in the sighting notch. The explosion, in that enclosed space, was deafening.

Piotr, hit on his left lapel, did not fall immediately. He was thrown back and swung to the left. Finding the effect comical, Aleksandr sent him swinging in the opposite direction, with a bullet in the right shoulder.

He wanted to hurl crude insults, in Russian, at this marionette that was falling apart before his eyes, but he did not do so, out of respect for death. At the same time, he thought, with a strange sense of voluptuousness: 'I'm shooting an unarmed man.'

Using the double action, he stuck a third bullet in the rib cage, again on the left, and Piotr swung back again, but now his legs were giving under him and he collapsed in a heap, as if he could not make up his mind whether to fall backwards or forwards. With a fourth bullet Aleksandr shattered his skull. Despite his fever, anger and panic, he had shot well. He gave himself good marks.

The echoes of the shots and the echoes of the echoes were still rolling round the orangery; the dust, raised by the deflagrations, was settling.

Aleksandr went down the wooden staircase and stopped over the corpse, which was giving off an unpleasant stench: the intestines had given way. Aleksandr did not know that this was a common phenomenon, he still believed that battlefields smelled of shed blood. 'So this Piotr was a coward,' he thought unjustly. 'That doesn't surprise me.' And, baring his teeth, he hissed: 'Bolshevik!'

As if he were not a Bolshevik himself.

The body had slumped to one side, so that one could see

where one of the bullets had left the body. The wound caused by the hollowed end was appalling; flattened and widened, the bullet had taken with it a large piece of meat; the fibres of the flesh and those of the superimposed clothes, shirt, jacket, mackintosh, were mixed together; the blood flowed out in rhythmic, but slower and slower splurts and mingled with the dust on the floor to form a crust.

Aleksandr went back up the wooden steps to get his briefcase. The tendons of his knees were trembling and he felt a slight nausea, but he remained in control of himself. However he noticed that his hands had started to tremble again when he ejected the spent cartridges and replaced them with four fresh ones. One of the two cartridges that he had not fired rolled into a dark corner, and it took him two or three minutes to find it again: it seemed very important to him, as if someone, by means of that cartridge, might have traced him back to his weapon.

Satisfied, he stuck the revolver in his belt, picked up his briefcase—a strange picture: a businessman wearing a revolver in his belt—and, making a detour in order not to get too close to the corpse, crossed the orangery and walked up the stone steps. He was now in no doubt about Marguerite's treachery; he was simply wondering what he would do with her; shooting her would have been a suitable solution, but the archetypes were strong: he did not feel capable of shooting at a woman.

Marguerite, tactful as ever, had decided to spare him a scruple of conscience: she was no longer in the small drawing-room and, as he walked round the ground floor, he saw that one of the large drawing-room French windows was open. There were footprints in the snow. He should have followed her, he would have caught up with her, but what was the use, since he knew that he would not kill her? The asp was a different matter altogether. He had hated him on sight and, anyway, he had no intention of ending up on the end of a tie like Gaverin. As he emptied the Smith and Wesson into that body, he had the feeling that he was settling a very old score.

Then it occurred to him that Piotr may not have come alone. But reinforcements were slow in coming. Maybe they were lying in wait in the park. He would see soon enough. He came back to the small drawing-room, strewn with the mess from the night before. The fire was dying. He looked out of the window: the Peugeot had disappeared, no doubt borrowed by Marguerite. Yes, the keys in the left pocket of his Burberry had gone.

Calmly, he used his handkerchief to wipe all the objects he thought he had touched, more because he had seen it done in films than for any practical reason. Then he went down into the orangery and, holding his breath, forced himself to look through the dead Bolshevik's pockets. First he found what he was not looking for: a VZ 62, a Czech sub-machine-gun, which, when folded up, was no bigger than an ordinary automatic pistol, but which was capable of firing 700 rounds a minute; he wanted to take it as a trophy, and above all because he liked fire-arms, but he reflected that he would not like to use a weapon whose peculiarities he was not familiar with. (If he had had more experience, he would have reminded himself that no weapon capable of such a rate of fire could have peculiarities that had to be taken into account, but this consideration escaped him: he had all the limitations of a good shot, and he decided not to take the Skorpion.) In another pocket, he found what he was looking for: car keys.

Then he wondered if he should bury the corpse, but that struck him as a complicated matter: he had neither a spade nor a pick, he was tired, his fever was returning . . . Anyway, it would not be enough to bury him: he would have to wipe up all the blood that was already coagulating on the flagstones. In any case, if the Geebee were after him, a corpse, abandoned in a *château* where no one would set foot until the spring, was not going to make the situation all that much more dangerous for him.

He left the *château*, making no effort at concealment. If there was an ambush, then let them shoot at him! He would reply. But there was no one in the park, no one in the drive, no one in Piotr's Volvo. He got in and started up the engine.

'And now where?'

At 2 p.m., Marguerite called her case-officer. There had been shots. She had been afraid. She had fled with the Peugeot.

'What happened?' Nikitin asked, calm as ever.

'I don't know. I don't know.'

'Fool. Take a grip on yourself and go back and see.'

'I'm afraid.'

'Afraid?'

He blew smoke rings to calm his own nerves.

'I'll make you more afraid than that. Do you want me to get you arrested by the French? Not the D S T. An unofficial police force. They'll make you spill the lot and then forget you in a block of reinforced concrete.'

Marguerite went back to the *château*. The Volvo, which had been at the end of the drive, had disappeared. At the limit of her strength, Marguerite thought that she would never be able to lift the gate. She managed to do so, at the cost of tearing her gloves, breaking her nails, and scratching the skin off her hands. She crossed the lawn once more. She no longer tried to avoid the brambles, but just tugged at her coat when it was caught, leaving shreds of it behind—never mind, never mind!

The orangery door had been left open. Marguerite went in . . . and backed out again a moment later. She vomited as she walked. She wondered whether her father had looked like that.

She ran towards the gate, tripped in the grass, in the snow, fell, got up again. Suddenly she was ashamed: 'I, a Communist! I, the daughter of a French army sergeant!'

She got a grip on herself.

She walked calmly, trying to see only what she really did see in front of her: trees, the gate, the opening, the Peugeot.

Once inside the telephone box, she realized that she, the perfect secretary, had no more change. What a nuisance! Silly fool: why did I put all those coins in the plate at mass? She drove on to the next village and found a petrol station open on Christmas Day. She got change, but now there was no telephone. She found one ten kilometres further on.

She called back, she made her report.

'Tell me,' said Nikitin calmly—clearly he was destined for a fine career—'when you went through Pontoise, you were left alone in a café for nearly half an hour?'

'Yes.'

'Why didn't you ring me then?'

Always blame mistakes on your subordinates and, on the pedestal of those mistakes, become a great man. Bureaucracies are all the same.

'You told me to use this number only in an emergency.'

'You should have known that this was an emergency. We'll try to repair the damage you've done. Come back to Paris. Call me again as soon as you get back. From a public telephone box, of course.'

From that line which, he knew, was not bugged by the French, Nikitin rang the resident on one of his secret numbers.

'Comrade Colonel . . .' He was looking for a jocular way of breaking the bad news. 'Petiusha's kicked the bucket.'

'Pity!' said Mozhukhin. 'He was a bright lad. It's the fault of those smart Alecks in the new Directorate.'

He rang Moscow.

In Moscow, night was already falling and the lieutenant-general was still pacing up and down. The orderlies and secretaries, despite the difference in their ranks, exchanged looks: their boss, usually so gentle and understanding, seemed today in a 'distinctly cannibalistic' mood, declared Sub-lieutenant Volodia Voznesenski with a fierce wink.

On hearing the news, Iakov Moiseich shut his eyes.

There are agents like that who give satisfaction all their lives and then suddenly go berserk! The new humanitarian norms of the Geebee don't apply to these extreme cases.

'Yet it was a good idea, *Hard Sign* . . .'

But he had no time for the moment to concern himself with *Hard Sign*, which would have to be put back on the rails as soon as possible. Meanwhile the set-up had got out of its operator's control, and there is a procedure for such cases that it was now up to Iakov Moiseich, Hidy-hat that he was, to set in motion.

With an expression of disgust on his face, he picked up his *vertushka* and called Directorate V.

'We must get him alive,' he explained. 'I don't know whether we'll try him after an interrogation, or whether we'll ask you to get rid of him for us, but we need to know what little cog has stopped working.'

Aleksandr drove the rest of the day without even being aware that he was doing so. The fever was undermining his strength, working its way through his body. Sometimes he turned on the heating, which blew warm and dry, sometimes he opened the windows which slashed him with cold; most of the time it seemed as if he was floating in air rather than driving a car, and yet, he was driving this car, which was stolen, perfectly safely.

During the seven hours or so he had been driving, the same operation was performed a hundred, a thousand times in his mind. He relived the moment of the murder. 'He was there . . . I was there . . . I called him . . . he turned . . .' He felt no pity. Out of curiosity, he tried to arouse such a feeling within himself, telling himself that, perhaps, Lieutenant-Colonel 'Piotr' had a family, but when one has broken a viper's back does one bother about its family?

He felt no remorse either. The weapon found on the dead man would have dissipated any that he might have felt, but even that was not necessary: asps are armed with their poison, that was enough. The image of what had taken place a few hours ago kept recurring to him: 'He was down there, I was up here, "Where are you?" And again "Where are you?" And the three semi-circular windows, and that human shape swinging back as it collapsed, tottering first one way, then the other, then back again, and then slumped, and then the brains were blown out. I held him at my mercy. I could have not . . . "Where are you?" And you, where are you now, Bolshevik? He wanted to tighten the screw on me. Dust raised by the movement of air. Dust forming a carapace on the trickles of blood. And the echoes that gradually died down and that pain in the eardrums. I wondered for a moment if I would stay deaf for the rest of my life. I reproached myself for not wearing my ear muffs. Or perhaps I did not reproach myself with anything at all: I'm making that up now. And again the asp in the gun sights. His face.

What expression did it have? Anxious, I think? Nervous? Or irritated?' Aleksandr wanted to insult it, that face that had already begun to rot imperceptibly, and the crudest expressions in the Russian language came into his mind, but he repressed them. You don't insult filth. He had kept in the shadows, like some Zeus releasing his thunderbolt in calibrated bursts. A flash, another . . . 'How many times did I fire? Four. Four times the hammer rose, fell, hit the percussion cap. The powder exploded, and the bullet, spun by the grooves of the rifling, like a top by its whip, sped through space. Well done, revolver, my friend. It was not for nothing I loved you. Should I have taken the Skorpion? What would I have done with it?' And the scene began again: the dark, triangular face, the ridiculous little moustache and once again the gun sight, triangle against triangle, cutting away part of that head doomed to rot very shortly.

Aleksandr stopped at the Porte d'Orléans. He recognized the café where he had had several contacts with Ivan Ivanich. He must not be seen there. Now he had to take decisions, and that struck him as almost impossible, with the fever throbbing in his head. The long road, as twilight turned to night, was behind him: all those trucks, with their headlights undipped, all those Christmas holidaymakers, all that travelling Babylon was behind him. He had got back, without incident. But he did not know where to go.

Marguerite's betrayal did not bother him too much. He was merely surprised that he had not suspected it earlier and, far from being irritated by the lack of trust shown by the Geebee, he found it rather flattering that they had thought it necessary to plant a full-time stool pigeon in his office. He did not kill her, as he should have, but one has to recognize one's limits, not strain one's voice too much. Nor was he under any illusion as to what awaited him if the Geebee got their hands on him: in killing Piotr, he had put himself outside the law; he could expect a bullet in the neck after questioning. But the Geebee did not know where he was; having got rid of Marguerite, the witness whom they had stuck to him like a blister, he would now find it easier to melt into the night. Furthermore, the very fact of having recognized her for what she was had cured him of his superstitious fear of his own service: the stoolies of the Geebee could be uncovered and the officers of the Geebee could be shot; it was just a question of keeping one's eyes open.

And first, of course, he had to get rid of the Volvo, which might be equipped with a secret transmitter, which would enable them to locate it. That was easy enough. He left it in the first gap he came to in the line of parked cars and, with his collar turned up against the cold that was swirling around him like a damp rag, his tweed cap pressed down to his ears, he walked at random down the Rue d'Alésia.

He quite enjoyed being alone, without a master. But, feverish as he was, he knew that he would not keep going long in such conditions: he would have to make his peace with the Geebee—which is usually not impossible—or go over to the French, or find a new protector. Meanwhile, he needed a retreat where he could collect his thoughts, reason things out and decide on the course to follow. If he had not been ill, he would quite simply have walked all night; walking is a great aid to reflection, and constant movements increase security, but he had hardly walked a hundred yards and he already felt that he would have to sit down somewhere and, preferably, lie down, in a bed, on the ground, anywhere, providing it was warm, very warm. He went into a café and ordered a grog, being careful to keep his face down so as not to engrave his features on the waiter's memory.

Where could he go?

Not to his apartment or to his office, of course: Marguerite would have informed them of the murder and those two places could now only be traps. To a hotel, under a false name? That, no doubt, would have been the most reasonable course, but Aleksandr could not convince himself that he would be safe in a hotel. How could he sleep knowing that the manager had a pass-key? The door can be bolted from the inside, true, but . . . the spectre of Gaverin floated before his eyes. Too many suicides have been found in too many hotels. He did not want to have to get rid of his passport, and don't hotels go through one's pockets? And how many receptionists would refuse to speak to a 'detective' who showed them what purported to be a photograph of a man on the run? Marguerite could describe Aleksandr's clothes in detail, and how could he change them? Not a hotel, thank you.

A police station? Yes, Aleksandr could give himself up immediately, but he had not yet decided to change sides, and he knew that the French would not let him stay neutral, that he would have to turn his intelligence, his experience, his training, against those who, three days before, were his masters and friends, against the excellent Iakov Moiseich, his amiable Mephistopheles.

Some friend of either sex?

He ordered a second grog and played over in his memory the film of all the faces, ran through the lists of all the names he knew.

He had no personal friends. Acquaintances, yes, kept up out of snobbery (my friend, the marquis . . .) or convenience (a yacht, a place in the country). There was no one he could trust among those people. Women? He had lost touch with all of them, except Jessica Boïsse, but he was not proposing to hide in the lion's mouth. He was left with professional acquaintances. He could hardly seek refuge with Fourveret! Johannès-Graf might hide him, but would want to know why. Monthignies would definitely hide him and befriend him at peril of his own life, but three hours later the whole of Paris would know. He thought of Divo. Yes, Divo would have the necessary courage, discretion and perhaps even wiliness. But if he explained nothing to Divo he would have the impression of failing in some internal code that was more precious than anything; if he told the truth, Divo would smile one of his slanted smiles and make some remark like: 'I see, the coat's on the right way round again.'

'For one side, I'm a traitor. For the other, a murderer,' he thought.

He looked at the good, ordinary folk around him and mused: 'These are good, ordinary folk, most of whom have never killed anyone. And even if they have, they don't show it.' But, then, no one could read it on his face that he was a murderer, could they? Much as one might caress a dog, he caressed his briefcase affectionately with his toe—the briefcase containing the Smith and Wesson that had interrupted the career and, incidentally, the life of Lieutenant-Colonel 'Piotr'.

373

' "Piotr" '! If only he'd let me call him Ivan, I would probably not have killed him!'

The situation struck him as highly paradoxical. He, who was regarded as a high-powered member of Parisian society, did not know where to find a bed for the night. He opened his address book, as he did whenever he was drawing up a list of recipients for his books, or guests for one of his parties. A, B, C, D . . . the names, the addresses, the telphone numbers followed one another: INV, WAG, MAI, JAS, BAB, ODE, for the old ones and 525, 329, 265, 254 for the more recent ones. Some numbers were preceded by no name, and he could no longer remember whose numbers they were. Some names failed to summon up a face. In the case of one or two he managed only to identify a scent. (Those women would no doubt have taken him in, if they had been alone that evening, but with the fever that now raged in him how could he pay a visit to a scent? There are men, it seems, who feel a quickened desire for cool flesh after committing a murder; he felt nothing of the kind.) He hesitated before the name of Kurnosov: he could request this kind of service of his comrade-in-arms, but the staff of the little hotel must have been penetrated already. Ah! There was Sacha de Fragance, the shady stage director, a playboy with greying temples, who had apartments and villas more or less everywhere; but Marguerite knew that Psar and he were fond of one another and his name would be one of the first she would give. Ah yes, he needed an address that Marguerite would not think of. That eliminated Perquigny, the small independent publisher, whom he quite liked and who clung to Psar's coat-tails because he regarded him as a man of the right. And it eliminated Bernou, too, the courageous editor of *Seconde*, who certainly had at his disposal a network of secret apartments and who would no doubt be up to playing the game of clandestinity in the hope of a scoop. It eliminated all the Agency's authors. It eliminated . . .

Aleksandr ran through the address book again and, this time, his eye was caught by a name that he had missed first time round.

Would he telephone her? It would be the normal, polite thing to do.

But he preferred to bet on the totally absurd.

That afternoon, there was a council of war at the embassy; Colonel Mozhukhin, the resident, Colonel Viazev, of Department V, and Major Nikitin, Marguerite Thérien's case-officer, conferred over tea. Two men had been sent to the Limousin to spirit away the corpse. Nikitin had rustled up a subordinate to question Marguerite. Viazev had set a trap in the subject's apartment.

As soon as Marguerite telephoned to say that she was back, Nikitin and his assistant took her to the Agency office. One carried out a search, while the other questioned her, then they changed roles. Nikitin assumed a tone of authority: 'Well, my girl, do you serve the people or don't you?' His assistant tried a more urbane approach: 'Surely, Mademoiselle, a young woman of your abilities . . .' Exhausted, suffering from a heavy cold, constantly blowing her nose in Kleenex tissues, Marguerite was as co-operative as anyone could have wished. Nevertheless it irritated her to see these men, who knew nothing about literature, ferreting through files that she had taken such care—and pleasure—in organizing. 'With their great paws! . . .' But in fact they were trying not to disturb anything, to be meticulous and understanding.

Marguerite, having for the sixth time gone over her employer's habits, acquaintances and eccentricities, could not help from time to time asking questions herself: 'But who was that gentleman? And why did he do that to him? I know M. Psar was a supporter of the extreme right all along, but now he's a murderer!'

The two officers avoided these questions and returned to the charge: 'Apart from Mme Boïsse what women did Psar see?'

As Marguerite listed the addresses where Psar might have taken refuge, Nikitin communicated them to the operation headquarters, which took the necessary steps. Viazev had put all his men on to the affair. All the part-time collaborators were up all night: a 'bug' here, a little 'plumbing' there. The men were all French: some worked for the money, others out of idealism, but they, too, of course, were paid, and had to sign receipts, against the day when their idealism started to flag.

The Volvo was found; it contained no clues. However its presence proved that the subject had returned to Paris. The computers of the airline companies and of French railways, questioned by paid informers, showed that no new reservation had been made under the name of Psar. No car-hire firm seemed to have any dealings with him. It is true, being Christmas Night, not many could be questioned. The Omega was parked near the Opéra, where Psar had left it three days earlier. And a telephone call to the *Pont-Royal* revealed that the camel-hair coat was still hanging on its hanger . . .

Marguerite, crying with exhaustion, despite the brandies she was being plied with, repeated tirelessly, on the verge of hysteria: 'He had no friends, no friends. Not a single friend.'

And she added, pathetically: 'He had only me.'

In some very secret way, she felt a new loyalty to him, since she had taken part in this man-hunt. In so far as she was doing all she could to help them find him, she no longer regarded herself as bound to see him as an enemy. It was now up to those two Russians to deal with the class enemy, to find him, and to take care of him as they saw fit; she, for her part, was free to remember the courteous, generous boss, who always knew what he wanted, and, of course, the lover.

In the morning, Nikitin decided to stop the interrogation. Marguerite was taken home and a reliable nurse was assigned to her who would look after her as long as it took her to regain possession of her faculties. This would prevent her from doing anything indiscreet, even if her fever got worse and she became delirious.

All day, the search continued, and the following night and the morning after that. No observation post showed any sign of the subject. No eavesdropper came up with any revealing allusion. Neither the trap maintained at the apartment nor the one that they had set up in the office had yet been sprung.

Aleksandr Dmitrich Psar, co-opted colonel of the Committee of State Security, at present on the run, had vanished.

In Moscow, Colonel-General Pitman, member of the Consistory governing Directorate A, began to show signs of impatience.

In Paris, Colonel Mozhukhin grumbled: 'Well done, Hidy-hats! They're destroying our profession, trying to take over the world without our good old friends espionage and counter-espionage.'

But he showed no less enthusiasm and application in tracking down Piotr's murderer—Piotr was a young fellow with a bright future ahead of him, whose only fault had been to allow himself to be transferred to the smart Alecks.

She was going to bed when the door-bell made her jump. She had to stand on tiptoe to look through the spy-hole. She did not recognize her visitor at first. She had only seen him once, last June, and his face, then so smooth and sleek, so poised, now looked haggard and crazy. Razor cuts marked his cheeks and neck. His eyes had a morbid brightness about them.

She opened the door nevertheless.

'Monsieur Psar?'

'Mademoiselle . . .'

His eyelids were creased with pain and his chin was trembling. His hands gripped the handle of a large black briefcase. He was wearing an English raincoat which was torn on one side.

'Mademoiselle Petit . . .'

'Yes.'

He bit his lips and creased his eyelids still more, as if he could scarcely see for fever.

'I'm terribly sorry to disturb you. At such an hour. I don't even know whether you're alone. Just say the word and I'll go away at once.'

It was comic, that elocution, that refined vocabulary, in the mouth of that ill-shaven man who looked so shaky on his legs.

Joséphine Petit stepped back to let this brave fellow in. She had no idea what he wanted, but she was confident that she would be able to defend herself if the need arose. She observed attentively the fine equine face in which she detected a scarcely repressed brutality.

He stopped in the middle of the one-room apartment looking around at the white-wood furniture, the divan-bed, which Joséphine had just turned down, the Braque reproductions on the wall, the severely arranged bookcase. He recognized several White Books.

'I've come . . .' he began, then broke off. He had quite a charming smile, surprising on that hard face.

'It's the simplest things that are so difficult to say, isn't it? You're interested in terrorism. And you refused to let yourself be intimidated or bought by me. That made me respect you, trust you . . . You are who you are. That's rare . . . I'm feverish. Nothing serious: I've caught a chill. But I need to think for a few hours. And to rest.'

She nodded. She realized that he was not his normal self. She felt a touch of compassion for him and no little curiosity.

'Why don't you go home?' she asked in a serious, concerned way.

He looked at her intensely, as if he had forgotten the reason.

'Ah, yes! Why not? Because, you see, I have to hide.'

He made a gesture, looking for another, less childish word. Then, not finding one, repeated: 'Hide.'

He looked at the small, square face with the stiff, bushy eyebrows, the thick skin, the dark, intelligent eyes. My God, how young this girl is! She was wearing a kind of white top, a kind of blue pair of trousers, ridiculous objects with barbarous names: *ticheurte, bloudjine*. He, Aleksandr Psar, had come to ask asylum from a twenty-seven-year-old dwarf of a girl in trousers.

She flung her arms apart, in a gesture not of hesitation, but of deliberation. True, she was interested in terrorism, but rather in the theoretical aspects of that social disease than in its more physical manifestations, but she was not a girl to shy away from practical activity if she was actually faced with it. She lived alone, she was answerable to no one, she had broken with her lover three weeks earlier because he had tried to impose on her his political convictions and his passion for slot-machines.

Later, she would wonder what kind of terrorism Aleksandr Psar was engaged in. She was strongly opposed to any violation of individual liberty and if this man was guilty of actions of this kind she would, as she had already foreseen, have a battle with her conscience; could she shelter a criminal, could she hand over to the police a man on the run? But she was well brought up, she knew that one did not ask questions of a guest before receiving him. One had to say yes or no straightaway, and that yes or that no must not be sullied with any such restrictions as 'I have only one room' or 'You wouldn't be comfortable here'. As a teenager, she had often deplored the fact that she had not lived under the Occupation or been old enough to take part in the Algerian War; here at last was an opportunity to act, a modest but definite one: would she reject it? Besides, this man was ill and, however little Joséphine Petit was given to sentimentality, she found it quite natural to offer help to those who expressed a need for it.

She shut the door, slipped in the safety chain and covered up the spy-hole with its little shutter.

'You ought to have a very hot shower and a grog,' she said, looking at Psar, who was trying to keep from shaking. 'It's through there. Obviously my pyjamas would be too small, but hang on: Ludovic left his. I was going to send them on to him.'

Her little studio-apartment was organized like the solution to a problem with three unknown factors. She climbed up on a pair of steps and found the pyjamas in a drawer at the top.

'Of course,' she observed, pulling a face, 'they're pink! Ludovic loved pink. But it's better than nothing.'

Aleksandr removed one hand from the handle of his briefcase to take the pink pyjamas.

'You'll need a towel.'

She climbed up to another drawer.

'Here, take this. It'll go with the pyjamas.'

As she passed the radiator, she turned the nob: the patient needed heat.

'Go on, then,' she said, seeing him standing there, still in his mackintosh. 'I'll see to the grog.'

He took off his Burberry with some difficulty. He clenched his teeth to stop them chattering. She noticed that he took his big black briefcase into the bathroom.

She glanced at the telephone. Should she call a friend? Say: 'If anything happens to me, remember that Psar, that night . . .' No. She did not feel that she had any right to give his name and, without a name, such a call would be nothing more than a sign of nervousness; and Joséphine was not nervous.

She would give her bed to the patient and sleep on cushions and blankets. She wanted to arrange them before making the grog, but thought that it might embarrass this man to see her sleeping on the floor: so it would be better to get him to bed first. She simply got her bedding ready in a corner, so as to be able to arrange it once she had turned out the light. The shower hissed, sounding like a husky siren. When it stopped, Joséphine called out: 'There's a new toothbrush in the medicine chest on the second shelf. The toothpaste is beside it. I hope you like mint.'

On second thoughts, she changed the sheets on the bed. She had three pairs; that way she would be able to put on a second clean pair tomorrow if Psar sweated too much during the night. She went and made his grog. The situation was beginning to amuse her: there was something so incongruous in a maths teacher getting mixed up in anything to do with terrorism. 'If my pupils could see me now . . .'

He came back, carrying his briefcase, his pink pyjamas half way up his calves and arms. He was shivering. She got him into the bed. She then gave him several aspirins and the grog, holding the cup for him so that he would not be afraid of spilling any.

'Now go to sleep,' she ordered.

He flopped back on to the pillow. She turned off the light. But one could still see, because the light was still on in the bathroom and came through the translucent glass in the door. A voice came from the bed: 'But where will *you* sleep?'

'Don't worry about that. Now what are you up to?'

An arm had emerged from the bed, groping for something: the briefcase. The hand opened the briefcase, got hold of an object and slipped it under the pillow.

'I'm in it now,' thought Joséphine Petit. 'Maybe I'm hiding a murderer. Well, if there's any shooting, I'll soon see whether I'm brave or not: I've always wanted to know.'

Next day, the visitor just lay inert. Jo did some shopping, came back, busied herself about this and that, read, wrote:

he might as well have been dead, except that he was breathing and sweating. The day after that he was still sleeping, his mouth open, his hair plastered down with sweat: he looked as if he had sea-shells on his forehead.

Joséphine made herself coffee, gathered up her notes, left written instructions ('There are eggs and a tomato in the refrigerator'), and went out without a sound. During the holidays, she was working on her doctorate with a girlfriend and, visitor or no, there was no question for her of changing her timetable. She would spend the day between the law of numbers and two yoghurts. Her friend was a good sort, politically emancipated (that is to say, not a Marxist), but it still annoyed her that Joséphine had not joined the union. That day, this irritation struck Mlle Petit as particularly childish. 'I'd like to see Edith with a killer in her bed!'

On her way back, the author of *The Psychoanalysis of Terror* made some carefully chosen purchases—duck in aspic, tinned crab—while repeating to herself over and over again: 'He may have flown.' Then she thought rather ruefully of Ludovic. But no, someone who expected her to mend his socks, just because of a few anatomical differences between them! . . .

She was relieved to find Psar looking at home and quite obviously better. A mixture of white and fair hair covered his cheeks; he had made the bed; he was wrapped up in a blanket that made his pink pyjamas invisible. Perhaps he had taken them off. The bathroom was spotless, the kitchenette shone like a new penny, and a bunch of tea roses had been placed on the white-wood desk, in a jug.

'You didn't go out, I hope?'

'No, I took the liberty of using your telephone.'

She looked with astonishment at this gentleman who took up at once so much and so little room. With the makings of a beard on his chin, he was beginning to look like a character in an icon, his brown eyes strangely veiled and much darker than his hair.

They had a pleasant little dinner. She liked to sit on the floor.

'Anyway, the table is so small: we're better on the carpet.' Sitting on the carpet, he looked a bit awkward, but he made the best of a bad job and she looked at him with mixed feelings, the most basic of which was that of a woman feeding a man because it was her nature to do so.

'Do you feel better now? Have you had enough?'

He was pale, much thinner than in June, but he was not shivering any more and his thoughts seemed to follow one another more logically. He had the good grace not to offer excuses for his intrusion, and not even to thank her in so many words.

'How's your book going?' he asked.

She—who had brought *zubrovka* specially for him, and served it any old how, not even chilled, without *zakuski*, in large glasses—she sighed: 'I took it everywhere. Nobody wants it.'

'Did you try Perquigny? He's got the wind in his sails and he's got guts. You should see eye to eye, the two of you.'

She jotted down the telephone number.

'Shall I mention your name?'

That made him laugh.

'Ah, yes. Perquigny still trusts me.'

Gradually, with the help of the *zubrovka*, they got on to more general subjects. Aleksandr told her about the mass they had attended.

'Are you religious, Mademoiselle?'

'Come on, call me Jo. Let's say that the existence of God does not strike me as a hypothesis that one has any right to reject *a priori*. What about you?'

'Yes. It's even beginning to pose some problems for me.'

In the end, she plucked up enough courage to ask to see his revolver. He showed her the Smith and Wesson and explained how it worked. She looked at the bulky weapon, fascinated. This expert in terrorism had never seen a revolver except in a shop window, had never fired a gun at all, except at a fair ground.

He ejected the cartridges, explained the difference between simple and double action. Jo's fingers were so short that she could hardly get her index round the trigger.

Fascinated by the weapon, as many are who are not used to them, she asked: 'Do you think this one has already killed someone?'

'It's quite possible,' Aleksandr replied coldly.

They were sitting on the floor, close to one another, almost cheek to cheek, and, once again, he was put off by the coarseness of her skin, while she was saying to herself, looking at his beard: 'I bet that prickles.' He was the first to move away, imperceptibly, then she did so too, asking another question about the working of this instrument composed of blue steel and light wood.

That night, he insisted that she should have the bed and she, out of negligence or for some other reason that she did not explain to herself, did not change the sheets.

Next day she awoke, much more aware than on the first evening of the responsibilities that weighed on her. She had fed him: he belonged to her.

'You worried me with your florist,' she said. 'Today you won't open the door to anyone, will you?'

He thanked her absentmindedly: 'No, no, of course not.'

They had their breakfast together, at the table, which was usually in the kitchenette, but which could be brought out into the room, so that one person ate in one room and the other in the other. Aleksandr noticed, with some horror, that the lady of the house dipped her buttered bread into her coffee.

'Today,' she said, 'I'll be back a little earlier.' (She would take some time off from the law of numbers.) 'What would you like for dinner?'

'Whatever you say.'

'Will steaks do?'

'Perfectly.'

When she had gone, he dressed slowly, as, in the olden days, one had to put on one's armour. He went to the window, which looked out over the Parc des Buttes-Chaumont, and, as he observed the suspension bridge, which swayed slightly, he buttoned his heavy gold cuff-links on to a shirt that was no longer clean at all.

He had come to a decision. He would not 'go home'. He would never 'see again' those dense birch thickets that he had never set eyes on. He would never hear those Russian bells, which were rung by working the tongue, and whose smooth, clear message echoed over the endless plains. 'I shan't go home, Alek, you go in my place.' But the father's hand had fallen back before it reached the son's cheek.

'You bequeathed me the duty to "go home", papa. You see that I can't. Forgive me.'

He felt no remorse concerning the false masters he had served. He was bound to them only by a contract, and it was they who had broken it. Russia remained: 'I don't love her any the less. I'm not going to kid myself that she has become something different. It will always remain the same language and the same black bread.'

If he had been able to keep going on his own—he still thought in these terms—he would have done so, but in fact there was only one outcome for him: to swing his will to the side where his flesh had already swung.

'I've never had any other choice but between two betrayals.'

He looked at his hands: 'And when I'm dead, it won't even matter to me if I'm buried at Sainte-Geneviève, where the corpses have made the soil Russian. My body, fed in France, will go to feed France.'

And as, in extremity, man always finds some consolation in thinking of mankind, he added this commonplace: 'I'm not the first exile—nor the last.'

His fever had gone, but he was still weak and the telephone directory felt a weight.

'Hello, I should like to speak to someone in authority. I have information to give concerning the Soviet networks in France.'

'Please hold the line, Monsieur.'

Another voice: 'Hello, yes?'

'I should like to speak to someone in authority. I have information to give concerning the Soviet networks in France.'

Another voice: 'Hello?'

'I should like to speak to someone in authority. I have information to give concerning the Soviet networks in France.'

'Yes, Monsieur. I'm terribly sorry, Monsieur. I'm not allowed to transfer calls. Would you give me a number where you could be called back?'

This childish trick irritated him. He guessed, correctly, that if he insisted, all the necessary transfers would be made, but he felt exhausted, all he was asking for was to be, literally, picked up. At the time, killing had had no effect on him, but in the longer term, he sensed a certain rottenness taking hold of him: it was contagious, death. He gave Joséphine's number and hung up.

A few moments later the telephone rang. A new, rather unctuous voice asked: 'Was it you who rang the ministry?'

'Yes, it was. I have information to give concerning the Soviet networks in France. Are you the person I should speak to?'

'Perhaps we could meet. You're in Paris: could you come over here?'

'I have reason to believe I'd be followed. I'm an influence agent. I'd prefer you to come here.'

He gave his name and address.

'Let's agree a password. Otherwise I won't answer the door.'

'You choose one.'

Aleksandr thought of a line of Laurence Durrell's which had struck him when he was reading *The Alexandria Quartet*.

'Vision is exorcism.'

Inspector Vaudrette, of Section A4, was forty-four years old, which was not young for a divisional inspector. His wife constantly bullied him: 'What about Paulus, why is he a chief inspector? You were at the police school together, weren't you?'

Vaudrette's two children concealed from their schoolfellows the fact that their father was a policeman; whenever they had a form to fill up, they wrote 'civil servant' under the heading 'father's occupation'. Fabrice owned more records than he could ever have bought or been given; Sabine slipped a box of contraceptive pills into her satchel with no other purpose, perhaps, than to impress her friends, but who knows?

For Inspector Vaudrette things were not going very well. Once, travelling second-class to Sète in line of duty, he had read a book that had made a deep impression on him: it was

L'Ami fidèle by Emmanuel Blun, the pocket-book edition. Blun probably had no other intention than to tell a story that would bring him fame and fortune, but this story changed Vaudrette's life: if he had picked *The Madonna of the Sleeping Cars* or *The Life of Van Gogh* off the spinner at the station bookstall, he would have remained an honest man.

Indeed, he had begun to tell himself that he, too, would like to have had a faithful friend like that, one who would have spared him certain blunders and ultimately given him the means of showing what he was capable of. Vaudrette was a dreamer. He could perfectly well see himself being summoned to the Matignon or even to the Elysée, where some bigshot, secretly alerted by the faithful friend, would tell him over his Régence desk: 'Vaudrette, we are thinking of setting up a new security service, a small one, mark you, very small, but modern, super-modern, beside which the D S T will look mentally retarded, and we thought that you had exactly the qualities required to run it.' But who would play the role of the friend? In Blun's book it was clear: only a Communist could have the necessary faith, the thrust and the brains for it.

As it happened, Vaudrette specialized in the surveillance of Communists, and now here they were in the government, against the will of the people, but thanks to the will of the people, work that one out if you can, it's almost as if in a democracy, the words 'will of the people' meant nothing. In any case it seemed a good moment to acquire a faithful friend in a faction that had joined the government after failing in the elections.

That was how it happened, without a great deal of thought going into it: at a diplomatic party, which Vaudrette was supposed to observe without appearing to, a lively young Soviet official handed him glass after glass of champagne while quoting Rostand to him: '*Nous, les petits, les obscurs, les sans-grade . . .*' ('Insignificant humble privates like us . . .') They arranged to go bowling together. The Russian was invited home to a dinner of sauerkraut; he reciprocated with a present of a video machine ('we diplomats can buy them for next to nothing'). One day at the sauna—for they went to the sauna together—his generous friend had asked for a list of addresses that it would have been boorish to refuse. (Anyway, some of them were in the telephone directory: so what did it matter?) On another occasion the diplomat had been entrusted by his bosses with the task of writing up the biographies of certain leading Frenchmen: it was difficult for him, but for Vaudrette it would be so easy . . . They had begun to play chess together, and although the Russian was very good at it, whenever he bet 500 francs that he would win, he lost. Mme Vaudrette found nothing to object to in this non-alcoholic, profitable friendship; besides, this Soviet diplomat had the manners of a Russian prince.

One evening, after a good *cassoulet*, Vaudrette went out to see his host part of the way home and, before they separated, they decided to stop at a brasserie for a parting beer. The Russian prince then said:

'You know, Klavdi Lvovich' (that meant Claude-son-of-Léon). . . 'Call me Volodia . . . You know, Claude, I think you and I understand one another. We're working for the same cause: the happiness of mankind. France, the Soviet Union, they are just intermediaries: what matters to us, to you and to me, is mankind as a whole. It so happens, however, that at the precise point in History where we now stand, the Soviet Union is better placed to work for that happiness. So . . . from one idealist to another idealist, I have a proposition to make to you. You know, like in that book you lent me, where the two friends always back each other up through thick and thin . . . If you ever hook a big fish, I mean something really big, I could lend you a hand. Not just every now and then: regularly, every month. And not through the tax man either, if you see what I mean. In case anything goes wrong, there's a rescue operation carried out by professionals. Two hours later, you'll be in Moscow. You know, it's a big city, a beautiful city. You could open a bowling alley. Obviously, to get a contract like that, you'd have to begin with something solid, if you see what I mean.'

'Am I to understand,' asked Claude-son-of-Léon, 'that if anything went wrong you might also export my wife?'

Volodia smiled, raising his eyes to the ceiling:

'That would be entirely up to you, of course. But for a woman of the age and character of Thérèse, it might be difficult to adapt to Soviet life, no? You're so young in heart, Claude!'

Since then, Inspector Vaudrette had adopted a rather superior attitude to Mme Vaudrette ('If only she knew what I've been offered'), took a firmer line with his children ('Not even sure that they're mine') and lived in a sort of dream. He had found his faithful friend. All the same, as a precautionary measure, he stopped wearing red ties.

Several times he thought he had hooked the big fish, but, while being quite willing to accept delivery of his goods, Volodia shook his head and left him to understand that this was not quite what he had in mind. 'Go on, Claude, keep trying, you're bound to hit the jackpot!' he would say.

Having received a call from this Aleksandr Psar—the name meant something to him, Thérèse had seen him on television and he, too, she thought, had the manners of a Russian prince—Inspector Vaudrette sat back in his chair and began to massage his forehead.

'I'm going to play this,' he said to himself, 'like a game of chess.'

Having rubbed his forehead for about ten minutes, he wrote out a card containing all the information he had just received and, crossing the corridor, knocked on the door of his boss, the head of Section A4, Deputy Assistant Commissioner Duverrier. Indeed Vaudrette had no doubt that his telephone, like all those in the building, was bugged. He now had the opportunity of a lifetime, but this opportunity was to be played with all the subtlety at his command, which his bosses had so far failed to recognize in him.

Duverrier, a pleasant man of hideous aspect, with a fat face covered with freckles and strawberry marks, bloated with growths, bristling with warts, swept the card to the end of the table, threw back his head, slipped his glasses down to the end of his pimply nose.

Vaudrette, respectfully leaning forward, watched him read it. To himself he bet a franc (his left pocket against his right) that Duverrier, nicknamed Fat Puss, would show the tip of his tongue and say: 'Thanks, I'll think about it.'

Fat Puss finished reading, looked at him over his glasses,

showed the tip of his tongue and said: 'Thanks, I'll think about it.'

Vaudrette left and transferred a one-franc coin from his right pocket to his left.

Instead of going back to his office, he took the lift. The policeman in uniform who supervised all comings and goings had a wasp-waist and a fine white moustache that had earned him the nickname of 'cavalry captain'.

'My respects, Captain,' said the inspector meekly.

'Mmmmmmmmmmmonsieur,' the 'captain' replied respectfully, with a most stylish bow.

Vaudrette walked about fifty yards and entered a café. He never went to the one directly opposite no. 13. No, he was clever, Vaudrette, and he suspected that his bosses had put an intercept on the telephone there.

He dialled a number that he had learnt by heart.

'Hello, Volodia? This time I've hooked a big one. But you'll have to move fast, because I . . .' He explained what it was about. Volodia sounded fairly impressed.

'I don't know, Claude. I'll see what my bosses say . . .'

Vaudrette went back to his office. Volodia may have pretended to hesitate, but this time he would have to play. An influence agent about to desert . . . The inspector took his MAB out of a drawer and blew into the barrel with a businesslike air. Fat Puss must be discussing the situation with Number One. Ten minutes would elapse before he gave the order to Vaudrette to go to the rendez-vous. And when he did arrive, there would be no one there: the Commies would have got their hands on Psar already.

Ten minutes went by, and twenty, and thirty. The right-hand pocket had lost two francs again. In the end the inspector went off to see for himself what was happening: Fat Puss was still closeted with the boss.

'And that,' said Vaudrette, patriotic all of a sudden, 'is how we keep missing the boat. It's hardly surprising that others beat us every time.'

The Deputy Assistant Commissioner had asked for an audience, which had been granted immediately.

'This is what Vaudrette has just brought, sir,'

'Vaudrette?'

'Vaudrette in person, sir.'

Fat Puss observed his boss with a mixture of attachment and detachment: attachment because he respected the old boy, who had risen from the ranks and got to the top, through push and charm, without being too much of a swine; detachment, because he was himself a happy man, he knew he had reached his ceiling and his ceiling was sufficient for him. There could be no question of going higher. He had humour and humour is a great drawback in a bureaucracy, especially when the left is in power. If he were removed from here, Duverrier would have retired, tickled the trout, played billiards and concerned himself no more with human greatness than he had ever done. Ah, yes! Duverrier, who had pulled off most of his jobs, including some particularly fine ones in subversive circles, who was regarded by his colleagues in the other services, and even at the international level, as an authority on counter-insurgency, could not help finding life, his job, his superiors, his subordinates and above all himself rather comical. He loved a good set-up like a savoury broth. 'Yum! How delicious! What fun we are going to have!' But he was also lucid: 'I'll never be Assistant Commissioner because I find everything funny: that's fair enough; an Assistant Commissioner has to be respected.' He meant it, too, but there was always that sparkle. Retirement would be enough for him. His two sons would manage: one was already a graduate in business studies, the other had his eye on the merchant navy; his daughters would keep him amused: one was at the Ecole Polytechnique, yes, yes, and the other would be a film star one day. His wife showed tenderness, a gratitude towards him that moved him whenever he thought about it, which was several times a day: 'Thanks to you, my lad, I shan't have had a single dull moment.' It would have been indecent to add to these advantages a career too brilliantly crowned: success was enough, and as M. Duverrier almost suffocated his humble chair under his weight, he observed his boss—a little wizened locust of a man who was swallowed up by his own armchair—with deference, indulgence and limitless understanding. If the corners of his frog-like mouth rose, he could not, indeed would not wish to, do anything about it: 'I am Deputy Assistant Commissioner, Section Chief, that's good enough for me. Let others have the bananas and their skins, sir, the dubious honours, the undoubted risks, the solemnity on tap twenty-six hours a day so as not to miss out the twenty-fifth, and three hundred and sixty-six days a year so as to be sure they don't come a cropper one leap year.'

'Here's another little item, sir. The transcription of a telephone conversation that Cavaillès has brought me.'

The boss could take in a page at a glance. That's why he was the boss.

'Didn't Vaudrette suspect anything?'

'Vaudrette is always suspicious and never enough, sir. He's a very little man, who can't see one obstacle beyond the next. He went into the third café, not the first or second, to ring the comrades. That's him all over. And he's surprised he has not yet been promoted.'

The boss read the page again, taking it slowly this time. Fat Puss was still squatting on the chair that was too small for him, the shadow of a smile floating not so much on his puffy lips, pointed up by a potential moustache, as in his eyes, which he liked to keep half closed in order to deserve his nickname, which he was really quite fond of.

'What do you suggest, Duverrier?'

Fat Puss got up, almost stretching. He always felt quite relaxed with his bosses. It was not just a matter of his age; he had got them to accept his apparent independence, that tone of his that was at once deferential and protective. He walked slowly in front of the enormous photograph, covering two walls, that represented the whole of Paris, then went and threw a somnolent glance at the real Paris through the triple bay window.

'There are several ways of playing this particular game of belote, sir. You know who Psar is. He claims to be an influence agent. I admit that I never suspected it, but let's suppose he is.

'You also know who Vaudrette is. With his little shagreen suits and his pink shirts' (Fat Puss was also wearing a pink shirt), 'we decided to keep an eye on him some time ago. For me, the crucial moment came when he gave up wearing red ties. Well, we've made the necessary enquiries, and he no longer has access to any top secret files, except a few that I have over-classified to allay his suspicions. I've already given you my interpretation of the situation: Vaudrette is waiting till he's got a dowry before going over to the other side. The shadows, the phone tappings, it all adds up. Right.

'As far as the comrades are concerned, we have picked up a whole flurry of activity over the last few days: increased radio traffic, communication through scramblers. There could be a connection.

'If you want us to pick up Psar, nothing could be easier: the comrades have to shift their bulk, while all we have to do is to pick up the blower and the local station will net him in no time.

'All the same, we had better get moving, otherwise we run the risk of finding nothing but mashed Psar or no Psar at all. Which in this game is, of course, another way of making a discard.'

'What would you do in my place, Duverrier? You're an old fox and I'd be sorry not to make the most of you before you retire.'

'I, sir? Simple as I am, I see the problem as a flow-chart with four boxes and double entry. We pick up Psar or we drop him; we gobble up Vaudrette, or we give him more rope.

'First box: we pounce. Vaudrette keeps going but we have Psar in the net: a big job, an influence agent spilling the beans, you can imagine the fuss. Letters of congratulation, promotion, the lot.

'Second box: we forget the whole matter or, a more perverse variation, we make sure we get there after the comrades. Vaudrette keeps going and Psar's had it. A bit trite, if you want my opinion.

'Third box: we try to kill two birds with one stone. Two big deals instead of one.

'Fourth box . . .'

'I was waiting for your fourth. I know my Duverrier.'

'The comrades get Psar, and the lions get Vaudrette. I know that that fool doesn't do us much harm, but it's a bit much having to keep him under surveillance morning, noon and night. Expensive, too.'

'According to you, Duverrier, we should therefore give the opposition time to get their hands on Psar, and then turn on Vaudrette for collusion with a foreign power? Wouldn't it be rather a pity to let the prey go, even if we did manage to catch the shadow?'

Fat Puss smiled. The boss loved elegant phrases. That's fair enough, only to be expected, that's what a boss is for.

'When one has four boxes, one has to be really out of luck if one can't knock up a fifth, even if it's a bit misshapen, out of the bits left over from the other four. The most we can hope for is to get Vaudrette prosecuted under one of the Article 70s, and where would that get us? Everybody will slap their thighs and cry that we've been penetrated, infiltrated, exposed. You can just see them, can't you, your friends in State Security, and the Yanks, and even more the British and Germans, who will no longer have a monopoly in leakages. Frankly, I can't see what's in it for us. If Vaudrette takes advantage of the opportunity and turns a somersault, all the better for his bank balance; as for us, we'll have the perfect vehicle for passing any piece of information, true or false, that we feel like passing off on the comrades.'

'I agree with you, Duverrier; I saw that, too, but couldn't we put Vaudrette in the saddle and still exploit Psar?'

'That's up to you, sir, but the question is what would we do with him? Do you remember that other affair? We'd been chasing after the guy for a whole year and spent a small fortune—all for what? To subject him to some infantile interrogation by an examining magistrate, have him sentenced just as childishly by the State Security Court, which released him inside two years, without his having divulged a thing, to speak of. This one will probably talk, but what's he going to give us? A few names, a few tactics we've been suspecting all along. After which, in the absence of any special tribunal, he'll be sent to the assizes, where he'll be duly acquitted for all that he's been a plague on the national consciousness for the past twenty-five years.'

'Acquitted? Why acquitted, Duverrier?'

'Because the procurator of the Republic will not be able to prove consequential damage.'

'What precisely do you mean?'

Fat Puss stroked his favourite wart, bristling with black hairs, with his finger tips. He showed the tip of his tongue.

'Well, sir, paragraph 3, article 80 of the Penal Code, the only one that allows us to take any action at all against influence agents, lays down penalties of imprisonment or detention of between ten and twenty years for whoever "maintains with the agents of a foreign power intelligence of such a nature as to harm the military or diplomatic situation of France or its essential economic interests". Let's for the moment overlook the imprecision of such terms as "intelligence" and "essential". But you will note that cultural, intellectual, spiritual, human interests are not even mentioned in our legislation: poisoning the minds of our youth, dislocating our educational system, undermining the family, sabotaging our Church, sullying our literature: all that is quite legal. Only our military, diplomatic and economic interests are protected. Moreover, we have to provide proof of the damage that has been done to them. Now M. Psar has done no damage to them whatsoever. If M. Psar were condemned, it would be a terrible judicial error of which we should be the first victims. The *Dindon déchaîné* would claim once again that we are locking people up for their opinions, and good French consciences would express their concern at our repressive measures. That is why, sir, until our legislation can be modified, as long as the crime of influence is not recognized as one of the most serious crimes of all—much more serious, in any case, than espionage in the strict sense—I would maintain that it is in our interests not to prosecute influence agents, if we don't want their prosecution to rebound against us.'

'In short, Duverrier, from the height of your experience and sagacity . . .'

'From the height of my little professional dung-heap, sir, this is what I should say: one of the comrades' influence agents has got on the wrong side of the comrades; let's leave the comrades to do the dirty work that we aren't capable of doing ourselves. Let's send Vaudrette to the premises, but in an hour's time. And then let's benefit from the right he will acquire for himself to the gratitude of the Union of Soviet Socialist Republics.'

The doorbell rang. Aleksandr stuck his eye to the spy-hole. A red-faced man stood there, his forehead deeply lined; he wore a leather jacket.

'Who is it?'

'Vision is exorcism.'

He had a slight provincial accent.

Aleksandr opened the door.

'Aleksandr Psar?'

'Yes.'

'Let's go.'

Aleksandr had his briefcase in his hand; he had already scribbled a message for Jo: 'Thanks, I'll ring you sometime.'

They got into the lift. The red-faced man smelled of something he could not quite identify: alcohol, aftershave, leather?

A black Citroën Pallas awaited them, the front passenger door open.

'Get in.'

Aleksandr settled into his seat.

The driver was a big, gloomy-looking individual. Another man was sitting in the back. He was smoking. He was wearing a white shirt and a dark suit. His face was veiled by the mauve smoke. The red-faced man got in next to him.

Aleksandr said: 'Messieurs . . .'

And he suddenly sensed that 'Messieurs' was not the appropriate term. There was a certain heaviness, a tension in the atmosphere that made the word 'messieurs' seem pitifully inadequate. He put his hand on the door handle. It did not move. The car was already moving along the Buttes-Chaumont.

The smoker said, in Russian: 'Take it easy, comrade. I'm Colonel Viazev, of Department V.'

The red-faced man leaned forward.

A needle was stuck into the back of Aleksandr's neck. His hand, which had reached inside the briefcase, slackened, everything inside him collapsed, he sank into darkness.

The Pallas took the ring road, left it and then stopped in a district full of warehouses, in front of the closed doors of a garage. The metal doors rose automatically, the panels sliding up into one another with much squeaking and shuddering.

The Pallas entered a huge hall with a glass roof. In the middle was an enormous truck, on which, in cyrillic characters, white on dark blue, was the word *Sovtransavto*. A strongly-built fellow with long legs and a short torso, wearing a smart Italian leather jerkin, was sitting on the footboard.

The metal door came down again, panels emerging from panels, the last one striking the concrete floor with a thunderous crash that set off long echoes buzzing through the garage.

The back of the truck was shut and the rear door was sealed with lead seals. The smoker had them removed. The doors were opened.

Inside was a cargo of wines and spirits. Between the cardboard boxes was a chest on the sides of which various labels had been stuck: Rémy Martin, Vieille Cure, Cherry Rocher, Chartreuse, Drambuie, Mandarine Napoléon, Fragile, This Side Up. This was merely an additional precaution, more a matter of decoration than of use, for nobody would open the truck until it had crossed the frontier of the Sovereign and Federal Republic of Bielorussia.

The red-faced man and the driver of the Pallas brought over the inanimate body of Psar, Smith and Wesson handcuffs on his wrists and ankles. He was placed in the chest, which was then shut. He would breathe all right. There was exactly the right number of holes as laid down in Department V's internal regulations.

With a loud bang the truck's container was shut again. The fellow in the leather jerkin took out his sealing pincers. The smoker watched him approvingly.

The seals were replaced. The fellow climbed up into his cab: it was easy enough with his excessively long legs. His team-mate muttered, rather nervously: 'Well, shall we be off?'

The smoker gave a last glance at the truck.

'Ready, Viacheslav?'

'Ever ready, Comrade Colonel.'

'Then off you go! And may the good lord go with you.'

The truck shuddered, vibrated and began to move. The metal door retracted again of its own accord and the huge machine, centimetre by centimetre slipped out into the street, where it caused a temporary traffic jam. One might have thought the entire garage was moving.

It was December 28. Before the end of the year Aleksandr Dmitrich Psar would be 'home'.

This and other Methuen Paperbacks are available at your bookshop or newsagent. In case of difficulties orders may be sent to:

Methuen Paperbacks
Cash Sales Department
PO Box 11
Falmouth
Cornwall TR10 10 9EN

Please send cheque or postal order, no currency, for purchase price quoted and allow the following for postage and packing:

UK
55p for the first book, 22p for the second book and 14p for each additional book ordered to a maximum charge of £1.75.

BFPO & Eire
55p for the first book, 22p for the second book plus 14p for the next seven books, thereafter 8p per book.

Overseas Customers
£1.00 for the first book plus 25p per copy for each additional book.

While every effort is made to keep prices low, it is sometimes necessary to increase prices at short notice. Methuen Paperbacks reserves the right to show new retail prices on covers which may differ from those previously advertised in the text or elsewhere.